Into the Sky with Diamonds

The Beatles and the Race to the Moon

in the Psychedelic '60s

An historical, fictional autobiography

Ronald P. Grelsamer

Hey Bulldog Press
an imprint of Authorhouse Press, Bloomington, IN

www.IntoTheSkyWithDiamonds.com

4th Edition 2020

authorHOUSE

AuthorHouse™
1663 Liberty Drive
Bloomington, IN 47403
www.authorhouse.com
Phone: 1 (800) 839-8640

Published by AuthorHouse 05/15/2020

ISBN: 978-1-4520-7053-7 (sc)
ISBN: 978-1-4520-7055-1 (e)

Library of Congress Control Number: 2010912299

Print information available on the last page.

This book is printed on acid-free paper.

Mal Evans
©*Paul Saltzman / (Contact Press Images)*

To Sharon, Dominique, and Marc

To Mal Evans

Acknowledgments

All my love and thanks to my wife Sharon and to my children, Dominique and Marc, for giving me the *time* to put this book together – and thank you Sharon for all the Beatle and space books that inspired me.

Eternal thanks, of course, to my parents, Nadine and Philippe, for their support and encouragement, and to my brother, Daniel, for always being there with a smile and a laugh.

Gareth Esersky, my agent from the Carol Mann Agency, has stood by me and guided me through the various phases of the project, and for this I will always be grateful.

A shout-out to my editor, Margaret Diehl, who went above and beyond with her research on Mal Evans.

Special thanks to my friends Alain Bankier, Michael Kubin, and Hillary Reinsberg, as well as Sharon, for reading version 1.0 of the manuscript and providing constructive criticism. A huge THANK YOU to Mark Amos and friends from the www.Beatlesbible.com Forum for the changes to the 3rd edition.

A special award to my colleague Steve Weinfeld, M.D. for his last minute tweaking of the book's title.

And finally, a very special thanks to John, Paul, George, Ringo, and the entire Apollo/NASA team for the thrills of a lifetime.

Table of Contents

The Japanese Fable

Many centuries ago, there lived a husband and wife blessed with an unusually tall, strong, and handsome son.

"How lucky you are!" said the villagers to the parents.

But war broke out, and the strong son was quickly taken away from his family and recruited to fight.

"How unlucky you are," said the villagers to the parents.

Brave and powerful, the son was soon decorated with the highest honors.

"How lucky you are," said the villagers to the parents.

He was seriously injured, however. He lost an arm.

"How unlucky you are," said the villagers to the parents.

War broke out again a few years later, and all able-bodied men were recruited to fight. They all died – save for the son with one arm.

"How lucky you are," said the villagers to the parents…

Introduction

For years, my friends and family have asked me to jot down my memories of my days at NASA in the 1960s.

Those were heady times. The Race to the Moon. The Beatles. James Bond. Vietnam. Hippies. Nixon. Drugs. The Rolling Stones. Race Riots. The Pill. Jimi Hendrix at Woodstock. The Kennedy assassination. Then another assassination. Then yet another.

I've always resisted writing my memoirs. Who has the time?

When I found an old shoebox with a trove of Mal Evans's letters, I finally gave in.

Mal was one of the Beatles' two roadies. He and I had struck up a relationship when we were both in Germany, before either of us could begin to fathom the wild ride we would soon be taking.

It was mostly a pen pal relationship, and in rummaging through the shoebox, I realized that I'd kept essentially all his letters.

He'd been convinced since the day we met that he and I shared an extra-terrestrial bond. This made him highly entertaining.

Who knows? Perhaps he was right...

1. Zanzibar

Only three more hours until liftoff, and natives brandishing spears and torches are blocking my Jeep. The office is in plain sight, barely a hundred yards away.

In three hours, I had better be at my desk; make that two. I'll need an hour to set up. It's been a month now since I arrived in this riot-infested area, which is only somewhat protected by Britain's Gordon Highlanders. My mission is to set up tracking stations for the Mercury missions. The very first orbital flight of an American capsule is about to take place. It will be unmanned of course, but many questions need to be answered. Will NASA be able to track the capsule in space? Will we be able to control any aspect of its flight?

Tracking satellites have not yet been invented. The only way to follow an object orbiting the earth is by way of earth-bound stations strung out around the globe. The stations lie along the anticipated trajectory of the Mercury capsule: the Bahamas, Zanzibar, Western Australia, Hawaii…

Months of planning and these natives with their toothy smiles are going to ruin it? I consider ramming through. But they're not coming towards me, and as I look more closely, they really aren't very threatening. They're just dancing from one foot to the other.

The tallest one of the bunch moves towards the Jeep, and I feel my fingers stiffen around the steering wheel. He is carrying a tall carved staff in his right hand, and a long mask covers the top half of his face. I don't know what kind of animal it represents, but it has two swept-back horns at the top. The man is bow-legged and barefoot. His clothing consists of a loose loin cloth, National Geographic-style. A year ago, it would never have occurred to me I'd be seeing this in real life. But the scene is real. I can just imagine the headlines: "NASA foiled by spear-wielding Africans." The Russians would laugh so hard we'd hear them in Florida. But just as I feel the first clench of fear, the man, just a few yards from the car now, breaks into a grin. The gap between the front teeth and the gold incisor give him away. It's Ouamadou, the house-keeper. I lean back into the seat.

"I take care of 'em," Ouamadou whispers to me. "Got something for 'em?"

Perhaps I detect a wink.

I get it. I reach into the dashboard and pull out a carton of Camels. The toothy grin widens. The breath is awful. Ouamadou spins around triumphantly towards his buddies while brandishing the cigarettes, the modern day war trophy. The road clears.

The office is nothing but an ugly concrete bunker, a leftover from God knows what war, paid with God knows whose foreign aid, meant to go for God knows what kind of food program. I call it the Palace. Inside, sad little light bulbs dangling from the ceiling illuminate drab green cinderblocks. My "office" is the largest room on the second floor. A large rectangular window looks out onto the desolate plains. It faces north, and there is little direct sunlight. Large non-descript wooden tables line three of the walls. They are covered with electronic equipment, including the latest model Teletype machine. The machine can transmit a phenomenal sixty words per minute. In short order, Teletype technology will be outdated, but for now it's state of the art. This machine is how I communicate with Chris Kraft and Gene Kranz back at Cape Canaveral, Florida.

The roof of the Palace is an electronic porcupine of tracking gear that I personally escorted here a month ago. I've been testing it and tweaking it on a daily basis. All of this for an approximately eight-minute test. I think of Olympic athletes who train for years just to perform a two-minute routine.

The chatter of the Teletype breaks the silence. My time has finally come.

"Liftoff successful."

A stream of numbers starts to come through, indicating the speed, direction, pitch, yaw, and roll of the capsule. Moments later it's my turn. Yes!!!! There it is! I cannot see, let alone hear the small capsule whizzing by at 17,000 miles per hour a hundred miles over my head. But there it is on my oscilloscope. The numbers are coming in clearly, and I dutifully transmit them back to the Cape.

Now for the crucial part: Can I change the pitch, roll, or yaw of the capsule from here on earth? Not that we engineers don't trust the astronauts, but it'll be necessary for us to have control over the capsule, should they become incapacitated. Upon arriving, I painted the three critical knobs red, white, and blue, so as not to make any mistake. Yes, of course, I can turn these knobs in my sleep, but at the decisive moment would my nerves betray me? I hadn't really thought so. However, I wasn't taking any chances.

I gently turn the white knob a few degrees clockwise. The readout indicates a three-degree yaw to the right. Yes! The ultimate remote control airplane! Briefly, I allow myself to remember being twelve.

I repeat the maneuver with the pitch and roll, teletype my success to Kranz, and my job is over. Time to pack up the gear. Good-bye Zanzibar. I make a mental note to leave Ouamadou an extra pack of Camels.

2. Hamburg

"Mr. Richtman?"

I looked away from the blurry forest and into the large face of the man sitting next to me. He seemed huge – 6'4" at a guess – with an engaging smile and thick, Buddy Holly-style, black-rimmed glasses.

"I noticed your name on the folder," he said, nodding towards a red file on my lap. The words "UFO" were lightly stenciled across the top right corner.

He had a British accent and introduced himself as Mal Evans. It was vaguely comforting to hear English in a bus full of boisterous Germans.

"Your name is… Robert?"

"Robert Richtman. I call myself Rob, but everyone knows me as Dutch."

"Dutch?"

"My father's Dutch. Van Reichtmann is my given name. I've shortened it."

"I see." He looked down, and his voice trailed off.

He perked right back up.

"Any Celtic ancestry?"

"Actually, yes, on my father's side. My grandfather once told me that our ancestors were from Brittany. With a name like van Reichtmann that didn't make much sense to me at the time."

"Ah…" Mal leaned back with an air of satisfaction. He paused.

"My ancestors were Druids, High Priests if you will." He glanced at me to see if I knew what Druids were. I nodded. "Reichtmann, Reichtman, Richtman, I think these are names that can be associated with a high priest from Brittany called Chyndonax, which is why your name caught my attention. Perhaps your ancestors were also Druids."

"Chyndonax? Sounds like a cartoon character."

Evans ignored me.

"You've heard of Stonehenge, menhirs, dolmens?" I nodded again.

Mal continued, "Did you ever think of who could have lifted those twelve-ton blocks or who laid them out in such a perfect astronomical pattern? Did you ever notice that, when seen from the sky, Stonehenge fits every description that's ever been made of a flying saucer? ... It's round ... Our planet may have been visited by other civilizations, don't you think?" His eyes brightened, and I had a moment of déjà vu. Had I met him... in high school... no, college maybe... there was a definite sense of familiarity.

I shifted the red folder onto my other lap. "Yes, who knows?"

Mal was a little forward, but he was animated, and I found myself drawn into his banter – Stonehenge, UFOs, extra-terrestrials, and the like – until, in the blink of an eye, we had pulled into Hamburg's bus station. I took him up on his offer to meet for drinks later in the week. Outside of my Air Force buddies, I didn't know anyone in Hamburg.

The Kaiserkeller was a dive along the Reeperbahn, an avenue within the red light district of the Baltic port of Hamburg. The fishnets and portholes lent an air of *faux nautique* to the joint, complementing the sailors and prostitutes who made up most of the clientele.

I joined Mal, seated at a small round table. Over the din of a rock'n'roll band, he picked up where he'd left off.

"Our ancestors were from Brittany. Stonehenge lies in southern England, but you can't look at these lands as separate countries. As I'm sure you know, there were Celtic tribes on both sides of the English Channel, including the part of France now called Brittany. This is why the language of Brittany is similar to Celt."

With a few beers under his belt, Mal was off to the races.

"Have you ever heard the term 'geoglyphs'?"

"No."

"Ancient carvings in the ground whose shape can only be appreciated from the sky. You find them all over the world. The Nazca plateau in Peru, the American southwest..."

Evans stared at the mug and twirled his beer ever faster.

"Of course, thousands of years ago, humans were completely earthbound. No airplanes, zeppelins, hot air balloons. So who could have drawn these figures, and why?"

Evans stopped talking and seemed to be completely absorbed by his beer.

"I'm sure there's a cosmic connection."

I was now more interested in the band playing behind Mal at the other end of the room. Five very young men in leather outfits were jumping around on a dilapidated stage. Actually, one of them stood with his back turned to the audience as he fussed with his instrument, while the three other guitarists did all the jumping. They were screaming so loudly I thought they'd cough up a larynx. One of the two singers would harangue the sparse crowd in a combination of English and German. He yelled out a nonsensical stream of gibberish and curses, sure that they would land on unappreciative ears. He was quite correct in that assumption. The handful of German sailors seemed to be paying no attention. The night was still young.

The band played exclusively American rock'n'roll. One of the singers, the other one, the one not shouting obscenities, sounded remarkably like Little Richard in his rendition of "Long Tall Sally." The bass player, the one who kept his back to the audience, wore sunglasses. I hoped his better days were still ahead; he just played single notes here and there. The drummer was the best looking of the bunch. He seemed to command the attention of the two fraulein waitresses, both blond and red-cheeked, one just a little plumper than the other. They were young. Could they remember WWII? It wasn't impossible one of their fathers had faced mine in battle…

Mal pulled me away from my disturbing thoughts. "You said you're here with the American Air Force? What exactly do you do?"

"Communications. I work on designing communications systems for fighter pilots."

"Planet Earth to pilots?"

"Yes, you could put it that way." This seemed to please him. "I'm a telephone repair man, so I'm in communications too." He chuckled at the little connection he'd just made. "I'm just here for the week-end. I work part time at a music club in Liverpool and these are my friends." With his thumb he gestured over his shoulder towards the stage.

I felt a stab of envy. Rock'n'roll was fun. At least I could say I worked for the Air Force.

Mal stood. "I've got to go, but let's get together again. I'd love to know more about your family."

My family: the Celtic Druids. I could just imagine what my father would say to that. I smiled and told Mal I'd be happy to see him again too. He left a few German marks on the table, took down my phone number, promised to call soon, and left.

I was about to follow, but the band suddenly launched into a vibrant rendition of "Summertime Blues." Then "Twenty Flight Rock." Then "Be-Bop-A-Lula."

Songs from the 50s.

Obviously an oldies band.

3. Strictly as a Favor

Beep... Beep... Beep... Beep... Beep...

Rarely have Americans been as frightened as they were when they awoke on the morning of October 5th, 1957.

The Beep... Beeps... were emanating from a 184 lb porcupine called *Sputnik*, the world's first orbiting satellite. It was a Communist Soviet satellite. The implications were immediately shouted from house to house all across America, as surely as if the British were coming. The Communists now had the capability of loading the skies with nuclear weapons that would be out of our reach. If they wanted to, the Russkies could rain nuclear bombs onto every American city. They could blackmail us. Take over our government. Pretty soon we would be dead. Or worse.

We'd be Kommunists!

There could be no worse fate. "Better Dead than Red" was the motto of the day. I believed it, and so did all my relatives and all my friends. The Communists saw us as decaying, decadent, and exploitive Capitalists, and we saw them as drab and totalitarian murderers.

The geopolitics of the day were straightforward for people like me. The world was divided into three camps: The Free World, the Communist World, and everybody else. In the Free World – mostly the United States and Western Europe – citizens could express their thoughts and choose their own beliefs without intervention from the government. The United States and Western Europe championed such beliefs. The Communists, on the other hand, believed that the State knows best. About everything. Communist governments were the arbiters of acceptability at every level of society. Topping the list of no-no's was organized religion, "the opium of the masses." Rock'n'roll, the corrupter of youth, could be found one rung below. Any citizen with an inclination to disagree with the Party could end up in Siberia (or embalmed).

Nikita Khrushchev was born in 1894, worked in the mines, converted early on to communism, slavishly followed Stalin, became head of the Communist Party in 1953, and took full control of the country in 1958. He was a short, rotund, blustery, in-your-face type of man. He was short on intellect and long on conviction. You either believed in his political system or you were evil. You were with him or you were against him. You either saw things his way or he would make you pay.

In 1956, he had been attending a reception at the Polish embassy in Moscow. He was so overbearing that a number of Western delegates had walked out. An infuriated Khrushchev lashed out: "History is on our side. WE WILL BURY YOU!" That same year, Hungary tried to throw off the Soviet yoke. Khrushchev sent the tanks into Budapest and had the leaders executed. A few years later, while addressing the United Nations in New York, he would bang his sandal on the table in a fit of anger. Americans had reason to be scared.

The Free world and the Communist regimes fought for influence in the countries that fell outside these two systems. Now the Communists had sent a rocket into space, and we hadn't.

For President Dwight ("Ike") Eisenhower, this was precisely the situation he'd been avoiding: America had long had the brainpower and the means to develop a space program; after all, had Germany's Wernher von Braun and his team of rocket scientists not defected to America in the waning days of World War II? Von Braun had been the director of Peenemünde, and he'd been responsible for the V2 rockets that rained death and destruction on Great Britain. But it was space, not war, that was his true passion. He liked to remind everyone that the Nazis had imprisoned him for two weeks in 1944 for professing too much interest in space and not enough in weaponry. Yet, not wanting to open up another front in the Cold War, Eisenhower had personally kept the lid on the idea of a space program. Having seen firsthand the ravages of war, he would do his utmost to steer the country away from dangerous confrontations. But presently, the Communists had made the first move; Eisenhower had no choice.

Unfortunately, America had more brainpower than rocket power.

Throughout the 1950s, Eisenhower had watched the various branches of the military fight over the development of ballistic missiles. The Army (with von Braun) had put forth the Redstone, the Jupiter, and the Juno. The Air Force had proposed the Atlas, the Thor, and their own Jupiter. Not to be left out, the Navy had developed the Vanguard, the Polaris, and, yes, they also had a piece of the Jupiter. Each branch of the military saw itself as the rightful owner of space. To the Army, rockets were a mere extension of their artillery. In the eyes of the Air Force, the skies and space were one; it even coined the term *aerospace* to emphasize the point. Finally, from the Navy's perspective, the invisible, submarine-based Polaris missiles were the ultimate weapons. The military fought bitterly among themselves for rocket superiority. Sometimes you wondered who the real enemy was!

And yet, American rocketry in the 1950s could be a sorry sight.

December 6th, 1957. In response to Sputnik, the United States invited the world to witness its rocket power. In front of an excited press corps, a Vanguard TV-3 rose a few inches off the launch pad before exploding in a massive fireball. The press had a field day: *"Flopnik!"* *"Kaputnik!!"* *"Stayputnik!!!"* they howled. The next few rockets did not fare much better.

Despite these failures, Eisenhower kept Von Braun at bay. He would reach out to him only if he had to. In the back of Eisenhower's mind, Von Braun was still the enemy.

October 1st, 1958, saw the birth of NASA, the National Aeronautics and Space Administration, which would coordinate all space endeavors. This would be a civilian agency; there would be no military connotation attached to it and no favoritism expressed towards any single branch of the military.

On December 17th, 1958, NASA announced the creation of Project Mercury, named after the wing-shoed messenger of the Roman Gods (and patron of gamblers). Project Mercury would test our ability to send a man into space or, more specifically, into earth orbit. No specific motive was given. What exactly the pilot would do when he got into space was of a secondary nature. The Soviets were doing it, and we had to do it better.

Project Mercury would require astronauts. (The Soviets would call their pilots cosmonauts.) At first it was felt that the job of astronaut should be open to anyone who was young and athletic. Unfortunately, such loose criteria opened the door to any crackpot circus clown looking for a thrill. Many at NASA were from the military, and not surprisingly, it was quickly decided that astronauts would be chosen from a pool of military pilots – candidates with a track record. To the chagrin of very few, this disqualified all women. There were many excellent women pilots and quite a few who'd expressed an interest in the space program, but none were in the military.

Right after Christmas, Eisenhower gave his stamp of approval to the selection process. 508 pilots met the criteria for the initial screen. The list was whittled down to 110 and divided into three groups. In January 1959, the first two groups were invited to Washington without being told specifically what the meeting was for or who would be there. They had been told to wear civilian clothes. Only as the meeting began were the astronauts informed of its purpose.

No one rushed to sign up.

The pilots would be leaving a secure position in the military for a civilian organization that could go belly up at any time. Would a true test pilot give up a plane for a tin can? A number of Air Force generals had discouraged their pilots from applying in the first place. Thirty-seven candidates backed out when it was explained to them that chimps would be the first to go up in the Mercury capsules. It didn't help that it was called a "capsule" rather than a spacecraft. Because of his age, Chuck Yeager had not been invited, and he sniffed the loudest. He was the test pilot's test pilot, famous for having broken the sound barrier in his orange *Glamorous Glennis*. "Don't forget to wipe the chimp poop off the seat!" he mocked.

More than one pilot took his cue from the master.

To the guys who hung in there, however, it was clear that if they were going to fulfill the test pilot's motto – *Faster, Further, and Higher* – this would be the ultimate opportunity.

The real selection now began. No one – not the doctors, not the astronauts, not Congress, not President Eisenhower – had the slightest idea what physical challenges lay ahead for the astronauts. Would the astronauts be able to swallow in space? Would their eyeballs pop out? Would blood pool in their feet or in their head? How much acceleration could they tolerate? Just how fit did you have to be to be an astronaut? What physical and mental traits would serve you best? In the absence of any definitive answers, NASA doctors decided that the strongest, the toughest, the most patient, and the most tolerant of abuse would make the best subjects; and abused they were. Thirty two candidates were taken to the Lovelace clinic in Albuquerque, New Mexico, where they were spun, whirled, drained, heated, frozen, and fatigued, not to mention poked, prodded, gyrated, and inspected in cavities never before visited by humans. They were subjected to greater and greater acceleration (Gs), until they passed out and their limbs dripped with blood from the broken capillaries. A sperm count was taken as a "fertility baseline."

The candidates were given multiple psychological tests, such as "give fifteen different answers to the question 'who am I?'"

The astronauts found the psychological tests more uncomfortable than the physical abuse. They didn't know what the doctors were looking for; and weren't their minds their own business? They gave away as little as possible. Pete Conrad expressed the general frustration when he was shown a white piece of paper to interpret. "It's upside down," he deadpanned. The doctors deemed Conrad a wise-ass.

In early April, seven candidates received a call informing them that they had been selected. Anointed rather. They were quickly dubbed the "Mercury 7."

Superficially, they were a remarkably homogenous group. They all resembled one another in their silver astronaut suits, all had All-American names starting with C, G, or S, and all were politically correct, 1950s style: White, Anglo-Saxon, Male, and Christian. No Rodriguez, Cohen, Jaleel, and certainly no Ivan. They were all happily married – at least on the surface. Gordon Cooper was separated, but he and Trudy were told to get back together and look happy. The irony was that in the end, only three out of the seven astronauts would remain married to their first wife.

Three were named after a profession: Cooper, Shepard, Carpenter.

Looking more closely, however, they were a varied lot:

<u>Lieutenant Malcolm (Scott) Carpenter, U.S. Navy</u>. More than a pilot, Scott was an adventurer and a bit of a poet, not ashamed of pondering the spiritual ramifications of humans going off into space. He had done his flying in prop planes, which sometimes left him the odd man out when comparing war stories with his hot-shot fighter pilot colleagues; but he could hold his breath under water more than twice as long as any of them, and who knew when that could come in handy?

<u>Captain Leroy (Gordon, "Gordo") Cooper, Jr., U.S. Air Force</u>: An airborne cowboy, not afraid to push the envelope – or a general's buttons.

<u>Lieutenant Colonel John Glenn, Jr., U.S Marine Corps</u>. Part pilot, part minister, part politician, part spin-meister. He was smoother than the rest, and he knew it. He would have been insufferable but for his genuine good-heartedness and loyalty.

<u>Captain Virgil (Gus) Grissom, U.S. Air Force</u>: Majored in engineering at Purdue; a decorated fighter pilot in Korea; an Air Force test pilot. At 5'5", he was the shortest of the group.

<u>Lieutenant Commander Walter (Wally) Schirra, U.S. Air Force</u>: No nonsense test pilot.

<u>Lieutenant Commander Alan Shepard</u>, <u>Navy pilot</u>; a pro at landing a jet on an aircraft carrier; known for rapidly changing from charming to chilly and back; the tallest of the astronauts (5'11").

<u>Captain Donald "Deke" Slayton, U.S. Air Force</u>. Another no nonsense test pilot, cut from the same cloth as Wally Schirra.

None of them was modest.

They formally met each other for the first time at a press conference on April 9th, when the Mercury 7 astronauts were introduced to the Washington press corps. Magellan, Columbus, Lindbergh, Vasco de Gama, and the Wright brothers combined could not have received a more enthusiastic response. These were our Knights in shining space suits, off to fight the Communist Dragon. The auditorium was packed. As each name was announced, reporters put down their pens and cameras. They clapped wildly, as if cheering on the home team in the World Series. And the astronauts had yet to accomplish a single thing. All they'd done was show up!

Typical of the times, the first question posed to the astronauts had no connection to space or even flying: How did their wives and children feel about all this?

Wives and children?

The guys were tough, brave aces, but they were completely unschooled in the practice of public relations and B.S.. They found themselves sweating in front of a press corps already eager for sound bites. Gosh, gee wiz, by golly. They all mumbled through this ceremony with the exception of John Glenn, who jumped all over the question like a hungry cougar.

"I don't think," he intoned, "that any of us could really go on with something like this if we didn't have pretty good backing at home, really. My wife's attitude towards this has been the same as it has been all along through my flying. If it is what I want to do, she is behind it, and the kids are too, a hundred percent."

Gus Grissom had the misfortune of following Glenn. He was a pilot and a patriot, not an ambassador or an orator. He was a whiter shade of pale as he began to stammer through whatever platitude he could conjure up. Could they not just give him a MIG to fire at?

And so it went for a couple of hours, as the new astronauts began to look back more and more fondly on the rectal probes and whirling centrifuges.

It's not possible to overstate the public's lionization of the Mercury 7 or the attention instantly showered upon them by the public and the press. They were the rock stars of their day with *all* the trappings that accompany such adulation. They snagged an exclusive contract with *Life*, arguably the most famous American magazine. *Life* tracked, reported, and glorified their every move. Unfortunately, with the possible exception of John Glenn, these pilots were no saints, and had no intention of living up to such an image. NASA would quickly have to master the art of damage control.

Another unwelcome aspect of their newfound fame was "the pep talk," the visit to the contractors who were building the capsules and rockets. The goal of the pep talks was to cheer them on and let them see a real, live astronaut up front and personal! None, except for Glenn, were fond of this dog and pony show. Gus won the prize for the shortest speech: Staring blankly into a sea of faces at the Convair plant, he thought and thought and thought before finally stammering, "Do good work!"

Gus received a standing ovation.

The euphoria associated with the selection of the astronauts was quick to die down. The sober fact was that relative to the Soviets, we seemed to be going nowhere. A month after *Sputnik 1*, the Soviets launched *Sputnik 2*, which was five times heavier than its predecessor, and housed Laika, a dog. (The animal lived for a week before its oxygen ran out.) In January 1959, the Soviet Luna 1 missed the moon by a few thousand miles, but nevertheless was the first object to leave earth's gravity. In September of the same year, the Russians scored a bull's eye, when Luna 2 impacted the moon; no small feat considering that the moon is a quarter million miles away and circling the earth.

In America, where the press was growing more restless and ornery by the day, the response to this accomplishment was swift. *Newsweek* published an article titled "How to Lose the Space Race." (The term "space race" had gradually crept into the American-Soviet lexicon alongside "missile gap.") To ensure that you'll be on the losing end, advised the magazine, simply "start late, downgrade Russian feats, fragment authority, pinch pennies, think small, shirk decisions."

****

Liverpool was a grim, gray city on the top left side of England. The pictures Mal Evans would send showed gray dockyards, gray buildings, gray ships, gray everything. It was with some shock that years later I would see a color photograph of the city. Why yes, there were reds and blues and greens and yellows... Liverpool had been a major world port and a key destination for American World War II supplies – and therefore a major target of Nazi bombing. By the end of the war, much of it was ash from which not one but two Phoenixes would arise.

By his own admission, Lennon had been a bully as a teenager. Not that he ever got into fights; he talked the talk, but would go home to get his laundry done. He had a prickly shell but a tender core. His father had left the family early on, and his mother, Julia, had abandoned him to the care of his aunt Mimi. As a young teenager, he discovered that his mother lived nearby, and she taught him the banjo; she was more of a pal to him than a mother.

Then, she was killed in front of his house by a speeding car. She had left him again, this time for good. He was seventeen.

Lennon got along well with his Aunt Mimi and Uncle George, but suddenly his uncle died. It seemed that all those he loved would desert him in one fashion or another. He failed all his major exams and was last in his class of twenty. He became an angry young man of sorts, but eager to be loved and appreciated. He would dress up as a Teddy Boy – the local gangster punks – but he wasn't one of them. The most he would do was take the collection box from church and use the money to buy beer. In fact, *real* Teddy Boys would regularly beat him up for dressing like them.

He wrote poetry, but didn't want to be seen as literary. Though near-sighted, he refused to wear glasses. His fingers were stained with nicotine. Neighborhood mothers warned their children to stay away from him. Surely he could have been voted least likely to succeed; the classic misfit.

Elvis Presley's "Heartbreak Hotel" would save him. From the moment he heard the song, his energies became focused on finding other American songs. And a guitar. Finding the songs was the easy part. Liverpool was still a major British port and home to throngs of sailors who brought back records from America. Before rock 'n' roll, they'd brought back country and western tunes, the inspiration for English skiffle – music played on sophisticated instruments such as the washboard and the comb. Finding a guitar that he could afford was harder.

Considering his fascination with word play, Lennon ironically had no particular interest in lyrics. His focus was on the beat and on the music. With his classmates, he put together a band called The Quarry Men, named after his school, The Quarry Bank. He was the front man. To say that his bandmates possessed limited talent would be a vast understatement. Lennon himself barely bothered to learn all the words to a song, resorting instead to his remarkable gift for improvisation. While singing on stage, John's bitterness seemed to evaporate.

Growing up in another middle-class part of Liverpool, Paul McCartney could not have been more different. He was well adjusted and well liked. His mother Mary had died of breast cancer when he was fourteen. He'd adapted to the tragedy better than Lennon would to his. He had a younger brother, Michael, to pal around with. He was close to his father, who played the trumpet in a jazz band and often took his sons to hear music.

Like Lennon, McCartney found himself drawn to American rock 'n' roll, and he also scrounged around for a guitar. Once he figured out how to string the guitar for the lefty that he was, he found it relatively easy to play chords and arrange songs. He could handily tune his guitar. He made an effort to memorize lyrics.

On July 6th, 1957, the two met at a fair through the efforts of a mutual friend, Ivan Vaughn. John's band was playing. John was sixteen and a half; Paul had just turned fifteen.

They chatted a few moments, and then came Paul's audition. He played the complicated "Twenty Flight Rock" from beginning to end. With panache. Lennon was impressed. The kid could play and he had a certain presence.

You never know when the biggest decision of your life is going to come around, and for Lennon here it was. Should he ask the kid to join the band? The bloke hadn't even asked to join. But surely that's what he was there for.

The pros and cons were obvious. The chap could sing, he could play a ton of chords, he remembered the lyrics, and he even tuned the fockin' guitar just before he started. Does an alpha lion invite another alpha lion into the pride? Lennon mulled it over a few days.

The chap was a year, no a year *and a half* younger, for chrissake.

But at least he would know who was boss… Lennon bicycled over to Ivan's. "By the way, tell Paul he's in." Strictly as a favor, of course.

McCartney, for all his cool, was elated. A band!!! No one had ever asked him! Not that he would ever show his elation to Lennon. He would join strictly as a favor.

The pair quickly recognized that their voices complemented each other, with Paul's melodious, choirboy voice playing off John's harsher nasal tones. At this stage, theirs was a working relationship, not truly a friendship. Lennon's real friend was a dreamy dead ringer for James Dean, a budding artist by the name of Stu Sutcliffe. Stu could talk for hours about painting and art, and this resonated with John. Stu even sold one of his paintings to an art collector! John promptly convinced him to buy a bass guitar with the money, and the Quarrymen had a new member. He'd never played bass before, but this didn't put him that far behind the others.

On the way to school, McCartney took bus line 81 together with scrawny George Harrison. George loved to practice guitar solos, his favorite being a tune called "Raunchy." Paul brought him over to meet John. For heaven's sake, this lad was even younger than Paul. What was this, a nursery school? George Harrison was in.

It was always a mystery to Cynthia Powell why she was so attracted to John Lennon. One year her junior, he reflected none of her own qualities. She was proper, polite, eager to please, and deferential to her elders. He was crass and mean. Her father had passed away, but, other than a dead parent, they seemed to have nothing in common. She had met John at his worst. His mother had recently been killed, and his staid and stern Aunt Mimi was raising him. He was now meaner and cruder than ever. Nevertheless, she found herself completely taken in by him – and he by her – and she would remain so her entire life.

In May 1960, the Quarrymen were hired to back up Johnny Gentle on a tour of Scotland. A tour!!! They changed their name to Johnny and the Moondogs for the purposes of the tour, one of many names they would hopscotch over in the course of the next few months.

Now, if they could only find a drummer.

For illustrations see www.intotheskywithdiamonds.com

4. Mach Schau!

As we awoke on January 1ˢᵗ, 1960, there was nothing to suggest any imminent changes to the new decade. Same President, same music. We were still fighting the Communists. All was generally well in a prosperous America. Only a few dark clouds peppered the sky. Racial repression persisted, as did the Cold War: In March, Negroes marched against segregation in Montgomery, Alabama, and in April, ten Negroes protesting on a segregated Mississippi beach were shot. An American U-2 spy plane was shot down over Russia. The pilot, Francis Powers, was captured.

The music scene was uninspiring, and I took little interest in it, except for the harmonious Everly Brothers. When I think of the time spent on my guitar learning the simple "Cathy's Clown" …

**

Prodded by a visionary administrator, George Low, NASA tentatively announced a program that could put a man on the moon. The program was baptized "Apollo." The program was nothing more than a daydream. There were no funds allocated to the project, and Low wasn't getting any help from the ballistic engineers: Rockets were blowing up left and right.

On July 29ᵗʰ, 1960, an Atlas rocket carrying an unmanned Mercury capsule blew up one minute into flight, and on August 21ˢᵗ the parachute on a Mercury capsule failed. The capsule disintegrated on impact with the ocean.

My buddies in the Air Force poured it on with their string of high-profile successes: Within days of the first Mercury-Atlas fiasco, the cool all-black X-15 rocket plane set two world records – one for speed (2,196 miles per hour) and one for altitude (136,000 feet). Now *that* was flying. In mid-August, an Air Force C-119 trailed a huge trapeze-shaped net and caught a falling satellite in mid-air. It was the kind of flight heroics that people love, whether they're engineers or average Joes in front of the TV.

As usual, though, the lion's share of the press went to the USSR. On the very day that the Air Force completed its catch-a-satellite routine, the Soviets sent into orbit a mini menagerie: two dogs, Strelka and Belka (dubbed "muttniks"), along with rats, mice, flies, plants, and fungi. After eighteen orbits, the whole ark came down safely. This marked the first successful recovery of biological organisms after an orbital voyage, and the implications for human flight were not lost on NASA or the American public.

In mid-August, the U.S. fortunately launched a communication satellite, ("Echo"), leading a suddenly upbeat American press to announce that we'd rejoined the space race.

****

Though raised in Providence, a stone's throw from Brown University, I had felt the need to spread my wings and had enrolled at Purdue in Indiana. I graduated with a degree in Engineering, then joined the Air Force as a communications specialist. As I'd explained to Mal, it had been my job to establish communication networks between controllers on the ground and pilots above. Now, at the tender age of twenty-three, a month after my return from Germany, I was contacted by Gene Kranz and invited to join him at NASA. He himself would just be starting work there. Kranz had been an engineer and supersonic Air Force jet pilot, and he'd been picked to be one of the flight controllers. He was an amiable, tough military type who favored the crew cut. (Today I suppose he'd favor a shaved head.) His eyebrows hung low over his eyes, giving him a perennially intense look. His palms tended to sweat.

I'd never been to Florida and was a little nervous. The humidity and stifling heat were rumored to be ideal breeding grounds for all sorts of organisms I could hardly pronounce. My friends joked that you practically needed shots if you were going to spend any time near Cape Canaveral. But my nerves were no match for my excitement. To be handpicked for a job in a high-profile new institution, my future career wide open... Suffice it to say, the guys I was leaving behind were envious. After all, it was in my lifetime that we'd first seen high-altitude planes. Now people flew to Europe or California at will. Who knew what could happen in the next twenty years?

Upon my arrival at the Patrick Air Force Base, a short athletic fellow, who looked to be in his thirties, walked briskly towards me, and thrust his muscular hand in my direction. His face would have fit neatly within a rectangle. He had two slits for eyes and also wore a crew cut. His face split expansively into a broad smile.

"Hi, my name's Gus Grissom. I'm assigned to drive you to the Cape."

His name meant nothing to me, but I was impressed by his mode of transportation: a shiny red Corvette!

He wore a short sleeve Ban-Lon sports shirt and aviator glasses – the astronaut's uniform, as I'd soon find out. (Everyone else at NASA wore white shirts and ties. And pocket protectors for the ballpoint pens.)

"I hear you went to Purdue," said Grissom. "I was Class of 1950."

There was something reassuring about being with a fellow Boilermaker. We had both majored in Engineering, he in Mechanical and I in Electrical, and the two of us had arrived at NASA by way of the Air Force.

We jumped into the Corvette, the rear wheels spat sand and gravel, and off we were. Gus drove too fast for me to appreciate the scenery. Maybe that was all for the better. I'm not sure I really wanted to see the alligators and snakes jawing and hissing as we invaded their territory. Using our alma mater as a springboard, we went through a thumbnail sketch of each other's lives: Upon graduation Gus was set to take a job at a brewery, but his mother, a dedicated teetotaler, would not hear of it. (How different his life might have been had he taken the job!) Instead he joined the Air Force. He flew one hundred missions in the Korean War, and, for saving a fellow pilot from an attacking MIG, he was awarded the Distinguished Flying Cross. He'd met fellow astronaut Gordon Cooper at the Wright-Patterson Air Force Base in Ohio; they were now best buddies. Oh, and he was married. Been married to Betty since he was nineteen, even before going to college. Had two sons, Scott and Mark. He had taken a ribbing in Korea for naming his F-86 Sabrejet *Scotty*. (Planes were supposed to be named after your best girl.) In college someone had mistaken the abbreviation of his name ("Gris") for "Gus," and the rest was history.

I told him about my family – my father played cello in the Rhode Island Philharmonic Orchestra, and I had two younger sisters – but mostly I asked questions. About NASA, his time in the Air Force, Korea. What I wondered, but didn't ask, was what it was like to marry at nineteen.

The launch area was not impressive. Mercury control was a squat, square, concrete bunker, maybe sixty feet long. A map of the world covered much of one wall. A little model of a spacecraft moved along a wire suspended over the map to simulate its trajectory. At various points along the map, circles were drawn over the locations of our tracking stations. A toy company could have made the whole thing.

Engineers walked with slide rules clipped to their belts.

At the back of the room were three rows of consoles. I'd be introduced to those shortly.

Two hundred yards away, in the middle of the launch pad, a black and white Redstone rocket pointed towards the sky. The rocket was a pencil of glistening metal, but the capsule sitting atop it looked like a heap of corrugated metal. Topped by its tall red escape tower, Gus commented that the whole thing looked more like a buoy than a rocket. "You get in with a shoehorn and get out with a can opener," joked one of the pad crew. The spacecraft's coarse appearance seriously belied its complexity. This little jewel from the McDonnell Aircraft Company in St. Louis involved 4000 suppliers and 596 direct subcontractors from twenty-five states. It consisted of 750,000 parts and seven miles of wiring.

Gus brought me past Fat Boys' restaurant and into the bar of the Holiday Inn in nearby Cocoa Beach, where I could be properly introduced to the rest of gang. That meant downing a few mugs of beer while comparing war stories. Of course, I had none, but my arrival gave all the others an opportunity to regale themselves all over again with tales of heroics and near misses. I was hungry for the details, even if they were exaggerated. My father rarely talked about his war experience. He'd make a joke or say something like, "We just did what we had to do."

The boss at Mercury Control was Christopher Columbus Kraft (no kidding). You would not have wanted to be stuck on an island with him, but he epitomized organization, and he surrounded himself with A-level staff. Every position in the hierarchy had a "handle" in the communication loop, and Kraft's position at the top of the pyramid was "Flight." It took me a while to understand that when people began their communications with the word "Flight," they were addressing Kraft.

"Flight" was a master at listening to multiple conversations in his headset and picking out just the information he needed – much like the orchestra conductor singles out the one problem instrument among the multitude.

Everyone around looked young. There was barely a grizzled temple in sight. We all reported to the "old man," Bob Gilruth, a big fellow from Minnesota, who must have been in his mid-forties. At the age of twenty-three, I was hardly out of place. Since there had never been a space program, and since we were just getting off the ground, so to speak, there were job openings everywhere. Past a certain level, it was hard to be un-qualified for the job. That didn't stop us from feeling special. It was a dream job for the young and cocky.

And yet, we still ignored many basics concepts. For example, by definition, an object that reaches earth orbit will circle the planet in-definitely. But how to tell if a capsule has reached orbit? If it has, what is its path? If it hasn't, where is it coming down? I hadn't been there two weeks, when Kranz and I were called into Chris Kraft's office.

"Get with the test conductors," he said, "and write a countdown. Then write some mission rules. When you finish give me a call, and we'll come down and start training." There. Just like that, Kranz and I would be responsible for something neither of us had ever done.

***

I had not recognized the man when he ambled in unannounced. Tall, broad, athletic, and good-looking, he smiled and pumped every-one's fist, as he made his way towards the back of the control room. Was he was running for office? The man was a perfect human speci-men. He could have fallen off the back of a Central Casting truck. Everyone but me knew exactly who he was. It was Wernher von Braun. You could pronounce his first name "Werner" or "Fairn-er," but you couldn't say "von brawn." It was "fon brown." Period.

The man had quite a history.

He had been a Nazi and was now working for the Americans. That was the short story.

The long story was far more complex and enticing. He had understood his life's work since childhood. As a teenager he had immersed himself in rudimentary rocket manuals, attached fireworks to wooden carts, attracted the attention of the police for posing a menace, drawn rockets in the margins of his classroom notebooks, and daydreamed of going to the moon. Yet for all the trouble he had caused as a teenager, in 1932, at the age of twenty, he began a secret dissertation for the army. The German army subsequently offered to fund his research, with the obvious understanding that Von Braun would design artillery rockets. This posed no moral conflict for this hyper-energetic young man from a military family. If he had to develop his moon rockets by way of the Artillery, so be it. He became the Technical Director of the Army Rocket Center at Peenemünde on the Baltic Sea, quickly displaying his greatest talent: coordinating enormous engineering projects.

1937 would be a watershed year in Von Braun's life. Hitler and the Nazis had now been in power for five years and controlled every aspect of military life. If he were to continue being the Director of Peenemünde, he would have to join the Party. His father advised against it, but on November 12th, 1937, Von Braun became Nazi Party member #5,738,692. Nazi policies mattered little to Von Braun. The moon beckoned and was his only master.

The start of World War II saw Von Braun pressured to come up with a practical rocket. The pressure was gradually ratcheted upwards as the war took one bad turn after another and Hitler became more desperate. Von Braun was briefly jailed when the Party determined that he was not sufficiently cooperative. To help speed his projects along, the Nazis assigned prisoners of the nearby Dora camp to the Peenemünde detail. The conditions at Dora were no better than in the worst of the concentration camps. Workers died of abuse on a regular basis. "What did Von Braun know about Dora, and when did he know it?" were the questions that would haunt him the rest of his life.

Von Braun's team finally came up with a rocket that could travel hundreds of miles with some kind of accuracy – the black and white V2 that destroyed much of the greater London area. By then the war was lost, and perhaps Von Braun finally came to wonder what exactly he was fighting for. In February 1945, Von Braun was ordered to organize the evacuation Peenemünde. Herding along his most trusted associates, he defected instead to the Americans. He was thirty-three years old.

Von Braun was sent to El Paso, Texas, and subsequently to Huntsville, Alabama, where he was placed on "town" arrest. Von Braun was still not considered trustworthy. Conversely, when traveling to Europe, he was given a heavy military escort for fear of kidnapping by the Soviets.

Only slightly embroidered by an exuberant imagination, his tales of space travel found a receptive audience in the America of the 1950s. His publisher, *Collier* magazine, handsomely supplemented his small Army stipend. He orchestrated a movie with Disney. A silver screen version of his life, *I Aim At The Stars*, was produced. The movie was a flop, but it became great fodder for comedians. Mort Sahl deadpanned, "I Aim at the Stars… but sometimes I hit London." On a more positive note, "Missile Man von Braun" graced the cover of the February 17, 1958, issue of *Time* magazine.

For all his public success, von Braun constantly needed funding for his rocket research. He had first resorted to his tried and true approach: convincing the military that his rockets would defeat the enemy – the godless Communists of the Soviet Union. Von Braun, however, had met with only modest success. The Navy and the Air Force were building rockets without him, thank you, and Eisenhower had not taken the Soviet bait. America would build whatever it needed to defend itself, and no more. *Sputnik*, of course, had changed all that. Von Braun was back in the game and loving it.

And here he was pressing the flesh. All were standing in receiving line fashion, except for Kraft. I shot a glance at Gene, who had sidled up to Kraft, and I instinctively decided I had better do the same. When von Braun strode towards us, he received a frosty reception. Kraft looked the other way. Gene extended an awkward handshake.

Was there a problem here?

A legend in our midst, and Kraft was giving him the cold shoulder!

Apparently, there was no love lost between the two, though the disdain was unidirectional: von Braun had no quarrel with Kraft, but Kraft prided himself on a hard day's work carried out in professional anonymity. He did not appreciate Mr. Spotlight-Seeking-Know-It-All's attitude. Not with all the blood on his hands. "Arrogance honed to a fine edge" was how Kraft would describe von Braun. Moreover, von Braun did not seem to care what flag he fought for, a pardonable offense perhaps in the scientific community, but unforgivable in the military. I could see Kraft's point.

The test launches continued to be a series of embarrassments.

It was the end of July – I had hardly been at Cape Canaveral a month – when I witnessed my first rocket launch, a Mercury capsule coupled to an Atlas rocket. A skydiver made a precise landing not far away just prior to the main event, generating a round of applause. A small voice at the back commented that it was too bad the daredevil had actually been aiming for Tampa on the other coast of Florida. We chuckled and turned around to see that the voice had come from a lovely svelte woman, who flashed a radiant smile at the sudden attention.

Things turned serious again as the countdown began. Liftoff proceeded normally, and then... one minute or so into its flight...........

Kaboom! The Atlas rocket disintegrated into a ball of flame. "That's our ride," joked future astronaut John Young.

Yeah! The astronauts couldn't wait to get into that baby!

The press continued to roast us in our own flames. In August, *Missiles and Rockets* ran the following piece:

> *NASA's Mercury manned satellite program appears to be plummeting the United States toward a new humiliating disaster in the East-West space race. This is the stark conclusion that looms in the minds of a growing number of eminent rocket scientists and engineers as the Mercury program continues to slip backwards...The program is more than one year behind the original schedule ... It no longer offers any realistic hope of beating Russia in launching the first man into orbit, much less to serve as an early stepping-stone for reaching the Moon.*
>
> *Despite precautions and improvements Mercury continues to be a technically marginal program that could easily end in flaming tragedy. Mercury, at best, is a technical stop-gap, justifiable only as an expedient ... Mercury*

has proven to be a trip down a dead-end road that U.S. taxpayers are finding themselves paving in gold.

This and other equally virulent opinion pieces pushed NASA into a defensive posture:

> *As most of you know, there have been some adverse comments in the press about the progress, or lack of progress, being made in Project Mercury ... At the same time there are number of people around our country who do understand how much work and how much blood and sweat go into an undertaking of this kind...*
>
> *Since the negotiation of the capsule contract, McDonnell personnel have averaged 14% overtime for an equivalent 56-hour week. McDonnell has assigned approximately 13,000 people in direct support of Project Mercury. In October 1959, production went on a 7-day week, three shifts per day ... Many have used essentially no annual leave ... When the MA-1 capsule was delivered to the Cape on May 23, 1960, this [Space Task Group] went on a 60-hour week. During the final month of MA-1 preparations, the launch operations crew was working a seventy-hour week,...*

Perhaps my job at NASA would turn out to be a dead end, but I decided to wait things out. I was twenty-three; I could afford to take a chance. I was growing to like it there. What's not to like about the beaches? There were so many birds – gulls, herons, egrets, pelicans, plovers – and so many I'd never seen before! Even if our rockets ultimately failed, I was getting the education and experience of a lifetime. But we weren't *going* to fail! We were Americans! We were the best!

I focused on the preparation of the Mercury capsule.

Our immediate concern was guarding against – and preparing for – the failure of this or that system. Systems that had never been tried in space. Back-up strategies were devised for nearly every aspect of the flight. If the air pressure in the capsule were lost, for example, the astronauts' suit would instantly inflate to a pressure of five lbs/in^2. The search for redundancy was also true in my area, communications. If one microphone failed, a second one would be available. If one radio frequency failed another would be available. And what if all voice systems failed? Morse code ... --- ... .

I was soon introduced to my other colleagues: the Western Electric radars, telemetry, Teletype, and control consoles that would be my tools from here on in. During rocket launches my console would be in the middle row next to the Teletype. In a sense, Teletype was the precursor to IM/text messaging: You typed as quickly as you could, a machine punched holes into a narrow paper tape, and your message was delivered by radio waves to an electric typewriter sitting at your destination. Communication was only as fast as your fingers.

In those early days it was even more cumbersome than that. All messages were first sent to Langley Air Force Base in Virginia, where some poor soul frenetically plugged cables into a huge board of jacks aimed at the rest of the world.

There were no communication satellites. NASA set up manned communications centers around the globe designed to track and communicate with an orbiting craft. I was part of that team. During the first Mercury flight, I would actually man one of these centers (the one in Zanzibar).

The tracking sites included the so-called major Go/No Go sites, in Bermuda, Australia, Hawaii, Mexico, and California. Major decisions such as continuation or discontinuation of a mission would be made as the capsule passed over these stations. The astronauts felt strongly about speaking to one of their fellow astronauts at critical times, so a Mercury astronaut was assigned to these sites. Because his task would be to *com*municate with the capsule, he would become known as the CapCom. At each Go/No Go site, the CapCom had access to a thirty-page Mercury rules book, including hypotheticals that were carefully underlined in green or red, depending on their Go/No Go status.

At the intermediate sites, controllers would track the position of the capsule, communicate briefly with the astronaut, and report back to Mercury Control. These intermediate sites would be located in the Canary Islands, Nigeria, Zanzibar, Canton Island, as well as on ships stationed in various oceans. In all, there were thirteen manned sites.

Some of these sites were outright dangerous. Rebellion was rife throughout Africa, with one country after another overthrowing the vestiges of colonial rule. Zanzibar was particularly tense, as I'd witnessed myself. There was no one over thirty at any of these stations. It wasn't that the loneliness, the danger, and the exotic nature of the locations appealed mostly to recent college graduates. Rather, NASA at this point was as likely to implode as it was to put a man in space, and few people with secure jobs were willing to risk their careers.

When a capsule flew over a station, there would be approximately eight minutes of contact. Then nothing but silence until the capsule passed over the next station. Needless to say, we tried to minimize the No Contact periods, and when all worked well, there were none; at least not for *single* orbit missions. Because the earth spins underneath it, a capsule passes over a different part of the earth with each orbit. It would take a few orbits before the capsule would come back over the tracking stations. This meant *loooong* periods of silence on multi-orbit missions. Murphy's Law dictated that many in-flight problems would develop during these No Contact periods.

Our communication system was laughably capricious. A construction crew would sever a cable, and, bam, there went Australia. Fog? Out went the Canary Islands. A sunspot? Good-bye Zanzibar.

It became clear that we would need to develop unambiguous language to communicate with an astronaut. Static could alter words and drastically change their meaning. Thus "continue" was changed to "GO," and "discontinue" converted to "No Go." "Yes" could sound mumbled and so became "Affirmative."

**

NASA had decided that the seven astronauts would become intimately involved with the development of the Mercury project. There would be plenty of work for everyone, since nothing had been developed.

I was hoping that Gus would be assigned to my section, but instead the assignment went to Scott Carpenter, who had done similar work while in the Navy. (Gus went to the manual control systems team.) It was our job to help Ground Control talk to an orbiting astronaut. We suggested, for example, that the radio be independent of the other systems. I did not have complete confidence in these miles of wires, and if all went to pot, I still wanted to be able to talk to my astronaut. It was one of my better ideas, and it would save Gordon Cooper's life during his first mission.

**

The dull-looking tin can masquerading as a spacecraft gave no hint of the many considerations that had gone into its design. In the first place, the capsule had to fit over an existing rocket and function as a nose cone! In fact, one of the original designs had called for the capsule to be a pointy cone.

When it was discovered that men would tolerate more Gs (acceleration/deceleration) lying down, it was decided that the seat would be turned ninety degrees to position the astronaut on his back during lift-off. This would have the added advantage of having him face forward during flight, not that it would make a big difference. It wasn't as if he were going to run into another spacecraft. A special molded couch was manufactured.

The parachute necessary to decelerate the capsule for a soft landing on solid ground was found to be too big to fit into the capsule. Ergo the decision to have the capsule "land" in water with a smaller chute. The word "splashdown" was coined.

Wally Schirra pushed to have "capsule" changed to "spacecraft."

Astronaut training seemed to be a continuation of the pilot screening process: The MASTIF (Multiple Axis Space Test Inertia Facility) at the Lewis Center in Ohio was a cage-like device into which the astronauts were strapped. The cage would spin around multiple axes, and the astronaut's job was to control the cage with a single control stick. There was the centrifuge in Pennsylvania, and, on a "lighter" note, the zero-gravity flights at the Holloman base in New Mexico. A plane, the "Vomit Comet," would climb at a steep angle and then plunge downwards. At the top of the arc, the astronauts would experience a few moments of weightlessness.

We needed to set up flight contingency plans. What would we do in the event of malfunctions? A team of five people was assembled to set up disaster scenarios. The director of that team was given the title "SimSup" (Simulation Supervisor). During simulation exercises SimSup would feed us imaginary malfunctions to which we would

32

have to respond. Our responses would result in real-time changes to the entire system. Today we would call this virtual reality. With increasing sophistication, these mind games would continue until the very end of the Apollo program.

In between all the fun and games, the astronauts took time out to gather at the B.F. Goodrich plant for a fitting of their astronaut pressure suits. One of the most famous NASA pictures was taken on that day: All of the Mercury astronauts are wearing their suits, the only time all seven astronauts would ever be required to be in their suits simultaneously. It was a true *Life* magazine moment.

****

I'd never really been interested in politics, but in the fall of 1960, it was hard not to pay attention. For one thing, I could now vote. The election would represent a changing of the guard, regardless of who won. Eisenhower had served his two terms, and our next President would be either Vice-President Nixon or Senator Kennedy. The two could not have been more different. Staid, stiff, and uncomfortable in a crowd, Nixon presented a stark contrast to the young, smiling, charismatic Kennedy. Nixon, however, represented the status quo – a status quo that the public by and large approved of. Much was made of standing up to the Communist Soviets, and much was also made of Kennedy's Catholicism. To the outside world it must have seemed puzzling that such a major distinction would be made between Protestant Christian and Catholic Christian, but such was the state of America.

In September we were treated to a new event, a televised debate between the two candidates. Most of the fellows around me were Nixon guys. He was a known, safe quantity. Who knew what Kennedy would do to our space program? Perhaps he'd take our budget and put it all into rockets aimed at the Soviets! Kennedy hammered away at the "missile gap," a concept based on the erroneous premise that the Eisenhower administration had allowed the Communist Soviets to pull ahead in missile firepower.

As the debate wore on, we started shifting in our seats. Between the lighting and the makeup – or lack thereof – Nixon looked like a gangster. Nixon was also suffering from a knee injury and shifted uncomfortably from one leg to the other. Kennedy was animated and engaging.

Afterwards, it was clear to me that Kennedy had won the debate. I wasn't going to take any chances though: I would vote for the team of Richard Nixon and Henry Cabot Lodge.

****

On September 27th, I received my first letter from Mal Evans.

I hadn't quite recognized the name on the envelope. A letter from England?

Liverpool, 27th September, 1960

Dear Dutch

It was nice to meet you. You're the first American I've ever spoken to at any length.

Nothing too exciting here. For fun, I've agreed to work part time as a bouncer at a club called the Cavern, here in Liverpool. "Club" is stretching it. It's a subterranean brick cave eighteen steps down. It's hot, dank, and claustrophobic, but people come here to listen to music. It used to be just jazz, but they've expanded to rock'n'roll. Friends of mine play here at lunch. I don't know if you noticed them at the Kaiserkeller in Germany, where we had a drink. The girls dig them, and they've got a nice little following. They're dressed in black leather from head to toe; they're billed as "Direct from Hamburg," leading some of the kids to believe they're German. The really big guys in Liverpool are Rory Storm and the Hurricanes, as well as Cass and the Casanovas.

The letter continued for another two pages, but it was at this point that I remembered who Mal Evans was. The big guy on the bus, the druid guy, that one. Yeah. I was surprised he'd written to me, though I remembered exchanging addresses. (I'd promptly lost his.)

His letter was a mishmash of stories about the group I'd seen in Hamburg and theories about Stonehenge and UFO's; I answered it with a description of being tapped by Krantz to work at NASA. He wrote back almost immediately and regularly after that. It's hard to imagine now – that kind of relationship springing up between two men who'd only met once – but things were different then. People had pen pals. One-on-one blogging. It was the only way anyone with an interest in the wider world could stay a part of it. It turned out that Mal was quite a prolific writer. That's what happens when you don't have a television! (Despite being a *communications* specialist I didn't own one either! Nor did any of my co-workers. Considering my position, I thought I should be entitled to one. As a business expense, of course.)

Mal's letter filled me in on what the Beatles' had done before Hamburg. He was amused by how often they'd changed their name – from the Quarry Men to the Beatals to the Silver Beatles, and finally to the Beatles. "Beetles" was an obvious nod to one of their rock 'roll' heroes, Buddy Holly and the Crickets, and they had tweaked it to "Beatles" to snatch the little "beat, beatnik, back beat" double entendre. Lennon liked the fact that "Beatles" could be further turned around to read "Les Beat," which sounded French and cool.

Their gig in Hamburg was their first break. Liverpool promoter Allan Williams had a German connection in the person of club owner Bruno Koschmider, a thug who ran seedy nightclubs. English bands were popular in the red light district of Hamburg's Reeperbahn, and after he'd exhausted his "A" list, Williams had sent over the Beatles.

Desperate for a drummer, Lennon, McCartney, Harrison, and Sutcliffe had induced Pete Best to join them on their overseas venture. He had a shiny-new drum kit and had taken some lessons. His mother, Mona, ran a popular little nightclub in Liverpool.

Hamburg lay on the northern coast of West Germany, and like Liverpool, was a bustling port city. It buzzed with activity, fed in large part by the American military bases. The St Pauli district was the Montmartre or Times Square of the city, and running down its nerve center was a seedy street called the Reeperbahn, complete with pulsating neon, sex shows, and brothels – one big celebration of extreme sexual behavior of every sort.

Dreaming of the big time as they arrived in this intoxicating atmosphere, the Beatles instead landed in a pit called the Indra (German for India), a dingy dive with exhausted furniture and a plastic elephant out front. Their "housing" consisted of a cubbyhole behind the screen of a nearby porn theater. No shower, no bathroom. The Indra's dressing room was the men's toilet.

Safe to say, Koschmider wasn't overly impressed to be hosting the Beatles.

The Indra could not even be compared to any of the Liverpool hot spots, for it was empty. It would be their job to bring in the crowd.

And they failed.

Not that they weren't playing well. They played their numbers to perfection. The chords were there, the beat was loud, the harmonies were passable. But sailors stuck their heads in and walked out.

Koschmider didn't have much patience for this. He stood at the doorway, gesticulated a little with his hips, and yelled "mach schau"!!!

Mach schau????

There was no specific English equivalent for this expression (it wasn't even good German) – but the meaning suddenly hit the band like a bolt of lightening. They got it. Create a show! Well, that was something they could do! They were naturals. All the while playing their guitars and singing their heads off, Lennon and McCartney began jumping and growling and bumping and swiveling; and … it worked. Soldiers and sailors came in and had a beer. Lennon had them howling with his imitations of cripples and goblins. He yelled at them, insulted them, called them 'Krauts', with no ill effects. Quite the contrary, the more he ranted, the more they loved it. Their audience was on the prowl for drink and sex, and was oblivious to any insult. The Beatles played all evening and into the early hours of the morning, seven days a week, to a crowd consisting of drunken sailors and whores. Diet pills nick-named Prellys kept them going, as did the constant flow of beer.

Lennon would later say, "we were born in Liverpool, but we grew up in Hamburg."

The Beatles sang, danced, jumped, crawled, screamed, gesticulated, and pounded out 1950s rock'n'roll for hours on end. And so it went on for the next five months.

Things improved a little.

In October, Koschmider decided that the Beatles could be moved up to his "big" club, the Kaiserkeller. This was the gaudy club with the fishnet and portholes where I'd first had drinks with Mal Evans.

The crowd was even rougher than at the Indra, and the club had its enforcers to keep the undesirables in line. The term "undesirable" was, of course, very relative.

There was still a chronic shortage of microphones. Being a lefty, however, McCartney could share one with Lennon, and still face the audience without pushing the neck of his guitar into Lennon's ribs. Head to head, the two could actually hear each other; they began to work on their harmonies. McCartney could hit the higher notes and gradually took on the loftier lines.

The Beatles alternated sets with another Liverpool band, Rory Storm and the Hurricanes. Rory Storm wasn't his real name. It was Alan Caldwell. He gave himself and all other members of his group stage names. To his drummer Richard Starkey he gave the name Ringo Starr.

On a hot summer night, the fates brought in a most unlikely character, Klaus Voorman, a stylishly dressed art student and musician. He was an "Exis," a loose group of literary, artsy students. "Exis" stood for existentialists. It's not clear what had brought Klaus to the Kaiserkeller, only what brought him back: the antics of these wild guys from England with their funny pompadours. He thought a friend of his should check out the scene. He returned with a perky blonde named Astrid Kirchherr.

Astrid also took a liking to the five maniacs on stage, in particular the bass player, Stu. She and Stu soon became an item, and in short order, the Beatles were hanging out with the intelligentsia of Hamburg. Discussions were of a higher caliber than their usual jabber, and the fivesome readily took to the German scene. A particular feature of Klaus and their Exis friends was their look: black leather pants, denim jackets, and… their hair combed forward onto their forehead.

Stu was the first to go along with this sartorial and tonsorial metamorphosis. Over the next few months the others followed suit. Pete Best was the only holdout. He would upgrade his clothes, but he wasn't giving up his pompadour. Girls flocked to him as it was; there was no reason to mess with a good thing. Standing apart from the other four did not bother him in the least. He hadn't grown up with them, and he didn't partake in their endless teasing, wisecracking, and horsing around. It just wasn't his style.

Fall found the Beatles still playing in Hamburg. With their Koschmider contract running out, they accepted an offer to move to the classier Top Ten. Contract or no contract, however, Koschmider played by his own rules. He was not pleased to see his star attractions move to another club. He tipped off the police that George Harrison was underage, and before long, the five Beatles were back on their arses in Liverpool.

Mal also had a lot to say about UFOs, the magnetic energy of Stonehenge, and other paranormal phenomena. I was interested in his ideas, but what did he really know? *I* was the one who was going to have real outer space experiences!

****

October saw Soviet Premier Khrushchev's famous sandal incident at the United Nations. He would crush us, he vowed. He had made this threat before, and he meant it. He wasn't scared of America, he wasn't scared of Eisenhower, and he wouldn't be scared of Nixon. Would Kennedy fare better? Yes, the American public decided, and on November 8th elected him President by a mere whisker.

I was 0 for 1 in elections.

And nervous. It wasn't clear at all that this new Administration would support the space program. After all, it was the prior Administration's project, and our progress was only slightly encouraging. I could easily see the new Administration canning the whole thing. The best part of Election Day was that our next rocket failure went un-noticed. "Little Joe 5" was the code name for this rocket/capsule combination. It failed sixteen seconds into its flight, when the escape rocket and the tower jettison rocket fired prematurely, shattering everything to pieces.

That wasn't even the low point of the year. That honor belonged to the November 21st Mercury-Redstone 1 (MR-1) flight.

NASA was inaugurating a new Mercury Control Center, and all the biggies were there. Bob Gilruth was there, waving his big cigar, as were Chris Kraft and Wernher von Braun. The plan was to fire a dummy Mercury capsule atop a Redstone rocket. An escape rocket at the top of the capsule was designed to whisk the capsule to safety in case of a launch emergency.

With each launch failure there had been increasing pressure to get it right. Kraft was as tense as a guy who's flunked his finals twice and is getting another chance. I kept getting him milk from the "roach coach" outside Mercury Control. This was a little truck that came by our palmetto swamp three times a day with basic foods. No beer. But milk was all Kraft ever asked for.

As the countdown began, all voices hushed to a whisper.

The countdown reached zero, a long flame erupted, and a huge cloud of smoke enveloped the rocket. We looked up to the sky, but the rocket had already disappeared.

Well, not quite. When we looked back down, and the smoke had cleared… the rocket was still on the launch pad!!!

The 83-foot missile had lifted a few inches off the ground, and then plunked itself back down! Considering all the fuel in its tanks, it was miraculous that it hadn't blown up.

As far as the escape tower at the top of the capsule was concerned, ignition had signaled liftoff. When the rocket shut down, it errone-ously sensed that the capsule was entering orbit. Right on schedule it shot up into the sky to disengage itself from the capsule. Normally, the rocket would have been over the Atlantic at that point, and the escape tower would have fallen harmlessly into the water. With the rocket still on the launch pad, however, the escape tower would perhaps land right on top of our heads!

It landed with a thud about a thousand feet away.

Not registering any acceleration, the capsule itself behaved as though it were at the top of its parabolic trajectory and entering the recovery phase. With a little pop, the parachutes deployed. Right there on the launch pad!

This was right out of a Three Stooges Movie!

Inside Mercury Control it was total pandemonium. "What the hell happened???" yelled Kraft. He was as red as the rocket exhaust. The booster guys reverted to German, as they hyper-excitedly called their base in Alabama. This seemed to infuriate Kraft even more.

The most immediate problem was the parachute, limply draped over the fully fueled Redstone like a half-unveiled work of art. A breath of wind could at any point topple our hot bird and cause it to explode.

Everyone had their pet solution: get a cherry picker and cut off the parachute, shoot holes in the rocket to allow the fuel to leak out, etc… Everyone gesticulated at once, and I thought Kraft would him-self explode.

"Quiet!!!"

He fielded the various proposals, and considering the forecast for calm winds, decided to simply wait things out. By the next day, the booster had depressurized on its own, the batteries were depleted, and NASA engineers were able to take down the rocket.

The mission would come to be known as the "four inch flight." The problem was found to lie with the disconnecting of a two-pronged electrical plug. To the press it sounded like pulling out the cord while you're vacuuming the carpet, and this led to another round of derision. *Time* referred to us as the "Lead-footed Mercury (program)." It went on to say, "Project Mercury's latest failure, third in a row, just about evaporated the last faint wisp of hope that the U.S. might put a man into space before Russia does."

As I wrote to Mal – with perhaps more technical detail than he'd want – the plug issue was actually more complicated. The prongs were *supposed* to disconnect, and were to do so with a delay of a few milliseconds. The system had worked to perfection during prior Redstone launches. This Redstone, however, was heavier due to an extended fuel tank. The rocket took off more slowly, and the delay was ever so longer. This triggered an abort signal, wherefore the shutdown.

Having identified the problem, we were able carry out a successful Redstone launch within a month. Nevertheless, as 1960 came to an end, it was clear that the Soviets held the advantage. The *New York Times* conceded first-man-in-space honors to the opposition and presciently looked ahead: "The first man in space will not be the last, and after the tributes have been paid to that first man and those who made his feat possible the more important question will arise of what man can do in space that is worth the immense cost of putting him there."

For illustrations, see www.intotheskywithdiamonds.com

5. Light This Candle

As the time of the first flight approached, it was only natural for the astronauts to wonder who would be the Chosen One. Of the five hundred or so pilots first considered for the Mercury program, this astronaut would be Numero Uno. He would forever be the first American in space, perhaps the first human. His likeness might end up on coins, stamps, dollar bills... The possibilities were endless. No one would care about the second fellow. Each of the Mercury 7 astronauts had good reason to imagine that he would be chosen. Humility was not a criterion of success among test pilots.

How the leader of the pack would be determined remained a mystery to me and to the astronauts. But we were all shocked when one important parameter was revealed to us: the astronauts themselves would vote, and their opinion would be seriously considered. Little did we know at the time how true that would turn out to be.

On January 19th, Bob Gilruth gathered the seven astronauts. The original plan had been to provide all astronauts with the same training, since in principle they were all equally qualified. To avoid the inevitable massive media attention that would laser down on the first astronaut, NASA had decided to wait until the eve of the first manned flight to announce his name. Even the astronauts would be kept in the dark until the last moment.

It quickly became clear, however, that this would be highly impractical. The prime astronaut and his backups clearly needed more training than the others. NASA decided to reveal three names. The trio would consist of the prime astronaut and his two backups. Cleverly, NASA did not indicate who would be the prime astronaut and who would be the backups. The media frenzy would then at least be split three ways.

Thus, on this day, the media were given three names in alphabetical order:

John Glenn
Gus Grissom
Alan Shepard.

Life magazine quickly dubbed them The Gold Team and the remainder, The Red Team.

All three aviation branches of the military were represented in the Gold Team: Navy (Al Shepard), Air Force (Gus Grissom), and the Marines (John Glenn).

Of course, in their hearts, the media already knew who the prime astronaut would be. It could only be Glenn.

****

Liverpool, 20ᵗʰ February, 1961

Dear Dutch,

It's been rough, but things are getting better.

Coming back to Liverpool with no permanent job in sight has been a major downer. To think that John, Paul, George, Stu, and Pete played all night every night for months — and then nothing. They even cut a record in Germany. Sort of. They were asked to play and sing backup on Tony Sheridan's "My Bonnie." They also recorded "Ain't She Sweet." Well, it was a record!

Back home, John stayed indoors and stared at the ceiling. The others tried to keep busy. Finally, as I think I told you in my last letter, they got a break with a gig at my place, the Cavern. What really kick-started things for them was a show they did at the Town Hall Ballroom just before New Year's. The girls went crazy, each part of their body seeming to keep a different time, and then they rushed the stage! I've never seen anything like it. Now the band plays every lunchtime and is developing quite a little fan base. The girls still go crazy. I'm working on getting in on the action! But really, their time in Germany has paid off. They've gotten quite slick and seem to anticipate each other's every move. Between the black leather outfits and their greaseless hair combed forward, they continue to look quite different from everyone else around.

What's new with space? Thanks for all the info. One day you'll have to tell me how you plan to communicate with the astronauts.

Mal

****

The girl who had made the wisecrack about the skydiver a few months back turned out to be Sally, a nurse working with Dee O'Hara, the head nurse in our operation. Sally was now eating Chinese with Kranz, myself, and a couple of the guys. As we opened the fortune cookies Sally pretended to read hers. "Astronaut who not change underwear after flight sit alone." We all chuckled. Kranz' shoulders did a little jiggle. It was fun to watch him laugh; it was a rare event.

As I swiveled my eyes to meet hers, I thought I caught Sally momentarily holding my look. Her eyes were green and almond-shaped and fringed with dark lashes; she wore her sandy-brown hair in a ponytail. Unlike the rest of us, Sally always managed to get out in the sun, not enough to be darkly tanned but enough for a healthy glow. Her skin looked warm.

**

You had to feel for Glenn. The next few months must have been excruciating. Not only did he have to train hard and deal with the pressures of being the front runner – El Chefe, El Excellente, Numero Uno, Da Man, Top Dog, and Top Gun all rolled into one – he had to secretly and graciously deal with the fact that he wasn't any of those.

His spirits had momentarily skyrocketed when he was picked for the Gold Team, only to nosedive just as fast when he found out NASA's first choice.

It was Al Shepard.

And Glenn wasn't even number two. Grissom was.

Flights two and three were designed to essentially be repeats of the first, and Glenn would be flying Number Three. That had to be eating him up. Shepard was an excellent pilot, but not exactly the friendliest. And Grissom? Great guy but couldn't put two words together! The way Glenn saw it, he had to have been torpedoed by the other guys' votes. Surely, he would have been chosen by the NASA brass. This was not completely true. Some, such as Chris Kraft, saw Glenn as the ultimate teacher's pet. Either way, I tipped my hat to him. The guy kept it together. Not a peep, not a wrinkle in his sunny behavior. A true professional.

The next day, John F. Kennedy was inaugurated. Many of us had voted against him. Even now, the thought lingered that Kennedy might see the Mercury program as a Republican extravagance, and junk it. Besides which, he was Catholic. Kranz, who was Catholic, was pleased. Many, however, were uncomfortable with the break in tradition.

Putting a positive spin on things, we had to recognize that Eisenhower had actually been rather nonchalant vis-à-vis the space program. In his last speech to Congress on January 16th, he had flat out stated:

> Further testing and experimentation will be necessary to establish whether there are any valid scientific reasons for extending manned spaceflight beyond the Mercury program.

Alas, Kennedy's choice for Special Assistant for Science and Technology, MIT's Jerome Wiesner, quickly dashed our fledgling hopes:

> We should stop advertising Mercury as our major objective in space activities. Indeed, we should make an effort to diminish the significance of this program… We should find effective means to make people appreciate … space activities other than space travel.

"Other than space travel?" What did that mean? More satellites? It was not a joyful day.

Considering the spotty track record of its prior launches, and notwithstanding the snickering of the test pilot community, NASA still thought it best to place a chimpanzee in a live Mercury capsule prior to sending up an astronaut. The Chosen One was Ham, a thirty-seven pound chimp. (HAM was an acronym for Holloman Aerospace Medical Center.)

Ham himself had endured a rigorous selection process, ending up Top Chimp in an arduous competition with five other wannabe astrochimps. The chimps were required to respond to certain stimuli by pressing buttons akin to keys on a keyboard. Each key would transmit a certain morsel of information back to ground control. Where most chimps would sit there with magnificently frustrating indifference,

Ham was a regular Mozart, even as he was shaken and whirred on the centrifuge.

Liftoff took place on January 31st. The Redstone did not blow up, but the flight was not an unqualified success. The rocket took off at too sharp an angle and so came back down too steeply. The poor chimp pulled 15 Gs instead of the expected 12.

Ham must have felt like bacon.

He landed quite a distance from the target, which meant a long wait for the rescue. Did I mention that the capsule was taking on water? When the scuba divers finally extricated the half-drowned Ham from the capsule, he was one gnarly chimp. We tried to explain to him that he'd fared better than Laika, the Russian dog who'd gone into space and never come back, but this didn't seem to placate him.

The media plastered his smiling face on the front page of every paper, but we knew the poor fellow wasn't smiling.

**

Our tracking and communications grid was now complete: Twenty one sites, including ships treading water in the various oceans, and five astronauts sprinkled around the globe at the Go/No Go sites, all ready to communicate with each other and with the capsule.

March 12th had been lightly penciled in as a possible launch date, yet Shepard's date with history came and went.

'*One more* test of the Redstone rocket' NASA had decreed! The doctors, moreover, were still not convinced that a human could survive space flight. Another animal flight was advisable. A presidential scientific committee headed by Don Hornig was rumored to be recommending another *fifty* chimpanzee flights. Bob Gilruth remarked that if this were true, perhaps NASA should move to Africa.

Shepard could hardly contain his anger: "We have them by the shorthairs and we're giving it away!" Wernher von Braun was equally frustrated. Asked what we would find on the moon if we ever went there, von Braun replied, "an empty vodka bottle."

Sure enough.

We awoke on April 13th to the news that the twenty-seven year old Soviet lieutenant Yuri Gagarin had successfully orbited the earth and had safely returned. The Soviets had proven that a human could function normally in space. It was a tremendous engineering and scientific achievement.

To us, it was a crushing disappointment.

The Soviet government gloated. "In this achievement, which will pass into history, are embodied the genius of the Soviet people and the powerful force of Socialism." Yes, "The powerful force of socialism"… Another reminder of what this whole competition was about. *(The Soviets were cagey too: they let it be understood that Gagarin had returned in his capsule, when in fact he'd parachuted to safety. According to the Fédération Aéronautique Internationale rules, a pilot has to return in his vehicle to qualify for an aeronautical record).*

NASA PR man, Shorty Powers, was pulled out of bed and given the news. Undoubtedly caught off guard and not at his sharpest, Powers could only come up with a lame sound bite, "We're still asleep down here." The American press jumped all over Powers' quote. "Russian in orbit! America's spacemen still asleep!"

I made sure to steer clear of Al Shepard. His comments were not recorded for history.

It seemed that whenever we took a step forward, the Soviets would take two. Our intelligence operations were non-existent, and we were being caught by surprise at every turn. It was frankly disquieting to read about the Soviet exploits in the newspapers just like everybody else. Combined with the constant attacks from critics, who didn't think we should even have a manned space program, there were clearly times when we had to wonder if it was all worth it.

The work was grueling. It sounded glamorous to be involved in a space program on the beaches of Florida, but the truth was far from glitzy. A launch, or even a launch simulation, meant being up by 2 A.M, fresh as the morning dew in front of our consoles. That meant getting to Mercury Control at 1 A.M.

There was very little late night partying.

As for the Florida beach, it was but a dream. Not only was there no time for sand castles, but the mosquitoes had first dibs on all the choice spots. For entertainment, Orlando was a short drive down Highway A1A (especially if an astronaut gave you a ride in his 'vette), but in all my time at NASA I went there once with Gus, and that was it.

The only good news coming out of the Soviet flight was that Gagarin had been our guinea pig. There was really no need for us to send up any more animals. Gagarin had proven that a human could survive a space flight. Even the doctors agreed to give us the green light, and Shepard's flight was set for May 2nd.

This should have been a time of joy and excitement, but it wasn't. We were smarting from having been beaten into space and particularly vexed to know that we could have easily sent up Shepard in March. Those ridiculous doctors had cost Shepard and the United States the opportunity to be first in space. (And as far as Kraft was concerned, it was von Braun's fault too for insisting on more Redstone tests!) The doctors weren't ridiculous at all, but they made for convenient scapegoats. They never seemed to be the pilots' or astronauts' friends anyway. All they seemed to do was ground them!

Things got worse. The very same week as Gagarin's flight, 1300 or so Cuban expatriates made a pre-dawn landing at Cuba's Bay of Pigs. With only lukewarm support from the United States Air Force, Fidel Castro's lilliputian army creamed them. It was yet another serious embarrassment for America.

Bad news comes in threes: On April 25th, we sent up our third Mercury-Atlas rocket – the very type of rocket earmarked to eventually boost our astronauts into orbit. A few moments after liftoff, Tec Roberts, the flight dynamics officer, laconically announced, "Flight, uh, negative roll and pitch program." There was barely a touch of anxiety in his voice. NASA had a very understated way of expressing disaster. For what he really meant was, **"Holy Sh..! The rocket hasn't rolled and pitched over the Atlantic! It's going straight up! That means it's going to come straight back down onto our heads!!!"**

It was the Range Safety Officer's job to push the button that would blow up the rocket in case of such a malfunction. Of course he'd want to give the rocket as much time as possible to correct its course. But he wouldn't want to wait too long ... what if the button itself malfunctioned? Hmmmm.

Forty-three seconds into the flight, a cloud suddenly appeared on Kraft's little black and white monitor. It was over; another belly-flop into the ocean of Atlas failures.

Back to the drawing board.

At least the escape mechanism worked. The capsule was whisked away by the escape tower, and was gently delivered to the recovery team by a set of perfectly deployed parachutes. Nevertheless, at this point there'd only been one successful Atlas launch in three attempts. Not a bad batting average in baseball, but lousy in rocketry, especially when a man would soon be perched at the top.

No one had to ask von Braun what he thought of these Air Force rockets.

There was one week to go before the first manned American launch. Hopefully the smaller Mercury-Redstone combination would fare better.

As late as April, the identity of the first astronaut remained unknown not just to the public, but to all of us at the Cape. Only Kraft, top doc Charles *("don't call me Chuck")* Berry, MD, and senior administrator Walt Williams were in on the secret. "Astronaut X in seclusion," shouted the headlines.

Now, on the eve of the launch, the secret was let out of the bag. To everyone's surprise it was Shepard.

Shepard?

Shepard???

No knock on Shepard, but what about Glenn?

Yes, Glenn had been correct. NASA had given considerable weight to the astronauts' vote, and Glenn stood out like an earnest goody-two-shoes. Too bad. Though Gus had been my sentimental favorite, I thought Glenn was the best choice. As qualified as the others, he best projected the All-American image and was certainly the most articulate.

At 2 A.M., on the morning of May 2nd, I was ready at my console. This was finally the real thing. As dawn approached, I began to feel little tingles of anxiety. It wasn't just the excitement of the moment, it was the weather. Langley, up the coast from us in Virginia, had no problem staying in touch with the thirteen relay stations as far as Australia, but the wind and lightning dancing around Florida played havoc with Langley's ability to communicate with *us*! At 7:30 AM, the flight was scrapped.

So much for our first manned mission.

We tried again on the next day, with the same result.

Each attempt meant a 1 AM wake-up call for all of us, including Shepard. Each time he had to don his spacesuit and squeeze into *Freedom 7*, the name chosen by Shepard. The *7* came from the fact that it was the 7th capsule to come off the production line, and of course, there were 7 Mercury astronauts.

**

Shorty Powers was a diminutive, dapper fellow with a big voice. His was an unenviable lot: his job was to feed the media's insatiable appetite for news with information that would be palatable to his bosses, the press, and the public. It was clearly in NASA's interest to put the best possible face on all events. (Shorty had already come close to losing his job over the "we're all asleep" fiasco.) As such, Shorty was constantly flirting with the edges of the truth, a problem the Soviets never had to deal with. His claim to fame would be his addition of one common term to the English language.

This would come in just a few weeks.

**

Why don't you guys light this candle!

May 5th, 1961.

As had been true twice this week already, the early morning traffic was astonishing. This was a town where you could drive down a highway and be the only car. There were barely any traffic lights.

I was somewhat prepared for the local traffic, but not for the television newscasts showing drivers around the country pulled off to the side of the highway, standing beside their cars and squeezing transistor radios up against their ear. This was going to be the most spectacular success in America since Lindbergh… or the most awkward boondoggle since, since, well since forever!

America was taking one of its biggest engineering gambles in full view of the country and of the world. The Soviet space program was veiled in deep secrecy, and the Russians waited for success before making any pronouncement.

My console was ready.

Once again, Shepard was awoken at 1 AM and went through the little routine that had been scripted for him: a shower, a shave, and a breakfast of steak, bacon, and eggs. At 2:40 AM he received a physical examination, followed by the placement of medical sensors, the location of which completed attested to Shepard's patriotism. He was now ready to slither into his pressurized suit. With military precision he entered the transfer van at 3:55 AM, lay down while his suit was purged with oxygen, and donned his gloves. At 5:15 AM, he ascended the gantry alongside the rocket. The pad crew applauded as he stepped out of the elevator, and Shepard dredged up a little smile.

Black and white pictures flickered on the monitors showing Shepard shimmying into *Freedom 7*. You didn't sit in a Mercury capsule as much as wear it. The sixty-five foot, thin, checkered, black and white rocket was awash in floodlights against the pre-dawn night.

Shepard shook hands with the pad crew, and the capsule's hatch was closed down over his head. The thud seemed more definitive than during the simulation. This was it. His ride to fame and American glory. Or his coffin. This could be his last hour, and Shepard knew it; he'd seen enough rockets blow up. There was no sugarcoating it. He would be riding a controlled explosion. At least it was a Redstone and not an Atlas, like the one that had blown up the week before.

Shepard quickly chased those thoughts away. Wedged atop the Redstone, his legs jackknifed above him, Shepard mechanically went through all the controls and procedures, as he waited through one delay and then another. First it was the weather, then an electrical inverter in the electrical system, then a computer at the Goddard center in Maryland. The hours went by. "Why don't you light this candle???" Shepard muttered in desperation.

Shepard was a big fan (and imitator) of comedian Bill Dana, and for relaxation purposes it was decided to pipe in some of his classic routines right into the Mercury capsule. It was a little bit surreal, like granting a guy his last wish before blowing him into space.

By 8 AM, we had all taken a few cigarette and bathroom breaks. Everyone at NASA was an inveterate smoker, and it was getting hard to see through the thickening cloud of cigarette smoke. This was not a place for second-hand smoke worryniks!

The only one who hadn't taken a bathroom break was Shepard. Right around now he began to feel a sensation that was as familiar as it was disquieting.

An unusual pronouncement came over the intercom: "I gotta pee."

Because the flight was scheduled to last just 15 minutes, there were no provisions for this little indisposition.

"Can't you wait?" I asked.

Ask a dumb question, get a dumb answer.

"D'you think I'd ask?"

This led to an unusual summit between doctors and engineers. If he did pee, would he short out all those wires glued to his skin? The consensus was that he would not. And what were the alternatives? Cancel the flight so Mr. Shepard could go to the little boys' room?

"You're GO for peeing."

Shepard may or may not have detected the smile on my face when I said this, but he didn't wait to be told twice. The pee pooled into the small of his back, as he waited for the countdown to proceed.

At 9:34 Eastern Standard Time, Kraft pushed the liftoff switch. The luminous torpedo was off!

"Ah Roger, liftoff and the clock is started" Shepard's voice crackled in my headset. "Yes sir," he continued, "reading you loud and clear. This is *Freedom 7*. The fuel is GO. 1.2g. Cabin at 14 psi. Oxygen is GO… *Freedom 7* is still GO!"

Trailing a pencil of fire, Shepard zoomed off into the stratosphere at a speed of over 5,180 miles per hour.

Thirty seconds into the flight, Shorty Powers announced to the world that everything was "A-OK."

A-OK?

Shorty had made his contribution to American lingo.

Meanwhile, the Redstone rocket with its two-ton Mercury payload roared more than 100 miles into space.

Eighty-eight seconds into the flight, *Freedom 7* tore through the transonic speed zone, and Shepard was buffeted about so violently that he could no longer read the dials. Soon enough the ride was smooth again. 142 seconds after liftoff, the booster shut down after having accelerated the capsule to 5,134 mph. The capsule separated from the rocket. A minute later the automatic attitude control system turned the capsule around to a heat shield-forward position. At the top of the parabola, Shepard enjoyed nearly five minutes of weightlessness before accelerating back towards earth. Shepard's one task had been to see whether he could change his capsule's attitude – up, down, left, right, and yes he'd been able to do so.

There was no practical window on his capsule, but he peered through a periscope that offered him a view of Florida that no one had ever seen. Despite a crushing 11 G re-entry, he maneuvered his capsule in rudimentary fashion and fired his retro rockets to slow his descent. The parachutes opened as planned, and Shepard landed safely in the Atlantic, 302 miles from his departure point, a mere fifteen minutes and twenty two seconds since liftoff – less time than it took me to get to work every morning.

Moments later he was securely on board the *Lake Champlain*.

We'd DONE IT! We'd sent a man 116.5 miles into space and gotten him back in one piece!

The drivers who'd pulled off to the side of the road threw their Fedoras in the air and whooped it up.

We might not have been winning the race, but we were IN it!

It didn't matter that Shepard's flight had been just a simple cannon shot to Gagarin's acrobatics. "U.S. hurls man 115 miles into space," blared the New York Times.

Shepard was a bona fide hero. Our first Knight's quest had been a success. For Shepard, this had been the *nec plus ultra* of any test pilot: he'd flown *faster, further, higher* than any American before him. He'd made the right choice.

**

Sally had been commandeering all my nighttime thoughts. I imagined the almond-shaped eyes that were always happy with the dawn of the day; I pictured her on the beach with her sandy brown hair in windblown disarray; I heard the soft giggle that followed her funny little quips, and saw a smile that in my fantasy melted into animal passion. The loose knot at the back of her favorite pink and white dress was practically an invitation. Finally, on this day, riding the enthusiasm of the moment, I mustered up the courage to ask her out.

Was I more thrilled by her acceptance or by Shepard's flight?

I took her to the fanciest place around, Fat Boys restaurant, where all of NASA seemed to be celebrating the day's events. Grissom had taped the front page of a newspaper to the wall. *"U.S. Scores Success in First Try to Put Man in Space."*

We talked about the mission and about Florida and where we came from. (Sally was from Ohio.) I remember the sheer happiness of sitting next to her, ticking off in my mind the signs of the trouble she'd taken for our date: a hint of perfume, a tad more eye liner, her hair pinned up. She couldn't get her hair to stay in place in the damp heat of the bar. I loved listening to her, never letting her know quite how much I enjoyed seeing her fuss with her hair.

Her eyes met mine and didn't slide away.

Everyone was excited and drinking too much. We were just part of the crowd, and the fact that it was our first date barely got any attention. On any other night I would have had to endure a lot of ribbing – or rather, Sally would've because it would have been her choice of me that inspired jests, not the other way around. I wasn't the only guy who'd noticed her, or even the first who'd asked her out. I didn't realize it at the time, but she'd already sweetly said 'no' to a number of suitors.

I know I drank too much that night because I told Sally about Mal and his theory of our Druid ancestors. She'd never heard of Stonehenge and didn't believe in UFOs, but it was a pretty good story, she agreed. I changed the subject and talked about Mal's job and his favorite Liverpool band. In my last year of college I'd been the guitarist in a band; I told her we wanted to be the Everly Brothers.

Sally nodded in approval. She'd listened to Chuck Berry's "Rock'n'Roll Music" over and over again when she was on the orthopedic ward recovering from a broken leg ("Riding my bike," she said. "No hands.") The hospital stay convinced her to become a nurse. She respected doctors, but nurses worked just as hard for less glory.

"So why exactly did you want to be a nurse and not a doctor?" I asked.

"Why exactly did you want to be an engineer... and not an astronaut?" she countered.

I was discovering a new side to Sally. I decided to change the subject.

Sally was passionate about her work, which I liked. Yet, she was never serious for too long – she loved to laugh and could forget the day's worries better than anyone I knew. She was so pretty and so sexy with her hair falling down, and to hear her sound like Florence Nightingale (another comparison she hated) made me want to leap across the table and hug her. I settled for holding her hand on the way out and, before the alcohol wore off, securing a Saturday night date.

**

Shortly after his flight, Shepard was invited to the White House for a personal congratulation from President Kennedy. He received a confetti ticker tape parade down the canyons of Wall Street in New York; grown men wept.

**

NASA's success was a strong morale booster for an American public that had heard nothing but bad news in recent months. It was also a great crowd pleaser abroad, and the swell of enthusiasm from the world community gave John F. Kennedy the seminal idea of his Presidency. Why not beat the Soviets at their own game?

The Soviets had for years used technology to promote the virtues of their political system, why not do the same? They had beaten us into space (just barely), but there were other goals to shoot for. The American public seemed completely captivated by the astronauts – as was he – and there would be no political harm in associating himself with the conquest of space. *Au contraire.* As long as NASA was successful, it could only be a win-win situation.

Kennedy gathered his scientific advisors as well as top NASA officials. The meetings did not go as smoothly as he would have hoped. Every option put on the table was expensive. We needed every possible dollar to build missiles to fight the Communists – at least such was the reasoning of some advisors. Sending men into space was a cute trick, but wouldn't win the Cold War. The idea of putting a man on the moon by the end of the decade was brought forward and nearly laughed out of the room. "To the moon, Alice!" someone quipped.

This was the stuff of science fiction, not science. In 1649 Frenchman Jean Baudoin had published "Voyage to the Moon by Dominique Gonzalès, Spanish Adventurer." Jules Verne, writing from his home in Paris, had launched three men to circle the moon in *"De la Terre à la Lune"* (1865). And, of course, there had been HG Wells's 1928 "The First Men in the Moon," in which a playwright and a scientist float up in a balloon and encounter the moon's inhabitants, the Selenites[1].

Science fiction or not, Kennedy liked the idea.

NASA engineers thought that we had the technological know-how to send someone to the moon. The goal could be set far enough in time to give us a chance of catching up to the Soviets and beating them.

The race would make Americans forget the Bay of Pigs. If all went well, Kennedy could ride the NASA rockets into a second term. There was, of course, no guarantee at this stage. NASA had sent all of one man into space for a grand total of fifteen minutes, and the Atlas rockets, the backbone of the Mercury program, were still blowing up at an alarming rate.

Still, on May 25th, 1961, Kennedy delivered the speech of our young lives to a Joint Session of Congress. He began his address with traditional issues: freedom, boosting of the military, civil defense programs, etc...

He then shifted into a different gear.

> "If we are to win the battle that is going on around the world between freedom and tyranny, if we are to win the battle for men's minds, the dramatic achievements in space which occurred in recent weeks should have made clear to us all, as did the Sputnik in 1957, the impact of this adventure on the mind of men everywhere who are attempting to make a determination of which road they should take.
>
> Now it is time to take longer strides, time for a great new American enterprise, time for this nation to take a clearly leading role in space achievement, which in many ways may hold the key to our future on earth.... For while we cannot guarantee that we shall

---

1   Selene, Greek goddess of the moon

one day be first, we can guarantee that any failure to make this effort will make us last ... We go into space because whatever mankind must undertake, free men must fully share."

Congressmen who were half asleep must have wondered if they were not dreaming, as Kennedy reached the climax of his speech and laid down the following challenge:

"I believe that this nation should commit itself to achieving the goal, before this decade is out, of landing a man on the moon and returning him safely to earth. No single space project in this period will be more exciting, or more impressive to mankind, or more important for the long range exploration of space."

"If we are to win the battle for men's minds." "No single space project will be ... more impressive to mankind." Yes, we would be in it for the same reason as the Soviets: winning the world over to our way of life.

London bookies wasted no time in giving Kennedy's challenge 1000 to 1 odds.

The effect at NASA, however, was like a shot of intravenous caffeine. The Administration was behind us, and money would no longer be an object. No more living day to day. No more relying on a roach coach for milk and sandwiches. We'd have a real launch site with a real cafeteria! Sally and I walked the beach that night and stared at the sky. A defiant Ms. Moon stared down at us through wisps of mercury clouds. She would be receiving visitors. But she would play hard to get.

The President's deadline was daunting. How were we going to get to the moon in just nine years and do so before the Soviets? The enemy had already sent a man orbiting around the earth, and we weren't scheduled to try anything like that until the fourth Mercury mission. Heck, we didn't even have a reliable rocket for such an adventure.

The answer was painfully simple: no more days off, no more 9 to 5, no more automatic lunch time, no Holidays except Christmas and New Year's, and no complaining. And no more marriage. At least that's

how it would seem to those who were married. Sally and I started referring to our fifteen-minute cafeteria lunch dates as "a night at the movies." If we managed to scrounge thirty minutes, we called it "a weekend
in Orlando."

Kennedy's speech opened the door to some very creative minds, for
NASA now had to decide how to reach our sister planet.

Before Kennedy and Congress could change their minds, the following plan was put forth: the Mercury program with its single astronaut wedged into his little capsule would test the basics. Could a
human survive in a weightless environment? (The Soviets seemed to
already have answered this in the affirmative.) Could we effectively
track and control a capsule? Could we communicate with a spacecraft?
Could we monitor an astronaut's vital signs at a distance? Could we
make a spaceship splash down where we wanted?

The second phase would be the Gemini program. The capsule
would be a bigger version of the Mercury model and would house two
astronauts. During the Gemini flights, NASA would test an astronaut's
ability to function in the vacuum of space, since astronauts would presumably be walking on the moon. The astronauts would test Man's
endurance in space to ensure that the three and a half day trek to the
moon and back would be tolerated. Gemini would also test the feasibility of "rendezvous" – the ability of two crafts flying different trajectories
to approach each other. Finally, Gemini would tell us if two spacecraft
could align themselves so perfectly as to physically link.

The third and final phase would be the Apollo program proper.
Three astronauts inhabiting the capsule would test the Apollo capsule
and the moon-landing spacecraft, the design of which remained to be
determined. This would all culminate in an American astronaut walking on the moon within the next nine years.

Just like that.

****

Hamburg, 10th July, 1961

Dear Dutch,

I heard Kennedy's moon challenge. Of course I thought of you. You're
going to be busy! Well, we've been busy too! We're back on the Baltic Sea!

The boys now play at the Top Ten, a classier place than the Cavern! It even has some well-known acts, at least by Hamburg standards.

I do see some storms on the horizon. (No pun intended: Rory Storm and the Hurricanes are here again too.) The problem is Stu. His heart is clearly not into playing the bass — or any instrument for that matter. He's into art, and now that he's re-connected with Astrid his mind seems elsewhere. His bass playing has never been more than elementary. Paul's pointed out to me that Stu always plays the root note that corresponds to the chord they're strumming. So when they play a G chord, he hits the G note, and when they switch to C, he plays a C, and that's it. Not much bounce or spark. He's also not making much of an effort to improve his play or find his own style, the way John, Paul, and George always do. The beer and amphetamines don't help their tempers either, and they've all gotten into fights. Stu begs off practice, saying he has headaches, and he spends all his free time with Astrid. It's fair to say he's not taking the band as seriously as the others.

Our friend Bill Harry has a new paper, *Mersey Beat*, covering the whole Liverpool music scene. He's really been helpful. Here's a sample:

> 'I think the Beatles are No. 1 because they resurrected original style rock'n'roll ...They hit the scene when it had been emasculated.... Gone was the drive that inflamed the emotions. The Beatles therefore exploded on a jaded scene. And to those on the verge of quitting teendom — those who had experienced in their most impressionable years the impact of rhythm & blues (raw rock'n'roll) — this was an experience, a process of regaining and reliving a style of sounds and associated feelings identifiable with their era. Here again, in the Beatles, was the stuff that screams are made of. Here was the excitement — both physical and aural that symbolized the rebellion of youth in the ennuied mid-1950s. Rugged yet romantic, appealing to both sexes ... affecting indifference to audience response, yet always saying "thank you." Reviving interest in, and commanding enthusiasm for, numbers that descended the charts way back.'

Harry asked John to write about the origins of the Beatles for one of his issues, and got back vintage John:

> 'Once upon a time there were three little boys John, George and Paul, by name christened. They decided to get together because they were the getting together type. When they were together they wondered what for after all, what for? So all of a sudden they all grew guitars and formed a noise.'

John certainly gave us a laugh. And speaking of a laugh, do you know what was funny? Watching John and Paul try to behave when their girlfriends, Cynthia and Dot, came over for a bit. I think John misses Cyn much more than Paul does Dot, but talk about cramping your style and having to be on your best behavior! Of course, the minute the girls leave the boys are back dipping into the cookie jar. What a place this is! I don't know if you were allowed to, um, "partake" when you were here, but the next time you come I'll show you around.

Mal

I continued to be fascinated by this glimpse into the day-to-day life of a rock band. His letters made me feel like I was there, or maybe I just wanted to be there – screaming girls, great music… There wasn't much to do after work at the Cape. The astronauts raced their cars. The rest of us watched. Mal's sexcapades, of course, were out of my league. For that, you had to be a rock musician or an astronaut. I was thrilled just to be with Sally.

Mal, for his part, couldn't hear enough about Florida. He was certain that girls in bikinis surrounded me all day long. He couldn't understand why I hadn't taken up surfing yet. Of course, I had made a point of telling him in every letter how many days of the last month had been sunny and warm. I had left out the hot and humid part.

Mal had an intriguing little post-scriptum for me at the end of his last letter:

"By the way, since you're aiming for the moon, you should know that it was once inhabited. It had volcanoes, an atmosphere, and even water. It might have spun faster than it does now, so the days and nights might not have lasted an entire two weeks. When the atmosphere disappeared, so did all the inhabitants — off to another galaxy. And did you ever think of what the earth would look like from the moon? Those living on the near side would see the earth as an unmovable, blinking blue eye in the sky. Dark — light — dark — light, depending on whether it was a "new earth" or a "full earth." On the far side, they wouldn't see the earth at all. Maybe they'd go their whole lives never knowing of earth's existence. By the way, 10 to 1 your astronauts find water if they dig deep enough. Do tell your colleagues."

I made a mental note specifically not to.

****

"Dammit, get Gus, forget the damn spacecraft"

On July 21st, it was my buddy Gus Grissom's turn to wiggle into a Mercury capsule atop a Redstone rocket. He had named it *Liberty Bell 7*, and it featured three items not present on Shepard's capsule: A trapezoidal window that was positively posh compared to Shepard's periscope, two awkwardly placed ports, and an entry/exit hatch fastened with explosive bolts. These allowed for an emergency exit after splashdown (a lesson learned from Ham's near drowning experience).

I had promised Gus's wife Betty that I would take special care of him, and that I'd call her as soon as I knew he was safe. Not that there was anything special I could do. My job was to talk and listen to him. Granted, as the Communications guy, I might be able to call her at home without having to put a dime in the phone booth.

Perched seventy feet above Pad 5, Gus was outwardly calm. Sally pointed out that his heart rate had not sped up much. Gus noted that the pad crew had left smudge marks on his window, as they peered in after closing the hatch. We promised him windshield wipers the next time around. I also told him that back at Purdue everyone was cheering for him.

Enough small talk. At 7:20 AM, Kraft fired the ignition switch, and Gus was outta there on a howling jet of flame. The scream of the rocket gradually simmered down to a distant purr; within a few moments silence had once again fallen over the Cape.

The flight was in every sense a carbon copy of Shepard's flight, and when *Liberty Bell 7* splashed down, it was time for high fives all around.

The celebration turned out to be a little premature.

Lewis and Reinhard were experienced helicopter pilots – top dogs of their specialized world. They had trained over and over for this, the final part of the mission. They had tracked the capsule as it oscillated under the parachute, and had zeroed in the moment it hit the water. As they went to grab the capsule, they saw the hatch blow open and Gus jump out into the sea.

The capsule was taking on water and slowly began to sink. Whom to pick up first? Grissom? *Liberty Bell?* Grissom? *Liberty Bell?* Grissom could swim. They went for *Liberty Bell.* The capsule was getting heavier and heavier, however, and was slowly dragging the chopper down. The motors whined at an ever-increasing pitch. All three wheels were in the water. Lewis slammed the throttle all the way. They started to make headway; but the moment the capsule rose above the water, it lost all buoyancy. It was heavier than ever. An emergency light flashed in the cockpit: metallic debris in the oil sump from excessive engine strain. Both the Sikorsky and the capsule were going down. Better to lose one craft than two. Lewis and Reinhard cut the capsule loose, and it peacefully sank in a foam of gurgling bubbles.

The drama was not over. Gus could swim all right, but the backwash from the helicopter was whipping up the waves around him. His helmet off, water poured into the space suit with every wave that broke over his head. He had a rubber dam around the neck, but it wasn't enough. Grissom's heart jackhammered away, as he slowly realized that he was drowning. It was all he could do to tilt his head back and keep his mouth above the waves. What a silly way to go!

Helplessly, we watched this on the monitor. "Dammit, get Gus, forget the damn spacecraft," yelled Kranz to no one in particular.

Finally, disgusted by the loss of the capsule for which they would catch hell, the copter and scuba teams turned their attention to Grissom. There was only one shark circling him. Nothing they couldn't handle. His spacesuit filled with water, Gus weighed nearly as much as the capsule! Exhausted, puzzled, and embarrassed, he was hoisted onto the helicopter. How did the warm Gulf Stream waters so quickly turn into an icy ocean of humiliation?

**

On the aircraft carrier, the hero's welcome he'd half expected was mysteriously absent. The capsule had been lost. NASA was already speculating that the hatch had blown open because Grissom had panicked and had hit the emergency switch.

Shorty Powers announced that the mission had been a complete success, which of course in many ways it had. The media, however, picked up on the loss of the capsule and reviewed in agonizing detail how Grissom had "screwed the pooch."

There was no ticker tape parade for Grissom.

He and Betty did not get invited to the White House.

What they couldn't know was that President Kennedy was still deeply involved with the fallout from the Bay of Pigs.

Gus was miffed, and I couldn't blame him. I think he also felt bad for Betty. Gus had already met the President, but not Betty. A trip to the White House would have been Betty's payoff. Not that she wasn't pleased to be the wife of America's second true astronaut, but Louise Shepard had been to the White House, so why not her?

Eventually, NASA would completely absolve Gus of all fault, and would give him plum Gemini and Apollo missions; but the media image of Grissom as a bit of a bumbling boob would persist. I felt a little pinch in my heart when years later I saw the movie *The Right Stuff.* There was Gus portrayed one more time as the oaf who'd screwed the pooch.

In July 1999, his *Liberty Bell 7* would be retrieved from the ocean floor, three miles down. Deeper than the Titanic. They never did quite figure out why the hatch blew.

Gus's adventure had an impact on our recovery protocols. From here on in, the recovery team would retrieve the astronauts first, the capsule second.

On August 6th, the Soviets sent up Captain Gherman Titov. He was originally scheduled for 3 orbits, but Khrushchev pushed it to 17 orbits. Titov could be seen via television chatting it up with communist workers. Nothing like turning the knife in the wound.

Shortly thereafter, the Communists erected the Berlin Wall, splitting the communist eastern half of the city from its free western half. Guards armed with machine guns sat in turrets overlooking the wall. Anyone trying to get from East Berlin to West Berlin would be shot. The stated purpose of the wall was to "block the way to the subversive activity against the socialist camp countries." Naturally, this subversive activity was nothing more than people trying to get out of the prison their society had become. The Cold War had just gotten colder.

The West was powerless. It was just another embarrassment, another symbol of our weakness. In our little corner at NASA, the reaction was swift: No more sub-orbital flights! Mercury-Atlas 3 would orbit the earth. John Glenn's hour had arrived.

On November 28th, there would be one last manned test of an Atlas rocket prior to Glenn's flight. Semi-manned. Simian-manned, to be precise.

Enos was one heck of a monkey. A graduate of the finest chimp school, Enos was another master of the console switches. Enos would be the first American mammal to orbit the earth and the first mammal to ride on the Atlas rocket. I'm not sure he appreciated the honor. He probably would have preferred going home to the wife and kids, knocking back a beer on the back porch.

The launch came close to not taking place. The telemetry was noisy, and there were numerous holds for repairs; I could see Walt Williams chewing on his pen. In the end, the takeoff was smooth; the Atlas did not blow up. Though the flight was cut short by one orbit, when it looked like the capsule was losing altitude (and proper attitude), Enos was brought back alive. The flight was considered a success.

Not everyone was enthusiastic. A few short circuits here and there had led Enos to receive painful electric shocks instead of banana chips, even when he'd hit the correct keys. The normally unflappable chimp had hammered away at the keys with ever increasing speed in an effort to avoid the shocks.[2] He really did deserve a few beers.

Shorty Powers announced that the U.S. was now ready to send a man into orbit. John Glenn would be at the controls. Major Donald "Deke" Slayton would follow him four months later.

****

But for the blue color of the envelope, I might have missed Mal's letter.

Liverpool, 10ᵗʰ December, 1961

Dear Dutch,

Aristocratic, elegant, fastidious, Jewish, queer, patrician, imperious, these are all terms that have been used to describe the new man in our lives. They're all true!

You should see the scene at the Cavern! It's still the same sweaty place, smelling of yesterday's ciggie, but it's packed whenever the Beatles play. I mean chock-a-block crammed. I have to turn people away at the door. On stage, the Beatles saunter about, they joke, they smoke, they banter with the audience — especially John and Paul. This is the hot ticket in Liverpool! Stonehenge isn't your average pile of rocks, and this isn't your average rock band!

Anyway, the other day, this bloke approaches the door with a purpose-ful stride. Cuts right in front of everyone. Says he must enter. He'd actually phoned in ahead of time asking for VIP admission. VIP admission to the Cavern!!! We'd all had a pretty good laugh. He's wearing a bloody suit and a foulard, for God's sake. I just couldn't say no. Not even the owner of the club dresses that way. Maybe we haven't paid our taxes or something.

But no, the chap just wants to see what all the fuss is about. People have come into his record store to see if he carries "My Bonnie," a record by a German band called the Beatles. Lo and behold, this band isn't German

---

2   Having recovered, Enos was rumored to have called Ham: "We're a little be-hind the Russians, but we're a little ahead of the Americans."

at all, and he discovers that they're a local band playing 200 yards away at our very own little dive.

Epstein (that's his name. Pronounces it Ep-Stine) stands incongruously in the swirl of this feral atmosphere and is smitten. His eyes take them in one by one, as they prance and curse and wail away on their guitars, and you can see the wheels spinning in his head, while he rubs his chin. He comes back repeatedly, and the guys at his store say he can't stop talking about the Beatles. This is amusing because the man's always been into musicals and "real" (classical) music.

For a week or so, his mind boils with indecision, and then the other day, at the end of the gig, Eppy, in his manicured suit, majestically walks up to the stage and puts forth the proposition that he wishes to manage the band. He can get them a recording contract. A recording contract!!!! The boys are impressed that an older, elegant, established businessman would take an interest in them. It doesn't matter who he is. The Cavern scene is getting to be a tad old for the boys. A record contract is the Holy Grail.

Mind you, other than running a small record department, after failing to become an actor and a dress designer, Epstein knows nothing about the record business. We'll see. Anyway he's the best thing that's come along in a while. John's most excited of all. He does tend towards excess. Paul is most circumspect.

Eppy goes on to arrange a meeting. Paul is late. "He's taking a bath," George announces. Eppy isn't happy. "He's *very* late!"

"And *very* clean" answers George!

Cheeky!

Epstein settles back in his chair and fidgets.

Paul finally arrives. Epstein looks each Beatle in the eye, his gaze resting fractionally longer on John. Paul examines Epstein's foulard and cufflinks with piercing suspicion. Epstein unhurriedly shuffles a few papers atop his desk. Then, pouring as much admiration and flattery as possible into his voice, Epstein places the palms of his hands flat on the desk and gets to the quick.

"Boys, I think you're terrific, I'd like to be your manager. I'll book you on tours; get you a recording contract. My take will be 25% out of which I'll pay for all the promotion. You'll get back to me on this as soon as possible, won't you?" He let the sentence trail off in the air. He rose to his feet, and after a little small talk, the meeting was over.

Eppy then did something very clever. Sniffing where most of the resistance might come from, he met directly with Paul's father and John's Aunt Mimi. Make the boys respectable! Earn a real wage! Sealed the deal.

And by the way, remember the bass player, Stu? He's decided to stay in Hamburg. He's engaged to Astrid.

With Stu back in Germany and expressing no particular interest in rejoining his mates, the band had to decide who would play bass. Pete is the drummer and doesn't know an A-chord from an acorn. George is committed to playing lead guitar with all those little guitar frills and solos he loves. John has enough trouble remembering the lyrics without having to remember bass riffs.

That left Paul.

Paul also fancies the guitar and the occasional guitar solo. He enjoys singing, which is difficult to do while playing anything but the simplest bass! But none of the others would budge. And so it was decided that Paul would play bass.

He's actually doing a pretty good job at it. He can jump around on stage, keep the beat, and sing. His bass lines now dart in and out of the chords the way his harmonies do. He's bought himself a lightweight, violin-shaped Hofner bass guitar that looks the same whether it's held by a righty or a lefty.

Epstein's very careful about appearances. He believes that if you're going to break into show business you have to look the part. Black leather is cool for the Cavern crowd (and sexy — I think it turns him on) but you ain't gonna make it with anyone else in town. He's making them wear matching suits. I thought John was going to have a canary when he heard this. Suits??? The antithesis of everything he stands for!!! Be like the Man????? He had a fit. He's rebelled by leaving his top button undone or by leaving his tie slightly askew. (Lennon's attitude reminded me of the astronauts, fighting back any way they could against rigid rules and regulations.)

Eppy's put down some other rules: no drinking or smoking on stage, and one hour sets, max. No dragging three-minute songs into fifteen-minute jams, and each show should feature only their best songs.

But Epstein's proved his worth. He's arranged for a man from Decca records to come to the Cavern. The man's coming from London! No one here's ever seen such a thing!

Merry Christmas and Happy New Year!

Mal

For illustrations, see *www.intotheskywithdiamonds.com*

6.   This New Ocean

Dear Dutch,

Lots of ups and downs here (no pun on the rocket business). The winter was tough. I don't think I've ever seen the boys look so down. They can't make a living just playing the Cavern. They borrowed money from Eppy just to get by. For the first time I heard them talk about getting a job just like everyone else. George mentioned becoming a bus driver like his Dad. Paul's had offers from other bands. Pete has a connection with a baker. Come to think of it, John never mentioned getting a job.

The man from Decca did indeed come to the Cavern, and he was impressed enough to invite the Beatles to London for a formal audition.

On the day before New Year's, the Beatles piled into Neil's shoddy van and drove down to London. There was no heating in the van; the four lay on top of each other in the back, taking turns at being on top. It was snowing hard, and Neil had never driven to London. He got lost. It took forever. The boys spent New Year's Eve walking the frigid streets of London and dreaming of 1962. I'm afraid it didn't exactly pan out as planned.

We arrived bright and early to a nondescript building in Broadhurst Gardens, which announced itself in discreet letters as being a Decca recording studio. They set up their gear in a cold, sterile room, punctuated by randomly placed partitions. Used to playing in the overheated Cavern, here they could practically see their breath. Instead of performing to a room full of dancing fans, they would be playing to a control room.

Eppy had carefully massaged the play list to show the breadth of their talent, but I wasn't crazy about his choices. There were three McCartney-Lennon compositions that didn't go over particularly well, and the rest were schmaltzy covers of classic songs that Eppy thought would impress Decca. He was keen on showing their versatility, but I think the folks at Decca were merely confused.

The boys were eager, but nervous. Their finger work was a little stiff, their singing just a little stilted, the drumming a little overbearing. Who can blame them? In the end, they were reasonably satisfied. Considering

69

the circumstances, they'd held up pretty well. No errant notes, no cracking voices. It was now time to pack up and head back north. And wait.

Brian sounded confident, but with each passing day he worried just a little more. He was right to.

Down in London, Decca was hesitating between Brian Poole and The Tremeloes —and the Beatles. The bad news finally arrived. Decca told Eppy that guitar bands were on the way out. They'd picked the Tremeloes. They'll never admit it, but I'm pretty sure Decca chose the Tremeloes for reasons that have nothing to do with music. They're not comfortable signing up a band featuring two front men. They're used to So-and-So and the So-and-So's: Cass and the Casanovas; Rory Storm and the Hurricanes; Cliff Richard and the Shadows, and so forth. A band with two lead singers seems unnatural — and they don't even know about George yet.

On top of that, we're from Liverpool. As you would say, we're hicks. The Tremeloes are from London, where any proper British person would be from. Is Decca going to bet on northerners with funny haircuts and a weird name?

When Brian broke it to the boys, they didn't take it well. This had been their big chance, and now it was over. Why did Brian make them sing those silly cover songs? Why didn't they simply rock the roof off the studio like they did at the Cavern? Why this, why that?

Brian's taken the audition tapes to Pye, Phillips, HMV, and Columbia, but it's been No Go. (I'm learning your lingo.) He's promised to keep trying, but there are only so many record labels around.

It's been a tough few months.

Right then,

Mal

****

Glenn's flight was scheduled for Jan 16th, then the 23rd, then the 27th, then February 13th, February 14th, and then February 16th. Rumbling clouds, sheets of rain — each time around it was either the weather or a mechanical glitch causing a cancellation. Each time, a few hundred reporters were forced to put away pens, pads, and cameras. Each time decisions had to be made with respect to twenty-four ships, sixty aircraft, and 18,000 recovery personnel around the world. Stay put or go home? Each time another heartache. A modern day Sisyphus. Yet every launch date had to be given the utmost attention.

Finally, on February 20th, things looked good. At 4:27 AM, I received word that the global tracking network was ready. Joking that he'd be fine even without any banana pellets on board, Glenn, decked out in silver armor from head to toe, radiated his usual confidence. He had to be worried, however. At this point NASA had a grand total of three orbits' worth of (un-manned) experience under its belt. An Atlas rocket – the type he was sitting on – had blown up 13 times already, two out of three times with a dummy Mercury capsule atop it. Including the last attempt.

Still, this was the moment he'd been waiting for. His initial disappointment at being passed over for the first Mercury flight had been compounded by NASA's initial decision to launch three suborbital flights. This meant that both Grissom and he were initially slated to duplicate Shepard's cannonball flight. For the public, it had been exhilarating the first time, mildly entertaining the second time, and would be borderline boring the third time. Spurred on by the Russians, however, and encouraged by the first two flights, NASA had decided that Mercury mission number three would be *orbital*. And that was Glenn's mission! He was now in a position to be the first American to orbit the earth! It was a great stroke of luck if it didn't kill him, a thought that brought him sharply back to reality.

By 6 AM, Glenn was wedged in the capsule. There would be over two hours of countdown holds, and like Al and Gus before him, Glenn had plenty of time to think back on his life, and mull over the consequences of a failed mission. The contract he and all the astronauts had with *Life* magazine would provide his family with some security in the short run. In the long run, Annie would get re-married. Glenn winced. It wasn't something he wanted to think about. He did his best to empty his mind of such distractions.

The Atlas rocket was significantly beefier than its Redstone predecessor, and condensation streamed down its sides like the impatient breath of a pawing bull. All three television networks were broadcasting from the Cape; forty million television sets were tuned in. Kraft polled each member of the mission team. Each would answer GO or NO GO depending on the readings on his console. With each GO, the anticipation in the room was ratcheted up a notch, climaxing with the now famous 10..9..8..7..6..5..4..3..2..1.

At 2:14 PM, Glenn was off.

"Godspeed John Glenn," mumbled Scott Carpenter, to which there responded a hundred unspoken amens.

The roar of the Atlas was deeper and louder than that of the Redstone. The black and white rocket lumbered through the roiling clouds of smoke, then gradually accelerated, and soon was off like an arrow. As it gained altitude, the Atlas gently rolled along its axis and arced southeast over the Atlantic.

In twenty seconds the Atlas reached 700 miles per hour, Mach 1, the speed of sound.

Teletype information from our necklace of tracking stations around the world indicated that the capsule was following its scheduled path, and Glenn himself reported that all was well. I took personal pride in the fact that we could hear him!

Glenn could turn the capsule to face forward or backwards. He took a moment to comment on the forty-five minute night, and he marveled at the continents and oceans that fled out from under his feet. He gazed down at the spangled lights of Perth, Australia, where all the lights had been turned on just for him.

As he passed over Canton Island in the South Pacific, Glenn had an unusual sighting.

"I am in the middle of a mass of thousands of very small particles…"

What the…? Were these space insects? Aliens? The Soviets hadn't reported such particles. We deferred to Kraft, who waved the whole thing off with this hand.

Moments later I received a most unexpected request from Kranz. "Dutch," he said, "President Kennedy wants to speak to Glenn. Can you patch him through?"

Patch him through? He must have seen the expression on my face.

"Dutch, he's THE PRESIDENT!"

Just then a more ominous call came in.

"Flight, Segment 51 just lit up."

Even the President would have to wait.

Segment 51 referred to the flotation collar that would keep the Mercury capsule afloat after splashdown. It was folded behind the capsule, wedged in under the heat shield. Strapped to the heat shield and to the capsule was the "retro pack," consisting of three little rockets designed to slow the capsule down prior to re-entry into earth's atmosphere.

"Segment 51" meant that the flotation collar had deployed. If so, it would be burned to a crisp during re-entry. More significantly, if the collar had deployed it meant that the heat shield was no longer attached to the capsule. No heat shield, no John Glenn. The capsule and its precious human cargo would be toast as soon as the capsule entered earth's atmosphere.

Unless, and this was a BIG unless, "51" were a false alarm. A little malfunction in the wiring could turn on the light in the absence of any problem with the flotation device.

We had our first full-blown crisis on our hands.

To believe the light or not to believe? The control room was suddenly abuzz with conversations.

There was no point in worrying Glenn, so we decided that, for now, this would be our little secret. Nevertheless, I ventured an innocent question: "John, everything OK on the panel? Hear any banging noises at the back of 'ole *Friendship 7*?"

"No, why?"

"Just checking."

Half the tracking stations reported seeing the same Segment 51 light, the other half did not.

"Does anyone have the number for McDonnell?" I made a note to establish a hot line to McDonnell for the next mission. If there were a next mission. Were Glenn to perish, this could be a very short-lived Apollo program. The critics would destroy us.

This was one scenario SimSup had not thought of. Virgin territory. Not knowing whether the light meant anything or not, we had to assume that it was for real and think of a solution. If we came up with an easy solution, we'd implement it. If the solution were too risky – or if there were no solution – we'd have to ignore the signal.

Communications from our tracking stations took an eternity to reach us, or so it seemed. It was probably no more than ten – fifteen minutes, but Glenn's life hung in the balance.

In the meantime, Glenn remained oblivious, at least for a while. He figured things out when every tracking station asked him the same question.

Max Faget, the main designer of the capsule, devised a plan involving the retro pack attached to the back of the capsule: At the conclusion of the rocket burn, Glenn was scheduled to jettison the rockets pack, leaving the heat shield to bear the brunt of the re-entry. The capsule would fall towards earth ass-backwards, and the heat shield would keep the 3,000° F temperatures from incinerating Glenn. Faget's suggestion was to keep the retropack strapped on after it had done its job.

"Does anyone know the aerodynamic effects of reentering with the retro package attached?" yelled Kraft. No one had a clue.

At best it would make no difference. At worst it would somehow ruin the heat shield or cause the capsule to spin out of control. Clearly, if any of the little rockets still contained fuel at the end of its burn, it would ignite during re-entry with devastating consequences.

It soon became clear that leaving the retropack on was the only option, unless we chose to disregard Segment 51.

There ensued a lively discussion between Walt Williams and Chris Kraft as to which course to take. "Lively" is putting it mildly. I estimated the heat shield upon re-entry would be only slightly hotter than their two faces. Williams didn't think we could ignore the signal, and didn't think leaving the retropack on would be a big risk. Kraft thought the signal was spurious. In the end, Williams pulled rank. The retropack would stay on.

Absent the entertaining chitchat between Williams and Kraft, the entire drama was played out before the American and world public.

As Glenn's capsule decelerated towards the ocean, we had our first tense re-entry. When a spacecraft re-enters earth's atmosphere, the speed and heat cause the particles in the air to ionize and ignite around the capsule. The result is a spectacularly bright orange fireball and, more significantly, a complete radio blackout. This was one problem that Kranz and I had been unable to get around. We would be completely out of touch with the astronaut during one of the most delicate parts of his mission. And now in particular, there was a reasonable chance that our astronaut would be cremated alive upon re-entry.

We knew roughly how long the radio blackout period would last. If we didn't hear from Glenn at the end of that period no explanation would be needed.

The waiting began. Glenn fired the retro rockets and began to experience the crushing Gs of deceleration. Chunks of material flew by through the orange curtain that surrounded him. Glenn worried that his heat shield was disintegrating. The capsule danced to and fro much more than he expected. At least his back wasn't feeling any warmer!

In Mercury Control, I studied the patterns of cigarette smoke drifting about the ceiling; anything to take my mind off Glenn's descent.

As we would soon find out, these re-entries all feel endless. And as the public would re-discover on Feb 1st 2003 with the disintegration of the Space Shuttle *Columbia*, there is no such thing as a routine re-entry.

"We have him!" shouted the CapCom from the destroyer *Noa*.

Friendship 7 had made contact with the ship. Glenn was safe.

He bobbed in the water inside the ever-hotter capsule-turned-greenhouse, and waited and waited. Seventeen minutes later, *Noa* pulled up alongside the capsule, plucked it out of the water, and plopped it onto the deck. Glenn blew off the hatch, and a clutch of eager hands extracted him from his pressure cooker. He'd lost five pounds in sweat and dehydration, most of it while waiting to be picked up.

Completing a flight that could have been scripted in Hollywood, Glenn returned home to a delirious welcome. He was now the reigning hero – a trip to the White House, a photo session with President Kennedy, an invitation to address Congress, and a New York ticker tape parade that was even bigger than Shepard's. (March 1st was declared "John Glenn Day" by New York Mayor Robert Wagner.) *Friendship 7* went on its own little world tour, millions of people in seventeen countries (and Hawaii) lining up one by one to peek inside the capsule. (The fourth orbit of *Friendship 7,* we joked.)

At NASA it was cigars all around.

The inspection of Glenn's capsule indicated that Segment 51 had been a false alarm. He was never in danger. Kraft felt vindicated, but he was not satisfied. He was "Flight," and the final decision should have been his to make. From here on in, if Webb, Gilruth, Low, and Williams wanted him in Mercury Control, they would have to butt out during the missions.

Agreed.

Basking in a little reflected glory, Kennedy capitalized on the moment to further his agenda:

"I know that I express the great happiness and thanksgiving of all of us that Colonel Glenn has completed his trip... I also want to say a word for those who participated with Colonel Glenn at Canaveral. They faced many disappointments and delays – the burdens upon them were great ... We have a long way to go in this space race. But this is the new ocean, and I believe the United States must sail on it and be in a position second to none."

**

Only one American stood glumly on the sidelines in total disbelief: Alan Shepard. His place in the sun had just been eclipsed. After just nine months! In less than one year, he had gone from Alan the Conqueror to Alan who? He had been designated the best of the Mercury 7, he had been the first to ride into space, and now astronaut #3 was getting all the glory. And it was goody-two-shoes Glenn, to boot.

Shepard had just been introduced to the Japanese fable. Who could have known that #3, not #1, would be the lucky draw? Shepard wondered whether anyone would remember him. He was right to worry. Does the average American today know the name of the first American in space (the first astronaut to receive a ticker tape parade, the astronaut who inspired Kennedy to launch the race to the moon, and one of just twelve humans to ever walk on the moon)? Strictly *Jeopardy* material! Just how much fame does one need to be remembered by the next generation? Ah, the Doppler effect of history...

Shepard was determined to jump back into training and get assigned to another flight. The Japanese fable, however, would strike him again. And again.

Deke Slayton was scheduled to follow Glenn into orbit. Flying the second orbital mission was somewhat of a vindication. He hadn't made the Gold team, but at least he was the best of the rest. Slayton was in the process of studying the new-fangled experiments concocted by the scientists, when he was called into NASA headquarters. He was off the flight, and Carpenter was in. Slayton was grounded. And not just for this flight. For all missions. Permanently.

Doctors (those doctors again) had discovered an irregularity in his heartbeat when he had first gone through the selection process in 1959. It was called idiopathic atrial fibrillation. No one thought much of it at the time, since Slayton had performed magnificently throughout his career. It hadn't bothered him as a hot shot test pilot pushing the envelope of the F-105 at Edwards Air Force Base, it had not hindered him in the centrifuge tests, and the doctors weren't even sure that it would bother him in space. But as the time for his flight approached, NASA became increasingly nervous. Sally reminded me that doctors had no idea what physical or emotional stresses an astronaut might be subject to, or what those stresses could do to a particular heart condition. Finally, NASA found a panel of cardiologists who would formally verbalize NASA's concerns: no one could predict the effects of space travel on atrial fibrillation. Why send up a man with an arrhythmia, when healthy alternatives were available?

It didn't take long for the other astronauts to come up with parallel theories for NASA's sudden interest in Deke's heart. The one I heard most often went like this: NASA was *getting even* with the uppity astronauts. For example, while Glenn was enduring one of his many cancelled flights back in January, he had gotten word that Vice-President Johnson wanted to visit Glenn's home in Virginia to console his wife, Annie. Along with fifty or so reporters, of course. Annie, who was shy and, worse, stuttered, frantically called her husband at the Cape. Glenn put out the word that Johnson was not to enter the house under any circumstance, even though he was already standing right outside on her lawn. NASA officials were seriously embarrassed. A government employee saying "no" to the Vice-President of the United States! Slayton's heart condition was now an opportunity for NASA to show the Mercury 7 astronauts who was really in charge.

I didn't buy that theory. I could see how NASA could ill afford to lose an astronaut in space. There were already enough variables beyond our control, why start behind the eight ball with a defective astronaut?

It was a bitter pill for Deke, and there wasn't a soul at NASA who didn't sympathize. The brutal selection process and all that training had just gone down the drain. He was bitterly disappointed, angry with the doctors, and embarrassed by his own anatomical failing. One moment on the verge of coming home a hero, and now a crumpled pink slip…

****

Three months hence and three thousand miles away to the North East, one of the Beatles would soon be feeling those same pangs of cosmic injustice.

****

What happened next surprised me nearly as much as Deke's sudden dismissal: Wally Schirra was Slayton's backup, but it was Carpenter who was chosen by NASA to fly Deke's mission. Schirra wasn't shy about making his displeasure known, and though none of us at Mercury Control – not myself, not Kranz, not even Kraft – was in a position to state an opinion, we secretly agreed with his outrage. No reason was given for Carpenter's sudden ascent and Schirra's demotion. The best I could come up with was that if fitness had been behind Slayton's bumping, NASA would want in his stead the man who best exemplified health. That was clearly Carpenter. It made perfect sense. Unless you were a pilot.

It was at that point, I think, that Kraft took an irreversible dislike to Scott Carpenter.

****

Liverpool, 20th July 1962

Dear Dutch,

THEY'VE DONE IT! A record contract with Parlophone. Eppy's come through!

But you have no idea how close they came to coming up empty-handed. Parlophone was their final attempt. There would have been no more doors to knock on. In fact, between you and me, Parlophone is a label known for comedy, not music, but at this point who cares?

The big moment came when George Martin of Parlophone agreed to audition the boys in person. Martin is a classical musician, who's made a name for himself recording comedy for this low-end label. Peter Sellers, the Goons, and the like. He is tall and urbane, a man of simple dignity and considerable presence. The boys played three of their compositions, "Love Me Do," "P.S. I Love You," "Ask Me Why," as well as the classic "Besame Mucho." Martin wasn't terribly impressed with their musical talent, but when they bantered about among themselves, it reminded him of something he was quite familiar with: the wacky humor of the Goons. The Beatles were effortlessly funny. They were naturals.

And of course they're always irreverent. As they listened to the playback of their recording, Martin asked the band members to critique themselves. Was there anything they didn't like? George piped in, "Well, we don't like your tie."

That was the real do or die moment. Could have gone either way. Martin saw that George was smiling, and after a seemingly eternal pause, he laughed.

That was it.

Martin has had absolutely no experience and categorically no interest in rock 'n' roll. But I think this proper, lanky fellow feels he can have fun working with our foursome.

On the downside, did I mention poor Stu? He died of a brain hemorrhage. The boys found out just as they were starting their last gig in Hamburg. They were devastated; John in particular. He laughed hysterically for a few moments — I've seen him do this before, when he's seriously distraught, but then he broke down. Paul and George feel very guilty about the way they used to tease and taunt Stu about his lack of musical talent. They think back to what a good friend he was and how he and Astrid gave them their look.

It's been a particular roller-coaster ride for John in every area of life. The record contract. Stu's death. And now, back in Liverpool, he's found out that he's going to be a father. That's right, Cyn is pregnant and they've decided to get married.

It was John's idea. He doesn't seem to mind the pregnancy or the wedding, I do think he loves her. The two who were upset were his Aunt Mimi and Brian. His Aunt couldn't imagine him getting married so young, when he doesn't even have a proper job, and Brian, well, for Brian it's more complicated. Brian fancies John, and somewhere deep down probably hoped that John might one day return his secret longings. This marriage, if nothing else, will delay that blissful day. (Frankly, I'd bet you Yanks land on the moon before John reciprocates.)

On a practical level, a married Beatle is a public relations nightmare. A girlfriend is bad enough, but a wife! And a child! How un-cool. How un-rock star-ish. Most of all, for the fans it's essential that the boys be carefree — emphasis on "free"!

Aunt Mimi and Brian acted on their feelings in opposite ways: Mimi was conspicuously absent at the wedding. Brian, on the other hand, personally arranged the affair and gave John and Cynthia indefinite use of his secret bachelor pad. He made one thing absolutely clear, though: the public was not to find out about the wife thing. No photographs of Cynthia would be released, and John would not be seen with Cynthia at any venue accessible to the press. This strikes me as being somewhat excessive. Who is going to recognize John outside the Cavern?

As for Parlophone, the contract has certainly lifted their spirits.

Now they have to record something! Martin wants them to record "How Do You Do It?" but the Beatles want to record their own compositions. We'll see.

Yours,

Mal

****

In the midst of preparing for the Mercury missions, everyone who worked at the Cape or at Langley was instructed to move to the new Space Center in Houston. We would be given thirty dollars a day for thirty days in relocation money. After that, we were expected to be moved in.

Congress had considered a number of sites across America to house this new Center, putting out a list of requirements and entertaining bids à la Olympic Committee. The suspense existed only in the minds of those who were totally ignorant of politics. Vice-President Lyndon Johnson and Albert Thomas, chairman of NASA's budget committee, were both from Texas. Houston was in Thomas' district. End of story.

For Sally and me the question was: should we live together? As soon as we heard about the move, we were both thinking about it, though I didn't know at first that she was too.

I looked at her lying across my bed, skimming the real estate ads in the Houston Chronicle. It was a Sunday afternoon, and she was wearing a sleeveless tee shirt and a pair of white slacks. She was barefoot, her toenails painted flamingo pink. I thought if I wanted to live with her, I should ask her to marry me, but I wasn't ready for that. I couldn't think of any reason *not* to marry her, except that I had decided in high school not to get married until I was at least 26, and that still seemed like a sensible plan.

But in 1962, living together without being married was not something a girl like Sally would even consider. What would her parents think? Her friends? Even the guys at work would look at her differently.

And yet. We were spending six out of seven nights together. I thought her car – a chemical-green '55 Nash Meteor her father handed down to her when she moved to Cape Canaveral – would be much happier if left behind in Florida. If we lived together, we'd only need my VW. (Mine was the little ugly car everybody loved. Even the VW advertising company made fun of it: "Ugly is only skin deep," "After a few years it starts to look beautiful," "Think small," "It makes your house look bigger," "Live below your means," "Do you earn too much to afford one?") My Beetle was cherry red, without the Day-Glo flowers and peace signs appliqués that would eventually adorn it.

"I could room with Betsey and Dinah again," Sally said, without lifting her eyes from the page.

"Hmm."

"Or I could room with you."

"Isn't that against the law in Texas?"

"We work for NASA, Dutch," said Sally sweetly. "I don't think we'll be arrested."

"But what about your parents?"

"I'm more interested in what you think," she said, looking at me now, her sparkling eyes holding a hint of doubt. That doubt undid me. How could she think I *wouldn't* want to live with her?

I got out of the chair, and lay down next to her on the bed. "Sally, will you be my roommate?" I whispered in her ear, and dopey as it sounds, it was actually a romantic moment. She laughed. "Yes."

A few minutes later she added, "You know, Dutch, I don't want to get married too young either." I'd always suspected she could read my thoughts. I was just glad she didn't do it too often. "As for my parents, it'll be *my* apartment. When they visit, you'll have to pretend to leave at night." I considered this for a minute. "They haven't even visited you here."

"No. They'll come once, just to see where I'm living. We'll need to take the couch from my apartment. They bought it for me."

"As long as we take *my* car," I said.

"Deal."

**

The new Mission Control Center (MCC) would be built near the Gulf of Mexico, half way between Houston and Galveston. The humidity, mosquitoes, snakes, and swamps around Houston and Galveston were not terribly different from those near Cape Canaveral, so this was no new sweat off my back. The MCC itself was set up on flat, dry, tree-deprived acreage. It consisted of a bland, chalk-white, aseptic group of two three-story high edifices, save one eight-story administration building. It could have been part of a college campus, a hospital, a factory, or a minimum-security prison. Inside, the walls were painted an unimaginative gray-green, and the décor could have stepped right out of my old Zanzibar Palace catalog. But it was home.

There wasn't exactly an abundance of accommodations near the new Center, so Sally and I rented an apartment out near Hobby airport. It was a long drive to work, and the countryside was empty and desolate, though Sally found it exhilarating. "There's so much sky!" she said. "Doesn't it make you feel bigger?"

Actually, it made me feel smaller and insignificant. I looked at that endless horizon, and thought of Mal's talk about UFOs. If they were to be found anywhere, I decided, it was Texas.

A big plus to our new location was that we had our own major league baseball team, and it was even named after us: the Houston Astros! And the team would play indoors in the … Astro-Dome *(and eventually on a new artificial turf called… Astro-turf!)* Somehow I felt we should have free tickets, but that just wasn't in the NASA budget.

Fortunately, we had more success than the Astros. The players looked like Lifesavers in their uniforms, and I think they were sub-consciously too embarrassed to play up to their full potential. (We, on the other hand, felt no shame at all at being dressed in the same white shirts, with the same plastic pocket protectors, and the same slide rules clipped to our belts.)

**

Scott Carpenter stood out from the other astronauts. He would actually contemplate the implications of Man's going into space – out loud – and he was the only one to take an actual interest in the space experiments that were being devised. He also sported the most toned physique. Not surprisingly then, according to Sally, he was the doctors' and scientists' favorite astronaut.

Unfortunately, the choice of Carpenter deepened the schism be-tween the scientists on the one hand, and the engineers and astronauts on the other. The former felt that our purpose in space was to ad-vance our knowledge of Man and his Universe (would NASA's Mission Statement not one day read "To improve life here, To extend life to there, To find life beyond," shades of Star Trek!). The latter were fo-cused on getting the machinery to work. This uneasy divide between equally meritorious camps would persist throughout the entire Apollo program.

At 7:45AM, on May 24th, Carpenter's Atlas booster blasted off on three pillars of liquid fire.

Whereas the previous astronauts had chosen straightforward, pa-triotic names – *Freedom, Liberty, Friendship* – Carpenter, in typical fashion, chose a name with multiple meanings: *Aurora 7*. Not only was it the name of the Colorado street he had grown up on, but "Aurora" was the Roman Goddess of the dawn, and weren't we at the dawn of a new age? Glenn was the only other astronaut who thought that was cool.

There was a quiet sigh of relief as the Atlas streaked into space without disintegrating. Carpenter's flight would be a repeat of Glenn's, i.e. three orbits and then splashdown. The major difference would be the addition of the experiments. These had been opposed by Kranz and by Kraft, who felt that the astronaut would still have his hands full flying the darn capsule, but the scientists felt that with each flight we should learn a bit more about ourselves and about space. They had prevailed.

Carpenter marveled at the sights only one other American had ever seen: the indigo skies, the horizon repeatedly aglow with raging sunsets, sunrises glowing a deep orange against the endless black sky, etc… With minimal effort, Carpenter turned the capsule one way and then the other. He pointed it straight down towards the earth. If he closed his eyes, he felt the same regardless of which way he was pointing.

Problems started during the second orbit. Flying over the Canary Islands in the Atlantic Ocean off the coast of Africa, Carpenter reported that his instruments were not in agreement with each other. The Teletype messages I received from Africa, Australia, and Hawaii all confirmed this.

In the meantime, Carpenter had experiments to carry out. These included the release of a multi-colored balloon to judge the effect of space on the reflection properties of colored surfaces, observing the behavior of a liquid in a weightless state to better design space fuel tanks and pumps, and one study completely designed to capture the public's imagination: "a distance measurement of the airglow layer above the horizon, its angular width, and a description of its characteristics." Carpenter actually relished this.

Juggling his job as a scientist and as a pilot, Carpenter struggled to keep the capsule from getting a "bad attitude."

Unbeknownst to Carpenter or to us at Mercury Control, one of the capsule's eighteen attitude thrusters was stuck in the "on" position. *Aurora 7* was gulping fuel as Carpenter struggled to keep the capsule in line.

It rapidly became clear that he was in trouble. He was running out of fuel. Kraft assumed that this was the result of poor piloting, and I could see the color gradually draining from his face. Carpenter was advised to turn his systems off for a while and just drift to conserve fuel.

Carpenter, however, needed every ounce of concentration and energy to keep the capsule on track.

Carpenter was also curious to investigate the "fireflies" that Glenn had seen at sunset. He discovered that if he hit the walls of the capsule, the fireflies would suddenly appear in space. They were obviously coming from the capsule itself. Carpenter swung the capsule around to get a better look; another bit of precious fuel expended and another rise in Chris Kraft's blood pressure. As *Aurora 7* hurtled over the Pacific for the last time, the controllers in Hawaii were practically wetting their pants: Not only was Carpenter essentially out of fuel, but the capsule's attitude was all wrong for re-entry. If he were lucky, he'd simply land "long," but the other possibility was that he'd fail to re-enter altogether. He would drift into a decaying orbit and die.

At this point, Kraft could have cared less about Carpenter himself. The death of an astronaut, on the other hand, would have potentially fatal implications on the infant Mercury program. We were perpetually just one tragedy away from seeing our funding cut.

Passing over California, *Aurora 7* was now in the hands of Al Shepard, CapCom of the California tracking station. This would be the last chance for NASA to give Carpenter any feedback on his position and attitude.

"I'm out of manual fuel," said Carpenter.

Shepard did everything he could to calm Carpenter.

"You have plenty of time, about seven minutes until .05G, so take it slow and easy." Carpenter, however, did not need any calming down.

"Roger. Okay, I can make out very, very, small farmland … pastureland below. I see individual fields, rivers, lakes, roads, I think."

Fields, rivers, lakes? Was he writing a travel guide? Did he not see the gravity of the situation? Was he courageously cool or irresponsibly oblivious?

The little vein on the left side of Kraft's forehead was furiously beating.

"Dammit, Dutch, keep his mind on the job. I think he's delirious."

There was not much I could do, though. It was up to Al to keep him focused.

"Recommend you get as close to reentry attitude as you can," Shepard calmly advised Scott.

And that was the end of the conversation. Carpenter would fire the retro rockets, and the period of radio blackout would commence.

At 17,000 mph, a delay of one second here or there translates to a vast distance. If Carpenter had any chance of landing anywhere near his target it was imperative that he fire his rockets precisely on time. He was three seconds late.

John Llewellyn, another precocious prodigy at Mercury Control, was in charge of tracking Carpenter's descent. We had all noticed the three second delay, and Llewellyn frantically pushed his slide rule through warp speed to calculate the new location of Carpenter's splashdown.

Kraft wondered what instrument of torture he would apply to Carpenter if he came out of this alive.

Another pack of cigarettes went up in ashes as we waited through the blackout period.

We announced to the press that Carpenter would be landing long, and we further announced that we didn't exactly know where yet. (This wasn't completely true. The exact location was given out on a strictly "need to know" basis.) Radio stations broadcasted the approximate landing zone, and every private plane and boat patriotically headed for that area. Planes were stacked up like dishes in the sink!

Suddenly: "I'm on the main chute at 5,000. Status is good!" It was Carpenter. He'd made it.

Llewellyn had him pegged 250 miles downrange from his target. It would take a while for Air Rescue personnel to reach him, but he would be fine.

Communications between Carpenter and his rescue team were spotty. Air Rescue announced that they had not located Carpenter, and as a result, CBS news anchor Walter Cronkite announced that we had a missing astronaut. This made for high drama, but only served to anger Kraft even more, if that was possible. We knew exactly where Carpenter was – Llewellyn had figured it out – what were they talking about?

Scotty's capsule splashed down at a rugged 22mph, dunking it 10-12 feet underwater before it bobbed back up. If it was going to take an hour to find him, Carpenter was not going to roast in a tiny rocking capsule, no sirree. He had seen how drained Glenn looked at the end of his mission. Who knew how long the rescue would *really* take? The Mercury capsule was a spacecraft not a ship. He thought better of blowing open the hatch, and instead slowly crawled out the top of the capsule. He wiped the back of his hand across his brow, threw the life raft onto the water, and jumped in.

Three hours later, the rescue team found him eating a candy bar, gentle waves lapping at the raft. He was missing only a guitar. Interviewed on the way back to the ship, Carpenter stated to the press, "I didn't know where I was and they [Mercury] didn't either."

Them's were fighting words to Llewellyn and to Kraft, who was already prepared to wring his neck.

Arriving on board the carrier, Carpenter was rather pleased with himself. He had ridden the bucking bronco and had managed to stay on. He had managed the fuel consumption beautifully, using every last drop at his disposal, and he had carried out the scientific experiments to the letter. He had even landed within striking distance of his target.

Expecting congratulations, he was not prepared for Chris Kraft's fury. Kraft's eyes bored into Carpenter the minute he walked in, and Flight proceeded to lash into him with ill-concealed hostility. In a little speech laced with expletives, Kraft laid out before him all of Carpenter's perceived transgressions. Palms outstretched Carpenter defended himself gamely, as he took in this unhappy earful, but Kraft laughed him off with a harsh bark. Before Scotty could say anything, Kraft had turned sharply on his heels, and was gone.

Though congratulations poured in from the White House and the entire country, Kraft specifically swore to anyone within earshot that Carpenter would never fly for him again. And he never did.

Carpenter hung around as CapCom, but seeing the writing on the wall, soon left NASA, and turned his attention to the Sea Lab program. He would become the only human to orbit the earth and explore the ocean floor. In 1965, he spent thirty days living and working 205 feet under the sea – a feat that, in many ways, was more challenging than his NASA mission. In the following years, he dived in most of the world's oceans, including the Arctic, worked with Jacques Cousteau, and wrote two novels, dubbed "underwater techno-thrillers."

In short order, NASA would be looking for astronauts of Scotty's ilk: adventurous pilots with an interest in science. Not yet, however. For now, they just wanted pilots. Carpenter was a man out of time. In my book, he was a hero.

**

We were just starting to think that we had caught up to the Soviets (they had not done anything in a year), when we read that they had just sent up not one, but *two* Vostok capsules. How they were planning to get to the moon remained a mystery, but by sending up two capsules it sounded like they were also working on rendezvous techniques.

And here we were, nowhere near the end of our Mercury program. We had yet to see one Mercury flight go smoothly, and the Communists were working on rendezvous. The only good news, if any were to be found, was that the two Soviet crafts appeared to have come only within three miles of each other. It was a significant accomplishment, but a three-mile gap is no rendezvous. Maybe the "bad guys" weren't so far ahead after all.

And speaking of moon voyages, it was one thing to *decide* to go to the moon, it was quite another to figure out how to get there. This was a little detail that needed to be cleared up before we invested the many years it would take to design and build all the necessary equipment. Consequently, it was critical that we quickly come to a decision. It was a subject that captivated the entire country, and it landed us on the August 10, 1962, cover of *Time* magazine (a whimsical cartoon featuring a mischievous, speedy little flying bug of a spacecraft).

Understandably, everyone had his pet idea of how to get to the moon. The most obvious approach was to send a rocket directly to the moon and have it come back to earth ("the direct ascent method"). Science fiction writers and comic books favored this solution. The brilliant Belgian writer Hergé had described exactly this feat in his beautifully illustrated '50s Tintin comic strip, *Explorers on the Moon (On a Marché sur la Lune)*. This approach was also my sentimental favorite. (Sally bought me a toy rocket ship and put it on our coffee table. Once,

I found it in my underwear drawer. She remarked innocently, "It's been awhile, you know. You work too hard.")

Alas, there was the real risk of the rocket tipping over upon reaching the lunar surface if it did not land on a perfectly flat surface; moreover, how do you fashion a heat shield for a rocket with three landing fins? Most importantly, a quick calculation revealed the impossibly large size of any "direct ascent" rocket, even to the ever-imaginative von Braun. Direct ascent was out. I took it well.

The most realistic option was to send a mother ship into space. A lunar craft would disengage from the mother ship, land on the moon, return to the mother ship, and be discarded. The crew would return to earth in the mother ship.

The plan was unanimously approved. Bickering, however, began when it came time to decide where exactly in space the mother ship and lunar craft would disengage and reunite.

The most popular plan at NASA called for these activities to take place in earth orbit. This plan was dubbed Earth Orbit Rendezvous, referred to by the mellifluous abbreviation EOR. John Houbolt, however, put forth a stranger-sounding option: The mother ship and lunar craft would travel in tandem to the moon; they would orbit the moon together, then disengage; the lunar craft would land on the moon, return to the mother ship, and be left in lunar orbit or sent back to crash on the moon; the mother ship would return to earth. This was LOR – Lunar Orbit Rendezvous. It seemed silly to send two craft to the moon, and this second proposal was initially given short shrift. It didn't help that Houbolt, as associate chief of the dynamic loads division, was far removed from the action, out at NASA's Langley, VA, facility. He appeared before every committee that would listen to him, to no avail.

As the engineers began to specifically draw out the specs of the various crafts and to calculate the risks associated with each and every particular step of an expedition to the moon (and back), Houbolt's proposal began to make more sense. NASA started to see things his way, and when Von Braun threw in this support, it was a done deal. LOR it would be.

We had barely been able to send a tin can around the earth, and already we had a multi-part plan to send a man to the moon and back. We didn't know how long a person could stay in space, whether a person could survive outside a spacecraft, whether we could ever manufacture a suitable spacesuit, whether two spacecraft could safely rendezvous, or whether we could start and stop a rocket engine in space.

To answer these questions NASA created project Gemini.

We drew up a list of accomplishments that would be required for a moon landing. Gemini would have to:

- demonstrate that astronauts could spend one to two weeks in space – the duration of the anticipated moon missions.
- demonstrate that the astronauts could function in the vacuum of space, i.e. outside a spacecraft. NASA would test this through a series of "space walks" (Extra-Vehicular Activities, EVAs in NASA-speak), whereby the astronaut would leave the capsule, perform a series of maneuvers, and return to the capsule.
- develop rendezvous techniques – the ability to bring two spacecraft side-by-side.
- develop the technology to *dock* two spacecraft.

Gemini is the third constellation of the Zodiac, named for the twins Castor and Pollux, brothers of Helen of Troy[3]. It was amusing to note the mixing of Greek mythology with the hard science of getting to the moon. Now all that remained to be done was create the rockets, design the capsules, figure out the math, and send the guys up!

***

Liverpool, 24th October, 1962

Dear Dutch,

There's been a lot of news here. I'm now the Beatles' road manager. As for the boys, wow! They spent the summer in Hamburg at the Star Club. This time they flew over by airplane. Eppy wanted them to go in style. (He told the Liverpool fans that the band was going on their "European Tour.") They were the headliners this time – and Eppy even arranged for them to meet... Little Richard! I think there may have been a little gay connection

---

3   In the myth, the twins shared the same mother (Leda) but not the same father (one was Zeus, the other a Spartan king). This meant that Pollux was immortal and Castor was mortal. When Castor died, Pollux asked Zeus to let him share his immortality with his brother. Zeus transformed them into the Gemini constellation.

there. They were very excited. They've taken the concept of "mach schau" to the next level: John showed up on stage completely wasted, naked from the waist up, with a toilet seat around his head. The crowd loved it. And guess what? In the studio they recorded one of their own compositions, "Love Me Do," with another one of their compositions on the B-side, "P.S. I Love You."

"Love Me Do" was originally sung by John, but when George Martin suggested John add some harmonica, the vocals went to Paul. John harmonizes here and there, when he's not playing the harmonica. It's gone to number 17 here in England! For a Liverpool band!!! And *no* promotion from EMI (the bastards). They must think that the Beatles are another one of George Martin's comedy routines. Good thing Eppy's gotten into the act. He ordered I don't know how many copies of the record for his own store, and has gotten everyone he knows to call Radio Luxembourg asking to hear it on the radio. And it worked! We all huddled around the radio the other day, and on came "Love Me Do"! Do you know the thrill of hearing your own song on the radio?

The Beatles are the toast of the town. No Liverpool band has ever gone so far in the charts; the Cavern has *recording stars*. You should see the line to get in. Of course I'm getting a lot of "mileage" from this, if you know what I mean.

There is one down note, though, and I have mixed feelings about this. The boys sacked Pete Best. It was cruel. They sacked him just as they were recording "Love Me Do." Can you imagine?

George Martin triggered the whole thing when he told Brian he'd bring in a session drummer to replace Pete. He doesn't much care for Pete's drumming; it's adequate for the little concerts the Beatles play, but not for the studio. Without batting an eyelash, the boys asked Brian to ditch Pete! They said they'd get the drummer from the Hurricanes to take his place. I don't think any of them ever as much as spoke to Pete. They left it to Brian to do the dirty work.

I've thought about it a lot. Pete's slogged it out with them for how long now? He's been to Germany, sweated it out with them through all their Hamburg gigs, played the endless sets, eaten the crappy food, slept on the cold floors, lived in misery with them day in and day out, and now, just when they're on the cusp of success, he gets the boot![4]

The boys have been pretty tight-lipped about this, and there are a few theories buzzing about. The obvious one is that the Beatles agree that he's not good enough. Another idea is that the other three Beatles have been jealous of Pete's success with women. (There are enough girls to go around. Really.) It's also been suggested that this is all because he's refused to wear his hair like the others, and doesn't hang out with them. (It's true that whenever the boys rib each other or slip into one of their absurdist Goon acts, Pete's not usually pitching in.) My guess is that they don't think he's good enough. You wouldn't know it to look at them goofing around on stage, but they're all very ambitious. The other factors just made the decision easier. Anyway, Pete's out. Got a job as a baker.

His replacement's a short feller with sad eyes and a funny nickname, "Ringo" (wears many rings on his fingers). Richard Starkey's his real name. He's from the Cast Iron Shore section of Liverpool and was with Rory Storm and the Hurricanes. He used to hang out with Beatles in Hamburg, and I think the boys got along with him better than they did with Pete. He's got this sullen, hound dog look, but there's nothing sullen about him. He's quiet, but follows the conversation keenly, and drops in humorous zingers quite fancied by the other three. He shaved his beard and now combs his hair à la Beatles. They're no longer drawing straws to see who's going to share a room with the drummer. As much as I like Pete, I must admit that the minute Ringo joined, it was like he'd been there forever.

The reaction among the Liverpool faithful has been swift — and negative. "Pete forever! Ringo Never!" is the chant, and some of the girls have tried to punch Ringo. (That's where I come in, of course.) I didn't think when I took this job that I'd be fighting with girls!

On a side note, I sneaked off to the Ealing Jazz Club to see another hot new band, the Rollin' Stones. Their singer has the largest mouth I've ever seen, and he snarls more than he sings. The girls dig him.

In the meantime, Eppy has spiffed up the Beatles' appearance for shows outside the Cavern. He's had them fitted with identical dark velvet-collared suits. John had to be dragged to the tailor again, kicking and

---

4 *and has the rest of his life to see what might have been- just like Deke.*

screaming, but Eppy found an ally in Paul, who probably has the best show-biz sense of the bunch. Leather fits their true selves better, but Paul and Eppy are probably right about the suits.

The new outfits haven't slowed the boys down. George moves back and forth between Paul's microphone and John's. Paul springs up and down. They all exchange winks, laughs, double takes, you name it. It sometimes looks like one big inside joke that we're peeking in on.

By the way, what's with the race riots?[5] Are they anywhere near you? I have to tell you, I'm on the side of the Negroes. Nat King Cole, Little Richard, Chuck Berry. Need I say more?

By the way, congratulations on your space success (aren't the Russians amazing?).

Mal

Amazing, my ass.
Well I suppose they were. What could you do?

****

Just in case the Free World had any inclination to protest the first anniversary of the Berlin Wall, the Soviets provided a made-to-order distraction. On August 11th, they sent up Nikolayev, and the very next day, from a different launch pad, they blasted Popovich into space. The two capsules came close to each other, and the cosmonauts merrily sang to each other. Nikolayev also took the time to toe his government's line on religion by commenting that he did not see God while orbiting the earth.

"Did it occur to him that maybe God isn't a visible person?" Sally muttered.

The double launch and apparent rendezvous were an impressive combination of feats, far beyond the reach of our Mercury program. We did not even have two launch pads...

The Soviets were quick to gloat: "Communism is scoring one victory after another in its peaceful competition with capitalism." The cosmonauts chimed in; standing in Red Square before a large crowd,

---

5   Whites had rioted when the African-American, James Meredith, enrolled at the University of Mississippi.

Nikolayev exulted, "The group flight in outer space is one more vivid proof of the superiority of socialism over capitalism."

Not quite.

The cosmonauts could barely have waved to each other. They hadn't been able to maneuver their capsules, and as such, couldn't rendezvous in the sense that we understood it. This was another notch in the abacus of Soviet deceit, but we had no way of knowing this at the time. We listened to the *New York Times* congratulate the Soviets on "a spectacular accomplishment, an amazing feat," and sucked it up.

In September, President Kennedy traveled to Texas to deliver a speech at Rice University. He was unpopular in Texas, and despite the presence of Lyndon Johnson on his ticket, he considered it important to establish a presence in the Lone Star State. He delivered his speech at Rice Stadium, with Gene and I sitting at the fifty-yard line. We'd heard that he was going to address the space program again.

Sure enough.

"Some have asked," he began, "why go to the moon? One might as well ask why climb the highest mountain? Why sail the widest ocean?"

It was good to see that he was still on our side. The space program was hardly a sure thing. We were two for two in near misses on our orbital flights. Either we were going to get it right or we were headed for a tragedy.

Dejected, but not abandoned by NASA, Deke Slayton received an unusual compensation for his sudden grounding. Since NASA needed a senior manager to oversee multiple affairs pertaining to the astronauts, the astronauts themselves – specifically Shepard, Grissom and Schirra – had put Deke forth as a candidate. If they were going to have a boss, it might as well be one of them. The proposal had been accepted by NASA and by Deke. As far as Deke was concerned, this would be a way to stay close to the action, maintain face, and most importantly, ensure that he remain in NASA's eye for the day he would be cleared again.

One of his first tasks had been to chair the panel that would select the next round of astronauts, and the time had come to make the announcements:

Neil Armstrong, civilian (formerly of Navy) (and Purdue Engineering graduate!)

Major Frank Borman (Air Force; did not attend Purdue, but
 born in Indiana)
Lieutenant Charles (Pete) Conrad (Navy)
Lieutenant Commander James Lovell (Navy)
Captain James McDivitt (Air Force)
Elliot See, civilian
Captain Tom Stafford (Air Force)
Captain Ed White II (Air Force)
Lieutenant John Young (Navy)

The selection criteria had been modified for this group. Since the
Gemini capsule was slightly larger than the Mercury capsule, the can-
didates could be taller (up to six feet). This was fortunate for Stafford.
They could be civilians, and this opened the door for Armstrong and
See.

Deke, Al Shepard, Bob Gilruth, Walt Williams, and Shorty Powers
met the new crop of astronauts at Ellington Air Force Base. Gilruth assured the space rookies that there would be plenty of missions for them
all (true indeed!). Deke filled them in on the rules and regulations:

"With regard to gratuities, if there is any question, just follow
the old test pilot's creed: anything you can eat, drink or screw within
twenty-four hours is perfectly acceptable." Gilruth blushed, and
Williams coughed a little. "Within reason, within reason," Williams
admonished.

None of the recruits were thinking "goodies" at that point. Each
was thinking of the moon. One of them would be part of the first lunar
landing crew.

If the new hotshot astronaut recruits thought that they would
immediately start flying cool machines, they were wrong. They were
immediately placed... in school. It was time to learn astronomy, ge-
ology, rocket propulsion, computer science, meteorology, space guidance, space physiology, and the like. The tradition continued of giving
each new astronaut a specific area to focus on. Communications got
Stafford.

**

Wally Schirra was pacing like a caged lion.

He had watched four lesser-qualified astronauts go up in space before him, and now it was finally his turn.

He would show them how it *really* was done.

He wasn't going to get distracted by namby-pamby White Coat experiments, nor was he going to gaze lovingly into a silly sunset. He was a test pilot, and his job was to fly the craft and land it on target. Fortunately for him, the flight plan called for few scientific experiments.

He named his spacecraft *Sigma 7*. Sigma is the Greek symbol for the sum of the elements of an equation and a symbol of engineering excellence. Engineering, not lyric opera.

As Schirra sat atop the Atlas, I don't know that he gave much thought to childhood memories, family, or any other distraction. As for Kraft, he looked positively relaxed. Schirra was the pilot's pilot. No one was going to have to coach or cajole him. *Sigma 7* was about to erase the memory of *Stigma 7*...

On October 3rd, splashing flame and smoke, Mercury-Atlas rumbled into space without a hitch.

As expected, once in orbit Schirra did not extol the virtues of space travel, and he did not reel off any colorful sound bites. Like other astronauts, he'd seen the last rays of sunlight quickly flicker and die over the horizon as he flew into the night, but this elicited no comment. In fact, he specifically avoided looking out the window except when called for by the flight plan. His goal was fly the perfect mission. He'd show them a thing or two about all that Gold team/Red team crap.

Both Glenn and Carpenter had reported serious heating within their spacesuits. Schirra, who'd been assigned to spacesuit detail, had devised a little water pump. Now, sure enough, Schirra began to feel uncomfortably warm. Time to try the pump – and it worked. Score one for the Red team.

Schirra got the GO for a second orbit. He soon confirmed Carpenter's assessment that Glenn's "fireflies" were nothing more than ice crystals coming from his own ship, not alien life forms.

Until this mission the capsule had flown in the automatic "chimp" mode, as Schirra liked to call it. As soon as it had reached orbit, the capsule had been programmed to turn 180°, position itself for re-entry, and hold that position throughout the mission. Maintaining this position used up fuel. Schirra had successfully lobbied to allow the capsule to drift up until the time of re-entry, at which point he (the PILOT) would fire the retro-rockets and align the capsule – er, spacecraft. He used his rockets sparingly throughout the flight (with what he lovingly referred to as micro mouse farts), earning him the GO to make six orbits.

As he positioned himself for re-entry, he received updates from Shepard on a boat in the Pacific, from Glenn in California, and from Grissom in Mexico. All systems were GO. He then passed over South America. NASA had a mini-tracking station in Ecuador. No astronaut was stationed there, and there was no scheduled communication between Schirra and that station. The station was there purely in case of an emergency.

"*Sigma 7?*"

Uh-oh.

Schirra noted no abnormal lights on the dashboard. This would not be a great time for an emergency.

"Yes, this is *Sigma 7,* I hear you."

"Do you have a message for the people of South America?"

@#$%^&*(), f'in A. Who did they think he was, Scott Carpenter? Did they really expect some lovey-dovey message about how beautiful South America looked from space?

"Buenos dias you-all" – and he was history. That's an advantage you have when you're hauling ass at hypersonic speed.

Schirra's re-entry was near perfect. He joked that he was aiming for elevator #3 on the recovery ship *Kearsarge.* In fact, he splashed down just four and a half miles from the carrier, in full view of the crew and reporters.

Following this textbook flight, Schirra waited by the phone for the call that would invite him for a leisurely visit to the White House, a fireside chat with the President, an address to Congress, etc, etc... i.e. all the benefits associated with the A+ perfect performance. He tried out a few speeches.

"Dear Congressmen and fellow Americans." No, "My fellow Americans, and dear Congressmen." Perhaps he would get Glenn to help him out.

The call never came. He would be directed to the White House, he would pick up his medal, but the reception was perfunctory. President Kennedy had war on his mind.

**

Having sized up the American President as weak when they had met in Vienna, Soviet Premier Khrushchev was now shipping ballistic missiles to Cuba. Every American city along the Eastern seaboard would be at risk for nuclear extinction, a serious bargaining chip in any future negotiation with the Americans. Eager to avoid another Bay of Pigs, Kennedy now made sure there would be no mixed signals. On October 22nd, 1962, he blockaded Cuba. He announced, furthermore, that if the Soviets failed to turn around he would fire on their ships.

The world held its breath, while the two super powers stared at each other "eyeball to eyeball," as Secretary of State Dean Rusk would say. Would there be a third World War in this century? With nuclear weapons?

Khrushchev blinked first. On October 28th, he called for his ships and missiles. The Cuban Missile Crisis was over. It had been a tense week. Plenty of people thought the Space Center would have been a choice nuclear hit.

**

As head of the astronaut office, Deke was given another plum job: making the crew assignments. If Deke couldn't walk on the moon himself, the next best thing was to decide who did.

His first job was to select an astronaut for the next, and probably last, Mercury flight. It should have been a no-brainer: Other than himself, Gordon Cooper was the only Mercury 7 astronaut who hadn't flown yet. Gordo, however, had a knack for making life tough for himself. He had awkward ways of making a point, and his actions tended to backfire. In full view of his superiors, he once landed his F-102 on a runway that was far too short for comfort. On another occasion, he took off in a plane that was low on fuel just to spite the airport that had refused to refuel him. He felt no compunction about piping up when he had an opinion. This works well in college, but it doesn't advance you in a quasi-military setting. Nevertheless, Deke officially recommended Gordo, and despite some grumbling, NASA agreed.

****

London, 19th December, 1962

Dear Dutch,

George Martin has invited the boys to record another song! They had wondered whether a #17 song on the hit parade would be enough to warrant another recording — and it has! They want to go with one of their compositions again, and they're mulling over a number of options. Right now they're leaning towards one of John's songs. Paul's working on the bass line and the harmony.

Happy Holidays!

Mal

For illustrations, see www.intotheskywithdiamonds.com

7.   Just Rattle Your Jewelry

Dear Dutch,

We have a hit!

Yes, "Love Me Do" broke the Top-20, but now the Beatles have <u>the Number One song</u> in three out of four music polls!

The song is called "Please Please Me." The Beatles first recorded it in a slow, bluesy fashion, but then Martin had them speed it up. A stroke of genius!!! I've enclosed a copy of the 45.

George Martin had the idea of capturing the Beatles' live sound on a long play record, and he trudged up to Liverpool with his recording paraphernalia. He quickly gave up when he discovered that the Cavern has the acoustic sophistication of, well, a cavern. The boys were disappointed, but Martin agreed to record their live set in the studio, and this will be the basis of their first album.

In retrospect, I guess the studio is not the place to get a live sound, because the excitement only comes through on "Please Please Me," "Twist and Shout," and "I Saw Her Standing There." You'll see.

The media have finally noticed us. Not just the *Liverpool* press, the national press. Maureen Cleave from London's *Evening Standard* wrote a piece titled, "Why the Beatles Create All That Frenzy," and here's an excerpt: "Their physical appearance inspires frenzy. They look beat-up and depraved in the nicest possible way." She goes on to describe John as witty, Paul as charming, George as handsome, and Ringo as "ugly but cute."

The boys are crisscrossing the country in Neil's van — a different city every night— and I have made a major decision: I'm going to travel with them and help set up their equipment as a full-time job. Eppy agreed. Neil and I make a good team. I hate to give up the Cavern gig, but this is more fun (lots of bird action, if you know what I mean).

Mal

Gus, of all people, had a record player; a rectangular box with a round hole, behind which lived a little speaker. You opened the lid, and there were the turntable and the needle-tipped arm. I pulled the small 45 RPM record out of the sleeve, and stared. The label was cherry red, with white lettering that spelled **PARLOPHONE**.

I had to find the plastic piece that would fit in the center of the record and allow me to center it on the turntable. Gus only had large 33 rpm LPs (33 revolutions per minute, "long play") records.

Gordo had the plastic piece.

Within moments of listening to the song, I was dumbstruck.

Peter, Paul and Mary were my speed. Chubby Checker's "Twist" had been my idea of a fast song.

This stuff was turbo-charged! It was a *wild* two-minute ride.

I listened to it again – and again. The song soared – then stopped – then started up again. The bass was pounding, the chord changes were fast, the harmonies were tight, the tone was hurried and exciting, and then that tremendous climax, and – whew – the exhaustion of that final chord. Anyone have a cigarette?

I wondered what effect "Please Please Me" would have on Sally. I had visions of her breaking out in maniacal dancing, like the Cavern girls Mal had described. I was curious about that loss of inhibition, respectable girls gone crazy. My curiosity remained unsatisfied. She said she liked the song – but she didn't ask to hear it again.

****

The astronauts tended to hang out together, but every now and then I'd find myself alone with an astronaut, most commonly in the cafeteria.

One day I found myself with Gordon Cooper. His flight was scheduled for May, and he was excited. He would be the last to fly in a Mercury capsule. He planned to take quality pictures from space and had drawn an unusual assignment: could an astronaut sleep in space? I wondered what kind of dreams a man would have so far away from earth, and thinking of that reminded me of UFOs, Stonehenge, geo-glyphs, the Nazca plateau in Peru... Would astronauts in space have any insight into these phenomena?

I debated whether to broach the subject with Gordo. These astronauts were pretty much the straight arrow types, and I could quickly lose their respect. I decided to tip-toe in.

"Gordo, think you might be able to see things from space that you just can't see on earth?"

"Like?"

I fidgeted with my glass.

"Patterns in the ground."

"You mean geoglyphs?"

My heart jumped. "Yes, exactly!"

"Well I'm sure we could. Heck, you can see them from airplanes!"

"What do you make of these geoglyphs?"

I could tell that it was Gordo's turn to be circumspect. He pursed his lips and narrowed his eyes, as he pushed a few carrots around on his plate. "I don't know, what makes you ask?"

I recognized his nervousness and it gave me courage. "You know, sometimes I think there could be extra-terrestrials."

I saw the muscles tense up in Gordo's face. He looked up at me, and then slowly swiveled around to examine the room. He leaned forward.

"Of course there are," he said, barely parting his lips.

So there it was. Like two members of a secret society who'd found each other, we suddenly found ourselves free to speak our mind. I jumped in.

"I met a guy in Germany who believes he's got connections to extra-terrestrials. He knew everything about my ancestors. It was the strangest thing."

"Well, I don't know about that, but I can tell you about UFOs."

"UFOs?"

"Yes, Unidentified Flying Objects, Roswell, and all that. I've seen them myself."

"Really!" This was better than expected. Seeing that he had a receptive audience, Gordo had relaxed, and was now in what, for him, would pass as an expansive mood. "Back in '58 two test pilot friends of mine were flying over New Mexico when they sighted a round metallic object flying in front of their T-33 jet trainers. Albuquerque Regional Flight Control had spotted the craft on their radar, but hadn't been able to establish contact with it. The guys noted that the object wasn't leaving a contrail, even though their own jets were. There was no evidence of exhaust from an engine. They sped up to catch up to this object. It had no wings and looked like a saucer. After a few moments of flying side by side, the craft sped up and out of sight. Though duly noted on the Albuquerque radar, and duly reported to the authorities, my friends never got any feedback on their sighting."

"Wow!"

"And I've had my own sightings."

"Really!!!" This was *far* better than I'd expected. The cafeteria had gradually emptied out, leaving us sipping our Cokes in a corner. To anybody walking in we were just shooting the bull, planning Gordo's Mercury mission.

"The first time was in '51. I was a second lieutenant assigned to the 525th Fighter Bomber Squadron at the Neubiberg Air Force base in West Germany. Communist MIGs would regularly buzz the base. One day the alarm sounds, no big deal, we all jump into our F-86s. We zoom to our maximum ceiling of about 40,000 feet, and the damn planes are still way above us! And traveling much faster than us! These weren't MIGs! None of us had ever seen these things before. You couldn't even call them planes. From where we were, we couldn't even see wings! They were, well, saucer-shaped!"

Good 'ole Gordo from Shawnee, Oklahoma, refilled his glass.

"This happened again and again. The alarm would sound; we'd rush up in our F-86s, only to be toyed with by these saucers. Sometimes they'd be in groups of three, or four, or even more! We'd be chasing them all over the place. Then they'd stop dead in their tracks, and just hover, as we'd zoom by above or below them!

"Eventually, we stopped chasing them. Our worst fear was that these were new Communist aircraft, and if that was the case we were in deep doodoo."

"Didn't you report this?"

"Of course, the senior officers reported it. I kept my mouth shut. Hell, it's not for a lowly second lieutenant to go filing reports of this kind."

"I'm surprised we haven't heard more of this."

"Who knows? I think the government feels we'd be too frightened if we knew the truth. Might upset some religious folk too. Not worth the trouble. Especially since we can't do anything about it! Better to focus on an enemy we can fight.

"Anyway, that wasn't my last experience."

Gordo was on a roll now. For a guy who never said more than two words, the length of his narrative was as remarkable as the story itself.

"In early May 1957, I'm flying as a test pilot at Edwards Air Force Base in the California desert. Now, Dutch, you know we pilots tend to be pretty much nose-to-the grindstone type of guys."

He was right. Test pilots from the Edwards Air Force Base were the best of the best. Top Gun. Focused.

"A new precision landing system has been installed on a dry bed lake. A couple of experienced cameramen, Jim Bittick and Jack Gettys, are taking pictures, as I practice landing my jet.

"When I land for the last time, they run towards me, asking if I'd seen the saucer touch down on the desert; I hadn't. 'Did you get pictures of it?' They had!

"This time I had the authority to call the Pentagon, which I did. I was told to develop the film, not to print any pictures, and to send off the negatives. They didn't say anything about not *looking* at the negatives! Sure as shootin', there were the saucers!

"Now do you think we ever heard back from the Pentagon? Nada."

Gordo pushed himself away from the table, and leaned back with the satisfied look of someone who's just stumped the audience. He then leaned forward and cocked an eyebrow.

"What do you think of that, Dutcho?"

Actually, I was stunned. This was far more than I'd bargained for. And here *I* was worried about looking loony.

"Gordo, I think that's great stuff. There's a lot we don't understand out there. Many Americans would be scared to death. But there are plenty of people who *would* be interested…"

"Don't go there."

Gordo's voice was stern. He'd reverted to Gordon Cooper, Air Force Test Pilot and Mercury 7 astronaut. Once again he leaned forward.

"Dutch, both our careers are over the minute anyone gets wind of these thoughts of yours. I see where you're going and I ain't saying you're wrong. I wish we *could* talk about it in public, but I can't and we can't. It's not happening. Just keep these thoughts to yourself. Got it?"

I sure did. It was now dark outside, and we both had work to do.

**

Actually, unbeknownst to Cooper, there was yet another Mercury astronaut who'd seen a UFO, or actually felt pretty strongly that he'd seen one. That was none other than hard-nosed Deke Slayton, and he had been fairly casual in talking about it – *after* the docs had already grounded him. Some time after my chat with Gordo, Deke told me that when he was a maintenance officer with the Air Guard, he saw a metallic disc while flying a P-51. The object kept evading him until it sped off at an ungodly steep angle. Deke reported this sighting, never heard back from anyone, and like Cooper, thought it wise to file the information somewhere in the back of his brain, and leave it at that.

Gordo and Deke would not be the last astronauts to report UFOs.

****

I played "Please Please Me" for the guys at work. They were nonplussed. Way too far from the country music they enjoyed most. Since my letter from Mal back in March, the Beatles had released a full length LP in England called *Please Please Me*. Though unreleased outside of Great Britain, it was an enormous hit at home, staying at the number one spot from May through December. Mal had sent it to me and it was quite a hit in my little apartment. It doubled my collection of LPs, and dramatically increased the usage of my newly acquired red and white record player. One of the highlights was Lennon's interpretation of "Twist and Shout," a vocal chord-shredding performance. And Mal was right: The third highlight was the opening number, "I Saw Her Standing There." The song opens with "one, two, three, fo-ah!" and quickly gives way to McCartney's breathless excitement. The guitars clang, the bass line bounces about, and the *oooooos* leap up the phonic scale into the falsetto-sphere.

I didn't bother to play the album for the guys.

Sally's favorite was "Do You Want to Know a Secret"? Gus actually liked that one too. Surprisingly, Lennon wrote most of the song. I didn't recognize his voice, and found out much later that Harrison was the singer. Nice of John to give George the song. After listening to the entire record, Sally and I came to the same conclusion: The most original aspect of the album was the variety of styles within it. It was hard to believe that a band that screeched out "Twist And Shout" and "I Saw Her Standing There" could also ooze out "Do You Want To Know A Secret" or "P.S. I Love You."[6]

****

Walt Williams was the Project Mercury Operations Director and the Number three guy at NASA. On the morning of May 8th, I sat across his desk in Hanger S, reviewing our latest attempt at communicating with astronauts during re-entry. On the other side of the Cape, the pad crew busily readied the Atlas rocket for the next day's Mercury mission. It was an otherwise peacefully hot and humid Florida morning.

An enormous explosion suddenly rocked the quiet of the day. As the walls shook, and the autographed picture of President Kennedy came crashing down, Williams and I hit the deck. Williams waited a few moments under his desk, while I lamely stuck my head beneath my chair. Neither of us spoke, as we both imagined flames shooting skyward and people dying. Had the Soviets attacked? Had the Atlas exploded? Was the rocket even fueled up yet?

"Think it's safe?"

"I don't know," I answered. "I certainly don't hear any shouting."

"If the rocket exploded we'd be hearing the fire engines," Williams reasoned.

"Think everyone's still hiding?"

We decided we could peak through the window. All seemed normal. Everyone seemed to be going about his usual business.

Williams picked up the phone, and what he learned didn't please him one bit. In fact he was livid. The explosion was nothing more

---

6   The Beatles gave "Do You Want To Know A Secret" to Billy J Kramer. In Britain the song went up to #2, right behind the Beatles' "From Me To You."

than Gordo flying his F-102 a few feet over the roof, and lighting his afterburner.

Gordo had just been told that the doctors wanted to cut one more hole in his space suit in order to add yet another goddam monitor. Didn't this violate the rule that nothing should be done to an astronaut's pressure suit just before takeoff? What if this new gizmo caused a leak?

Gordo had just been doing a little venting. The pilot's way.

Williams didn't see it that way. His Kennedy autograph was ruined, and Cooper was a reckless ass. Certainly he couldn't be trusted for the longest Mercury mission ever. Williams ordered Cooper off the flight. Al Shepard would take his place.

Shepard was momentarily caught off guard but none too unhappy. In fact, he was quietly ecstatic. His fifteen-minute cannon ball shot two years earlier now seemed rinky- dink. He rubbed his hands at the thought of doing some *real* space flying.

Conversely, Cooper looked like a guy outside a delivery room. The normally cool Oklahoma kid paced about furiously, and there was no talking him down. Cooper could see years of training go down the drain just 'cause some deskbound bureaucrat couldn't take a little joke.

I felt as proud as I'd ever felt to be part of the NASA team, when Glenn, Grissom, Carpenter, Schirra, and Slayton all banded together in support of their colleague. A direct call was placed through to Kennedy, who by now had come to know all the astronauts. Cooper himself had given the President a tour just a few weeks before. It might seem risky, calling the President of the United States about something like this, but the astronauts felt a certain kinship with JFK. And anyone who'd make his own brother Attorney General would certainly respect loyalty. Glenn spoke to the President and prevailed upon him to call Williams.

At 10 PM, we got word that Williams had relented. I'm guessing he got another autographed picture.

May 15th was Gordo's day. The plan was for him to spend a full day in space, more than double Schirra's nine hours. After some much-publicized hand wringing over what to name his capsule, he'd finally settled on *Faith 7*; reasonably pious and innocuous enough, as far as I was concerned. NASA, however, saw ghosts around every corner. What if Gordo and capsule were lost?

"NASA loses Faith," the headlines would scream! Gordo won out on that one too. I couldn't help but wonder if he was imagining headlines like, "UFO destroys Faith."

Strapped in his seat, Gordo sat through the usual pre-dawn delays. And then we were treated to an unusual event: Gordo fell asleep. He's about to be blasted off on an Atlas rocket and he's cuttin' z's! Having nonetheless woken up in time for the final countdown, Gordo and his Atlas booster hammered off into the Florida sky.

No pilot will ever admit to a physical ailment; that would be a sign of weakness. Yet, he had barely reached orbit, when Cooper made the following admission:

"My face feels real flush."

Sure. He'd gone from crushing G forces, during which time his heart was pumping in overdrive to get blood to his brain, to sudden weightlessness. His heart was still pumping furiously for no particular reason. It was precisely the kind of thing the doctors had worried about when they grounded Deke. Dr. Berry now leaned way forward in his seat. It was *his* ass in a sling right now. Fortunately Cooper seemed to be functioning normally – at least for him, as Walt Williams would point out. His heart rate gradually returned to baseline.

Gordo had a real camera on board, a lightweight Hasselblad. Not that he had to. NASA's position was that "if an astronaut desires, he may *(may!)* carry a camera." It had not dawned on NASA yet that the stunning view of earth from up in space would be a public relations bonanza. Glenn and Carpenter had taken their Instamatic® cameras, for Pete's sake! Same as *my* camera! Cooper marveled at the fact that he could leave the camera suspended in mid-air as he tended to other tasks. He commented that in his weightless state he also felt no pressure on his back when the capsule was pointing up, or on his harness when the capsule pointed down towards the earth. He had no sense of angular velocity. It was as if the capsule were still and the scenery was turning around him.

Gordo was the first astronaut for whom sleeping in space would be an issue.

Could a weightless person sleep?

Gordo was up to the task. (He'd been practicing on the launch pad, after all.) He told me it was his favorite experiment. The scary part was waking up to find his arms floating in front of him with his hands dangerously close to all those switches on the control panel. That was something they'd have to work on.

Gordo's oxygen consumption impressed the doctors. It was but a third of what they had expected. We later figured that it had to do with the fact that Gordo was the only lifetime non-smoker among the astronauts. Schirra and Shepard smoked right up to the launch pad!

The flight was picture perfect. Cooper had been given a list of experiments to carry out, and he'd methodically gone through the list without breaking a sweat. Like the astronauts before him he marveled at the sights – the horizon set on fire by the blazing sun and the stars tossed up against the black firmament, and like his predecessors, he marveled at the impossibly tiny details he could make out below, such as streams and fields.

In the middle of his 19th orbit, the re-entry light came on.

That little green light had no business being on. It was ironically a pet peeve of Gordo's that these lights would come on for no reason. You would think that after Glenn's flight, the engineers would have addressed this problem! Gordo repeatedly threatened to take a hammer to these control panels, and one day had entered the training capsule to find a little toy hammer dangling from a switch. He could have used that hammer just about now.

We'd seen that same light on our own panels, and thought that Gordo had had an emergency and was initiating re-entry.

He didn't know it quite yet, but there was indeed an emergency. One by one, Gordo's systems were shorting out: telemetry, cooling, air purification, gyroscopes, even the clock. We were losing all ability to gauge the position of our speeding capsule or anything else about it or its astronaut. Most significantly, Gordo would soon be poisoned by his own carbon dioxide.

In Mercury Control, this new development suddenly stilled the low level murmur of multiple conversations – a silence immediately replaced by the loud chatter of people huddled around the various consoles.

We weren't very good at hiding the fact that we were completely in the dark. Ever since Glenn's adventure, we had decided that an astronaut should be in on everything that was being discussed in Ground Control, and Gordo could tell that we were stumped. On the twentieth orbit we beamed up the bad news: There was a complete power failure on board his capsule. Faith or no Faith, *Faith 7* was a dying ship, and he would be dead too if he didn't get his butt down to earth ASAP.

The only reason we could even speak to Gordo was because the radio battery was separate from the rest of the electrical system... I was more than a little proud of that one. I wondered if Carpenter stationed out at the Hawaii center was thinking the same thing. Hopefully we'd be able crow in a few hours.

For Cooper this situation could potentially be a dream come true, assuming he survived – an opportunity for an astronaut to fly a spacecraft on his own. With telemetry out, he could expect no help from the ground, and with all the automatic functions out, he would be doing it all himself. He would align his capsule's angle of attack by way of the horizon, and judge his yaw (left-right) against a zero-yaw star. He would actually be using all that astronomy stuff he'd learnt since joining NASA and be an actual *astro-naut*. As for the oscillations caused by the thrusters, he would have to damp them himself to prevent the capsule from spinning out of control. So much for the "spam in the can" and "wipe the chimp poop off the seat" stuff! So much for the scientists who felt that it was unnecessary to have a human in space. Oh yeah? Machines would do the job just as well? Take that! What would your darn machines be doing now???

Meanwhile, the cabin temperature had risen to 130 degrees, and worse than that, the carbon dioxide levels in his suit were above the maximum limits. Cooper would soon get groggy.

And where would he land?

In the jungles of Africa? In the middle of a city?

Hopefully somewhere on water!

I had fleeting visions of the capsule parachute dangling from the Empire State Building or the Eiffel tower.

Cooper passed over Glenn's station in the Western Pacific and quickly filled him in. Glenn didn't bat an eye. He'd been there before. They quickly went over re-entry procedures. Long ago the two of them had had their differences when it came to the proper behavior of an astronaut, and they'd had words. None of this mattered now. Cooper had to return alive.

"Catch you on the next orbit."

"I'll be firing the retros," answered Cooper.

Cooper swung the capsule around so as to point its backside directly in the direction of its fall. As usual, any significant deviation of the capsule to the right or to the left, and it would fry.

Because of the high CO_2 count, Cooper's breaths were now shallow pants.

As he passed over Africa, Cooper readied himself to fire the retro rockets. The three retro rockets pointed in different directions and were scheduled to be fired at ten second intervals. Thus, with each firing, the capsule would lurch to one side. Cooper would have to anticipate that and manually make the requisite adjustments. He had reviewed this with Carpenter over Hawaii.

Just east of Shanghai, Cooper was once more in contact with Glenn, who now began the countdown. Cooper followed on his own wristwatch in case he suddenly lost contact with Glenn.

"Five, four, three, two, one, FIRE!"

Four minutes into the burn, Cooper jettisoned the retro pack – the same pack that Glenn had decided to keep during his own flight. The capsule rattled as it hurtled back to earth at 12,000 miles per hour, Cooper fighting to maintain the capsule at a zero yaw, 34-degree downward angle.

All things considered, Cooper was remarkably on target. If only he could hold the capsule steady, he was on track to splash down off Midway near our old friend the *Kearsarge*. Schirra had landed just four and a half miles from the ship, something he was very proud of. For Cooper it was a win-win situation: even if he landed 100 miles away, his safe return would be a major triumph.

Then came the blackout period. Even in the best of situations it was nerve-wracking. It seemed to drag on forever. And forever.

Stationed in Hawaii, Carpenter was the first to make contact.

"Doing fine!" Cooper shouted.

At 50,000 feet Cooper manually released the preliminary chute (the drogue) and at 11,000 feet he released the main parachute.

Cooper plunked down in the Pacific, just five miles from the *Kearsarge.*

As he alighted onto the red carpet, he was greeted by thunderous applause.

And who was there to greet him in Hawaii? None other than Walt Williams, eager to meet the latest hero.

"You *were* the right guy for this mission!!!" offered Williams, as he furiously pumped Gordo's arm with both hands. It must have been a sweet moment for Gordo.

Cooper was accorded a medal ceremony in the Rose Garden, President Kennedy himself pinning a medal on Gordo's chest. Sitting tall in his open limousine, Vice-President Lyndon Johnson then led him down New York's largest ticker-tape parade ever, even bigger than Glenn's!

**

At his press conference Cooper was asked an unusual question.

"Did you see any UFOs?"

Cooper's eyes momentarily met mine.

"No, next question."

He was telling the truth. He also was not about to put his career on the line by venturing into those waters.

As for the cause of the multi-system shutdown aboard *Faith 7,* it turned out to be slightly embarrassing. Cooper had peed all over the instrument panel. Not directly, of course. There had been a malfunction in the waste disposal unit, and a fine mist of urine had permeated the air and infiltrated the instrument panel. We decided not to leak this information to the press.

**

NASA was still basking in the glow of Cooper's flight when the Soviets announced the launch of Cosmonaut Bykovsky. We waited for a special event, but there was none... until June 16th. The USSR announced with great fanfare that Cosmonaut Tereshkova was now also being launched into space. *Valentina* Tereshkova. A woman! Much was made of this. Soviet women were equal to men; the Soviets were a more advanced society, and so forth and so on. We sweated that one out (we had a great deal of practice by now), and were relieved to see that woman or not, Tereshkova did not have the capability of maneuvering her capsule to rendezvous, let alone dock with Bykovsky. *(Too bad for Bykovksy. A little space docking might have broken up the monotony. He was said to have quite a thruster.)* Ironically, after reaping all the public relations benefit of having a woman in space, the Soviets would not send up a woman in space for another nineteen years. Maybe their women weren't that equal after all.

****

London, 24ᵗʰ August, 1963

Dear Dutch,

I'm VERY excited about the boys' fourth single.

I didn't think their last single, "From Me to You," was quite as exciting as "Please Please Me," but it went right to number 1. They tried an endless number of guitar intros, until George Martin had the idea of having them hum an intro (da da da, da da, dum dum da). Paul was very proud of the chord changes right at the bridge ("I've got arms (Gm7) that long to hold you and keep you by my side, I've got lips that long to kiss you and keep you satisfied" (G augmented)). He saw it as a breakthrough in their songwriting, like a driver who's just figured out how to downshift! They included their high ooooos ("and keep you satisfied, oooooooo"), and guess what? That drives the girls *nuts* in concert, especially when the four of them shake their heads in unison. Go figure.

Anyway, the boys are HOT. Girls are everywhere. They hang out in front of the studio, they hang out in front of their homes. I don't know how the girls find out about the dates and times for the recording sessions. Eppy books them as the "Dakotas," the name of one of his other bands, yet the girls still find out. Though the music whips them up into a frenzy, everyone pretty much agrees that the hysteria in general has nothing to do with music. It's about sex appeal and, well, sex. Thinking of the Beatles turns their moral compass south, so to speak.

The other day, the girls broke into the EMI building *en masse*, and we had to call the bobbies in! Eppy was running around saying, "oh dear, oh dear," and was literally wringing his hands. (The boys don't like having him around in the studio. It's ironic that he just happened to be there that day.) The boys laughed at the sound of the girls running about in the building, though they never made it into Studio Two (actually, one did, and Neil tackled her as she was getting close to Ringo!). Hearing the girls scream made it feel like a concert, and I think it gave the boys a little extra energy."

I was reading this letter on the couch, while Sally made dinner. I watched her, and tried to feel deprived that I didn't have hordes of screaming girls after me. I shook my head. Out of my league. I went back to the letter.

If you're not familiar with fan mail, it's a sight. Sacks of mail come in, and the boys devote time to answering the letters. Neil and I help of course. Most of the mail comes from Liverpool, where they are heroes.

I don't know how good a businessman he is, but Eppy has an eye for promotion. He's hired Tony Barrow to help with press releases. Tony came up with the term Fab Four, and the moniker seems to have stuck. He's arranged for *Beatles Book* to be published monthly — a magazine presenting the Beatles' daily activities, preferences, and desires through the rosiest of rose-colored glasses (no mayhem there, no madness, and certainly no excess). John was asked to describe where the Beatles got their name, and of course couldn't, or wouldn't, just come up with a straight answer:

> Why Beatles? Ugh, Beatles how did the name arrive? It came in a vision — a man appeared on a flaming pie and said unto them, "From this day on you are Beatles with an 'a.'" Thank you Mister Man, they said, thanking him.

Now, of course, ALL the recording labels have sent out their scouts to see what they've been missing in the Northern lands. Every band with a guitar has a contract. EMI's Columbia has signed Gerry and the Pacemakers (they're on Columbia, and we're still with Parlophone!). I think I may have told you that George [Harrison] whispered in Dick Rowe's ear that Decca should sign up the Rolling Stones; then there are the Hollies and a bunch of others.

The single just released the other day is really good. If "From Me to You" went to number 1, this one has to do as well. Paul had the idea of introducing a third person into their lyrics. He and John got tired of always writing about themselves (I love you, you love me, etc...). He's talking to another fellow about the bloke's girlfriend. A little unusual. Anyway, who really cares about the lyrics? The song starts with a cascade of drum rolls and launches right into the chorus, "She Loves You Yeah, Yeah, Yeah." George has sharp little guitar phrases throughout the recording, and he thought up a little 40s style harmony to end the song. (George Martin didn't care for it, thought it was corny, but the boys prevailed.) Paul tells the funny story of his father thinking the lyric should have been "She loves you yes, yes, yes." Other than that, the boys have kept the harmonies and the requisite *oooooos* (can't go wrong with that).

I forgot to tell you: In April John's wife Cynthia had a baby boy, Julian. Peter Brown [Brian Epstein's assistant] says it was a long and difficult labor. John managed to call the hospital that night, but didn't get to see Cyn and the baby until they were about to leave the hospital a week later. Then, the moment he came back from touring a few weeks after that, he went on holiday to Spain with Eppy. (That certainly started some rumors, but there's nothing to them. I think John just likes the way Eppy indulges his smallest whim.) But Cyn was pretty upset about the whole thing. Can't blame her. Not to mention that John is still an angry guy, frequently drinks too much, and even punched a fellow out. Eppy smoothed that out with a few quid.

Paul meanwhile has shacked up with a seventeen-year-old actress, Jane Asher. He loves the fact that her father's a doctor and that the whole family is into the arts and theater. This is a family that, up until now, Paul could have never dreamt of joining. He lives in a room upstairs, next to Jane's brother Peter. Sort of strange. Paul doesn't let this relationship interfere with his other amorous activities — anymore, for that matter, than John's marriage does his.

We had a formal photo shoot the other day. Photographer Robert Freeman came to the hotel and used the dining area as a studio. The light came in from a side window, casting a half moon effect. The left side of the boys' faces was bright, while the right half was dark. John stood up front, with George behind his left shoulder and Paul directly behind George's.

Paul's face looks smaller than George's, which looks smaller than John's. To get a roughly square picture that would fit an album cover, Freeman placed Ringo on a sitting stool in front of and slightly to the right of Paul. The four of them wore dark turtlenecks and none smiled. Maroon drapes created a dark background. The result is much closer to the artsy pictures Astrid used to take in Germany than to the happy-go-lucky pictures you see on most popular albums. They plan to use the picture on their next album.

Rumor has it that the boys are going to be offered a spot on the BBC programme called Pop Go the Beatles. And six months ago we were wondering where our next meal would be coming from...

Cheerio,

Mal

****

Attorney General Robert Kennedy had been pushing hard for a Negro astronaut. The term Negro, incidentally, was not derogatory. Americans of African descent were called by their ethnic label rather than by their skin color or direct origin (the equivalent of "Caucasian," rather than "European American" or "White").

No dice. Captain Edward Dwight of the Air Force came closest. I had heard that he really *preferred* a career in the Air Force, and did not particularly appreciate the political efforts to push him into NASA, but who knows? It would be a while before something other than the White, Anglo-Saxon, Male, Christian astronaut would come out of the Astronaut Casting box.

On October 14th, NASA announced the third class of astronauts:

Major Edwin "Buzz" Aldrin, USAF (Air Force)
Captain William Anders, USAF
Captain Charles Bassett, II USAF
Lieutenant Alan Bean, USN (Navy)
Lieutenant Eugene Cernan, USN *(from Purdue!)*
Lieutenant Roger Chaffee, USN *(from Purdue!)*
Captain Michael Collins, USAF

R. Walter Cunningham, civilian
Captain Donn Eisele, USAF
Captain Theodore Freeman, USAF
Lieutenant Commander Richard Gordon, USN
Russell Schweickart, civilian
Captain David Scott, USAF
Captain Clifton C. Williams, USMC (Marines)

Aldrin had come to his interview dressed in a coat and tie wearing his flight wings and Phi Beta Kappa key, prompting Gus to ask why he was wearing his résumé. But the guy was solid. In fact they all were, and they came from a variety of backgrounds: Seven Air Force, four Navy, one Marine, two civilians, eight test pilots, two former pilots now engaged in research (Cunningham and Schweickart), one pilot with a PhD from MIT (Aldrin), and one with a degree in nuclear engineering (Anders). It was hard not to be impressed. On paper these fellows were even more accomplished than the original Mercury 7.

[The Japanese Fable would have its way in the most extreme fashion with this group of fourteen: three would orbit the earth, three would orbit the moon, four would walk on the moon – and four would be killed. If you were an astronaut and you were given these odds, would you hold 'em or fold 'em?]

**

Deke started to plan for the crew assignments; sometimes I helped him. In theory all astronauts were equal. They'd made it through arguably the toughest screening process ever, and there was no reason why any of the astronauts couldn't perform any of the anticipated tasks. Some guys, however, seemed more athletic than others, while others seemed to be particularly sharp pilots. Since there would be two astronauts per Gemini mission, we also tried to put together the most compatible pairs. We had to keep in mind that the Apollo training would start in short order, and if some of the astronauts distinguished themselves we'd want them available for Apollo. Finally, there was the unwritten seniority rule. All things being equal, astronauts who'd been there longest would get priority.

Deke was about to pencil in Shepard for the first Gemini flight when the bombshell landed. The docs grounded Shepard. He had developed dizziness, and was diagnosed with Ménière's disease, a condition that affects the ear and can lead to dizziness and/or vomiting.

In the misery-loves-company category, Deke got all warm and fuzzy towards Al and invited him into the Astronaut office. Deke had approximately three hundred people working under him, and he needed help. Grudgingly, Al accepted. He would never give up on his quest to go back into space. Nor would Deke. They would both continue to list their names on the roster of astronauts. They would both eventually be successful.

****

London, 1st November, 1963

Dear Dutch,

I knew it. On Sept 14 "She Loves You" hit Number 1. The song just exploded onto the charts. The people at EMI say they've never seen or heard of anything so spectacular. "Yeah, yeah, yeah" is now firmly associated with the Beatles. In France, their fans are referred to as the "yé-yé."

But the big news has been the "Sunday Night at the Palladium." The "Palladium" show is Britain's biggest TV variety show. Everybody watches it, just like your *Ed Sullivan Show*. Anybody who is anybody in showbiz appears on that show. There is little if any rock'n'roll, but I don't think producer Lew Grade had much of a choice. The boys have the number one single in the country, the number one LP, and the number one EP [a four-song disc].

The Beatles appeared at the Palladium in October — topped the bill no less, and it was pandemonium. The police were needed to reign in the fans outside. Even the press got into the act.

Did they ever. The papers have gone completely overboard. The Beatles are front page news everywhere; you can even see me in a couple of pictures. Neil and I have become bodyguards! The *Daily Mirror* screamed out "Beatlemania" on the front page! Interestingly — and I think the boys are a little disturbed by this — the only thing anyone ever talks about is their hair and their effect on teenagers!

It's true that it's become mass hysteria. The Beatles are touring England (and Europe soon), but the concerts seem to be little more than scream fests! The girls shriek at the top of their lungs from beginning to end — I doubt they hear any of the music, nor do they care.

The press has also picked up on the fact that they can always get a good quote from the boys.

Reporter: Do you rehearse?
John: Paul does, the rest of us don't.

Reporter: The French have not made up their minds about the Beatles. What do you think of them?"
John: Oh, we like the Beatles.

Not everyone approves of the Beatles. The conservative newspapers point to the "yeah, yeah, yeah" as a symbol of how vapid the whole Beatles phenomenon is. (And in a sense, it really is. Too bad nobody's listening to the music.) As far as they're concerned, the Beatles simply fill with nonsense the empty heads of our mindless teenagers.

And yet, here's what the *Daily Mirror* has to say: The Beatles are "four cheeky- looking kids with stone-age hair styles." They are "as nice a group of well-mannered [!] music makers as you'll find perforating the eardrums anywhere." Talk about a backhanded compliment!

You know what I say to that?

So what!

Yours,

Mal

Curiously, Brian Epstein couldn't convince Capitol to release "She Loves You" in the United States. Eventually, the obscure Swan label took it on and released it in America, but Swan had no promotional funds, and the song disappeared like an ice cube in a bubbling pot. The same went for Vee Jay's *Introducing the Beatles*, a variation of *Please, Please, Me* with a sickly, jaundiced picture of the band on the cover. The press was entirely negative. *Newsweek* found their music to be "high-pitched, loud beyond reason, and stupefyingly repetitive." Dick

Clark played "She Loves You" on his hit television show "American Bandstand" – and the audience laughed. It was fair to say that, in America, the Beatles were still dead in the water.

It was hardly surprising. The concept of introducing a British rock'n'roll band to America was ludicrous. Rock'n'roll was *American* music to be exported abroad, not the other way around. To boot, Capitol had no history of success with rock'n'roll. While Decca had Bill Haley and Buddy Holly, and RCA had Elvis, Capitol had dipped their toe into the rock'n'roll waters with Gene Vincent, and his career had gone nowhere. Capitol had therefore been quite content with the presence of Frank Sinatra, the Kingston Trio, and the like in their large stable of hugely successful, non-threatening performers.

Also, based in Los Angeles, Capitol had recently signed a band right out of their backyard that appealed to a younger crowd. This band extolled the virtues of California beaches, tanned bodies, white teeth, and surfing. Their second single, "Surfin' U.S.A.," had been a Top Ten hit in the spring of '63. These, of course, were the Beach Boys, Capitol's own little nod to the teenage market.

Capitol had no need for a British rock'n'roll band with bad press, funny hair, and that awful coleopterous name. Couldn't they at least have the common sense to call themselves the Royal Four or something to that effect?

London, 26th November, 1963

Dear Dutch,

It can't get bigger than this!

The Beatles have released their fourth single of the year, "I Want To Hold Your Hand," and it's another #1 song. In fact they've knocked themselves off the #1 slot with their own song. Apparently the last time this happened was in your country when Elvis's "Love Me Tender" bumped "Don't Be Cruel" back in '56.

Brian has once again trekked to the U.S. hoping that Capitol will take an interest. (What's wrong with you people???)

In early November the Beatles were the featured artists at the Royal Command Performance, attended by the Queen and a clutch of Royals. The Prince of Wales Theater was ringed with police, and it wasn't completely clear to me if they were there to protect the Royals or the Beatles!

Marlene Dietrich was present, as well as a host of other acts nobody cared about. (At least _we_ didn't.) When the Beatles were announced, the place went wild. The Queen clapped a little.

They sang "From Me To You" – starting the song before the curtain was completely open, "She Loves You," and "'Til There Was You." Then, just before "Twist and Shout," the finale, John got cheeky. He even blushed, which I've rarely seen. "For our last number I'd like to ask your help. The people in the cheaper seats clap your hands, and the rest of you, if you'd just rattle your jewelry." After first checking the Queen's reaction, the whole audience laughed.

Except Brian. He was relieved.

Right before the performance, John had told him that he was going to say, "the f'...g rest of you can just rattle your jewelry." John could do that.

The next day, the papers were once more all about the Beatles. The Beatles this, the Beatles that. It's now official, by the way: This madness surrounding the boys is called *Beatlemania*.

Yours,

Mal

P.S. The boys are about to release their second LP called *With the Beatles*. I've enclosed a copy.

I was very happy for Mal, but I was a little too busy to listen to the LP. The picture of the "boys" on the cover didn't look anything like I'd remembered them. Then again, I'd hardly been paying attention at the time. They did look a little strange with their long hair combed forward.

Things were heating up on my end. President Kennedy had just come by for another visit of Cape Canaveral, and two of the Mercury astronauts, Gus and Gordo, had given him a personal helicopter tour. I was thoroughly tickled to be part of the group that he waved to when he walked into the control room. His hair was tousled. He pocketed his dark sunglasses, and as he shook hands with everyone, I was reminded of Von Braun's visit: the same ease, the same comfort with everyone he met. Both the more mature guys and the young'uns could claim him as one of theirs. I suppose that's how you gain superstar status.

In just a few days, Kennedy would be going to Dallas where he was going to give another speech pertaining to the space program. Perhaps the thought crossed his mind that one day the space center could be named after him. What President doesn't think of such things? If so, he couldn't have thought it would be so soon.

****

Heathrow Airport, London

He sat impatiently in his seat wondering why they would not let the passengers deplane. A huge mob seemed to have invaded Heathrow airport. They were probably there to greet the Queen or the Pope. No, a rock'n'roll band? Returning from Sweden? What kind of band gets such a delirious reception? And he, Ed Sullivan, the impresario of all impresarios, had not heard of them? Perhaps he should try to book them for his show. To attract such a crowd surely they had to have some special appeal. The American rock'n'roll scene was quieting down, and maybe the public would go for something new. He wouldn't audition them; talent wasn't an issue. He made a note to book them for February. There was an opening on the 9th.

****

Stockton-on-Tees, 22nd November, 1963

Dear Dutch,

I can't tell you how sorry I am about your loss. We're all honestly crying. I've tried calling you, but the line is busy, busy, busy. I can understand.

We arrived at the Globe Cinema today and expected another boisterous greeting. *With the Beatles* was just released this morning.

But everyone's wearing a long face, and as we got off the plane, we heard the news about President Kennedy. I really don't know what to say other than I'm so sorry and so sad. I'll write again when I've collected my thoughts.

Mal

On November 22nd, 1963, time had stood still as we learned of Kennedy's assassination.

Sally and I were on the way to work and had noticed that everyone was holding transistor radios up to their ear. I attributed this phenomenon to a big game I'd somehow missed hearing about. I didn't pay it much mind because we were in the midst of discussing Thanksgiving. In any case, I had no radio in my car.

When we got to work, the place was eerily quiet. In the control room everyone was huddled around a television, and, shockingly, Gene was crying.

Walter Cronkite had just told the nation that it was official. John Fitzgerald Kennedy was dead. He'd been killed in Dallas. The assassin had shot him from a window.

Kennedy *dead*? It wasn't possible. He'd been in this room only a week ago.

What was going to happen to the space program? I bit my lip at the thought of how selfish I was. He'd gone to Dallas to press a little flesh in unfriendly political territory, and he'd paid for it with his life. And so young. A wife, two young children.

Of course our astronauts put themselves at risk for a similar fate on every single space flight, but the President!

We suddenly felt vulnerable and aimless. At least the world was with us; flags were flown at half-staff all around the world. Even in France.

It was Friday, and no work was going to get done. We left early. We all felt like zombies.

The remainder of 1963 was draped in a spirit of mourning that no holiday cheer could overcome. Sally and I spent more on each other for Christmas than we'd planned – we both admitted that we'd had the same idea – a little retail therapy, but it didn't work. Neither of us had voted for Kennedy, but he'd become *our* President. All the astronauts had their stories of their meetings with him. His charm; his jokes.

I spent Christmas reading Ian Fleming's latest James Bond thriller, "On Her Majesty's Secret Service," and Peter Seller's *Pink Panther* provided a little laughter at the movies. The real world, though, remained a downer. Sally took down the Christmas decorations. She said she couldn't stand having them up even until New Year's.

President Lyndon Johnson assured the country that all policies would remain intact. He would continue to push for racial equality, and, and – and yes, it was critical that we fulfill JFK's dream of reaching the moon by the end of the decade.

****

At the EMI studios in London, the mood was different. Mal was ecstatic: Lennon and McCartney had been named the outstanding English composers of the year by no less than the *London Times*. Of the two composers, William Mann had written "they have brought a distinctive and exhilarating flavour into a genre of music that was in danger of ceasing to be music at all." The *Sunday Times* hailed them as "the greatest composers since Beethoven" (yeah, roll over Beethoven!).

A year earlier they'd been complete unknowns.

Having lifted the lid off the Liverpool/Manchester music box, the British had discovered a vibrant rock'n'roll scene: The Rolling Stones, the Dave Clark Five, the Animals, the Yardbirds… This was a tight-knit community. Sitting in one day with John Lennon and Paul McCartney, Mick Jagger and Keith Richards were shocked to see the duo polish up the choppy, Bo Diddley-esque "I Wanna Be Your Man," right there under their very eyes. They nodded in approval and recorded it. A top twenty hit! Didn't seem so hard.

Perhaps they'd give songwriting a try.

**

Overlooking the vast expanse of Los Angeles, Alan Livingston was slowly changing his mind. The President of Capitol Records had never liked anything by the Beatles, and in fact, he still didn't. "I want to hold your haaaaaaaand." Who stretches out words like that? And a one-octave leap between the words "your" and "hand"? It was unlike anything he'd ever heard before, and to his ears, it sounded awful. He'd signed *Frank Sinatra* ten years earlier, for God's sake.

Following in the footsteps of a song whose lyrics consisted of "She loves you yeah, yeah, yeah, She loves you yeah, yeah, yeah, yeah," this newest song (and its "composers") made absolutely no musical sense to him. As president of Capitol he'd been inclined to nix the Beatles again. He'd dismissed the *New York Times* article "Britons succumb to Beatlemania," but now could not escape the screaming headlines of *Variety.* The showbiz paper extolled the British success of "I Want to Hold Your Hand," the first song in Britain to sell more than a million copies prior to its release; this had only happened once in America – in 1957 with Elvis Presley's double-sided hit "Hound Dog"/"Don't be cruel." "She Loves You" had also sold more than one million copies in Britain, and the Beatles second album had sold more than a half million copies within a week of its release. In a market one-third the size of the U.S., the Beatles had as many million-dollar sellers as the entire American recording industry.

And they were coming to America.

Against his better judgment, Livingston gave in. He signed up the Beatles and Capitol's marketing department instantly went into high gear. Promotional packages were sent to the four corners of the country. Capitol executives were ordered to don Beatle wigs when meeting clients. Avid radio stations clamored for more records.

With an idiot's delight Capitol realized it had the whole enchilada.

For illustrations, see *www.intotheskywithdiamonds.com*

8.   Now Twice Tonight

I remember where I first heard the song as clearly as I recollect Kennedy's shooting. Perhaps it wasn't a coincidence. The song lifted me out of a low-grade funk that books and movies had failed to resolve. Was I wearing a lampshade? I don't know. But Sally and I were pleasantly plastered at our friends Tom and Linda's New Year's Eve party – a mix of NASA and neighborhood people, good beer, a dangerous punch, and spicy chili – when the radio DJ announced a song from a new British band. "Oh yeah, I—I-I, tell you so-o-omethin'…" The beat was snappy, the voices loud and harmonious, the beat unrelenting; I knew exactly who this had to be. I looked around. Everyone was dancin' and clappin'.

It had entered the charts on December 26th at the respectable number 46 position, but the ride had only just begun. By the first week of January, the song was at number 3, and by February 1st, 1964, it sat atop at Number 1.

I had to call Mal.

Did he know?

Of course he did. The Beatles had received a nighttime telegram in Paris informing them of their first American hit, and this had triggered a massive pillow fight at the decorous George V hotel.

With a hit on their hands, Capitol cranked up their entire promotional machine into even higher gear. And the Beatles were coming to town for the *Ed Sullivan Show*! What timing!

I no longer needed Mal to tell me what his "boys" were up to. They were everywhere. They seemed to have essentially hijacked every newspaper and radio around. That was bad news for those who didn't care for them, and that included most adults and nearly all the music critics. Frederic Lewis of the *New York Times* wrote, "Beatlemania, as it is called, affects all social classes and all levels of intelligence." Under the headline "Beatlemania," *Newsweek* wrote: "They wear sheepdog bangs … the sound of their music is one of the most persistent noises heard over England since the air-raid sirens were dismantled…" W. Williams of WNEW in New York chimed in with, "They want to hold your hand – a lot of people would like to hold their noses." And of course there were the steady comparisons to Moe of the Three Stooges and persistent claims that they were corrupting young girls (a steady refrain since the earliest days of rock'n'roll). At least some critics, like John Wilson, had a little fun with this: "Twenty-nine hundred Beatlemaniacs gave a concert early last evening … accompanied by the thumping twanging rhythms of the Beatles, an English rock'n'roll quartet … Through their first two selections, the audience maintained a sustained falsetto baying."

But the Beatles sold records like crazy. While a popular song would sell perhaps 250,000 records, "I Want to Hold Your Hand" had already sold far over a million. And quickly.

In anticipation of their arrival, Capitol rush-released an album that combined their current hit with songs off their first two albums. Since the titles *With the Beatles* and *Introducing the Beatles* were already taken, they named the album *Meet the Beatles*. It wasn't particularly original, but it didn't have to be. Capitol pinched the cover from *With the Beatles* and softened it with a bluish tint. I quite liked it. It was creative and quiet; the Beatles, calm and serious in the eye of their own hurricane. Though John and Paul were clearly the driving forces in this band, you would have never known it from the cover. (Brian Epstein had put up one heck of a fight to get Capitol's approval. They had pushed for the more typical color picture of the four Beatles frolicking about.)

I'd only listened with one ear to *With the Beatles*, but this time I was on top of it. And Mal didn't have to send me a copy; I went out and bought it. My very first Beatles album! (*I didn't tell the fellows at work*).

The first song was "I Want to Hold Your Hand." I'd heard it incessantly on the radio at this point, but hadn't gotten tired of it. I thought the second song, "I Saw Her Standing There," was just as good. Sally had played it over and over when we received the first album, and I hadn't tired of it either.

"It Won't Be Long" was no slouch, and in fact had been the first song on their recent British album. Lennon is in the lead in this "call and answer" type of song, with every backup *yeah!* screamed three notes above Lennon's shouts and sounding more excited by the minute.

128

Side 1 ended with "All My Loving," a typical rock'n'roll you're-leaving-so-I'll-miss-you song. The melody, the arrangement, and the delivery, however, were compelling. Lennon strummed urgently, high up on the neck of his guitar, McCartney thwacked a galloping bass line, and sang in his soon-to-be classic combination of earnestness and vulnerability. And of course, there was a little *"oooooo"* falsetto at the end. It was a perfect little pop/rock song. As with "I Saw Her Standing There," I thought it could have easily been released as a single.

Side 2 was less exciting but rich nonetheless. There was Harrison's melancholy "Don't Bother Me," a somewhat dour counterpoint to the enthusiastic gregariousness of the other songs. The song pegged him early on as the quiet Beatle. "Little Child" was a harmless composition, and the lone clunker in the bunch, "Till There Was You" from *The Music Man*, followed it. The song worked well in the musical, but on a rock'n'roll album???

After the more tachycardic "Hold Me Tight," the Beatles gave us their own version of "I Wanna Be Your Man," the song lateralled earlier to the Rolling Stones.

Lennon's piano-driven "Not a Second Time" finished off the album. Surprisingly, it was one of the few songs to get any serious musical acclaim. British music critic William Mann waxed lyrical, writing that "one gets the impression that they think simultaneously of harmony and melody, so firmly are the major tonic sevenths and ninths built into their tunes, and the flat submediant key switches, so natural is the Aeolian cadence at the end" – not that any of the Beatles nor their audience were in a position to understand a word of this.

For anyone paying attention to the song credits, these songs were all written by the Beatles (save for "Till There Was You"). The Everly Brothers and Chuck Berry had written their own songs, but this was nevertheless unusual in the rock'n'roll world. Not even the King, Elvis Presley, had written his most famous songs.

February 7ʰ, 1964.

The fateful day arrived as Pan Am flight 101 pulled into New York's Idlewild Airport (soon to be renamed John F. Kennedy airport). Despite the success of their most recent single, the Beatles were a nervous lot. America had been the graveyard of all the preceding British acts, including England's earlier number one act, Cliff Richard and the Shadows. "We can always turn around and go home again," hedged John as they approached the airport.

The sight of the crowd awaiting them at the airport immediately washed away whatever fears they harbored. In these more innocent days, teenage girls had packed the airport's roof and terraces, and were ventilating their lungs from the moment the plane was announced.

As John, Paul, George, and Ringo stepped out of the plane, they were greeted with the hysteria they'd grown accustomed to. Their eyes darted towards each other, and they broke into a knowing smile. This they could handle.

At the press conference, the throngs of reporters were not so kind. These journalists were not teenagers ready to swoon and give in, and they were naturally suspicious of what looked like a silly, dopey-haired gimmick. It was hard for them to even tell who the leader of this four-headed monster was. Little by little, however, they found what their British counterparts had already discovered: the Beatles were irreverentially and nonsensically quick-witted and made for good copy.

Reporter: Are you going to get a haircut?
Beatles: We had one yesterday.

Reporter: What do you think of Beethoven
Beatles: We love him, especially his poems.

Reporter: Do you hope to take back anything with you from America?
Beatles: Rockefeller Center.

Following the press conference, the Beatles were whisked off by limousine motorcade all the way into Manhattan, complete with siren-blaring police escorts front and back.

The stately Plaza Hotel overlooking the southern end of Central Park was hardly prepared for the onslaught about to take place. Epstein had honestly, if not disingenuously, booked the band under their individual names, names that hardly resonated with this storied preserve of the Establishment. Used to dealing with dignitaries and the fashionably wealthy, the venerable hotel was uncomfortably thrust into the limelight by fans in full throat laying siege to the hotel. From inside the hotel, disc jockey Murray the K issued regular bulletins that alerted his radio fans to the Beatles' every move. In the meantime, cooped up inside and listening to a steady stream of their songs on New York radio, the Beatles were enjoying themselves immensely.

But George was feeling more and more ill by the hour, and it soon became clear that he had a bona fide flu. He *had* to be well in time for the big show! Consequently it was the Fab 3 who took a photo-op/sightseeing tour of Central Park.

The band eventually needed to make their way to the CBS studio, where the *Ed Sullivan Show* was to take place. In order to avoid the wild, pubescent hordes outside, the Beatles' took their tradition of great escapes to another level.

They rode the elevator to the basement of the Plaza Hotel; they shot through to the basement of the adjoining building, into a tunnel under 59th street and onto an underground subway station across from the hotel; they then scampered up the steps of the subway station, spilled out onto the street (behind the backs of their adoring fans), and jumped into a waiting limousine.

This had *not* been a fun week for Ed Sullivan. Though thoroughly accustomed to complete marching bands and circus animals traipsing across his stage, he was being undone by three guitarists and a drummer. The rush of requests – 50,000 or so for just 700 seats – had been overwhelming, and he found himself repeatedly apologizing to this and that VIP.

On the evening of the performance, the marble-faced Emcee nevertheless got into the spirit of things, slapping on a Beatles' wig as he warmed up the crowd.

Sally and I tried to guess how many songs the Beatles would play. We hoped at least two. Three would be hogging the show. They had to play "I Want to Hold Your Hand"; it was their #1 hit. The other would probably be "She Loves You," though it wasn't on their American album, so maybe not. As for the third song, the most likely candidates were "I Saw Her Standing There," "All My Loving," and "It Won't Be Long." The first two were McCartney's songs and the latter was

Lennon's. Lennon was the leader of the band, but McCartney's songs were somewhat better, so I was curious to see which it would be.

None of the songs on the B-side of the album were a candidate, especially not "Till There Was You." Finally, I figured that the Beatles wouldn't appear until the end.

I was wrong on most counts.

After an opening ad for Aeroshave and Griffin Liquid Wax, the stodgy Sullivan strode onto the stage. Comedian Alan King had once said that Sullivan does nothing, but does it better than anyone else. Indeed, though his eye for talent had propelled him to the top, Sullivan was no charmer. Tonight was no exception. Cocking his right shoulder back, he mumbled and fumbled through his intro at breakneck speed. (Was he nervous too?)

"Now yesterday and today our theater has been jammed with newsmen and hundreds of photogs from all over the nation, and these veterans agree with me that this city never's witnessed the excitement stirred by these youngsters from Liverpool who call themselves the Beatles.

"Now twice tonight you will be entertained by them, right now and in the second half of our show. Ladies and Gentlemen *(swings his right arm stiffly to the left)*, **the Beatles!**"

The roar of the crowd continued unabated as the Beatles launched into their first song.

"Close your eyes and I'll kiss ...."

McCartney's song.

They performed it crisply, with Harrison singing into McCartney's microphone on the harmony. (There were no harmonies on the studio version of the song.) I thought this extra harmony added a nice touch – except that Lennon was essentially left off camera during the entire song.

The Beatles took a bow at the end of the song, and my heart sank as I recognized the intro to their next song.

How could they play the only song from their album not written by Lennon, McCartney, or Harrison, a song so un-Beatle- like that few of their fans could possibly like it? Brian Epstein apparently thought this song would appeal to a broader audience. Baloney. The "broader" audience had already written off the Beatles as a noisy, hairy gimmick, and was not going to be charmed by McCartney blinking his eyelashes to "Till There Was You." Nevertheless, there he was crooning away. Harrison played a credible classical guitar solo in the middle. Lennon was nearly iced out again. Actually he might have preferred to be completely ignored, given what happened next: The word PAUL appeared across the television screen as Paul sang. Then RINGO, as the camera focused on Ringo; then GEORGE and finally JOHN. And not just JOHN; no, it read JOHN *Sorry Girls, He's Married*. Without his glasses, John probably couldn't read this on the monitors, but Brian Epstein must have died a slow death. So much for hiding the wife.

As the song mercifully ended, the Beatles finally launched into the good stuff. "You think you've lost your love..." This was the whole package, complete with the *ooooooooos* and the head shakes. THESE were the Beatles the fans had come to see, and the crowd shrieked its approval. McCartney and Harrison shared a microphone on the left side of the screen, while Lennon assumed his typical wide-legged stance off to the right. The CBS producers seemed to like this McCartney-Harrison combo, the cameras cutting to McCartney and Harrison whenever they sang together. Starr was also quite photogenic, and he got plenty of air time.

The Beatles shared the evening with a comedian, a magician, a comedy team, and the cast of the Broadway show *Oliver!* This was consistent with the show's unstated motto of pleasing everyone some of the time. Ironically, the featured singer of the *Oliver* cast was none other than Davy Jones, future singer on the Beatle-spoofing television show *The Monkees*.

When the Beatles returned in the second half, they played "I Saw Her Standing There" (sung by McCartney) and, finally, "I Want to Hold Your Hand."

Monday morning saw a heated discussion over at Mission Control, the likes of which I'd never seen before. Were the Beatles any good? Did they look ridiculous? Were they *dangerous*?

I gave Alan Bean credit for voicing his opinion in the minority. He liked their music and didn't give a darn about their hair. I agreed with Al, but was more outwardly timorous. After all, my immediate boss, Gene Kranz, was in the other camp. He was flat-out outraged by the Beatles. "They look like the Three Stooges, they can't sing, they yell, and they're even more dangerous than Elvis Presley because there are *four* of them and because they only LOOK innocent [well, at least he was right about that], etc..." Chris Kraft was right along side him bemoaning the sad state of Western culture. We weren't talking about religion or politics here, so no one was worried about political correctness. Everyone in Mission Control had an opinion. The temperature rose, and the air was filled with fingers pointing and little bits of spittle. With some exceptions here and there, you couldn't help but note the divide between the men my age and the older ones who'd passed thirty.

The mainstream press remained merciless. Sniffed Jack Gould of the *New York Times*, "the pretext of a connection with the world of music ... was perfunctorily sustained." His colleague Theodore Strongin concurred ("The Beatles vocal quality can be described as hoarsely incoherent") and so did McCandlish Phillips: "They may yet become the vocal scourge of the whole Western world ... They were brought to their present pre-eminence in latter-day vaudeville by artful contrivance."

Having said that, regardless of what any critic or anyone at Mission Control thought, the *Ed Sullivan Show* was an unqualified success – much more so than anyone could have imagined, and the Beatles were now off to Washington. Snow had grounded their plane, leaving Brian Epstein to scramble for a train.

London, 1ˢᵗ March, 1964

Dear Dutch,

What a zoo this trip to Washington was. The press made an impassioned about-face, madly clamoring to get on board – literally. *Newsweek, Time, Life*, the major television networks – <u>everyone</u> wanted a piece of the action. Brian was a master at controlling access to the band, and the boys were fabulous at clowning around, striking poses, and throwing out more one-liners.

Reporter: What do you do when you're cooped up in your rooms
between shows?
Beatles: We ice skate.

Reporter: Do you have a leading lady for your upcoming movie?
Beatles: We're trying for the Queen.

As for the show itself, well let's just say I'd never seen anything like it and hope never to again. The stage at the Washington Coliseum was setup like a boxing ring minus the ropes, and every few minutes the four of them had to turn clockwise to face another part of the audience. Ringo would climb down and turn his drums himself! (In the film taken by the Maysles brothers you'll see me helping him.) Paul's microphone wasn't working well, so the harmonies sounded like crap — not that anyone noticed.

The low point of our trip to Washington, believe it or not, was the invitation to the British Embassy. This was not the kind of crowd the Beatles enjoyed mingling with, and when one woman decided to cut off a lock of Ringo's hair as a souvenir for her grand-daughter, that was it, we were out of there!

We played Carnegie Hall in New York. Brian had once again booked them under their individual names. At the time of the booking, the Carnegie front office had thought the foursome were a classical ensemble, and they were no more pleased than their colleagues at the Plaza to find out the veritable nature of their quartet.

Then we went off to Miami. None of us had ever felt such warmth and sunshine; it was a real thrill. We were offered a ride on a really fast boat, and some millionaire lent us his house (with his own pool!). Maybe your Florida experience was a little different.

There was a publicity shoot with the boxer Cassius Clay, who will soon be fighting another Negro, Sonny Liston. The boys were none too thrilled. They didn't know this famous boxer, and it's becoming evident that celebrities are looking to boost their visibility by attaching themselves to the newest act in town.

The boys taped a segment for a second *Ed Sullivan Show*. They introduced the American public to "From Me To You," and they sang "This Boy." It took guts to sing that three-part harmony song! — especially with John, Paul, and George always getting mixed up between the "this boy" and the "that boy" parts of the song! As you might have seen, the boys appeared a third time on Ed Sullivan, but this was a tape of two songs they recorded on the 9th before their live show ("Twist and Shout" and "Please Please Me").

We're off to England. We had a *darn good time.*

Mal

P.S. I hear we're going to be featured on the cover of *Newsweek* magazine.

And so they were. *Time* magazine also weighed in. To wit their February 21ˢᵗ, 1964, article, "The Unbarbershopped Quartet." "The Beatles are great. The Beatles are different. The Beatles are cool, cool, cool, cool, cool … At Carnegie Hall … they boomed their electrified rock'n'roll into the wildly screaming darkness … no press agent can light a blaze like that … the Beatles are being fueled by a genuine, if temporary, hysteria … They are pure and classic idols. All they have to do is lift their arms or shake their waterweed hair to provoke screams that would blot out an all-clear signal … If they are asked why they think they qualify as, well, four Rockmaninoffs, they disarmingly concede that they have no real talent at all."

"Concede." Right. They obviously understood a thing or two about PR.

As for the choice of songs during the *Ed Sullivan Show*, I could better understand the McCartney slant the night of their first performance: Lennon sang "Twist and Shout" and "Please Please Me" on their third show, and in the end there was a reasonable balance.

****

Gus was a happy guy. After "screwing the pooch" on his Mercury mission, he'd immersed himself into the Gemini program. He had spent so much time at the McDonnell plant in St. Louis that the capsule was coming to be known as the Gus-mobile. And now he'd been tapped to fly the first Gemini mission sometime in early '65.

****

London, 16ᵗʰ July, 1964

Dear Dutch,

It's been busy, to say the least.

I noted in the papers that our friend Cassius Clay beat Sonny Liston for the heavy weight title. Were you rooting for him?

Barely a day after their return home, the Beatles were back at work. Paul had had an idea for a song and he'd worked it through with John and George M. As with "She Loves You," it started right in with the chorus. George Martin agreed that the song had potential — a bit of a toe-tapper, and he rushed them into the studio. They should strike while the iron was hot, he advised.

"Can't buy me lo-ove, can't buy me lo-ove, no no no, nooooo!!!....." The song indeed shot right to the #1 position.

There wasn't much time to celebrate.

The Beatles had a movie to shoot! I'll reveal the plot another day, but here's an amusing tidbit: as the filming ended, the picture still had no title. "Beatlemania" was a leading candidate, but no one was thrilled.

Then, one day, Ringo complained about having had a hard day's night. We had a title! Yes, Ringo talks in titles and doesn't always realize that he's funny.

[Ringo was also the Yogi Berra of the band:
<u>*Reporter:*</u> *"Why do you get more fan mail than the other Beatles?"*
<u>*Ringo:*</u> *"I dunno, I suppose it's because more people write me."]*

But still, we had no title song!
No problem.
No sooner had the title of the movie been chosen that John and Paul returned to the studio, song in hand.

Twwwwannnnnnhhhhg. George came up with a devilish chord to open the song, quite distinctive and effective I might say, and there you had it, another #1 song (in the U.S. too, no?). It's mainly John's song, but he and Paul alternate lead vocals, Paul taking the high notes. The song doesn't appear in the movie itself; it was written too late. It's tacked on at the beginning and at the end like a pair of musical bookends.

It's fair to say that the Beatles can do no wrong: Paul suggested the title "In His Own Write" for a collection of John's literary doodles; the book quickly won an award. John was the invited guest at the Foyles Literary Lunch on the occasion of Shakespeare's four hundredth birthday. He was so hung over (this would never have happened to Paul) that when it came time for him to speak, he just got up and said, "Thank you very much. God bless you" — and sat down. The crowd had hardly settled in, and no one seemed to have heard him clearly. One guest suggested out loud that he'd said, "You've got a lucky face," and word quickly spread around the room of this brilliant witticism. The audience burst into applause. Can you believe it???? When you're hot you're hot!

137

John's not the only one with a book. Brian [Epstein]'s written a book called *A Cellarful of Noise*, which John goes around calling *A Cellarful of Boys*. This literally drives Brian to tears, and we feel for him. And there's more. With that look that can eviscerate you, John once told Brian that he should have called his book *Queer Jew*. John really crosses the line; he does so quite often with just about everyone around here. We know he's sensitive and even insecure deep on the inside, etc... etc... but really, he should know better. (I'll deny I ever said this.)

Brian's not totally innocent either. He flies off the handle on a regular basis. As Tony [Barrow] says, all the toys come out of the pram when Brian gets mad. I think everyone around here's gotten fired and then re-hired at least once. Eppy's personal life — or lack thereof — colors his whole world. It's not just that he's queer. If that were all there were to it, he could quietly find a fellow and have a steady relationship. It would be illegal, but he'd get away with it. No, he exults contradiction: everything about him is elegant, refined, and measured, but in his private life he only goes for guys who physically hurt him, cheat him, or blackmail him. Tough to get a relationship going! On some level, Lennon's cruelty probably appeals to him.

On a more cheerful note, the music scene in England is hot. The Dave Clark Five have a hit with "Bits and Pieces," and "Needles and Pins" is a hit for the Searchers. There's Chuck Berry's "No Particular Place to Go," the Animals are on the map with "House of the Rising Sun." (I think their lead singer, Eric Burdon, has the best voice around); your Beach Boys are making waves with "I Get Around." Ever hear of the Zombies? Their moody, breathless hit "She's Not There" is cool, I can send you a copy. Roy Orbison is going to have a smash with "Oh Pretty Woman," (you heard it here first). I also heard a band called the Kinks record a song called "All the Day and All of the Night." A very raw sound; kind of like it. Another British act, a singer by the funny moniker of Petula Clark, is singing a tune called "Downtown." John thinks it's rubbish; Paul likes it. I think it's catchy, but I can see John's point. Even your guys at NASA will like it. (At least their wives will!) Remember Jane Asher, Paul's girlfriend? Her brother Peter has formed a band — Peter and Gordon they call themselves — and Paul's given them a song, "World Without Love." The song's gone to #1! You know you've made it when even the songs you're giving away are going to the top of the charts! And Paul just turned twenty-two.

Next month we're off to America again. The schedule looks prepos-
terous: We'll be playing thirty concerts in thirty-two days in twenty-four
cities. All this on the heels of the tour we just completed in Scandinavia,
Hong Kong, and Australia. In Australia, it looked like the whole country was
there to greet us. People were saying there was a bigger turnout than for
the Queen. Then again, as George says, she doesn't have a hit record. The
most unnerving part? When we got to the airport, each Beatle was plunked
down into his individual Austin Mini with shocking bright letters spelling out
his name across the side of the car.

JOHN – PAUL – GEORGE – RINGO

They didn't like being split up. They were also asked to don blue capes
that had been made for them in Hong Kong. It rained. When they got to
the hotel their skin was blue!

As soon as we returned to England, it was off for a triumphant return
to Liverpool for the premiere of *A Hard Day's Night.* It was a little awkward,
waving from your motorcade to people you've known since you were a child.
I thought I caught a glimpse of Pete Best.

Perhaps we can touch base when we go through Houston.

Yours,

Mal

Everything Mal said rang true. The public's passion for the Beatles
continued unabated. The Beatles' latest single, "Can't Buy Me Love,"
quickly rose to the top of the charts — even before its release. The advance sale of two million records had sufficed. The sudden, stratospheric popularity of the Beatles led every company with any right to
any morsel of Beatle music to press vinyl around the clock. Too much
was still not enough for the Beatle-hungry throngs. As a result of this
feeding frenzy, the Beatles, in the spring of '64, had scooped up the
top five spots on the hit parade. This did not even include the future
classic "I Saw Her Standing There." At #2 and #3 were the relative
oldies, "Twist and Shout" and "She Loves You." "I Want to Hold Your
Hand" was still going strong at #4, and the recycled "Please Please Me"
chugged along at #5. The Beatles had nine other songs in the top 100…
All this assured the presence of a Beatle song on the airwaves at any
time of day or night.

Not everyone was thrilled. For every ecstatic person under thirty there lived someone over thirty who saw the foursome as the Four Horsemen of the Apocalypse, presumably bringing decadence, corruption, blasphemy, and bad music. To this right wing of America, the Beatles were clearly part of a communist plot to debauch our youth. Amusingly, these same Beatles were banned in Russia for being crass exports of a bourgeois capitalist society.

The Beatles triggered these visceral reactions without uttering the slightest incendiary word. "I want to hold your hand"? "Close your eyes and I'll kiss you"? "With love from me to you"? "I'll never dance with another"? In fact, were they not downright polite? Please this, please that, "Please Mr. Postman," "Please Please Me," "Oh please, say to me ..."

In contrast to an in-your-face revolutionary like Bob Dylan, the Beatles at that point hadn't the slightest interest in discussing current events. What they had was *attitude*. It was about now, not the future or the past. It was about joy, not caution. It was about love, not fear. It was about irreverence, not respect. Men with long hair? "Well, we got rid of that little convention for them," Paul would later say. The long hair was an unspoken act of rebellion against world order and was instantly perceived as such. And therein lay the rub.

Troubling much of the public was the rowdy, uncontrolled (some would say demonic) joy and call to freedom that rang in their accented voices when they sang. Part of the public saw the threat and thrill of the 1950s kicked up a notch by strange-looking foreigners. And what an effect on women these corrupters had! Teenage girls would take complete leave of their senses and be transported to an entirely different level of consciousness. They were possessed! Was this voodoo? What secret spell were these Beatles casting? What mass debauchery was this going to lead to? *(Very little actually, compared to the imminent release of the Pill.)* Elvis may have swiveled his hips, but he was a church-going mama's boy. He may have threatened a little, but he always stayed on the right side of the line. As wholesome as their lyrics might have been, the Beatles were perceived as being on the other. Some said they even smoked marijuana. The most famous evangelist in America, Billy Graham, felt obligated to jump into the fray: The Beatles are a reflection of the "uncertainties of the times and the confusion about us."

Capitol released a second album, cleverly titled "The Beatles Second Album," consisting of songs released in the U.K. a year earlier: "She Loves You," "Thank You Girl," "You Can't Do That," "I'll Get You," "I Call Your Name" (later covered by the Mamas and the Papas), and a host of covers including, most famously, McCartney's searing vocal performance in Little Richard's "Long Tall Sally." The cover of the album consisted of unattractive sepia pictures, and I decided to save myself the $2.50. I could always get "She Loves You" and "Long Tall Sally" from Mal.

At the end of July, *A Hard Day's Night* was splashed across the silver screen of seven hundred movie theaters across the country, and fans got to share the lives of their heroes up close and personal. The music, the mayhem, the British accent, the wit, the banter, a touch of surrealism – it was all there, a fan's delight. Each of the four Beatles was portrayed as a caricature of himself: John was witty and clever, Paul charming and attractive, George a quiet thinker, and Ringo the loveable runt of the litter. If nothing else, the movie engrained these images in the mind of the public, and such would be their public persona for the rest of their days.

Comic writer Allen Owun cobbled together a script that highlighted a week in the Beatles' lives, culminating with a concert performance. There wasn't much of a plot: Trailing a swarm of fans, the Beatles jump for their lives onto a moving train. They're on their way to a gig. On the day of the concert, Ringo is talked into wandering off in town to find himself, while the others are left to frantically look for him. The film was shot in black and white, partly to save money, partly to give the movie the feel of a documentary.

The artistic high point of the movie takes place when the Beatles burst out like schoolboys from the claustrophobic confines of the theater where they've been told to stay put by "The Man." They stick it to The Man by clowning, cavorting, and leap-frogging in an open field to the sounds of "Can't Buy Me Love." The film speeds up and slows back down; camera angles come from every direction – very avant-garde.

The movie ends with a concert, and of course the fans in the movie shriek along. Adding to the effect, the fans in the *movie theaters* would bray along hysterically!

Lo and behold… a critical success. The same critics who mercilessly panned the music of the Beatles a few months earlier were now tripping over each other in praise. I was amused by the apology that preceded many a review: "So help me I resisted the Beatles as long as I could" (A. Sarris, *The Village Voice*), "This is going to surprise you" (B. Crowther, *The New York Times*). Sarris went on to call the movie "The Citizen Kane of juke-box movies." "The legitimacy of the Beatles phenomenon is inescapable," praised *Newsweek.* Most reviews likened the Beatles to the Marx brothers and expressed surprise at their comedic talents.

The original purpose of the movie was of course to sell records. It didn't disappoint, though in America the record released by United Artists was an ill-advised mix of original songs and instrumental renditions of earlier Beatle songs. For the first time, here was a Beatles record you couldn't play nonstop from beginning to end. Sally and I would practically flip a coin to see who would get up to go lift the arm of the turntable past the instrumentals.

Nevertheless, it was worth it. In addition to the title track, you had McCartney's "And I Love Her," stand out Lennon-McCartney harmonies on Lennon's "If I Fell," the jaunty "I'll Cry Instead," and the high-octane, head-shaking "Tell Me Why."

Within a month Capitol had its own *Hard Day's Night*ish record out on the American market, curiously called *Something New* – curious because there was very little that was new. Five of the tracks were from the movie and already available on the United Artists album. There was the cover of Carl Perkin's "Matchbox" and the novelty song "Komm Gib Mir Deine Hand" featuring the Beatles singing in German their hit song from the previous year (a nod to their Hamburg fans). In the end there was but one new standout song, McCartney's "Things We Said Today." Lost on a lackluster album following a time of intense Beatle market saturation, this would be one of the few Beatle gems to slip by unnoticed and destined for relative obscurity[7]. Opening with a fast ta-ta-dum strum of the guitar, the song is a tale of separation, thematically linked to "All My Loving" – both starting on a mournful minor chord and both serving as blueprints for future McCartney ballads.

It wasn't worth buying the album for one song.

---

7   Joining the later "For No One"

The British *Hard Day's Night* album was another story: In addition to containing all the original songs from the movie, it featured "Things We Said Today" and "I'll Be Back" – in all, 13 original, mostly A-level Lennon-McCartney compositions.

In August, the Beatles landed on the cover of *Life* magazine for the first time. The story focused on the only "mature" adult of the group, Brian Epstein.

****

London, 15th October, 1964

Dear Dutch,

This last U.S. tour was a catalog of "can you top this?"

I was glad we could talk a few moments when we flew through Houston. Sorry we couldn't have a beer. I can honestly say there wasn't a free moment. You know I would have loved to visit the Space Center.

Houston was in fact quite memorable. I don't know if they wrote any of this in the papers, but at the airport fans broke through the fence and climbed onto the wings of the plane! In Dallas security officers brandished their rifles right there in the open. (Are we a rock'n'roll band or a Communist delegation?) In San Francisco the driver didn't pull away fast enough, and the roof of the car started to buckle from the weight of the fans. In Indianapolis, Ringo forgot to tell anyone that he wanted to drive on the Indy 500 racetrack (which the authorities allowed him to do), and we were all frantically looking for him; it was right out of *A Hard Day's Night*.

But my favorite stop was Kansas City.

Charles O. Finley, the eccentric owner of one of your baseball teams [Kansas City Athletics], was determined to have the Beatles play in Kansas City. Unfortunately, Kansas City was not on the tour list, and the Beatles had but one day off between concerts in New Orleans on September 16th and Dallas on the 18th. Finley was determined to snatch the Beatles for the 17th.

Barbra Streisand had to date received the highest payment for a single performance: $35,000. Finley offered the Beatles $150,000! It was an offer Epstein couldn't refuse.

"Oh, and one more thing," Finley said. For an extra $1,000 could the Beatles sing "Kansas City"? No? How about $2,000? $3,000? At this point Lennon stepped in. His eyes narrowed and his jaw tightened and he just said "no." Finley had bought their lone day off and now he was trying to buy the song set?

On September 17th, the Beatles played to a delirious Kansas City crowd. Finley wore a Beatle wig, and the back of each ticket read "Yeah! yeah! yeah! Today's Beatle's fans are Tomorrow's Baseball Fans [sic]."

At the end of their set, the Beatles announced that they would play one more song. There was a pause as John peered towards the owner's box. Paul started in:

"Aaaaaaah Kansas City, coming to get my baby back home, yeah, yeah..."

Another highlight was meeting Bob Dylan. Have you heard of him in Houston? Somewhat rebellious and moody folk singer. The boys have really been into his music. During our New York stopover, he paid a visit and introduced us all to marijuana. The funny thing is that he thought we were already devotees, based on the lyric in "I Want to Hold your Hand": "I get high, I get high, I get hiiiiiiiiigh." John was a little embarrassed to point out that the lyric is actually "I can't hide." The effect of the weed was immediate. We were all laughing hysterically over nothing. Paul thought he'd just seen The Light and had me writing down all the thoughts rushing through his mind.

But really, there were many ridiculous aspects to this tour. The entire trip was one long, high-pitched shriek. Nobody, not even the boys themselves, could hear any of the music or any of the singing over the screeching, head-spinning, fist-biting, panty-wetting teenagers that lined every road and filled every concert hall. Their voices barely made it past the first few rows before disappearing into the night. In Vancouver, Paul hit a really sour note during "If I Fell," and when they got to the line "I couldn't stand the pain," they all started cracking up. Nobody noticed. Every now and then they would just stop singing — and nobody noticed.

People are gathering up the bed sheets that the Beatles have slept in, cutting them into little squares and selling them! Same with the towels that they wipe their brow with in concerts!

The funny questions from the press continue:

Reporter: Do you like topless bathing suits?
Ringo: We've been wearing them for years.

Reporter: Does every city look the same?
John: No, some have trees, some don't.

Everyone wants autographs; everyone from the Governor down to the bellhop. Not for themselves, but for their kids. It's the ultimate present for little Suzie who's got everything already! All these people wait for us the moment we arrive in town. At the airport. At the hotel. At the concert hall. They aren't all there to get autographs. Some want a little more. I must say, the unbridled physical desire of the fans (and sometimes that of their mothers) is a thing of dreams.

Neil and I do the screening, and after listening to their excited chatter, we're more than happy to satisfy their libidinous ardor. We've learned what kind of girl each Beatle likes, and we get the rejects. That sounds harsh, but really! There are so many of them. Not even four healthy young rock'n' roll stars can handle it.

The press people are pretty cool. We allow them into our inner circle and give them access to breaking stories, and they keep our dirty little secrets under wraps. Brian's made it clear to the press how important the "lovable moptops" image is. Same with NASA, right?

We have two weeks of so-called vacation during which the Beatles have to produce another album in time for Christmas, and then we're off on a five-week tour of England. After that, we're booked three weeks solid for the Christmas show at the Hammersmith Odeon (good for me — there's no travel involved), following which, two weeks later, the boys are due to shoot another movie. And that will mean another soundtrack. Track, track, track. Hard to keep track...

Your friend,

Mal

Mal was certainly right about the press. Our astronauts were rascals, every one of them (except John Glenn, clearly). They were choirboys, however, as far as NASA was concerned, and the media played along. This cozy arrangement would go on for many years, as it did with the Beatles.

****

On July 27th, 1964, it was announced by the White House that a few military advisers were going to Vietnam. I wouldn't have noticed, but both my dad and Sally's dad commented on it. They both said the same thing: good thing I was working for NASA in case this turned into another Korea. Of course, personally, I thought there was no way we'd get involved in another Asian war; not unless Red China attacked us directly.

****

The loudest arguments and debates in the halls of NASA dealt not with the details of the missions, not with the selection of this or that crew, and not with the selection of this or that rocket.

No, voices were loudest when anybody discussed science.

The role of the scientist-astronaut had yet to be defined, and the battle lines were clearly drawn: The scientific community, which participated heavily in every aspect of the Apollo program, felt strongly that scientists needed to be included in the astronaut corps so as to reap the maximum benefit from the program. Most pilots, on the other hand, felt that science projects detracted from the missions. They were seriously disinclined to baby-sit some brainiac scientist during the serious and dangerous business of flying a new spacecraft.

A logical compromise was reached: There would be no scientist assigned to any crew while the spacecraft and equipment were still being tested. Once things had settled down, however, and we'd sent enough crews to the moon to consider the spacecraft reliable, NASA would send up, say, a geologist. In the meantime the astronauts would be pilots first, scientists second; they would be taught enough science to carry out basic experiments.

In October of 1964, NASA announced that the next group of astronauts would include scientists. This effectively ended the astronaut-scientist debate.

For now.

**

While we argued these weighty issues, the Soviets launched their first manned Voskhod *(Sunrise)*. It carried *three* astronauts. We had no idea that this Voskhod was the same old Vostok, with three smaller seats simply taking the place of the previous two. Even the names Vostok and Voskhod sounded the same.

Voskhod was only up in space for a day, and it didn't advance anyone's knowledge, but it was enough to make us feel like laggards again.

Khrushchev chatted with his sardined cosmonauts, telling them that they "glorify our homeland, our people, our party, and the ideas of Marxism-Leninism [by] which our state stands and [by] which we achieve all the things we have."

It was a proud day for Khrushchev.

Or *would* have been. For hardly had Voskhod reached orbit, that Nikita *we-will-bury-you* Khrushchev had himself been politically buried. On October 12th, Khrushchev was unceremoniously ousted and replaced by the stone-faced Leonid Brezhnev. *Pravda* ("Truth"), the official Russian newspaper, bleated "[we condemn Khrushchev's] hare-brained schemes, immature conclusions, hasty decisions, actions divorced from reality, bragging, and phrase-mongering..."

Talk about eating your own.

On the very same day, China exploded its first atomic bomb. The Cold War was now a three-way street. I began to think about my father's worries more seriously, but not, I admit very much more.

In America the center and the left held sway. It was obvious that we needed Civil Rights legislation, and Lyndon Johnson, once master of the Senate, now twisted every arm in site to push through legislation that would bring racial equality. In the same spirit, there grew a groundswell of community action that sought to bridge religious and social divides across the country. Although Houston was still, in most respects, segregated and prejudiced, we were slowly becoming progressive. It helped that Johnson was a Texan. Even with JFK's death and the horrific images of the Ku Klux Klan still fresh, there was a palpable optimism about what would later be called "The Great Society."

Not everyone was in step. Preacher Billy James Hargis would bluster, "The liberal churches today preach ... socialist gospel. Or, in the vernacular, they preach the gospel of Martin Luther King, instead of the gospel according to Matthew, Mark, Luke and John ... I believe in God and Satan ... I believe God gave us America. I would rather see my children destroyed ... than the thought of them having to live under a communist slave state ... you don't achieve ecumenical unity without compromise, and compromise is evil! ... Internationalism, liberalism ... are nothing but an attack on man's correct relationship with God. It is concealed atheism. *Don't talk to me of liberalism, it is a double standard, it is Satanic hypocrisy!*"

While this philosophy of life rang true with a certain segment of the population, and still does, for most it was reason enough to run the other way. The likeable Barry Goldwater ran on this presidential platform in November 1964 (defending "extremism" in the name of liberty) and was trounced by Johnson. He was going to lose anyway. No one was going to beat Kennedy's torchbearer.

****

Around Thanksgiving a new Beatle song took me by surprise. Mal hadn't said anything about "I Feel Fine," but before you knew it, it was Number One on the charts, and therefore heard around the clock. Mal would explain to me later that Lennon, upon leaning his guitar on his amplifier, had created an electronic buzz that kept getting louder and fuzzier. This so-called feedback was the bane of the recording engineers, but the Beatles decided that they liked it and excitedly chose to introduce their song with this unusual sound; this would be the first use of feedback on a record, the very feedback that would be teased and tweaked by Jimi Hendrix and all the hard rock guitarists to follow. The song then opened more traditionally with a catchy little guitar lick played in tandem by George and John throughout the song. The lyrics were inconsequential. I thought the flip side of the record was more interesting. Called "She's a Woman," this bluesy tune was cranked up with a powerful bass line and delivered with a gritty McCartney vocal.

The two songs made for good listening; in my apartment, at least, if not at NASA. Sally and I, with our Beatles' records and odd mixture of friends, were beginning to feel like we led double lives.

That fall, Martin Luther King was awarded the Nobel Peace prize. What was the world coming to? Wasn't he always getting arrested? I had yet to understand the concept of protest as an action *for* peace. I don't know that any of us at Mission Control had ever paid much attention to King. Then again, we didn't get out much.

I was more aware of the music scene. *Fiddler on the Roof* was a hit on Broadway. The Rolling Stones – a splashy hit on their hands with "Time Is On My Side" – got their own shot at the *Ed Sullivan Show.* In contrast to the Beatles, the Stones had their roots in jazz and blues. Mick Jagger and Keith Richards had connected on a train upon seeing the record albums the other was holding. Mick and Charlie Watts had played together in a band called Blues Incorporated, and Brian Jones along with Bill Wyman had recruited them to form this bluesy rock band. Mick Jagger now assumed the rebellious, bad-boy mantle reluctantly shed by John Lennon. The fact that they were solid musicians was irrelevant to the public or to American producers. At this point Ed Sullivan and everyone in TV land was eager to put forth anyone from Great Britain as long as they had the accent and the hair. Just about every British act, big and small, would have their fifteen minutes of fame on *Ed Sullivan, Shindig* or *Hullaballoo,* American variety shows featuring every possible style of music.

As much as we might have poked fun at the Beatles' hair, there was no question that men in general were now wearing their hair longer. Of course, we at NASA were hardly "men in general," and this gradual slide towards longer hair would bypass us completely. But across the country, barbershops were closing. The "wet look" with its hair creams, tonics, and the like, was finished. From this point on, through the end of the century, 80% of American barbershops would close.

Over Christmas I took Sally to a film that would be the second most popular movie of 1964, even though it came out less than two weeks before the New Year. It featured my favorite hero in his third appearance on the silver screen and was called *Goldfinger.*

To fans of Ian Fleming's *James Bond* books, the arrival of the racy *Doctor No* the year before had been cause to celebrate. Future Bond trademarks were already present: the *James Bond Theme,* complete with jangly guitar and blaring horns, the introduction "The name is Bond, James Bond," and the Martini was already shaken, not stirred. When Ursula Andress – "Ursula Undress" – emerged from the waters, she did for the bikini what the Beatles had done for the electric guitar. Nobody knew or cared that her voice was dubbed. At NASA we were particularly keen on Doctor No's fiendish plan to topple an American rocket by way of a radio beam. It wasn't so farfetched: Around launch time, a Soviet "fishing trawler" spiked with every possible radio and radar antenna always seemed to be lurking at the edge of our national waters.

Doctor No was a surprise hit. Flush with success producers Broccoli and Saltzman had ramped up the follow-up, *From Russia with Love*. We were now treated to an opening scene just *prior* to the credits, the singing of the movie's theme song by a popular performer (Matt Monro), and a gadget suitcase provided by Q. (Surprisingly, the producers changed the order of Fleming's books. "Doctor No" (the book) is the sequel to "From Russia with Love.")

I could have never imagined it, but *Goldfinger* was even more spectacular than its predecessors. For the first time, Bond took on the mantle of the larger-than-life espionage hero, cool enough to flirt and crack jokes while facing death.

The German actor, Gert Frobe, played the villain, Auric Goldfinger[8]. His English was limited, and as with Ursula Andress, his voice was dubbed. Also featured were the ultimate bad guy, Odd Job (he of few words and the guillotine bowler hat); Jill, the striking nude victim suffocated in gold paint from head to toe; the pretty villainess with the naughty name (Pussy Galore); the nasty weapon (the genital-threatening laser); a knock-out musical score belted by Shirley Bassey (and produced by George Martin!), and what gadgets! The best of the lot was Bond's Aston Martin DB5 equipped with machine guns, a revolving license plate, a retractable bullet-proof shield, a wicked tire shredder, and of course, the piece de résistance, the ejector seat on the passenger side. All of these were naturally put to use at various points in the movie.

The screenwriters threw in a little line at the beginning of the movie to make it completely *au courant*: Bond comments that drinking improperly chilled champagne is like listening to the Beatles without earmuffs. The producers didn't have to worry about alienating teenagers: most were not allowed to watch such racy material.

Left out of the movie was Auric Goldfinger's connection to the perennial bad guys, SMERSH (a real Soviet agency) and the fictional SPECTRE (SPecial Executive for Counter-intelligence, Terrorism,

---

8   Auric: pertaining to gold.

Revenge and Extortion). The popularity of the Bond films would, in short order, spawn a whole alphabet soup of acronyms, including the television show *The Man From U.N.C.L.E.* (United Network Command for Law Enforcement) fighting THRUSH (the Technological Hierarchy for the Removal of Undesirables and the Subjugation of Humanity). There was but one degree of separation between *The Man from U.N.C.L.E.* and James Bond, the name of the protagonist in the television series, Napoleon Solo, having been suggested by none other than Ian Fleming.

****

I finally got my first look at the Gemini capsule. It was somewhat disappointing. It looked much like its predecessor, although at nineteen feet long, it was visibly bigger. Someone joked that it looked like a Mercury capsule that had thrown away the diet books. It was somewhat roomier inside with approximately the wiggle room I had in my own VW Beetle. Of course it had seat belts, which my Beetle lacked. Heck, I was lucky to have a gas gauge (standard only as of 1962 on VW Beetles)!

Looks aside, as 1964 drew to a close, NASA still had its hands full. Glitches remained in the testing and design of the Gemini capsule. During a test of the ejector seats, the hatches failed to open, and the seats bore right through the capsule. "A hell of a headache," astronaut John Young commented, "but a short one."

****

Shortly before Christmas, I noted a new Beatle album in the stores, futuristically called "Beatles '65." I figured Mal would send me a copy.

For illustrations, see www.intotheskywithdiamonds.com

9. I'm Not Coming Back In

Sure enough, the day after New Year's, a record from Mal arrived in the mail. But it wasn't *Beatles '65*. I'd seen the album in store windows; the cover art showed the Beatles holding umbrellas. Instead, the album I was holding read *"Beatles for Sale"* and was adorned with an unsmiling picture of the foursome. Their faces were downright uninviting. You couldn't even say that the photograph was artistic like the cover of *Meet the Beatles*. The top of Harrison's hair gave his head a pointy look, and that was it for levity. The *Beatles '65* record being sold in the U.S. was yet another made-for-America mish-mash of various British releases.

The note from Mal indicated that he thought the band was getting a little tired, a little stale, and he apologized for the number of songs not written by the Beatles themselves. I don't know that I would have personally noted anything amiss. Yes, there were a number of covers, but how many songs can you write in a year? Mal was sorry that the Beatles had left out a McCartney composition called "That Means a Lot," feeling that they should have axed "Mr. Moonlight" instead. I couldn't form an opinion on the former since I had never heard it, but certainly agreed about the latter. This was the first Beatle recording I'd ever heard that was awful to the point of skipping to the next song whenever it came around. The low point was the skating-rink organ solo. "Mr. Moonlight" was not even one of their own compositions, so the motivation for releasing it remained a mystery. Lennon sang his heart out, but it wasn't enough. A real stinker.

"I'm a Loser" caught my attention. This was certainly an unusual rock'n'roll song. I would not have paid it any mind but for what Mal had once told me: Although cheerfulness would often break through when he performed, Lennon was hardly a happy person. Never had been. He was still the poster child for the angry young man. Neither fame nor money was changing any of that. In fact fame and money made things that much more frustrating. He had feelings for his wife, but he had mostly gotten married out of duty. He lived in a big house outside of London; it gave him no satisfaction. Being home meant being physically and spiritually isolated from the rest of the world. Cyn was sweet, but what was there to talk about? She neither stretched nor stimulated him. Sex was mechanical; the action was more interesting on the road. The cuddly Beatle image repulsed him more and more. He was turning into the rich, phony Man that he'd railed against his entire life.

"Yeah, I see what you mean," said Sally when I talked to her about this. "He sure has it rough."

I didn't think her derision misplaced, exactly, but my own reaction was more complex. Part of me was relieved to know that not even John Lennon had it all; but a larger part of me felt grateful for the music, and so wished him well.

"I'm a Loser" was sandwiched between two songs whose lyrics were just as bleak: In "No Reply" Lennon sees his girlfriend cheat on him, and in "Baby's in Black" he can't get a girl's attention. The time to go beyond I-want-to-hold-your-hand had clearly arrived.

For all its melancholy lyrics, "Baby's in Black" featured some of my favorite Beatle harmonies, especially on the middle-eight ("Oh how long will it take ...")

The album shifted temporarily into high gear with "Rock'n'Roll Music," a hell-raising Chuck Berry cover – better than the original in my opinion. I couldn't tell if it was Lennon or McCartney singing *[Lennon]*.

There were no new singles released off *Beatles '65*. Nevertheless, the album shot up the charts, and the Beatles' assault on AM radio continued unabated: In February, "Eight Days a Week" hit the charts. The title was another one of Ringo's little catchphrases. The song starts with a fade *in*. Quietly it begins then gradually rises to a normal volume; it seemed to be tailor-made for radio DJs. That was the song's only original aspect. Other than that, it was a little ditty that I'm guessing Lennon or McCartney thought up while doing the dishes or painting the walls. (I must admit, it worked for Sally and me.) It was catchy and it flew to the number one position.

***

Assigning crews was supposed to be easy for Deke. The commanders of the Gemini missions would simply be a repeat of the Mercury 7 sequence (Shepard, Grissom, Glenn, et cetera). Unfortunately, the

Mercury 7 had become the Mercury 6, when Deke himself had been knocked out of the program. It had been down to the Mercury 5, when Glenn ascended to an iconic status that only a biblical scholar could truly appreciate and had been taken out of the rotation. It was whittled down to the Mercury 4, when Carpenter became *persona non grata*. Finally, the seven had imploded to a measly Mercury 3, when Shepard had woken up with his Ménière's disease. Thus Grissom was an obvious choice to command the first Gemini mission. Picking the subsequent commanders would require more thought.

Deke chose Frank Borman to fly with Gus; then, from one day to the next, he mysteriously swapped Young for Borman. Although it created quite a buzz in the NASA hive, it was not that much of a mystery as far as I was concerned. The party line was that the two egos could not fit in that Gemini capsule. My feeling was that after an hour-long *tête à tête*, Grissom decided that Borman was too much of a straight arrow. They would have to practically *live* with each other for weeks on end, and Gus liked to have a little fun.

As Grissom and Young prepared for Gemini's debut, the wind was once more taken out of our sails. On March 18th, 1965, Moscow announced that two astronauts had gone up in Voskhod 2 (back to just *two* astronauts), and that one of them, Alexei Leonov, had actually… walked in space! They provided grainy black and white film to prove it.

It had not been much of a walk, it had been more of a "float," but we were beaten. The Soviets poured it on. "SORRY APOLLO! The gap is not closing, it is increasing … The so-called system of free enterprise is turning out to be powerless in competition with socialism in such a complex and modern area as space research."

Powerless? Yeah, right. We all had a few ideas where the Russkies could stick their spacecraft. Of course, they had a major advantage: by simply reading our newspapers, they knew everything NASA was planning, down to the time, the place, and the color socks the astronauts were wearing. We, on the other hand, could not begin to penetrate the Soviet Union's veil of secrecy. It was all "Grand Designer this," "Grand Designer that."

Still sore about the bad rap he had gotten for the sinking of his Mercury capsule, Grissom had decided to name his newest capsule *Molly Brown*, from the popular musical of the time *The Unsinkable Molly Brown*. His second choice had been *Titanic*. Jim Webb did not appreciate this self-deprecating jab and mandated that it just be "Gemini 3." In fact, from here on in, the capsules would no longer have any names. NASA would tolerate Roman numerals. The formal, generic, in-house appellation for all these missions was "CapsuleRocket-flight number." Grissom's first flight, for example, had been Mercury Redstone 4 (MR-4), Glenn's flight had been Mercury Atlas-6 (MA-6), and Grissom's current mission was formally referred to as Gemini Titan-3 (GT-3). It was announced to the press that Gemini 3 would lift off on March 23rd.

It had been nearly two years since the last Mercury flight, and we were all ready for action. There had been two unmanned Gemini flights, each of which had gone well but for the total blackout at the Cape as soon as GT-2 had taken off. The press had been allowed into the room, and for the first time, TV crews had been there to film us. It was a dress rehearsal for our return to space. As soon as the Titan blasted off, EVERYTHING went dark. Only the tiny lights on the intercoms punctured the darkness. By the time the lights came back on, the mission was over; Hodges' team in Houston had tracked the whole flight.

I joked that perhaps next time Kraft should bring along a flashlight. Predictably, he did not see the humor in this. (You'd think I would have known by now.)

There had been a few changes in Mission Control: Kraft could no longer be present every moment of these longer flights, so he created teams that would work in shifts. Each team would be identified by a color; Kranz chose white. I was now on the White Team.

We worked seven days a week in submarine-like confinement, and sub-surface tensions were bound to flare up every now and then – and they did. Unresolved, for example, was the issue of who would be in overall charge of the remote tracking stations. Slayton and Shepard felt strongly that it should be the CapCom astronaut. Kraft felt equally strongly about one of his own staff manning that position. A compromise was reached, but not before a few fellows nearly came to blows. The CapCom would communicate with the crew; Mission Control staff would be in charge of the flight plan.

At 5:53 AM on March 23rd, Gus and John were picked up with customary precision and driven the six miles to the medical trailer. Sensors were pasted here, there, and everywhere over their body, the astronauts donned their long johns and passed off urine samples to Dee and Sally. (Were they screening for drugs?) On Pad 19, site of the launch, backups Schirra and Stafford busied themselves checking and double-checking all the switches of *Molly Brown*.

At 7:06, Gus and John clumsily climbed into the van for the three-minute ride to the launch pad. The huge metallic gantry supporting the rocket was painted bright orange, contrasting starkly with the white Titan rocket and the blue Floridian sky. Personally, given the patriotic flavor of the space program, I would have painted the gantry red. Nevertheless, it was hard not to be awed. Compared to the Redstone and the Atlas rockets, at 109 feet the Titan seemed enormous.

Up the elevator the astronauts went, and into the White Room they entered. They were met by the "pad fuehrer," Guenter Wendt. After receiving their final inspection, they entered the spacecraft, John first, followed by Gus.

At 7:34 AM, the hatches were sealed shut, and the countdown began. There was a little hold as the pad team checked a possible leak in one of the Titan's first stage oxidizer lines, but the countdown moved smartly thereafter.

You didn't have to be a mind reader to know what Gus was thinking. There were of course Betty, Scott, and Mark to worry about. Once again, the life insurance would tide them over in case of disaster. For Gus, though, having been accused of "screwing the pooch" the last time around, it was time to show the world what Virgil Grissom could do. This was the moment he'd been waiting for. He wasn't nervous; he was *eager*.

9:24 AM. Ignition. The large hold-down arms of the gantry kept the rocket in place, as the thrust gradually built up. This was the two-second "launch kill" period during which the computers would go through the final performance checks. Any perceived malfunction would initiate a shutdown of the entire launch system. Otherwise, the bolts would fire, and in a single motion worthy of any synchronized ballet move, the hold-downs would rise and pull away. At this point there was liftoff, and there was no turning back.

Gus immediately noted the difference with the Mercury-Redstone launch: He hardly felt the rocket rise until the g's kicked in. Scorching the stratosphere, the Titan slowly rolled along its axis as planned. Gus eased his hands off the ejection ring.

I couldn't help but laugh. Gordo was the Cap Com. The Titan had barely taken off, when he whooped it up: "You're on your way *Molly Brown!*"

Molly Brown?

The press loved it. NASA did not. Another strike against Cooper.

Gus and John were mesmerized by the sight of the earth below them. John wanted to take a picture of Bermuda, but by the time he got his Hasselblad lined up, Bermuda was a memory. They were hauling the mail.

The first moment of terror occurred shortly thereafter. They had barely passed the Canary Islands off the coast of Africa, when the oxygen pressure in the cabin and in their suits suddenly dropped. They had seen this before in their simulator, and they quickly diagnosed a failure of the electrical converter system. Gus made a mental note to pat himself on the back for having insisted on backup systems. As they flipped to the backup converter, all returned to normal.

Next up, a sea urchin fertilization study. (Did Gus ever think he'd be doing this when he signed up for astronaut school?) Gus had to turn a handle to start the experiment.

The handle broke.

The next task was downright enjoyable. NASA had prepared a number of meals, which were now to be savored and critiqued by our first two extra-terrestrial culinary experts. The food was dehydrated and was to be reconstituted with water. There were applesauce, grapefruit juice, chicken bits, and last but not least, not-too-hateful brownies.

John also had a little surprise for Gus: a corned beef sandwich slipped to him by Wally Schirra just before launch. What a treat! But uh-oh… Schirra and Young hadn't counted on the crumbs.

Once again, Kraft was not amused, and this quickly escalated into a crumbfest in a teapot. Crumbs could get into the capsule's intricate machinery, the mission could fail, the astronauts could lose their lives, NASA would be embarrassed, funding would be cut, etc, etc… Even certain Congressmen chimed in on the lack of discipline at NASA. Young was worried that he might be shown the door. Fortunately, this was the only snafu of the flight; calmer heads prevailed, and Young was spared Carpenter's fate.

The splashdown again proved eventful for Gus. The engineers had decided that the capsule should strike the water at an angle in order to minimize the impact. To that end, one of the straps connecting the capsule to the parachute was to be released shortly before splashdown. The snap of the strap, however, flung Gus so hard that his helmet was punctured when it struck the instrument panel. Gus emerged from his daze to find fish swimming outside his window. My God, he was under water! This was *Liberty Bell* all over again! Then he realized that he was moving *through* the water: The parachute was still connected to the capsule; he hadn't disconnected it, and the eighty-five foot, orange and white parachute was now a well-trimmed downwind sail. Gus quickly reached for the parachute release mechanism, and the capsule bobbed up to the surface. Back at the Cape, an Air Force band welcomed the astronauts home to the tune of *The Unsinkable Molly Brown*.

Despite the little hiccups, it was a most successful mission. Gus was awarded his second Distinguished Service Medal, and this time around, the President of the United States himself pinned it on his chest. And Betty got her trip to the White House.

****

Obertauern, Austria, 20ᵗʰ March, 1965

Dear Dutch,

I am writing from the chilly Austrian Alps. That's right, Austria. We're filming a movie. In color this time! And I have a little part — I'm a disoriented English Channel swimmer, who pops up everywhere the Beatles go. "White Cliffs of Dover?" I ask repeatedly. Make sure you don't go to the loo, or you'll miss my little cameos.

The title of the movie was going to be *Eight Arms to Hold You*, but was changed to *Help!*, which fits in better with the plot. John's written the theme song. It reminds me of "I'm a Loser" in that John continues to be very down on himself: "When I was younger so much younger than today, I never needed anybody's help in any way; but now these days are gone, I'm not so self assured ... every now and then I feel so insecure... Help, I need somebody, help, not just anybody, *Help!*"

It's not going to dawn on the average person that John is writing about himself, but to many of us here, it's pretty obvious.

The plot is slightly mad, but makes for good fun: A fan gives Ringo a ceremonial Indian ring belonging to a cult. The bearer of the ring must be painted red and sacrificed; Ringo can't get it off his finger! The boys try many an amusing trick in an attempt to do so. The cult chases the boys through England, the Austrian Alps and the Bahamas, where there just happens to be an Indian temple. Two mad scientists are also interested in the ring, and they join the chase. There's a lot of typical Beatles banter:

Scotland Yard Superintendent: So this is the famous Beatles? ... and how long do you think you'll last?

John: So this is the famous Scotland Yard, eh? Great Train Robbery, how's that going?

Fun aside, I was very concerned when I heard that part of the filming would take place around an Army base on the Salisbury Plain. I could understand the producers' thinking: no fans to worry about! But the Salisbury Plain is where you find... Stonehenge! Is this not sacrilege? I thought about it the first night, staring at the famous stones. A mystery in place for thousands of years, and here we were with this frilly movie. And then, in the light of the half moon, I thought I saw a glow. Maybe just my imagination. Maybe not. But I got it. This was no coincidence; I was sure of it. They were here. Perhaps we'd be touched by the light? Would I be different by morning? I definitely wasn't, but I do think the others were. George was the first to be affected. He has quite suddenly taken an interest in all things Indian: the Indian sitar (a vertical, stringed instrument with a bulbous body), and more importantly, Indian religion. I've had to run all the way to London to bring him books!

I looked up from the letter. "Sally, I think Mal's gone 'round the bend."

"I thought he was already there."

"He seems to think the Beatles have been anointed by either aliens or our druid ancestors, I'm not sure which."

"Makes as much sense as anything else." Sally liked Beatles music, but could be a bit tart about "Beatlemania."

I imagined aliens cavorting on the moon and sending messages through Stonehenge. I went back to Mal's letter.

"I'm not sure why, but we filmed in the Bahamas *before* going to Austria, even though the Bahaman scenes appear last in the movie. The boys were therefore under instructions to stay out of the sun, so as not to appear tanned in the Austrian scenes! They had a good time anyway. Perhaps too good. An acquaintance plied them with marijuana, and they spent their days giggling. Tears would be streaming down their faces, they were laughing so hard, and I would smoke cigars to block out the smell. The seeds planted by Dylan last summer sure have bloomed! This pharmaceutical hilarity has followed them to the Alps. Good thing perhaps, because George is petrified of the skis. No stuntmen here except for a chairlift scene!

The *Help!* album will be very good. Keep a lookout for "Ticket to Ride" and make sure to catch my film debut!

Cheers,

Mal

****

The Gemini capsule and Titan rocket had worked to perfection, crumbs notwithstanding, and it was now time to take the next big leap forward into... nothing.

Literally.

The original flight plan for Gemini called for an astronaut to don his space suit, open the hatch, and stand up. Period. Leonov's "space walk" had changed all this in a hurry. If we couldn't get ahead of the Soviets, we had to show that we were at least keeping up. During the next Gemini flight, an astronaut would be asked to step out into the vacuum of space.

The space walk wasn't just PR. If an astronaut was going to walk on the moon, we had to establish that he could survive – and function – in space. There had been precious little testing for this, and the doctors had been furious.

The risks were enormous. Sally liked to enumerate them for me, the various paths to a quick death in the vacuum of space:

No air. No air, no oxygen; no oxygen, no life.

Cold. On the dark side of the earth, the cold can rip the skin off your bones.

Heat. On the sunny side, the skin burns like shrimp on the barbie.

But, in fact, the quickest killer would be the atmospheric pressure, or rather the lack thereof. Pressure keeps our bodies' gasses in solution. As every scuba diver knows, if the pressure diminishes quickly, the gasses come out of solution and form bubbles in the blood stream. This phenomenon is called 'the bends.' (You bend over in agony.) The bubbles, depending on their size and number, can block off blood vessels, causing anything from aches and pains to strokes and death. An astronaut suddenly exposed to the vacuum of space would experience the violent explosion of the air in his lungs and bowels.

Chief Dark Cloud! Sally was worse than the doctors!

Actually, she was in favor of the mission. It was just automatic for her to defend the doctors, and why not? She spoke their language.

"It's a good thing we know how to design spacesuits," I said. Not that I had any special knowledge of how well they'd work, but I had faith in our guys, and they lived up to it. The spacesuit engineers were some of the unsung heroes of the Apollo program. It wasn't easy to make something protective enough for such a harsh environment, yet flexible enough to allow motion at the joints. *And* resistant to micrometeorites.

The arguments at the upper levels went on and on, until the final word came down from Gilruth and company: "GO."

**

Lasting four days, this Gemini-Titan 4 mission would be the longest American mission to date. In fact, it would be longer than all prior missions put together. Consequently, the astronauts would have to worry not just about eating and peeing, but pooping too. Up until then the astronauts had been fed a low-residue diet for a couple of weeks, and they had then hoped for the best. Now, for the first time, an astronaut would potentially respond that he was "indisposed" when contacted by the CapCom at Mission Control. When you realize that in zero gravity anything squeezed out just stays put, you ... never mind.

From my point of view, the major event was the development of the round-the-clock shifts – three eight-hour shifts to be led by Chris Kraft (Red Team), John Hodge (Blue Team), and Gene Kranz (White Team). Marta sewed a white vest for Gene in honor of his team color. During the White Team's shift, Gene would now for the first time be called "Flight."

The CapCom at Mission Control would be rookie astronaut Roger Chaffee. Roger was bright and friendly, and he'd been assigned to study the Lunar Module. He wasn't likely to fly on any Gemini mission, but he'd probably fly on Apollo. For now, he would be one of the direct links between Mission Control and the astronauts in orbit.

Two of the newest recruits were tapped for this mission, Jim McDivitt and Ed White. They quickly set about naming their capsule *American Eagle*, but even more quickly, NASA shot it down.

Relentless in their desire to leave their mark, Jim and Ed came up with another idea: they would sew the American flag on their space suit. *That* idea actually appealed to NASA, and the American flag was thereafter *de rigueur* on every space suit.

White was one of the tallest and most athletic of the astronauts, and he was therefore chosen to be the space walker.

On June 3rd, White came to bat. After going through an endless checklist, the astronauts dropped the cabin pressure to zero, took a deep breath, and opened the hatch of the Gemini capsule. *Above them only sky.* White unfolded himself out of his seat, gathered up his umbilical cord, and stood up in the capsule. Appearing to work in slow motion, he eased himself out of the spacecraft ... and floated free. Feeling none of the effects of slicing through the sky at 17,000 miles per hour, he drifted around staring directly at the bejeweled firmament above and the gleaming blue orb below. White was supposed to stay out only twelve minutes, but he was having such a grand time that after a few moments he announced, "I'm not coming back in." When he was finally ordered back after twenty-three minutes, he said, "It's the saddest moment of my life."

At that moment, for the first time, I felt a twinge of envy. Floating in space – scuba diving and skydiving rolled into one. It must have been the ultimate thrill.

The fact is, White had no idea how close he was to never coming back in. Only one human before him had ever lived through a similar experience, and right about now Ed could have used some advice from him.

Leonov's space walk had been no cakewalk. The pressure differential between the inside of his suit and the vacuum outside had stiffened the suit to the point that he could barely bend his knees and elbows. More importantly, the suit ballooned so much that it blocked his return into the Soyuz capsule. He became overheated from exertion and then found himself stuck half in and half out of his spacecraft! Out of desperation, and on the verge of passing out, he opened a valve to let some air out of his suit, a move that could have instantly killed him. Exhausted, but alive, he collapsed into his seat.

His worries were not over: The capsule's automatic stabilization system failed, and Leonov and his fellow cosmonaut had to take over control of their capsule. This led to an extra orbit, and since each orbit takes a spacecraft over a different part of the earth, the cosmonauts landed 600 miles from their intended target. They ended up stuck in a Siberian fir tree, where they spent one long miserable night. A hungry bear tried for hours to get at them, making this Soyuz capsule the only spacecraft to return to its base marked by bear claws.

If only we'd known. The jokes, the morale boost! Sure, we would have felt sympathy for Leonov, but... bear claws. That would have put us in a fine mood. As far as we knew, however – and we only knew what the Soviets were willing to tell us – Leonov had carried out a successful space walk. End of story.

It was now White's turn to relive Leonov's nightmare. He was able to eventually cram himself in without opening any valves, but it was close.

It didn't seem to spoil his mood any.

We took a page out of the Soviet's book and announced a perfectly successful space walk. In fact, we had beautiful color pictures of both White floating in space and of Mother Earth below. Even Leonov didn't have any of those! To boot, for the first time we had an international audience, as the launch was broadcast to twelve European nations via the Early Bird satellite. Published around the world, these breathtaking pictures were a smash hit and contributed to the erroneous notion that the Americans had been the first to walk in space. Nobody at NASA was about to complain. It was about time we got a little recognition.

***

London, 12ᵗʰ June, 1965

Dear Dutch,

We were all in for a surprise today when Brian burst in excitedly. He triumphantly confirmed that the Beatles were to be the recipients of an MBE medal (Member of the British Empire).

We British have an entire list of Royal awards. The MBE is pretty much at the bottom, but it's a Royal award nonetheless! And why not? The Beatles have become super-salesman for everything British: British Jaguars, British Mini Coopers, British mini-skirts, British everything!

Predictably, the only one of us who isn't thrilled is John, who feels that, once again, the Beatles are selling out.

At the same time, John's the one most ticked off by the various veterans of war who now want to turn their medals in. "Cheapened," they say. John told the press that veterans got their medals for killing people, while the Beatles got theirs for entertaining. What was wrong with that? I'm guessing Tone *[Tony Barrow]* didn't get to screen that quote before it went out!

George piped in that any veteran who wanted to turn in his medal should send it directly to him, so that he could give it to Eppy. MBE, he joked, should stand for Mr. Brian Epstein. We all agreed. Brian was proud enough as it was, but a part of him longed to be with them receiving a medal. His dedication, perseverance, and gentleman's touch had been a big part of the Beatles' story. He confided to me that he wasn't given the award because he is homosexual and Jewish. At least that's how he sees it. I do feel sorry for him. Someone also brought up Pete Best's name. Poor Pete just can't escape. Every day, another reminder of what could have been.

In May the Beatles performed at the BBC for the last time; they've outgrown it.

You would think that as premier rock stars, Lennon and Harrison would be tripping the light fantastic. The two other Beatles certainly do. Paul and Jane make the rounds among the artistic and literary intelligentsia in swinging London, while Ringo and wife Maureen hobnob with the likes of Richard Burton and Liz Taylor. But George stays mostly in his estate, calling around to find out where his flirtatious girlfriend Pattie is, and as I think I told you, John is holed up at home with wife Cynthia. Decorated by Brian Epstein's interior designer, their home is a rather cold, forbidding mansion outside of London in Kenwood. John spends his time in the attic's music rooms, the only cozy rooms in the house. A little electric train set connects the various rooms and provides John with distractions. When he isn't upstairs in the music rooms, he lays on the couch doing this or that drug, much to Cynthia's horror. In an effort to improve their frosty relationship, she's partaken a few times, but these have all resulted in what they call bad trips; she's more a pint and a ciggie kind of bird. So she can only watch in dismay as John whittles away the hours in a drug-induced haze.

Every now and then, John pops out of his perpetual trance and goes to town with either myself or Tony Bramwell (the other Tony), one of Eppy's assistants. They hit one party then another, drop in on Mick Jagger and Keith Richards, who share a flat in London, and stay out 'til the wee hours. Then it's back to his Kenwood prison until a Beatles' engagement lures him out. It's no wonder that, when he sits down to compose, Lennon is no longer thinking in terms of 'boy meets girl.' It's more like "get me out of here!"

We thought we might tour Russia, Hungary, Poland, or one of the other Communist countries. Like the right wing in your country, the Communists think the Beatles will corrupt their youth, the difference being that the Communist governments have the power to ban all Beatle music. There is an underground, but it's way underground. People caught with Beatles records are in deep trouble. So we won't be touring Eastern Europe. Instead, this August we start another American tour. Only thirteen concerts in nine cities this time! We play the Sam Houston Coliseum on August 19th after stops in

New York, Toronto, and Atlanta. Hey, I know who Sam Houston was! Anyway, we can see each other then. If not, perhaps you could stop by the studio one day.

Yours,

Mal

Mal had been right about a number of things: *Help!* was indeed silly and it did not see the critical acclaim received by *A Hard Day's Night*. But many a part would qualify today as a music video. (The surrealistic snow scenes playing behind "Ticket to Ride" were the artistic highlight of the movie.) The title song was one of three Number One hits spawned by the (British) album of the same name. It had an urgency to it, consistent with the opening lyrics, "Help! I need somebody, help! not just anybody…" There were clean descending guitar arpeggios, courtesy of Harrison, and McCartney's background lyrics were out of phase with Lennon's, an original and very effective touch.

> *"and now I find*
> > and now I find, ….
> *my indep…*
> > my independence seems to…".

"Ticket to Ride" was a hit, as Mal had predicted, and had gone to the top of the charts in early May. On some levels it was a characteristic Beatle song, featuring Beatle harmonies and a little guitar riff that opens the song and repeats itself throughout. What set it apart from other Beatle songs and from other songs of the day, however, was the big, slow, heavy bass sound first heard on "She's A Woman."

"You've Got to Hide Your Love Away" was a poignant Lennon song with a pretty recorder-like instrumental, again revealing a down-in-the-dumps rock star. He had dipped his toe into the pool of unhappiness a year earlier with "I'll Cry Instead" ("I've got a chip…"), jumped in with "I'm a Loser," and was now completely wallowing in self-denigration.

But Mal completely missed the biggest song of the album. He wasn't alone. The song was relegated to the next-to-last spot on the record, one step above the raucous cover of Larry Williams' "Dizzy Miss Lizzy." The song in question has an unusual history: McCartney woke up with a tune in his head; he thought he'd heard it somewhere before, but maybe not. No one around him seemed to recognize it. He doodled with the lyrics. The song sat around for a while, and McCartney would periodically return to it. The beginning of the song called for a word with three syllables. "Scrambled eggs" would do at first. As it neared completion, the Beatles tried various arrangements with the usual drums and guitars and harmonies, but soon realized that the song would sound best with just an acoustic guitar. George Martin felt that a string section would be appropriate, though very unusual for a Beatle song. In the end, none of the Beatles other than McCartney participated in the recording. This was a first. Despite a lack of interest in England, Capitol demonstrated foresight for once when it released the song as a single in the U.S. It was a brilliant move. In addition to shooting up to Number One, it dispelled the notion that the Beatles' music was no more than shouting and wiggling.

The song was "Yesterday."

It's a pensive song about a paradise lost, sung in simple, unadorned fashion with just a twinge of regret as if the singer were leafing through an old photo album. Contrary to Lennon's recent works, this song was not autobiographical in the least. The twenty-three year old McCartney had imagined a person completely unlike himself, tapping into the emotions of an older, wizened man whose life has gone wrong. The song would become one of McCartney's many signature songs. Perhaps more importantly, it opened up the Beatles to an entirely new audience – the over-thirty generation[9].

The spring of '65 saw the return of the Rolling Stones. There would always be those who preferred their raw, angry image, and the Stones would become the Beatles' closest rivals. Behind the rivalry, however, lay a basic friendship from the top down: Rolling Stone producer Andrew Loog Oldham, for example, was Brian Epstein's friend. This would

---

9   "Yesterday" was recorded on June 14th 1965 during a remarkable studio session that also included McCartney's blazing vocal on the frenetic "I'm Down." The juxtaposition of two such disparate vocal performances is likely to have few equals in the history of recorded music.

lead to an unusual agreement, whereby the Beatles and the Rolling Stones would alternate releases so as not to compete with each other.

The music scene was not *all* about the Beatles and the Rolling Stones, only mostly.

Still breaking new ground alongside the Beatles was Bob Dylan, the anti-singer, anti-hero, whose hyper nasal voice would have been impossible to listen to but for the extraordinary lyrics and clever melodies. He was part poet, part activist, and you just had to notice. If you were over a certain age, you stared at your record player to see where the problem might be. If you were young, you thought he saw around corners.

A folk/gospel band, the Byrds, thought they could do better than the master. And in some ways, they did. Using the same twelve-string electric Rickenbacker guitar that George Harrison played, their leader, Roger McGuinn, together with future star David Crosby (Crosby, Stills and Nash) created a smooth, harmonious version of Dylan's "Mr. Tambourine Man," releasing it even before Dylan himself. It was an instant success.

****

I recently came across the following memorandum dated August 14th, 1965, and signed by NASA's James Webb:

> When we are dealing with matters, which affect the way elements of these programs are viewed in many different countries by many different nationalities, we cannot leave to the crew the decision with respect to these matters of individuality.
>
> In this case … I have a very strong concern about the "8 days or bust" motto. I wish it could be omitted. If the flight does not go 8 days, there are many who are going to say that it was "busted." Further, whether we get the 8 days or not, the way the language will be translated in certain countries will not be to the benefit of the United States.

This brought back to mind another Cooper imbroglio: Gordon Cooper and Pete Conrad, the astronauts selected for Gemini V, had hit upon the idea of a mission patch. It wasn't completely original; every Navy air squadron had one, but it would be novel for an astronaut. Since the mission was scheduled to last a record eight days, Gordo and Pete designed a patch with a pioneer's wagon and the motto "Eight Days or Bust."

Wherefore Webb's memo. The whole idea of a custom patch went directly against the spirit of depersonalization that Webb was looking for.

Strike three (or was it four?) against Gordo.

NASA compromised. The covered wagon was OK; the motto had to go. NASA followed up Webb's memorandum with a list of criteria and guidelines for these so-called Cooper patches. For all the grief he got, Cooper had actually started a trend. But it would be a Pyrrhic victory.

At 5'6", Pete Conrad was the shortest astronaut and also the funniest. I loved working with him. He and Gordo were a nutty pair. Contrary to Gordo, though, Pete could tweak people without ever causing major flaps.

In addition to setting an endurance record, Gemini V would be the first mission to use a fuel cell, a self-replenishing battery based on the chemical reaction between oxygen and hydrogen (H_2 + O = water + electricity).

As the launch date rolled around, so did rapidly moving storm clouds. While Cooper and Conrad sat in their capsule, a bolt of lighting suddenly knocked out power to the entire pad. All arms in Mission Control went up simultaneously in despair. The Mission would have to be scrubbed – and yet danger remained.

This was a replay of the four-inch flight from a few years back. We had a fully loaded rocket sitting on a launch pad, with two astronauts at the top of the hot booster and lightning flashing all around. There was no question of just waiting things out this time. We had to get the astronauts out. There was only one problem: lightning had knocked out the gantry and its elevator.

Eventually we located a cherry picker and plucked out the astronauts.

The weather was more propitious the following day; we had an effortless launch, followed by a smooth couple of orbits.

On the third orbit, Cooper's breath went out of him as he noted a severe drop in the fuel cells' oxygen pressure. Just as suddenly, the cells ceased to function outright. Naturally, at that particular point, Gemini V was flying in one of the communication dead zones.

Cooper made the only decision he could: he powered down the capsule, leaving on just the bare essentials.

And waited. He'd been through this before.

The capsule was now in a drift mode – and so it drifted for what seemed an eternity.

Cooper sat there thinking of the corners that were being cut in the name of the artificial timetable set by a President, now long gone. For better and for worse, this quest to get to the moon had become the crucible of American know-how. *And* we were in a race with the Soviets. Worse even than not landing on the moon by January 1st, 1970, there was the specter of the Commies getting there first and winning what had unofficially become the ultimate prize. Consequently, standard engineering tests were being chopped out to meet the deadline. Cooper himself had suggested testing the fuel cells at low pressure – an idea nixed by Bob Gilruth. He wondered sourly how Gilruth would now handle sitting in his seat, drifting through space in a faulty capsule. Political decisions were coming home to roost.

Gordo was finally able to come in touch with a relay station, and we instantly went into high gear. There were only two options: aborting the mission and bringing the capsule back to earth, or allowing the capsule to drift a while longer, while a solution could be found. Aborting the mission would prove a serious embarrassment, a colossal loss of money, and a major setback to our goal of reaching the moon by the end of the decade. Still, if NASA failed to bring the capsule down in a timely manner and the astronauts lost their life, the repercussions could be even greater.

Heads. Tails. Heads. Tails.

As we debated the issue, the astronauts noted that the pressure in the fuel cells had leveled off. It remained dangerously low, but did not seem to be going any lower.

Mission Control decided to allow Cooper and Conrad one more orbit.

It was the right choice: The astronauts discovered a problem with a heater, which they fixed. The fuel cells came back to life. Score another for those who believed in *manned* space missions.

On the fifth day of the mission, Gemini V broke the duration record for a space flight, a record previously set by the Soviets.

This record came at a price for Cooper, who was still longer on piloting skills than on people skills. The capsule was cramped, and every conceivable object literally floated about. Cooper and Conrad were constantly packing and unpacking; the simplest chores took forever. Cooper got testy. At some point Dr. Berry asked him if he was getting any exercise. (He was supposed to exercise with a bungee-type cord.) He answered along the lines of, "I hold Pete's hand once in a while; I use the cleansing towel when I pinch off a bowel movement, and every now and then I chew gum." Dr. Berry didn't say anything, but I distinctly remember how he bit his lower lip as he turned towards Kraft.

On the piloting front, things couldn't have gone more smoothly. The Apollo capsule and the lunar module would one day have to meet up in space (rendezvous) and physically link (dock). In order to rendezvous, the astronauts would need to change orbits to match the orbit of their target.

No astronaut had ever done this before.

Cooper and Conrad fired their thrusters, and behold! They had switched from a circular to an elliptical orbit. It was indeed possible.

The astronauts had been told of a meteorite shower that would pass within view of the capsule. They would be the first humans to witness this from space. Of course this front row view could turn deadly if a meteorite wandered into the capsule's path.

And then it happened.

BANG!!!

It reverberated through Mission Control like a cannon shot across a valley. The astronauts reported no obvious damage. It was concluded that a meteorite the size of a grain of sand had probably struck the capsule. A grain of sand flying at 30,000 miles per hour! And with energy being proportional to *mass x velocity²*, that's a heck of punch!

Along the lines of multiplying a tiny number by a large one, Gemini V landed a hundred or so miles short of its target. The reason was somewhat arcane: NASA engineers entered into their calculations an earth rotation of 360 degrees in a twenty-four hour period. Earth, however, rotates 359.999 degrees per twenty fours, a tiny difference except when multiplied by 120 orbits. Had Cooper not expertly altered the descent of the capsule, Gemini V would have landed 250 miles short of its target in the Atlantic Ocean. As it was, the rescue was flawless. All it took was a regiment of twenty-eight ships, 135 aircraft, and 10,000 people. I was glad not to be involved with *those* communications!

We'd come a long way from the Instamatic® camera. Gemini V carried *twenty* different cameras and assorted types of film. One camera featured an enormous telephoto lens; from outer space you could photograph a license plate. I was particularly intrigued to find out what those pictures would show.

They were confiscated.

Cooper in particular was incensed. He spoke directly to Lyndon Johnson.

"*I* ordered them classified," said the President.

And that was that.

Putting together various bits of information, Cooper and I decided that some of the pictures were probably too revealing, specifically the pictures of Area 51 high up in the Nevada desert, a top top-secret area, off limits even to the highest level test pilots.

Extra-terrestrial research, for sure.

Given his prior experiences with UFOs, Cooper was particularly intrigued – perhaps too much so for his own good. Following his chat with Lyndon Johnson, Cooper was never again assigned a mission within the Apollo program. Cooper probably wasn't going anywhere anyhow, but this was great fodder for the UFO conspiracy buffs. I'd have to run it by Mal.

Obscured by this little sideshow was the fact that the mission had been very successful. When Gemini V broke the record for longevity in space, it was the first "first" for an American mission. NASA never looked back. We would be first in every important category from this moment on, all the way through the Apollo program.

***

London, 10ᵗʰ October, 1965

Dear Dutch,

"Yesterday" made it to #1 in America? I hadn't seen that one coming. It wasn't released as a single here.

Sorry you weren't free the one day I was in Houston! You say they don't let you out when a mission is imminent? But there's always a mission!

Who am I to talk? No one around the Beatles sees the light of day. It's a plane, a hotel, a concert, a studio recording, an interview, a movie, another studio recording, another concert. It doesn't end.

I have two big memories of our American tour:

On 15 August, we're in New York. We get into a giant helicopter with one huge propeller up front and another in the back, and we fly over a baseball stadium. The pilot swoops around once "so we can get a really good look." (George and I are just about passed out from fright.) As we come down low, thousands of flashbulbs go off — all these kids with their cameras. We land near the stadium, get into an armored car, and now we are IN THIS ENORMOUS STADIUM! The noise is phenomenal. The boys are pumped! They have never played in such a big place in front of so many people[10]. They play a bloody fantastic set, perhaps the best I'd ever seen them play. Paul's spinning around on himself, John's running his elbow up and down the little keyboard, it's sticky hot, they're sweating like crazy, they're laughing, they're hooting, they're hollering (in harmony, of course), and generally having a grand 'ole time. They unplug their guitars, Paul waves his bass guitar high in the air, and we're off.

As we left Shay [Shea] stadium, we all agreed that this had been the most fun concert ever. My ears were ringing for hours.

My second memory is that of L.A.

---

10   nor had any other musical act.

Every movie star, past, present, and future was there to see and be seen with the Beatles.

And then...

It was arranged that we would meet Elvis. THE Elvis. My childhood hero. We all idolized him. The Beatles had tried to meet him before, but been brushed off, which they didn't take too badly; he is the KING after all! The meeting would take place at his home. (The word "home" is an under-statement.) First, it would be just the boys and Elvis, no press, no nothing. Colonel Parker, his manager, said he would be there, so naturally Brian said he would too. Elvis' handlers would have to be there, so Neil and I had to go. Before you knew it, it was all of his guys and all of our guys.

You're going to love this: We get lost on the way there (no surprise), and the boys, enjoying their usual illegal substances in the backseat, seem to have completely forgotten that we're going to see Elvis! They're making jokes like dafties back there, while I'm hoping they aren't completely off their heads. When we pull up at the gates, Paul goes, "Oh yeah, we're going to see Elvis," and they fall out of the car laughing.

They got their nerves back at the door. Elvis was wearing a red shirt and skinny grey pants. The boys and Elvis plopped themselves down in a big living room. And I mean BIG. There were pool tables right there in the room! I don't know if that's normal in America, but that blew us away. One of the pool tables even turned into a craps table. And then there was the biggest telly I think we'd ever seen — and in color! The colors weren't very natural, but who cares? Then the coup de grace: one of Elvis' boys would say, "watch, I'm going to say abracadabra, and the channel is going to change — and we'd hear a click and the channel had changed. He did that a few times. The trick? A little box with buttons. You push a button and the channel changes. I want one!

Here they are, the biggest star of the '50s with the biggest stars of the '60s. (Too bad Frank Sinatra wasn't there to represent the '40s!) They chitchat about touring and concerts, and the conversation seems to be petering out. Someone had the brilliant idea to bring out some guitars. Paul sat at a piano. Elvis grabbed a bass guitar, which seemed a little strange. Paul liked that. He could perhaps exchange a few bass riffs with the King. Elvis can't sing and play bass simultaneously (score one for Paul,

I thought), so he switched to a regular guitar and sang one of his songs. George and John showed him how to play "I Feel Fine."

At around 10 PM, Priscilla was brought out for a few minutes and then taken away. Paul thinks Elvis was afraid one of them would make a pass at her, which even the Beatles would never dare. Maybe he just didn't want her around.

After a few more songs, the evening ran out of steam. Elvis isn't much of a conversationalist. Perhaps he's shy, perhaps he's not very articulate, perhaps he felt threatened. Who knows? Maybe he didn't think the Beatles were that interesting or funny or articulate either. The boys shot a few sideways glances at each other, and I announced that it was time to go. On the way out John shouted, "Long live the King," as he dove into the limo.

For me, it was a jolly good day! (I don't think Elvis will miss the little ashtray.)

As I left the studio on Friday, Paul and John were still babbling over *Highway '61*, Bob Dylan's new album. To me, although the lyrics are always stimulating, the songs tend to drag on. Dylan could use Paul and George Martin for a little production! But John and Paul are quite excited. They argued a bit over who would take it home. John won.

The two of them have gotten into a bit of a routine now: Paul goes out to John's house in the suburbs and they hammer out a song. One of them usually has an idea for a song, and they then throw lyrics and chords at each other until the song's finished. Sometimes the melody's nearly complete before they even have the first lyric. That happened to Paul last year with "Yesterday," and that's what just happened with a new song called "Drive my Car." Other times it's the reverse. John recently wrote a song in which he goes down memory lane, and thinks of places he's been to and how they've changed and what they mean to him. Paul helped with a couple of the lines, after which they set it to music.

We go back to the studio in October. EMI expects us to have an album out by Christmas...

Yours,

Mal

****

On September 20th, we announced the crew for Gemini 8: Decorated combat aviator and X-15 test pilot Neil Armstrong *(did I mention that he went to Purdue?)* and Air Force Captain Dave Scott. I've heard it expressed through the years that NASA knew all along that they wanted Armstrong to be the first man on the moon, and that the crew rotations were manipulated to give Armstrong the best shot. There was, however, absolutely nothing at this point to suggest that NASA thought more highly of Armstrong than the others. On the contrary. While Dave Scott was the first of his group to be picked for a prime crew, Armstrong was the last. Borman, Lovell, White, McDivitt, Conrad, Stafford, and Young all flew before him.

It was time to address the third and fourth goals of the Gemini program: rendezvous and docking. Wally Schirra and Tom Stafford were tapped for this next Gemini mission. The mission would require superior piloting abilities, and NASA had all along seen Wally Schirra as the ideal candidate. Seconding him would be the amiable and equally talented Tom Stafford from the second group of astronauts. Having been assigned to Communications, Stafford had spent quite some time with me, and I had loved every minute. A smile always creased his broad face, and the peculiar hoarseness in his voice identified him anywhere within earshot. He had been an Air Force test pilot and instructor, and had a résumé filled with pilot heroics. In fact, he'd instructed fellow astronauts Borman and McDivitt. He was bright enough to have been accepted to the Harvard Business School, where he'd been enrolled all of three days before suddenly getting the nod from NASA.

The mission would be simple in concept, though infinitely more difficult in its execution: An unmanned Atlas rocket would be sent into orbit shortly before Gemini VI; the top stage, dubbed Agena, had been outfitted with a docking mechanism. Gemini VI would chase it down, meet up with it, and then dock.

For linkage to take place, generally speaking, two spacecraft must orbit in the same plane. Their orbits can be circular or elliptical; both capsules can be in a circular orbit, both can be in an elliptical orbit, or one can be in an elliptical orbit and the other in a circular orbit. A great deal of fuel is expended when a capsule needs to move right or left. The entire maneuvering fuel of the Gemini capsule, for example, would be used up to move the craft just one mile. Due to the earth's rotation, a delay of only one second would put a second capsule three miles too far to the left, and any rendezvous would be impossible. The timing of the second launch relative to the first therefore had to be perfect.

On the morning of October 25th, the Agena-Atlas rocket took off. A few miles to the north, on Pad 19, Schirra and Stafford readied themselves for their own blastoff. It was Tom's first flight and he was naturally a little edgy. His heart rate said so.

For Schirra, it had been three years exactly since his first and only venture into space; he was itching to get back into it. Flying in drift mode might have been fun, but no piloting skills had been required. As for changing orbits the way Cooper had just done, well, big deal... Changing orbits and speeds so precisely that you could align perfectly with another craft and oh so gently dock with it at 17,000 miles per hour, now THAT was piloting. And he was psyched. Finally, a chance to...

UH-OH !!!!

There were suddenly no telemetry readings from the Agena. Location, speed... nothing.

"Canary Islands, do you have Agena?"

"Negative"

We waited for the Agena to pass over the Carnavon (Australia) tracking station.

No joy.

The damned thing had probably exploded shortly after its separation from the Atlas.

We all kept our distance from Schirra as he climbed out of Gemini. Talk about all dressed up with nowhere to go!

There was no other Agena to send up. It would take months to manufacture a new one. What could Gemini VI possibly hook up with?

**

The Singing Wheel was a watering hole a mile west of the Center on Highway 3. In both success and defeat it was a favorite among flight controllers. Its particular feature was a slanted floor, the angle so steep that you couldn't lean back in your chair without risking a major egg on the back of your noggin. Nelson Bland, the owner, didn't need to be told whether it was a day to celebrate or a day to forget. If we came in quietly he knew. And he also knew well enough to discreetly keep a running tab...

Today was a day to lick our wounds with the help of a couple of Lone Star beers. The failure of the mission represented months of lost time. The problems with the Agena hadn't been our doing at Mission Control, but of course any failure reflects on the entire team.

The ray of sunshine, the *deus ex machina*, suddenly came from McDonnell's senior management. Why not have Gemini VI hook up with the Gemini VII capsule, which was due to launch in a couple of months? Gemini VII Commander Frank Borman had no intention of playing fender to Schirra's flying bumper car and quickly vetoed the idea. The concept, however, remained intriguing. It was decided that the two crafts would rendezvous, but not dock. The concept of a four-American rendezvous was very appealing to NASA. This was something else to beat the Soviets with. Less than three days after the Agena failure, President Johnson announced the plan to the American public. Seizing on the two numbers, the Press breathlessly dubbed this "*The Spirit of '76.*"

Wow, four astronauts, two spacecraft, what joy, what excitement!!! What a horror. I hated it.

How was I going to communicate with *two* spacecraft? One was bad enough. Should we have two separate CapComs? A different call signal for each craft? Teletype for one, real-time for the other? At some point I stopped whining, and we figured it out.

There were logistical issues, such as how to send up two rockets within a short period of time. We had gotten into the rhythm of sending up a manned rocket every couple of months, but now the two would have to be fired within nine days of each other. Preparing a launch pad was time-consuming, and we would have the added stress of monitoring Gemini VII up in space while getting Gemini VI ready for launch.

Guys were pulling double shifts, and this was bound to fray some nerves. Having overslept one morning, John Llewellyn raced to Mission Control in his Triumph, only to find all the parking spaces taken. He drove his car onto the walkway, across the grass, and up the front steps.

No, he wasn't congratulated, he had his parking privileges revoked. Determined to have the last word, he next came in on horseback.

It was a slightly incongruous sight at a Space Center.

****

According to Mal, November 11th saw a marathon recording session. The deadline for the next Beatle album was upon them, and they were still three songs short. Going with just eleven songs was unthinkable; twelve and thirteen wouldn't do: seven songs to a side, no more, no less. The Beatles first resurrected "Wait" from the *Help!* sessions.

Paul created "You Won't See Me."

John dreamt up "Girl," showing once again that he who hated schedules and commitments actually wrote some of his best material under the pressure of a deadline.

The sessions remained light-hearted throughout and were filled with continuous, absurd banter. Mal recalled:

It's the most fun when one of the guys screws up — sings a wrong note or flubs a chord. The others all gang up on him in mock anger. They take on every possible tone and accent. Sometimes I have trouble keeping up! The other day they were working on George's "Think For Yourself." John couldn't get the harmonies. First he couldn't get the three notes in "close our eyes." He sang it in every which way, never getting it right, much to the amusement of the others. George Martin just waited patiently. (He's good at that.) Then John tried just humming the melody "dum dum-dum," at which point he realized that these were the same notes that start off "Yesterday." Well, that started them on a wild version of "Yesterday" the likes of which you would not believe.

John finally gets it, but now he's having trouble with the line "and you've got time to rectify all those things that you should."

After a few takes, Paul intones in a school teacher's voice, "OK, let's take it from the top and run it!" John flubs it again, but before anyone can say anything, he jumps up and starts gesticulating like a mad revivalist preacher. "It's Jesus, our Lord and Savior who gave his only begotten bread for us to live and die on. And that's why we're all here, and I'll tell you brethren: There's more of them than there are of us! And that's a-why

180

there are so few of us left!" John's got an audience; even George Martin is smiling. He barrels on, "Condemn thou the thoughts of man!!!"

Still in the school teacher mode, Paul yells out, "Look! Terence, if you want to resign from the amateur dramatics, do!" John slips into one of his favorite roles, the prim spinster. He flutters his eyelashes, "Oh I'm so sorry, I feel so stupid," he whimpers, "I don't know what to do." Even Ringo jumps in: "That's crap, John" he bellows after another failed attempt at the harmony. John curses and looks down at him from over his glasses. "I will be pleased to see the earthman disintegrated." In mock hysteria Paul implores his mates, "I can't go on, I really can't. Come on, let's do this bleeding record!" They still don't get it right. "Just what key are you in, Jack????" Paul blurts out to John.

George good-naturedly sings the line for John.

John takes a break. He goes to the lavatory singing, "do you want to hold a penis?" to the tune of "Do You Want To Know a Secret?"

When he gets back, they run through the line again, a capella this time. John nails it. Paul springs off his sitting stool. "That's it!!!!!!" John takes on his deep American voice, "you should'a gotten me then, boy, I was movin'..."

On another note Paul's completely taken over George's song "I Want To Tell You." It's a humdrum song to which Paul's added a musical intro (it's becoming his specialty), a harmony that's nearly louder than the melody, and of course a clever bass line. And what do you know, an everyday song produced into another little Beatle jewel.

I'll be curious to hear what you think!

Mal

****

Of all the Gemini flights on the drawing board, one was going to be a horrible bore for the unfortunate astronauts. And that would be the (un)lucky Gemini VII mission. It was important to confirm that astronauts could tolerate a one to two week stay in space, since that would be the duration of the moon missions. Gemini VII was therefore scheduled to be a flat-out endurance run. Two weeks, to be specific.

Frank Borman and Jim Lovell drew the lucky assignment. Actually, as space virgins, they were thrilled to draw any Gemini assignment.

Lovell was my type of guy. He was just as capable as Borman (he'd graduated first from the Naval test pilot school, in the same class as Conrad and Schirra), but he had a more easy-going manner and a good sense of humor. His nickname was "Lucky" for the scraps he'd gotten himself in and out of. His most famous misadventure dated back to his days as a Navy pilot.

On the way back from a nighttime training run off the coast of Japan, he had gotten separated from his squadron by a thick layer of clouds. He locked onto the pre-arranged radio signal, only to realize too late that he'd actually locked onto a Japanese airbase a long ways off. Out over the icy Sea of Japan, under an inky sky, running out of fuel, he desperately needed to get back to his aircraft carrier, the *Shangri-La*. As much as he squinted, however, he couldn't decipher the tiny lettering on his maps. It was time to put to use one of his inventions, a little penlight that would plug right into his instrument panel. The result was as unexpected as it was unfortunate: A short-circuit of *all* the lights, including those that illuminated the instrument panel. He was now in total darkness, screeching along at five hundred miles an hour ... and seriously lost.

Pondering his misfortune and anticipating the slow death that would come with ditching the plane, parachuting into the waters, and then either being eaten by a shark or dying of hypothermia, Lovell's eyes gradually acclimated themselves to the darkness. Suddenly, he noted green phosphorescence below. It was laid out in a straight line.

The wake of the carrier!

Lovell followed the trail until he could make out the lights of the ship. He placed the penlight in his mouth to get a vague view of the dials dancing in front of him.

Now came the hairiest part: landing on that tiny, bobbing landing strip without a clear view of his instruments. It was hard enough when you had full control of your plane!

As he swooped down towards the carrier, Lovell suddenly noted a red light below him and off to the left. What other boat or air... his WING!!! He was seeing the reflection of his wing off the water! He was skimming the waves and headed right for the stern of the ship!!!

"Pull up, November Papa One, PULL UP!!!" he heard them yell in his headset.

The engines screamed in pain as he violently jerked the plane towards the sky, narrowly avoiding the *Shangri-La*.

On his second pass, he had the opposite problem.

"You're way high November Papa One, WAY HIGH!"

The hell with it, he thought. Dropping like a stone, he thundered onto the deck and blew two tires, the tail hook catching the last cable and bringing the plane to a violent stop.

"You won't believe what just happened to me…"

Applying to NASA the first time around, he had made the first cut but hadn't made the final round. He wasn't going to be one of the Mercury 7. He had tried again in '62 and this time he'd been successful. Now here he was, about to stay in space longer than any human ever had.

Liftoff was set for December 4th. The thrill of a lifetime for Borman and Lovell! Tedium, however, soon set in.

They were glued to a space about as big as the front of a sports car. Some sports car! This vehicle was a dull grey without so much as a fiery decal, and you couldn't even feel the speed. There were no in-flight movies.

There was also the small issue of having to eat, pee, poop, work, sleep, and exercise in their seat for two straight weeks. Fun! There might not have been any gravity in space, but there sure was odor.

Occasionally they could peel off their spacesuits. Only one of the two needed to be suited up at any given time; but getting in and out of the suit was a major endeavor. Houdini would have sweated!

**

December 12th, 1965.

As Gemini VII passes high over Florida, Schirra and Stafford are strapped down below in Gemini VI, ready for blastoff. As the countdown approaches zero, neither astronaut is nervous. They just want to get the show on the road. Their rendezvous target is approaching directly overhead.

10…9…8…7…6…5…4…3…2…1…

Liftoff !!!

No. Wait!

The engines have shutdown!

"No liftoff! No liftoff!" I yell.

Wally has only to pull the D-ring to eject them the hell out of there before the Titan explodes.

But all is quiet.

The shutdown has taken place during the two-second "kill" phase that starts with ignition. The hold-downs haven't released, and the Titan is still attached to the gantry.

Schirra has sat tight.

Good move.

Nobody has great confidence in these ejector seats, especially at low altitude.

Back goes the erector to fetch the two astronauts. Not ejected, but certainly dejected. Wally's not talking.

Flocking like locust, the engineers quickly identify the problem as a failure to remove a dust cap from some widget within the motor. A gazillion dollars to ready this rocket and it's all about a dust cap. Years later, another 10 cent piece of equipment, an O-ring, would take the life of the Challenger Space Shuttle crew. But today, we are lucky in our bad luck. There are no fatalities.

Gemini VII was up there for the long haul, so Gemini VI would get another bite at the apple.

Three days later Schirra and Stafford were off into space.

Finally some visitors! Borman and Lovell were thrilled. It was now day eleven of their mission, and they'd gone through each other's jokes many times over.

Gemini VI (now re-baptized Gemini VI-A, or GT-6A) was flying in a slightly lower orbit than expected. As unfortunate as this might have been for the Slide Rules who planned and calculated these things, the suboptimal position of the capsule immediately offered Schirra an opportunity to strut his stuff. Some directions were coming from Mission Control – a three second burn here, a one second burn there – but this was piloting!

278 miles from its target, Gemini VI-A's radar locked onto GT-7. The hunt was on. From thirty miles away, flying in total darkness over the Indian Ocean, the crew of GT-6A caught the lights that had been added to the shell of GT-7 specifically for this purpose. As GT-6A

nosed forward within a mile of its target, both spacecraft burst into sunlight. Little by little, the distance between the two capsules narrowed until the two spacecraft, moving faster than a rifle bullet, were flying side by side.

Schirra and Stafford were in for a bit of shock: Borman and Lovell had grown beards. But of course: they'd been up there without shaving for eleven days!

Deciding to liven things up a bit, Schirra and Stafford produced a "Beat Army" sign to tease Borman, the West Point grad. This was photographed and was a big hit back on earth.

Astronaut humor!

Then we were in for another surprise. Schirra suddenly announced that his radar was showing an object coming from the North.

Another object? From the North?

An object circling the earth in a north-south direction is said to be in polar orbit. There were no such satellites that we knew of.

Was this a Russian object?

President Johnson needed to call Moscow urgently. Time was of the essence.

"How far away?" I asked.

I then heard a very unusual sound in my headset. Could it be? Yes, they were jingles. Jingle bells!

"Ho Ho Ho," Schirra bellowed.

Ha Ha Ha. The joke was on us. Yes, Christmas was near.

So near yet so far for poor Borman and Lovell. For while Schirra and Stafford returned to earth shortly after their little get-together, Borman and Lovell still had three days to go. Three *looooong* days to go.

The ability to get a spacecraft to chase another within touching distance was a *major* technological advance. It was a true engineering first, and Jerry Bostick in Mission Control celebrated by handing out American flags. Considering how far behind we'd been just a short while ago, it was a proud moment for America.

**

It was time for the Japanese fable to make its appearance again.

Although just over a year away, the first manned flight of the Apollo capsule needed a formal crew assignment.

Because the capsule would no more than circle the earth a few times – a shakedown cruise, so to speak – there was no need for more than one veteran astronaut. Deke selected Gus to be the commander. The other two would be the rookies Roger Chaffee and Donn Eisele.

The announcement had Donn Eisele practically tap dancing.

Then, just before Christmas, Donn hurt his shoulder during a zero-g simulation flight. Nothing dramatic, but enough to keep him out of training a couple of months. Deke slipped a happy Ed White into his slot.

Donn's face was three feet long. How unlucky could he be? Or was he?

****

Rubber Soul was the second Beatles album I actually went out and bought myself. I must have felt rich that day and figured I could spring for the $2.50. I didn't want to wait three weeks until Christmas. The cover was intriguing. No smiling faces. All brown and black colors, but at least it was somewhat artistic. The four Beatles were stretched out like El Grecos. Mal would later clarify the choice of this photograph: the album-sized box onto which the Beatles' pictures were being projected suddenly tipped backwards, therefore elongating their faces. "That's it!" they'd all shouted. They loved the distortion, and thus it was. None of them are looking at the camera except for John, who's got a wry, sardonic grin on his face, like he knows something wicked, but he's not going to tell you. His hair is so long that it curls up at the bottom like a girl's. I didn't much care for that.

The title of the American album was the same as that of its British counterpart (released concurrently for once), but as usual, the song selection would be different. Paul had invented the title, a double, perhaps triple entendre. He'd heard musicians talk about phony soul, plastic soul – white musicians trying their hand at American soul music. Plastic soul became *Rubber Soul*. The lettering on the album was twisted into a rococo style that would soon be representative of the sixties.

The first song of an album generally sets the tone, and Capitol Records in the U.S. made a bold choice: they discarded "Drive my Car," the amusing, foot-tapping lead song from the British album, and in its stead transposed from the British edition of the *Help!* album the song "I've Just Seen a Face," a country-folk ballad with gentle, spiraling acoustic guitar riffs. And indeed, there would be nothing to twist and shout about the rest of the way. Capitol USA had decided to highlight the Beatles folk-rock, introspective side. In another era this might have been called "Beatles Unplugged." It marked the end of the "early Beatles," and depending on one's taste in music, it signaled the end – or the beginning – of the true Beatles genius.

"Norwegian Wood" was Lennon's rendering of a complex affair with an imaginary woman (an amalgam of the many he'd had). Not only would this bird not let him sleep with her (he "… crawled in the bath"), but in the morning he'd woken up to find that "this bird has flown." Eager to try new instruments, the Beatles had added to the soundtrack Harrison's new toy, the sitar. Mal said the studio was full of odd instruments, and the Beatles tried them all. Studio 2 had turned into a music laboratory. Every permutation of instrument and gadget seemed worth a try. On "Think For Yourself" McCartney had plugged his bass guitar through a fuzz box and loved it. I paid particular attention to the harmonies on this song, especially of course when it came to "close our eyes" and "you've got time to rectify all those things." What was so hard?

In a beautiful collaboration between McCartney and Lennon, the Beatles had set to music Lennon's nostalgic recollection of days gone by – perhaps Lennon's answer to McCartney's "Yesterday." "There are places I remember …" sang Lennon in "In My Life." The words had come to him fully formed in a dream. He didn't so much write the song as channel it *(what a gift!)*. McCartney wrote most of the music, this being one of the rare occasions where Lennon and McCartney conformed to their stereotypes – Lennon writing the lyrics and McCartney the music. George Martin added a little jewel of baroque piano in the middle of the song. He couldn't play it as fast as he wanted to, so he recorded it slowly and sped up the tape; a harbinger of things to come.

The lyrics to "The Word" also offered a peek into the future, though the merry melody could make you overlook the words completely. The love Lennon sang about was no longer physical love. This was no longer the physical love expressed in the "She Loves You" days. This was the cosmic *Love* and one-ness of the universe that Lennon had discovered through pot, acid, and, Mal would say, Stonehenge; a love difficult to express in words, but which could perhaps be communicated through song. This discovery had been an epiphany for Lennon, and in typical fashion he was now outright evangelical: "Now that I know what I feel must be right I'm here to show everybody the light." This was the first song he'd ever written with a specific message. From here on in, eager listeners would be scouring his songs for messages, whether they existed or not.

Mal was proud to inform me that on "The Word" he plays a few chords on the Hammond organ. (Multi-tracking, as we know it today, did not exist. Sometimes an extra hand was needed.) "Movie star, rock musician, what next?" he wrote.

The love ballad of the album was McCartney's "Michelle." Opening with a simple descending guitar lick, the song quickly turns into a lilting ballad with a twist of French. Within a month of *Rubber Soul's* release, twenty different artists had covered "Michelle"! The Beatles themselves never released it as a single – one of the many classic Beatle tunes never released in such a manner.

As popular as *Rubber Soul* would be, none of the songs from the album would be heard on the radio; not "Norwegian Wood," not "Girl," not "Michelle." FM radio did not yet broadcast rock'n'roll, and AM only played Top 40 hits.

Not that there was any lack of Beatle music on the air. Coinciding with the release of *Rubber Soul*, Capitol released a Double A single – a song for AM radio on both sides. Capitol couldn't decide which was the stronger of the two songs and had decided that both songs should be considered for airplay. One song featured a killer guitar lick starting on the lowest note you can play on a guitar, courtesy of John Lennon, and the other highlighted a clear-cut blending of the Lennon and McCartney styles, with McCartney writing and singing the verse, and Lennon the bridge. These were "Day Tripper" and "We Can Work It Out," respectively. Being partial to the guitar, I went with "Day Tripper." They'd had to change the lyrics from "she's a cock teaser…" to "she's a big teaser…" but we all got the message. The boys could no longer be accused of being cutesy.

Sally went for the urgent but gentle conflict and resolution of "we can work it out." Between the two songs, you really couldn't go wrong.

**

London, 10ᵗʰ December, 1965

Dear Dutch,

It's been ages since we've had any kind of time off. The last time we had more than one free day was back in '62! Since then we've been in the studio, on the road, at the press conference, on the movie set, in front of the telly cameras, at the BBC radio, and God knows where else, every f...'in minute of every week. We've been passed through hotels, stuffed into limos, thrown into armored trucks, not to mention plucked, picked, and pummeled by hysterical fans.

Finally, it looks like we have some free time to look forward to. After this British tour, that is. Ringo and I plan on hitting a few pubs, though pubs aren't the only places we're getting our minds twisted these days. It started with the boys' dentist. I don't suppose I've told you about him. Did you notice that John no longer has a chipped tooth? You probably haven't looked that closely. All the boys have been spiffed up a bit, dentally speaking — can't show your face on American telly with British teeth, doncha know! Some time ago we were at a party hosted by said dentist, when the bloke dropped LSD (a.k.a. lysergic acid) into our coffee. Nothing happened for a while, but then WOW! Everything became distorted. We went to a nightclub, and a little red light in the lift caused John to start yelling, "the lift is on fire! The lift is on fire!" It was hysterical. We sat at a table that was a mile long, but it was just an ordinary table, really. There were thousands and thousands of people all wearing masks... but frankly just a regular number of patrons wearing no more than standard makeup.

The biggest changes brought on by LSD were to our self-perception. When George took LSD he was suddenly in love. Not with anyone in particular, but with the whole cosmos. In ten minutes he felt he'd experienced a thousand years. His soul had left his body. It was now free and unbound. You'll appreciate this: he said he felt like an astronaut on the moon looking back at earth from his awareness. He could see his body as if it weren't solid. He was just an energy soaring through time, an energy that just happened to be in this body at this particular moment.

It made me think, I'm telling you. After what I saw at Stonehenge, I wonder if anything happens by chance. Is extra-terrestrial energy being channeled through the Beatles? (Don't tell anyone I said this, please — including my wife, Lil. She's not into this at all.)

John has completely embraced this LSD. He loves the fact that the drug was developed to control people (or so John thinks), when in fact it sets you free (or so John thinks). LSD is certainly affecting John's music. I don't know, however, that the stuff he's strumming on his guitar these days can ever make it onto a Beatles record. On the plus side, tripping with George has brought the two closer together; this is finally an area where George can be John's equal.

Merry Christmas and Happy New Year!

Yours,

Mal

Mal was leading *some* life, but I wasn't completely jealous. My evenings with Sally, when we weren't working, were spent listening to music, having friends over, or watching TV (we'd finally gotten a set). We could swim with *Flipper*, indulge in *Combat, Get Smart,* or get *Lost in Space* (a NASA favorite). I even liked *I Dream of Jeannie* though I kept telling Sally I was watching it for her sake.

It was a good holiday season. Even Santa was singing "We Can Work It Out."

For illustratiowns, see www.intotheskywithdiamonds.com

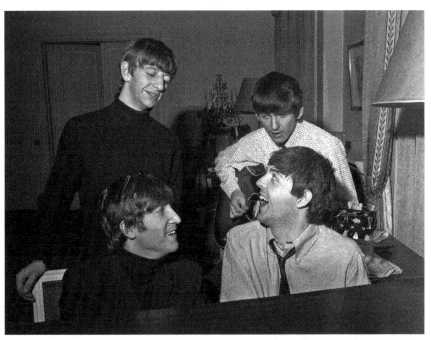

Photograph by Harry Benson

Photograph by Harry Benson

"I Want To Hold Your Hand" has just reached the #1 position in the U.S. charts. In the decorous Parisian hotel, the George V, the Beatles celebrate with a massive pillow fight.

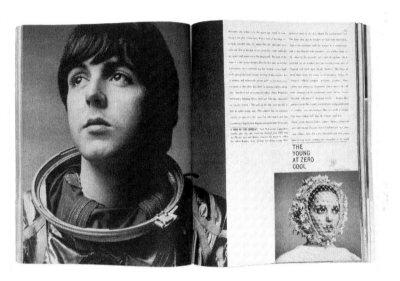

From Harper's Bazaar, January 1965,
Courtesy the Richard Avedon Foundation

The Beatles in India. Lennon and McCartney compose for the *"White Album," while Ringo ponders the rhythm.*

The Lunar Module, attached to the Command Module, attached to the Service Module. The SPS (Service Propulsion System) rocket is on the right, at the back of the Service Module.

APOLLO 11 LIFTOFF . . . JULY 16, 1969 — 9:32 A.M. EDT

Apollo 11 lifts off *(Neil Armstrong signature)*

10. Get Him In!

Elliott See was the quiet one, Charlie Bassett the extrovert. They were both ace pilots, sharp, and well liked. And now they were in luck: they'd just been assigned their own flight – Gemini IX. One stroke of the pen, and these men *and* their families had been raised to iconic status. One could argue that it was even more important to the wives. NASA was a civilian organization, but there were many military aspects to it. The status of a pilot's wife, for example, was completely dependent on her husband's rank and accomplishments – and an astronaut wasn't truly an astronaut until he'd flown a mission. Years of raising a family on her own and waiting dutifully (or resentfully, who knows?) for hubby's occasional visit would at last pay off when he flew into space. Thus, for Elliott & Marilyn See and for Charlie & Jean Bassett, Gemini IX was the payoff. At the impromptu party to celebrate their good fortune, we could all see the excitement in the women's faces. The astronauts were better at keeping their cool, but nobody could mistake the extra confidence in their step.

A space walk was scheduled for GT-9 as well as the usual bevy of ground breaking (space breaking) accomplishments. Marilyn See and Jean Bassett would soon bask in their husbands' glory, and their lonely years would finally see some recompense. Maybe not a trip to the White House like Betty Grissom and the other Mercury wives, but at least respect within the NASA family and within their *own* families. Many of the astronauts' wives had endured criticism for marrying military pilots – men considered by protective parents to be reckless fellows. Finally, they would have their "I told you so" moment. Their children could go into school and say, "my dad's an astronaut – he's been in space!"

On the morning of February 28th, 1966, at half past seven, the Japanese Fable swept into the picture in dramatic fashion.

The ones I felt most sorry for, really, were Marilyn and Jean.

There was no place at NASA for a *nearly*-astronaut widow. There was no special prestige for the wives of astronaut wannabes, no special status for women whose husbands came *this* close to flying in space.

In fact, after the funerals, I never saw them again.

Sally cried for the children.

See and Bassett had been scheduled to fly to the McDonnell plant in St. Louis where their Gemini capsule was being assembled. Naturally they piloted their own T-38, See up front, Bassett behind him. It was raining when they left, and snow flurries started en route. Visibility worsened. They came in low and slow. Suddenly, out of the fog, an industrial looking building jumped out straight in front of them. See banked sharply to the right. Too late. The plane struck the roof of a hangar.

The building they'd struck was McDonnell Building 101 – the one they'd come to visit.

I can only imagine the shock and horror of the McDonnell workers – first at being struck by a jet, then to discover in the wreckage the earthly remains of their expected guests.

See and Bassett never flew in space, but they were buried at Arlington.

**

Buzz Aldrin couldn't quite figure out what was going wrong.

He had an immense grasp of detail, he'd gotten a Ph.D. from MIT, and he'd been selected into the astronaut corps. Nevertheless, he'd only been assigned as a backup for Gemini X. That put him in line for the Gemini XIII prime crew assignment – except that *there was no Gemini XIII*. Gemini *XII* was the last scheduled Gemini flight!!!

He – Major Edwin "Buzz" Aldrin, USAF – had been given a dead-end job! Was no one out there paying attention to all he had to offer??? Did nobody realize that his mother's maiden name was Moon, for heaven's sake?

Being a backup for Gemini X turned out not to be so bad after all.

One man's loss is another man's gain (corollary of the Japanese fable). No sooner had See and Bassett been buried, than their backups Stafford and Cernan stepped into their shoes.

And whom did NASA designate as the new Gemini IX backups?

Why, the former Gemini X backups: Lovell and Aldrin.

YESSSSS!

Aldrin would put in his time as a Gemini IX backup, then fly the Gemini XII mission. It would be the last Gemini mission, a mission without any special objective at this point, but it would be a mission nonetheless.

****

It was an intense time at NASA, and my only distraction was music. I had not heard from Mal in a while and was taken slightly aback when, towards the end of February, the unmistakable sound of a Beatle song suddenly appeared on the radio. The harmonies were as perfect as ever, the guitar solo crackled with electricity, and the bass line was a song in itself. The lyrics were existential, about a man wondering who he really is and what he's all about. Lennon was the singer, and I had to assume it was his song. The song provided me with a few minutes of reflection every time it came on the radio. The song was "Nowhere Man." It had not been released as a single in the U.K., where instead it had appeared as just another song on *Rubber Soul*.

It didn't go unnoticed by my colleagues that I was quite fixated on the radio. But who could resist? The Rolling Stones had just released "19th Nervous breakdown," Nancy Sinatra sang "These Boots Were Made for Walking," the Beach Boys were fresh off "Barbara Ann," and teenage newcomer (Little) Stevie Wonder, a blind Negro wunderkind, had his own "Uptight (Everything is Alright)."

Out in San Francisco, Stewart Brand, a Merry Prankster and future publisher of the Whole Earth Catalog, held the first ever Trips Festival. It was a gathering of social dropouts sporting Beatles-style long hair (or longer) and clothed in flowery garb, beads and scarves. They smoked marijuana, dropped acid, and grooved to the Grateful Dead and to Janis Joplin. These dropouts called themselves "hippies."

I loved the music and was attracted in the abstract to the idea of freedom from convention, but I was put off by the style. I couldn't imagine myself with hair down to my shoulders, in paisley, beads, and sandals. Frankly I couldn't imagine *any guy* looking like that, except as a joke. There were a few hippies in Houston, but they were tame compared to their San Francisco counterparts, and we rarely saw them. Sally and the other women at NASA were wearing their skirts shorter, though – and I didn't hear anyone complain.

****

199

See and Bassett's death had temporarily focused our attention on Gemini IX, but our immediate concern was Gemini VIII.

Armstrong and Scott would have a mighty full schedule: Gemini VIII was to combine an extended space walk with the docking of two spacecraft, the original Gemini VI mission. The Gemini VI-A mission had been a great photographic and public relations success, but in the end, the capsule had only ("only"…) rendezvous-ed with another craft. It had not physically docked.

Neil Armstrong was no stranger to dangerous and exhilarating missions. The X-15 was a black arrow of a plane that flew to the very edges of the atmosphere. It had stubby wings that were too short to allow takeoff from a runway. A B-52 bomber carried the plane aloft, released it from under its wing, and allowed it to scream off into the stratosphere. This had been Armstrong's "trainer" plane.

On March 16th, 1966, GT-8 took off uneventfully as did the Atlas-Agena rocket. Armstrong and Scott circularized their orbit, caught up with the Agena, lined up along its axis, and clamped the nose of their capsule around the nose of the Agena. Another space first for Team USA. Mission accomplished.

Congratulations were in order all around, especially for Armstrong, Scott, and all the Slide Rules. Months of eye-blurring calculations had handsomely paid off.

Gemini VIII quietly slipped between two tracking stations while we busily patted ourselves on the back. The capsule was presently invisible and out of telecommunication range.

Imperceptibly, Gemini-Agena began to wiggle out of alignment. First one way, then the other. The oscillations increased. The astronauts were on the night side of the earth, and these disturbances were occurring in total darkness. Surely this unplanned motion was stressing the docking latches. As the pitching and rolling worsened, the astronauts considered the frightful possibility that the capsule could rip apart.

There was no use calling for advice as Mission Control was blind to their predicament. It crossed Armstrong's mind that had the capsule been torn asunder at that very moment, no one on earth would have ever known what happened.

Given its track record, the Agena seemed to be the likely source of the problem. Armstrong decided to disengage from it.

He was successful.

The problems worsened.

The capsule now began to roll and tumble in a way that the astronauts hadn't felt since their days in the centrifuge. Faster and faster the capsule spun, like a barbeque spit rolling down a hill.

The problem hadn't been with the Agena: It was with their own capsule!!!

As they passed over the *Coastal Sentry* located off the coast of Japan, contact with the astronauts was finally re-established. "We have serious problems, we're tumbling and have separated," Armstrong announced, "We're rolling up, we can't turn anything off." The hair stood up on the back of CapCom Jim Fucci's neck upon hearing Scott's report.

In Mission Control we froze in disbelief. The euphoria of a few moments ago quickly evaporated, and the cigars were quickly slipped back into the drawers. We couldn't see what the problem was. Kranz stared unblinking at his screen. I aimlessly snapped switches up and down on my console.

The veins in Armstrong's temples throbbed with quickening pace. He and Scott would soon pass out. Perhaps it was his piloting skills, or maybe his pilot's intuition, or possibly it was just plain luck. On the verge of blacking out, Armstrong flipped off the thrusters. The tumbling calmed down. And so did their heart rate. Slowly, very slowly, Armstrong activated the small re-entry thrusters over the nose of the capsule and re-aligned his capsule.

When he momentarily re-activated the main thrusters, the capsule again began its frightening tumble. So that's where the problem was. Without the main thrusters, the astronauts were left with just the mini re-entry rockets; the mission would have to end right there.

We'd have to wait another sixteen hours to get them down in one of the pre-planned splashdown areas. For the astronauts, that meant sixteen hours with minimal fuel and a limited ability to communicate with us[11]. The other option was to get them down NOW, and hope that a recovery team would get to them in a timely fashion.

That was not really a choice. Gemini VIII had to come down asap.

---

11 The capsule would shortly enter the part of the flight where communications could only take place every ninety minutes.

An exhausted John Hodge passed the baton to Kranz; Gene donned his white vest. We were on.

Every possible communication mode was activated – smoke signals, carrier pigeons, Pony Express… – while we jump-started all recovery teams around the globe. As best as we could calculate, the planned splashdown would occur 500 miles east of Okinawa. This assumed that the re-entry thrusters had the requisite fuel.

**

Comfortably resting in the western Pacific, the sailors of the USS *Mason* figured they'd drawn a cushy assignment. Then came the call, and suddenly they were scrambling to crank up the boilers. The carrier frantically raced to its new destination.

Fucci relayed to the astronauts the long string of de-orbit data and recovery call signs.

As they passed over the Congo, GT-8 fired its retros, and that would be the last we would hear of them until the end of the blackout period.

Kraft called for some extra milk, and we waited…

I think we all felt we'd done our best, however that didn't make it easier. There was a peculiar kind of guilt in knowing that we *had* done all we could, but it was the guys up there who'd pay the ultimate price if things went wrong.

Then suddenly, "Houston, we have contact." I took a deep breath.

They'd made it.

Their eyes were veined with blood, and they had to bob in the water for more than an hour before the *Mason* could get to them, but they were safe.

The sun was up. It would be a beautiful day.

"MAJOR SUCCESS" shouted the press.[12] Reporters could always be counted upon to put, ahem, a friendly spin on the situation. We had managed to dock two spacecraft!

And it was true. It *had been* a major success.

---

12 There'd been full television coverage, but some people complained that it had preempted the new hit show *Batman*.

One person who wasn't completely appreciative was Dave Scott. He was relieved to be alive, not to mention thankful for being presented with NASA's Exceptional Service Award, but he quietly felt gypped out of the space walk he had trained so many months for. The good news for Scott was that NASA quickly moved him into the Apollo training group, which meant that they still had faith in him. Armstrong, meanwhile, was assigned the seemingly lame job of backing up one of the last Gemini missions. On the plus side President Johnson approved a raise for Armstrong and his fellow space travelers: $6 a week more. Armstrong never did reveal what he was going to do with all that extra money.

**

NASA was optimistic about the possibility of eventually firing up twenty Apollo missions and a space station; Mars wasn't out of the question. NASA would need more astronauts.

On April 4th, we announced the recruitment of the following candidates:

Vance Brand, civilian
Lieutenant John Bull, USN
Major Gerald Carr, USMC
Captain Charles Duke, Jr. USAF
Captain Joe Engle, USAF (X-15 pilot)
Lieutenant Commander Ronald Evans, Jr., USN
Major Ed Givens, Jr., USAF
Fred Haise, Jr., civilian
Major James Irwin, USAF
Don Lind, civilian
Captain Jack Lousma, USMC
Lieutenant Bruce McCandless II, USN
Lieutenant Tom "Ken" Mattingly II, USN
Lieutenant Commander Ed Mitchell, USN *(born in Roswell, New Mexico, ground zero for the UFO movement. Hmm. Had Mal's guys infiltrated NASA?)*
Major William Pogue, USAF
Captain Su Roosa, USAF
John Swigert, Jr., civilian

Lieutenant Commander Paul Weitz, USN
Captain Al Worden, USAF

It was a good mix and a testament to our recruiting skills that the vast majority of these men actually went on to fly in space.

There were now fifty-seven astronauts! And that did not include Slayton and Shepard, who still harbored their own dreams.

At the Cape, von Braun was busy putting together the monstrous Saturn rocket that would take men to the moon. The rocket would be made in stages, and those stages would need to be very, very carefully stacked on top of each other near the launch pad.

A fifty story concrete box just north of Pad 34 on Merritt Island, the Vehicle Assembly Building (VAB), was built specifically for this purpose. It had its own micro climate. I recall it being foggy inside on a day that was no more than overcast! On May 25th, 1966, five years to the day since Kennedy's "Send a Man to the Moon" address, a Saturn rocket tentatively poked its head out. It would be snailed along to the launch pad on a platform which itself was a small mechanical wonder: a flat tractor the size of a football field, able to carry a 6 million pound rocket up and down a three mile road – without tipping more than an inch in any direction!

****

London, 10th May, 1966

Dear Dutch

Well, it's spring again, which in England basically means you get more rain in the day and less at night. My life as the faithful dogsbody grinds along. I'm not complaining! My mum finally gets it that I'm better off with the boys than driving a lorry.

The Beatles are back in the studio. They started with their strangest song to date. Inspired by Timothy Leary's "The Psychedelic Experience," John wrote a dreamy, one chord mono-tone song. The first lines, in fact, have been lifted entirely from the book.

"Turn off your mind, relax and float downstream It is not dying ... Lay down all thoughts, surrender to the void, it is shining / That you may see the meaning of within, it is being."

He wanted special sounds, and on this first day back, he pushed producer George Martin and new recording engineer Geoff Emerick to the limit. The Beatles were introduced to ADT [Artificial Double Tracking] and they completely took to it. Paul, in the meantime, was inspired by avant-guard musician Stockhausen to experiment with tape loops, sounds that go around and around when studio tape is spliced to form a loop. George Martin and Emerick located three tape recorders in three different rooms and connected them all to play Paul's loops. I was stuck in one of the rooms, turning the bloody tape recorders on and off without even seeing or hearing what was going on in the studio.

The boys have also completely gotten into testing the sound of an instrument when played backwards on a tape recorder. The cymbals, for example, make a short sucking sound. The guitars whine.

This particular song was going by the name "Mark I" and then "The Void" until Ringo was overheard making one of his famous malapropisms, "Well, you know, tomorrow never knows." John and Paul got a kick out of that, and it's currently the title of the song. I don't know that the song will ever see the light of day; it is definitely strange and certainly not commercial. I've never heard anything like it. The boys had fun recording it, though; a real team effort.

On a lighter note, the boys were asked to pose for a picture destined to grace *Yesterday....and Today*, another one of your made-for-North America records, a mix of singles and songs that should have been on your other records. Brian hired Australian photographer Robert Whitaker for the session. Whitaker has a reputation for being outrageous, and this fit in well with the Beatles' mood, especially John's. The Beatles' "cute" image troubles him to no end, and he was thrilled to meet a kindred spirit. It was Whitaker's idea to have the Beatles dressed in butcher smocks, holding decapitated dolls. George wasn't so keen on it, but John was jazzed. That would show 'em!

I had my doubts. I know you Yanks.

Capitol actually released the album with that cover until the higher-ups saw it and halted the presses. You have to love the note that was sent out to the music industry:

"The original cover, created in England, was intended as "pop art" satire. However, a sampling of public opinion in the United States indicates that the cover design is subject to misinterpretation. For this reason, and to avoid any possible controversy, or underserved harm to the Beatles' image or reputation, Capitol has chosen to withdraw the LP and substitute a more generally acceptable design."

Truth be told, everyone but John was somewhat relieved. Lil, me ole lady, summed up the general opinion: "It's just not how people think of them. They're cheeky boys and we love that, but you also know they'd be good for a cuddle." I made her swear never to say that to John. (Dutch, here's a secret: Capitol has simply pasted the new cover onto the old one. You can steam off the new cover — a bland picture of the boys standing 'round some steamer trunks — and find the original!)

We've been recording some seriously good material in the studio. Paul has a beautiful song about a lost love, called "For No One" ("and in her eyes you see nothing, no sign of love behind the tears, cried for no one, a love that should have lasted years"). He wanted a French horn for the solo in the middle. George Martin got the numero uno French horn player in the country, Alan Civil, to come in. Paul hummed the melody he wanted — apparently a difficult one for a French horn. Civil's rendition sounded great. George Martin was beaming. And then Paul asked Mr. Civil if he could do it better. Ouch!

The most fun, though, was "Yellow Submarine." Wait until you hear this one. Paul came into the studio with this idea for a Ringo song. Donovan stopped by that day. Everyone was in a wacky mood. The afternoon was spent coming up with lines for the song and dreaming up every possible sound effect. I'm in there too!

We're a bubbling cauldron of creativity! Seriously, I can't imagine a better job, though just between the two of us, they could afford to pay me a little more. But never mind that. You should really come by one day.

Yours,

Mal

I hadn't thought about what Mal was being paid, but I could see that it must be difficult to work for guys who suddenly become rich and famous beyond anybody's dreams. Sally and I were doing okay, but we still had to budget. It helped that the news was full of hippies seemingly able to live on nothing and having fun doing it.

****

Coming up to bat at the Cape were Tom Stafford and Gene Cernan. Always extending himself when it came to chatting with the guys in the trenches, Cernan was a Mission Control favorite. (Did I mention that he went to Purdue?)

As usual, their mission had been planned months ahead of time, long before the flight of the previous mission. The mission called for an even more ambitious space walk than the one Scott never took. Why not? White had shown the world how easy it was. Rather than use the hand-propelled gun that Scott would have used in his aborted spacewalk, Cernan was to strap on an elaborate, geometric Buck Rogers backpack imaginatively called the Astronaut Maneuvering Unit (AMU). The mission again called for a rendezvous with an Agena rocket.

On May 17th, all systems were GO for both the Atlas-Agena and the Gemini-Titan.

It wasn't to be.

A failure of the Atlas shortly after liftoff led to the loss of both the Atlas and the Agena.

No replacement Agena was readily available, but this time, in its back pocket, NASA had the sexy-sounding Augmented Target Docking Adaptor (ATDA). The rocket's nose consisted of a long, dunce-like cap. The shroud would open up, peel away, and reveal a docking collar.

On June 1st, the Atlas-ATDA took off without a hitch, and a few hours later, in circular orbit 160 miles above, it awaited a visit from GT-9.

All wasn't well. As the ATDA passed over Bermuda, telemetry data couldn't confirm that the shroud had opened. If the shroud was closed, there could be no docking. NASA decided that the mission had enough objectives, big and small, to warrant giving the thumbs up. The astronauts could practice different rendezvous tactics, and there was still the space walk.

Stafford and Cernan were shoehorned into the Gemini capsule. For Cernan this was the big moment. Stafford had been there before, and as it turned out, in more ways that one. Indeed, three minutes before liftoff, a computer malfunction caused us to cancel the flight. We were starting to feel snake-bit. For the second time in two weeks, Stafford and Cernan slowly twisted their way out of the capsule. (It's a great deal harder when a mission has just been canned.)

Two days later we were back at our stations. As the countdown proceeded, the buzz in the room once again gradually tapered off to a hush, disturbed only by the ticks of the clocks and the clicks of the pens. Kranz was sporting a brand new white vest put together by Martha for better luck; it featured a gold and silver brocade over white silk. He was pretty good-natured about the teasing.

Burning a clear white path through the azure sky, GT-9 was finally off. Regrettably, the good luck of the launch did not carry over into space. As they caught up to the ATDA, the astronauts noticed that, as half expected, the shroud covering the docking mechanism had not completely deployed. It was open all right, but not all the way. Stafford described the ATDA as "an angry alligator." Consideration was given to cutting the strap that held the shroud half closed, but the idea was dropped.

GT-9 would focus on the spacewalk. After all, through six Gemini missions we had a grand total of a single twenty-minute spacewalk under our belt.

The right-hand hatch opened, and out popped Cernan.

The first few moments were unremarkable; Cernan floated up much as White had done. He allowed himself a few seconds to marvel at the scenery. I hope he enjoyed it, because that was the end of the fun part.

Cernan quickly discovered the difference between a space *walk* and a space *float*. White had merely floated about. Cernan needed to purposefully move from point A to point B, and in trying to do so, he encountered some nasty surprises: If he moved his arm too quickly, his entire body would rotate and rotate and *rotate*. If he leaned forward too quickly, he would tumble and tumble and *tumble*. And so forth.

After a few moments of having gotten absolutely nowhere, Cernan was exhausted.

Topping things off, his visor fogged over.

To let Cernan cool down, we decided to wait for the capsule to pass into the night. Having given up on the first part of the mission, we were most reluctant to give up on the second one.

Things were not looking good. Cernan was expending huge amounts of energy doing the simplest things. His limbs moved with terrifying slowness, and yet, as if gripped by invisible fangs, the smallest muscle twitch would send him off balance. His body would turn one way, while he twisted his head the other way to compensate. His heart rate was stratospheric; his body temperature was on the rise; his breathing was labored; his communications were interspersed with grunts. It was painful to listen to. Although he'd managed to half strap himself into the AMU, it was clear that he would be too fatigued to do anything with it.

Dr. Berry and the medical team thought Cernan should quit while he was still alive. For once, it was hard to disagree with the doctors.

Cernan pre-empted us: "Tom, I'm going to call it quits. Nothing seems to be working."

End of mission.

Cernan, however, was not back in the capsule yet. Sweat was pouring into his eyes, and he had nothing to wipe them with. His visor was fogged over but for a small area near the tip of his nose. He inched forward towards the hatch. As the visor fogged up, he would wait a few moments for the tiny area in front of his nose to clear up.

Two hours and ten minutes after exiting the capsule, an exhausted Cernan had finally heaved and fought his way back in. The space walk from hell was over.

Of course, NASA and the friendly press were able to put a positive take on the fiasco, what with our second rendezvous and our second space walk, but we had accomplished neither of our two goals. There would be a great deal of pressure on the next guys to get it right.

**

That would be John Young and Mike Collins, both destined for Apollo fame.

I thought the mission plan for GT-10 was quite bold, considering the failures of its predecessors. After docking with an Agena rocket, Collins would perform two space walks, during which he would retrieve a package mounted on the Agena. *(We joked about what he might find when he opened the package. Superman comics? The Hardy Boys? Silly putty? In fact, it was a micrometeorite-measuring device.)* The astronauts were to then change orbits and hunt down the other Agena, the one left behind by Armstrong and Scott.

On July 18th, Young and Collins took off uneventfully. Within six hours they had docked with the Agena. They were 468 miles up – a new altitude record. Collins opened the hatch and floated out. Mindful of Cernan's experience, he maneuvered away from the capsule. He began to blink and then blink some more. His eyes were becoming frankly itchy, and the blinking was interfering with his concentration. He recalled no simulation for this situation; he decided to say something. Remarkably, back in his seat, Young was experiencing the same phenomenon.

Nothing like an itchy orbit!

Damn! Collins had to come back in. More huddling in Mission Control. We discovered that the lithium hydroxide used to absorb the carbon dioxide from the exhaled air was being blown right into their air hoses.

This was easy to correct, and the next day Collins would have another chance at the space walk.

This time he was successful! He retrieved the package and returned to the capsule without incident.

Problems began anew with his next space walk. He was supposed to deliver an instrument package to the Agena, but the umbilical hose wrapped itself around him, making each move clumsy and laborious. He began to heat up and perspire just as Cernan had. Mike was going nowhere fast, and, reluctantly, the decision was made to cut the space walk short. Even that was difficult. Collins could not get back into the capsule! Young himself eventually floated out to unwrap the hose that had snaked up around Mike's leg.

On earth the mission was hailed as a major triumph – of course. *Life* trumpeted the altitude record and published stunning pictures taken from higher up than any man had ever been.

Meanwhile, it was obvious that work remained to be done on the space walks.

We had two Gemini missions left to figure it out.

****

From where I sat, all appeared to be going well in Beatle-land. Summer marked the release of perhaps my favorite song to date, "Eleanor Rigby." This was McCartney's song from A to Z. No other Beatle was involved except for the background vocals. George Martin had written a score calling for classical instruments only – no guitars or drums. The song told of a lonely spinster who dies unnoticed by all but the priest.

Being a foursome afforded the Beatles creative liberties that would have been off limits to an individual rock' n' roll performer. Had McCartney written "Yellow Submarine" in 1976 rather than 1966, it would have been used as further proof that he'd gone soft. But written for Ringo, it was simply another daffy piece in the Beatle puzzle. It would be the B-side of "Eleanor Rigby."

The two songs appeared on their new album, *Revolver*. For the first time, the cover didn't feature a picture of the foursome. Instead, their German friend Klaus Voorman had sketched their portraits and within the drawings had interspersed small black and white pictures of the band.

This was by far their most varied and sophisticated album to date. In addition to "Eleanor Rigby," McCartney contributed "Here, There, and Everywhere," "For No One," "Good Day Sunshine," "Got To Get You Into My Life," and "Yellow Submarine" (with help from his three bandmates and Donovan). John pitched in with "And Your Bird Can Sing" (a sublime, multipart guitar performance) and "She Said She Said."[13] George was given the honor of opening the album with "Taxman." (McCartney played the quirky guitar solo.)

"Here, There, and Everywhere," "For No One," and "Eleanor Rigby" formed a gripping trio of love, loss, and loneliness that is argu-ably unmatched on any other album.

---

13   With honorable mention to "I'm Only Sleeping," and "Dr. Roberts."

"Good Day Sunshine" and "Yellow Submarine" were good fun. "Taxman" provided social commentary.

"Tomorrow Never Knows," the first song recorded and the last song on the album, was the pick of the litter for the critics of the day, and remains so today. Not in my book. The song is one long drone with funky sounds in the background. The lyrics urging the listener to let everything go didn't do much for me, and the song isn't particularly enjoyable whether you're relaxing at home or driving about. Perhaps if you're stoned it's a different story, but that's not something I could relate to. The song was fortunately placed at the very end, where it would do little harm. Another minor disappointment was the gradual disappearance of the trademark Beatle harmonies. The band seemed to have moved past that. In the end though, with or without harmonies, it was difficult not to play the album over and over again. It didn't seem that a Beatles record could ever get better than *Revolver*, and to many people it never did.

I tried to draw the guys at the cafeteria into discussing the record. More than ever, I consciously felt different.

****

London, 1st September, 1966

Dear Dutch,

This has been one of the worst periods in our lives.

It started well enough in June when we toured Germany. We went to Munich and took a private train to Hamburg. It was the train that Queen Elizabeth and the other Royals used! Me mum got a kick out of that. John did a whole routine pretending to be all our various female relatives getting the flutters — you would have wet your pants. The staff wasn't used to the likes of us. We listened to the Beach Boys' "God Only Knows" and a copy of Dylan's latest album, *Blonde on Blonde*. (Paul laid claim to it this time.)

But Hamburg wasn't the same. For one thing, the boys couldn't just go for a walk anymore. They were surrounded by a phalanx of security personnel that kept the crowds at a distance. The Star Club was fading. Astrid Kirchherr, responsible for all those early Beatle pictures, not to mention their famous haircut, now makes ends meet as a barmaid. George complained about all the "best friends" suddenly coming out of the woodwork. Girls I don't remember were saying we spent a night together. You don't know whether you just forgot 'cause you were blind drunk (which has happened a time or two, I suppose) or whether they're making it up... it's beyond embarrassing to think someone might invent spending a night with me. It was just a wee bit awkward, but obviously the experience was far more emotional for the boys.

"There are places I'll remember, all my life, though some have changed..."

We left feeling slightly dispirited but excited about moving on to Japan. Geishas, Hiroshima, transistor radios! It wasn't a place I could wrap my head around, if you know what I mean. I'd been to Hong Kong, but that's almost British, doncha know. Many sour notes awaited.

The first thing was, the flight got screwed up. Because of a typhoon in the Pacific, we were grounded overnight in Alaska. The Alaskans were perfectly hospitable and were thrilled to have the Beatles, but naturally nobody had made any hotel arrangements. Eppy was out of sorts and spent his time barking out orders.

Don't worry, we got beds. And food. No dog sled rides, though. Ringo was obsessed by the stuffed polar bear they had behind glass at the airport! I think if it'd been for sale, he would have bought it. Anyway, somewhat bleary-eyed, we finally arrived in Tokyo. The military presence was something else. Armed soldiers manned every intersection. For us!

The Beatles rode in a shiny white 1950s limousine, while Brian sat in a pink one! We were put up in the Presidential and Imperial suites at the top of the Tokyo Hilton, which would have been really cool had the whole hotel not been turned into an armed camp. The top floor was entirely cordoned off by soldiers. For the occasion, the elevator was programmed to stop at the floor below ours. After passing through stone-faced soldiers (all of them about 6 inches shorter than I am), we were allowed to walk up the one flight to our suites. There, we were essentially held prisoners. The Beatles were given kimonos to wear (John was quite fond of his), and a steady stream of craftsmen paraded their wares before us. The Japanese promoter was a cool guy: He gave me and Neil our own movie cameras! The boys got Nikons; seems the Japanese are very proud of their cameras. I was happy to sample their version of fish and chips — "sushi."

Well, you know prison isn't our style. Paul and I managed to don disguises and scamper out the service entrance in our great-escape style, but the bobbies caught up to us. Guess what? The Tokyo Police Commissioner does not have a sense of humor. He threatened to withdraw all police and army protection. This didn't really worry us, but it should have.

The Beatles played a few sets at the famous Budokan where the crowds were respectfully enthusiastic. For the first time in a long while, the boys could actually hear themselves sing. And here was a crowd that could appreciate the bow from the waist at the end of the show! This Budokan gig, however, was a much bigger problem than anyone in Japan had led us to believe. The Budokan is still a holy site to some Japanese. They use it for religious services and martial arts, which George found very ironic, and they consider the playing of rock'n'roll' within these hallowed halls to be a desecration. A nationalist group had vowed that the Beatles and their entourage (that's me) would not leave the country alive. Wherefore the army.

Given this sticky atmosphere, we looked forward to the Philippine part of the trip, which was supposed to be relaxing. The boys have a big following in the Philippines. They were to play two concerts while enjoying some warmth and hospitality.

But if we thought Japan was bad... Imelda Marcos, wife of the all-powerful President Ferdinand Marcos and sometimes more feared than Ferdinand himself, had invited the Beatles to join her and a select group of 300 children at her palace prior to their concert. This visit was to take place during the only hours earmarked as downtime during our tour. The invitation wasn't communicated to Brian ahead of time, and when some dour soldiers from the Palace informed him that very morning, he was irate. He refused to wake up the boys, who knew nothing of this until later.

The concerts were problem-free and left the boys in good spirits.

Then came the first ominous sign: our police escort had vanished. When we got to the hotel the gates were locked! A mob started attacking the car, banging on the windows, and screaming; and believe me, these weren't Beatle fans! Vic Lewis, Eppy's contact person in Manila, shouted, "Drive on! Smash the gates down," which the driver did. Then we ran into the hotel like criminals on the run.

Meanwhile, Philippine television depicted a forlorn Imelda surrounded by 300 sad-eyed children. She let it be understood that these children were cripples and orphans and that the Beatles had spit in the eye of the nation.

Brian rushed to the television studios to offer an apology, but the sound was mysteriously cut off just as he started to speak.

Then, the fit really hit the shan. Vic Lewis was dragged out of bed that night and brought to the police station, where he was interrogated. "Why did the Beatles snub Imelda Marcos?" Can you imagine, a rock'n'roll band causing so much trouble over so little?

The next morning, I ordered room service for everyone. We waited and waited and waited. Finally I went downstairs, and the entire hotel was empty!!! The halls were dark and the elevators weren't working. No guards, no security, no bellhops. Two cars and two sour drivers waited outside. I read the headlines in the newspapers: "BEATLES SNUB PRESIDENT." Back upstairs, all one saw on television was the story of the Beatles insulting the entire Philippine nation.

So much for rest and relaxation. It was time to get out.

We got reservations on KLM flight 862 to New Delhi, there was no time to lose. When we jumped into the cars unharmed, we thought we'd made it under the wire. We were wrong. Another mob awaited us at the airport. Without security to protect us, we were all pummeled as we made our way inside. The terminal had been cleared out (!!!). A single army officer languished over each page of our passports and papers. As the time for take-off neared, we were ushered into an empty room. I say "ushered," but in fact we were pushed around with rifle butts. The screaming hordes could be heard just outside. Ringo got pushed so hard he nearly fell to the floor, and when I stepped in to calm things down I got smacked around with their sticks. I still have the bruises!

We started to wonder if we'd ever make it to the plane. Bad time not to have our own charter!

They finally let us go, but we had to carry our own luggage and gear all the way to the end of the tarmac where the authorities had sequestered the plane. What a sight!

We'd barely plopped ourselves down in a mass of sweat, when the police came aboard and gestured for Tony Barrow and I to follow them. 'Tell Lil I love her!,' I yelled. Brian pleaded with the pilot to wait just a little longer, but the pilot had had it waiting for the Beatles (obviously a Stones fan). Tony reappeared as the doors were closing. They'd made him pay a "leaving Manila tax" that amounted to the Beatles' entire Philippine earnings. Bastards!

On the flight from New Delhi to London, John commented that he was through with touring. Who could argue? Of course no one took him too seriously either. In fact, we were about to go back to America.

As you know, things in America went from bad to worse, and now I really think it may be a while before the boys tour again.

Keep in touch!

Mal

"Things in America." I knew what Mal was referring to.

In the spring, Lennon had given an interview to his intimate friend Maureen Cleave of the *Evening Standard*. They had gotten onto the subject of religion, a subject clearly far removed from his area of expertise. Lennon, however, was more spiritual than most would have given him credit for, and he began to muse out loud on a topic he'd clearly thought about beforehand. He had no warm feelings for organized religion. "Christianity will go. It will go. It will vanish and shrink. I needn't argue about that. I'm right and I will be proved right. We are more popular than Jesus now. I don't know which will go first – rock'n'roll' or Christianity. Jesus was alright, but his disciples were thick and ordinary." This quote raised no eyebrows in Great Britain. Who cared about a rock star's thoughts on religion – especially in the case of John Lennon, who made it a habit of being irreverent? And in Britain Lennon's statement perhaps held a kernel of truth. The interview – one of dozens of Beatle interviews published on a regular basis – slid under the radar unnoticed.

In July, the article appeared in the *New York Times* magazine and hopped around the American press, again without much fuss.

Just before their August tour, however, the interview was reprinted in the teen magazine *Datebook*, with Lennon's most egregious remarks plastered on the cover. That did it. A firestorm of controversy erupted. It might have been read with some amusement or boredom in much of the country, but in the Bible belt the reaction was fierce. As Ringo would say, it was as if someone had taken Lennon's quote and shot it to the moon. (I liked the analogy.) Beatle records were burned in enormous public bonfires, stations banned Beatle songs, and parishioners were threatened with excommunication if they attended a Beatles concert. In South Carolina the Grand Dragon of the Ku Klux Klan nailed Beatles records to burning crosses and dared the Beatles to come to America. Reverend David Noebel, hyperventilating in a pamphlet called "Communism, Hypnotism, and the Beatles" warned, "We are in the fight of our lives and the lives of our children … let's make sure four mop-headed anti-Christ beatniks don't destroy our children's emotional and mental stability and ultimately destroy our nation."

At first, Lennon made light of the situation by pointing out that the public had to first buy his records before they could burn them, but the situation was no laughing matter. Promoters were on the verge of canceling concert dates, and the Beatles themselves were being physically threatened (again!). Something had to be done. Maureen Cleave herself came to Lennon's defense, saying somewhat disingenuously that it had appeared to her that Lennon actually deplored the loss of religious spirit among the young. This fell on deaf ears.

The attitude among the guys at NASA was, "Isn't Lennon an arrogant bastard?" Personally, I thought he was simply being honest, if undiplomatic, and since when are rock stars supposed to be diplomatic?

Brian Epstein suggested that Lennon release a taped apology:

> You had a serious and long talk about religion (in which you are very interested), and the quote came out of the fact that you were astonished and surprised that Christianity in the last 50 years in this country [England] has gone off in its appeal. When you said the Beatles are more popular than Jesus you were not trying to upset anyone, but merely suggesting that your appeal is more immediate. (Do not go back to the disciples being thick.) You could conclude with 'Profound and sincere apologies to Americans and to all people throughout the world, who may have misinterpreted this quote, which was taken out of context.'

This recording was never made, and upon the Beatles' arrival in Chicago, all eyes were on Lennon.

This time the press was not friendly.

They wanted an explanation and a formal apology. Lennon appeared pale and edgy as he stepped to the microphone. "If I said television was more popular than Jesus, I might have got away with it. As I just happened to be talking with a friend, I used Beatles as a remote thing, not as what I think – as Beatles, as those other Beatles, like people see us. And I just said "they" as having more influence on kids and things and anything else, including Jesus. But I said it in that way, which was the wrong way. But, I'm not saying that we're better or greater or comparing us with Jesus, as a person, or God as a thing, or whatever it is. I just said what I said and it was wrong, and now there's all this."

This had clearly been painful for Lennon. For a man who was normally quick-witted and succinct, this sounded like a lot of double talk. But at least it was over. Or so he thought.

The press persisted. "Are you prepared to *apologize?*"

Lennon thought he just had. He gamely trotted on.

"I'm not anti-God, anti-Christ, or anti-religion. I was not saying we are greater or better. I believe in God, but not as one thing, not as an old man in the sky. I believe that what people call God is something in all of us ... I wasn't saying the Beatles are better than God or Jesus. I used "Beatles" because it was easy for me to talk about the Beatles."

Was Christianity shrinking? "It just seems to me to be shrinking. I'm not knocking it or saying it's bad. I'm just saying it seems to be shrinking and losing contact." Paul swooped in to the rescue, "and we deplore the fact that it is."

As the feeding frenzy continued unabated, Lennon gave up.

"I wasn't saying whatever they're saying I was saying. I'm sorry I said it, really. I never meant it to be a lousy anti-religious thing, I apologize if that will make you happy. I still don't know quite what I've done. I've tried to tell you what I did do, but if you want me to apologize, if that will make you happy, then okay, I'm sorry."

That didn't sound like much of an apology, but it seemed to appease the mob. Had this whole flap really ever been about Lennon? A few months back, *Time* magazine had run an issue titled 'Is God Dead?' and no one had gone around making bonfires out of *Time* magazines. Lennon's remarks were probably the flashpoint of a growing reaction to all that rock'n'roll now exemplified, including (and perhaps, especially) a relaxation of traditional morals.

Lennon, in his "apology," went on to discuss America's involvement in Vietnam, making comments which, to my surprise, went totally un-noticed.

Apology or not, the tour was tainted from the start. In Cleveland, they played outdoors in the rain. In Memphis, the KKK threatened outside the stadium, while indoors, with everyone worried about a sniper, someone threw a firecracker on stage. In New York, Shea Stadium was no longer sold out. The tour ended in rainy, wind-swept San Francisco. As usual, no one, including the Beatles, could hear the music. John, Paul, and George gamely strummed their guitars and shook their heads, while Ringo trudged on semi-rhythmically behind them. It was August 29th, 1966. It would be their last concert.

According to Mal, the flight back to London was somber. Lennon had had it, and he announced again that his touring days were over. This time, the other three agreed. For George, the most religiously inclined of the four, this was specific evidence that Christianity had lost its way. The East beckoned. George would repeat to anyone and everyone that he'd always wanted to be successful, but he'd never sought fame. For Lennon, this would be the last time he would be persuaded to retract an opinion. If the public or the press did not agree with him, that would just be too bad. No heaven. No religion. Those were his opinions. Period. In fact, perhaps he'd write a song about that one day.

****

Had Sean Connery been able to sit down with the Beatles in the summer of '66, the five of them would have had much to commiserate about.

They were arguably the five most popular people in the world, and outside of politics, certainly the five most well known. Relative to their remarkable fame, they were also five of the most professionally unhappy. The Beatles were tired of behaving like marionettes in front of shrieking teenagers, and Sean Connery was tired of being James Bond.

Connery's Manila had been Japan.

He'd arrived to film his fifth James Bond movie. He was enormously popular in Japan, yet there had been a serious disconnect between the large crowd of eager reporters and Connery's relative disinterest. When he finally came down from his room to meet the press, it was not the suave "shaken not stirred" James Bond they were expecting, but a frumpy, grumpy toupee-less Connery.

"Is this the way James Bond dresses?"

"I'm not James Bond, I'm Sean Connery and I like to dress comfortably."

He bantered amiably enough about Japanese cooking and the Japanese O-Furo baths. Then he'd had enough. Unfortunately, there was another question.

"What do you think of Japanese women?"

"Japanese women are just not sexy," replied Connery.

This was not well received, but it hardly mattered to Connery. He'd already decided that this would be his last Bond adventure.

****

We were far behind schedule on our space walks and we had just two more Gemini missions to sort things out. On September 12th, it was Pete Conrad and Dick Gordon's turn. Pete was a panic. A smile and a cackle. That gap between his front teeth made it easy to pick him out in an often-homogeneous group of astronauts. He and Gordon were a perfect match. They'd been shipboard roommates on the *USS Ranger* before coming to NASA and had developed an intuitive feel for each other's moves.

Their first mission was to track down, catch up to, and dock with an Agena rocket *within their very first orbit*. This would eventually be required of a lunar module taking off from the moon in its chase of the Apollo capsule above.

We made it. One hour and twenty-five minutes after liftoff, Conrad confirmed the docking.

Next was the pesky space walk that had proven so difficult for Cernan and for Collins. Among Gordon's many tasks, he was to connect the Gemini capsule and the Agena with a tether. NASA had allotted four hours for the astronauts to don their spacesuits. They were ready in an hour – and waited. When the time finally came to open the hatch, Dick discovered a problem with his visor. He got himself all sweaty fixing it and sounded pretty beat even before leaving the capsule. We'd heard this song before. Losing his grip upon leaving the capsule, he drifted off, and Conrad had to pull him back by way of his umbilical cord.

Attaching the tether proved more difficult than expected because of Gordon's inability to gain any kind of footing. To achieve an element of stability, he clumsily positioned himself astride the docking cone.

"He looks like he's riding a bucking bronco!" joked Pete.

Dick, however, wasn't having fun. The temperature in his suit exceeded the system's ability to cool him down, and he was soon exerting himself and perspiring to a dangerous degree. Dr. Berry winced as he watched Dick's heart rate race into the red zone. Gordon finally attached the tether to the Agena, but once again it was painful to listen to.

"Get him in!" yelled Kraft. After just thirty-three minutes of extravehicular activity, Gordon was called back in. It wasn't going to be easy. As we knew, squeezing into the Gemini capsule required effort, and Gordon was incoherent with fatigue. Pete would later say that watching Dick try to fold himself back into the capsule was the only time in space he was ever truly scared. Dick finally made it in.

NASA had another docking and undocking under its belt, another space walk, and a new altitude record (850 miles). It was time for Gemini XI to come home.

The splashdown landed the astronauts closer to the carrier ship than any previous flight.

Another major success.

Except that we still hadn't figured out how our astronauts could maneuver and work in space. This would be a critical aspect of any Apollo mission, and there was but one Gemini flight left to solve this.

****

I hadn't heard from Mal since the summer, and his letter took me by surprise. The Beatles' "Paperback Writer" had gone to Number #1 in June. I had not cared much for the song until I had heard it on a quality sound system. The bass drives the song, a feature that was completely lost on my little turntable. I had heard rumors that the Beatles had disbanded, but I had been too busy to check with Mal. Another rumor had it that the Beatles were put off by the competition. There was indeed plenty of it:

"You Don't Have to Say You Love Me" (Dusty Springfield), "Paint it Black" (Rolling Stones), "Daydream" and "Summer in the City" (Lovin' Spoonful), "Sloop John B" (Beach Boys), "Rainy Day Women" (Bob Dylan), "River Deep Mountain High" (Ike and Tina Turner), "Sunny Afternoon" (Kinks), "When a Man Loves A Woman" (Percy Sledge), "Eight Miles High" (Byrds), "Reach Out I'll Be There" (Four Tops), "Bus Stop" (Hollies), "Good Vibrations" (Beach Boys), "Gimme Some Loving" (S. Winwood/Spencer Davis Group), "You Keep Me Hangin' On" (Supremes), "Sunshine Superman" (Donovan), "Bang Bang" (Cher), "California Dreaming" and "Monday Monday" (Mamas and Papas). The biggest newcomers were a New York group, the catchy-sounding duo of Simon and Garfunkel ("Sounds of Silence," "I Am a Rock," "Homeward Bound," "Hazy Shade of Winter").

Despite all the talent, I somehow doubted that the Beatles were intimidated.

**

London, 10th November, 1966

Dear Dutch,

I'm much more relaxed than the last time I wrote. In fact, I'm positively mellow (don't you love that word? How do you feel about "groovy"?) Following last summer's disasters, we all went our separate ways.

Paul and I went to Africa on safari, and upon our return, Paul wrote a score for the musical The Family Way. George went to India to study with Ravi Shankar and to explore all things Indian. He is looking to answer the age-old questions, "Why are we here; where are we from; where are we going?" He believes with all his heart that he will get these answers in India.

For a long time John sat home stoned, withdrawn from the world. His get-up-and-go had got up and gone. Much as Cynthia tried to engage him, John was still BORED. He turned down all invitations to write, talk, sing, emcee, etc... Finally, he took a small part in one of Dick Lester's movies, How I Won the War, an anti-war movie that suits his political inclinations. It was filmed in Spain, and Cyn was upset that he would spend his 25th

birthday away from her, but I don't think it bothered him very much. He finally invited her to join him.

Cyn's a fine person, goodhearted, stable, down-to-earth (and blonde) — attractive qualities when John was younger — but I'm afraid she's not exciting enough for him now. Not challenging enough. He was always somewhat the artist and rebel, and then these last few years — well maybe it's the drugs.

On the movie set John sat around all day not doing much of anything, but it gave him time to write a dreamy song about his childhood. I've listened to him play it on his acoustic guitar, and it is indeed very different. Very spacey, a slightly more tuneful version of "Tomorrow Never Knows." He calls it musical psychoanalysis. "No one I think is in my tree" — he always wondered whether he was crazy or a genius. "Sometimes, no, always, think it's me" — he halts, he's not sure, but yes he is, it hurts to lay bare his feelings, but he will. I like the song, but it made me want to take him out for a few pints. You know. He's got everything, but he feels lonely and confused. Paul and George *[Martin]* are going to have fun with this one.

John's also finally given in to wearing glasses. Nothing fancy. Wire-framed, army-issue glasses that he used for the movie. They make him look a bit scholarly or artistic, which I think he enjoys.

He did go out with me once (or rather, I went with him) on a visit to John Dunbar's Indica gallery. He hadn't washed or shaved in a few days; he claims that he was "lured" to the gallery by the promise of an orgy. There was no orgy, but he did laugh at some of the exhibits. There was a ladder leading to the ceiling. When you climbed to the top, there was a spyglass[14] that allowed you to read a tiny word scrawled on an equally tiny piece of paper. The word read, "YES." John liked the positive message. Then there was a board with a hammer and nails partially imbedded into it. John asked if he could nail one in. The artist answered "no," because the exhibit didn't open until the next day. Dunbar was nearly apoplectic and he yanked her to the side. "I'll let you hammer one in," she conceded to John — "for five shillings." Dunbar turned pale, but after a short, awkward moment, John smiled and answered tit for tat: "I'll give you an imaginary five shillings, and I'll hammer in an imaginary nail."

---

14 Magnifying glass.

The artist is Yoko Ono, a diminutive, un-smiling woman whose name — she made a point of telling us — means "ocean child." (That's pretty, but don't ask me why, I immediately thought "squid.") She's just moved from New York where she hasn't had much luck. I think I know why.

You should see her book of "poems" called "Grapefruit." On each page is a suggestion: "Draw a map to get lost." "Stir inside of your brains with a penis until things are mixed well." I ran out to get a copy for my parents.

John is drawn more and more to the offbeat. Is this the effect of Stonehenge? I know I'm obsessed with the subject, but if you'd been there... What we think of as reality is a lot bigger than we think. But you don't want to hear my ramblings. Did I ever tell you about John's car? His yellow Rolls-Royce? He's got a microphone connected to a loudspeaker. The windows are tinted. When he's inside, and people try to peek in, he'll yell, "Get away! Get AWAY from the car!" Or on the way home from a recording session late at night, he'll shout, "It is foolish to resist! it is foolish to resist! Pull over!" — and we leave a trail of houses suddenly lighting up. It's quite amusing, especially when you're sozzled. Once, we were on our way to the studio going through Regent's Park, when Paul spotted Brian Jones [of the Rolling Stones] in his Austin Princess. That's all John needed. Summoning his most official voice he screamed, "Brian Jones, do not move! You have been under surveillance — you are under arrest!" Brian practically drove off the road, but he quickly recognized the car. He was a good sport about it. In fact he's agreed to come in and play the sax on one of our songs[15].

There have been many rumors about the Beatles, in case you lot hadn't noticed. The only one with any truth to it is that the Beatles will stop touring. It's driving Eppy batty. Since there's been no formal announcement, he's had to fend off offer after offer, dreaming up one excuse after another. And what will become of him if the Beatles really stop touring? It's becoming a small obsession with him.

I have to say, I'm kind of sorry myself. Filipino dragon ladies aside, I get a kick out of seeing the world. That's not something a bloke like me is going to do any other way. I don't kid myself that Paul will take me on safari every year!

---

15 "You Know My Name (Look Up the Number)"

Don't believe the rumors about the Beatles breaking up. They're getting back to the studio shortly.

Cheerio,

Mal

****

There was but one Gemini flight left – Gemini XII, piloted by Jim Lovell and Buzz Aldrin. The mission without a goal had become a critical flight. It was now or never for a successful space walk. Cernan, Collins, and Gordon had all struggled. The three unwilling space acrobats agreed that better footing would be the key to future success. Without it, just about any maneuver would set an astronaut spinning. The outer shell of the capsule was therefore fitted with little boxes that Aldrin could slip his feet into.

NASA also decided that Aldrin would train while immersed in a pool to roughly approximate a floating sensation and a lack of contact with the ground. It remained to be determined if that would be good enough.

On November 11th, 1966, Lovell and Aldrin blasted off. The radar quit on them, and they had to dock like sailors with 'ole faithful (the Agena) using sextants and charts. Finally, the moment of truth arrived. Aldrin bobbed out of the capsule. With the new handrails and foot supports, he carried out *all* planned activities without breaking a sweat. *(He knew all along that he would.)* He performed three space walks. This was true success.

As they ambled towards the launch pad, Lovell had sported a sign on the back of his spacesuit that read "THE". Aldrin had worn a matching sign that said "END". And indeed it was. The Gemini program was over. Overall, it had been a remarkable success. The Gemini astronauts had proven that Man could survive in space, could walk in space, could track down another craft, and could dock with it.

1966 had been a heady year. Five missions! Plenty of close calls, but no fatalities. Would we be so fortunate with Apollo?

There had barely been a peep from the Soviets. How could they have allowed us to slip so far ahead? It just wasn't their style. We discovered later, years later in fact, the drama that had unfolded behind the Iron Curtain: the Grand Designer, Sergei Korolev, had died and there'd been no one to fill his shoes.

We knew none of this, nor did it matter. Our job was to forge ahead. We looked forward to 1967 and the start of the final phase: **Apollo**.

For illustrations, see www.intotheskywithdiamonds.com

11. *FIRE!*

Project Appalling

The Apollo program was traveling a bumpy road. The construction of the capsule was behind schedule. It was probably the most complicated piece of machinery ever built, and as of January 1967, there were still sixty discrepancies between the plans and the actual capsule. And it wasn't just the capsule: so many changes were being made, that the simulator didn't always match the spacecraft. The simulator had even seen Grissom hang a lemon on it. Nevertheless, as imperfect as they were, capsule and simulator were felt to be serviceable; training continued inexorably on.

The talk of the town, actually, was the crew of the *second* Apollo mission.

Apollo 1 had been settled long ago. That crew would consist of Gus, Ed White, and the rookie Roger Chaffee. Chaffee had spent a great deal of time in Long Island, NY, at the Grumman factory where the lunar module was being assembled. Unfortunately for Chaffee, the Apollo 1 flight plan didn't call for a lunar module, if for no other reason than none would be available until the third manned mission. Nevertheless, Chaffee would get some space experience under his belt. He would simply have to wait to make use of his lunar module know-how.

Apollo 1 would circle the earth over a fourteen day period, while the astronauts checked out its various systems. Apollo 2 would mostly be a repeat of Apollo 1. This had Wally Schirra, the commander of the mission, seriously irritated. Surely NASA could come up with a better flight plan! No, this is what NASA wanted and the brass were not going to be cowed by Schirra. One day I saw him come out beet-red from Deke's office, but frankly, Deke had no viable options. He couldn't simply assign Wally to the Apollo 3 mission, the one that would be testing out the lunar module. This mission had already been assigned to Jim McDivitt.

Yet after listening to Wally bellyache incessantly, everyone finally agreed with him that the Apollo 2 flight would be redundant. But in the category of "beware what you ask for," Apollo 2 was cancelled outright.

Wally was given the "opportunity" to back up Gus on Apollo 1. No one was around when Deke made Wally this offer, and it was probably a good thing. Someone could have gotten hurt. Backing up Gus? Again? He'd backed him up on Gemini 3, and he was going to play second fiddle yet another time???

I had to hand it to Deke. I don't know what he offered Wally, how he flattered him, or what he promised him, but Wally accepted. Rumor had it that it concerned a moon landing.

There was already a semi-official office pool pertaining to the first moon landing and the make-up of that crew. The fifth Apollo mission would be the first to possibly land on the moon, assuming that missions one through four were close to flawless. I put my money on the sixth mission; I didn't see how five straight missions could be so close to perfect. As for the crew of that first moon landing, it was really too soon to tell. The names you heard bandied about included Grissom, Schirra, Borman, McDivitt, Scott, White, Stafford, Young, Cernan, Conrad, and Gordon – guys with flight experience who seemed to be tight with Deke and Al. Having been Mercury astronauts, Grissom and Schirra would have the inside track. Here, I put my money on Gus. It wasn't just that he was my personal friend and fellow Boilermaker. I just sensed that Deke preferred him to Wally. After Gus and Wally, it was a crapshoot.

Meanwhile, it was time to get Apollo 1 off the ground.

**

It all happened so quickly.

Like many days seared in memory, January 27th started off deceptively ordinary. Sunrise, alarm clock, coffee, comb, newspaper, radio. Just another day.

The launch of Apollo 1 was a little less than a month away, and the prime crew (Grissom, White, and Chaffee) was set to go through a "plugs out" test, meaning all conditions for blast-off would be simulated. Gus, Ed, and Roger would be in their suits, pure oxygen would be pumped into the capsule, and all electrical cables to the capsule would be disconnected. The capsule would be running on its own power. Only one item was not simulated: the fueling of the Saturn V rocket atop which the capsule sat. With no propellants, cryogenics, or pyrotechnics around the pad, it was classified as a low-risk event.

Wally and the rest of the back-up crew had gone through a "plugs-in" test the day before. (The cables connecting the capsule to the tower had remained connected.)

At 1 PM, the astronauts were strapped into their seats and the hatch was closed. The countdown began.

As usual, one little glitch after another bogged things down. Particularly annoying was a recurring communication breakdown between the blockhouse and the Apollo capsule. "If I can't talk with you only five miles away, how are any of us going to talk to you from the moon?" Gus fumed. He wasn't talking to me personally, but being in charge of these transmissions, I couldn't help but feel the sting. There were hundreds of communication panels, each studded with forty-eight talk-listen buttons. If you wanted to speak to the fellow next to you, the communication would ricochet through the various boards before landing in your neighbor's ear. I could feel Gus's pain. The simple fact was that the low power microwave system we used was more effective in space than on earth.

Earlier in the day, Kranz and I thought one of us might slip into the capsule to see what could be improved upon. The Apollo capsule was large enough to accommodate another person in the "sleeping quarters" under the three astronaut couches. We'd thought of this in the past, but we'd always had too much to do in the blockhouse. Sure enough, looking at the task list that morning, it was clear that once more there would be no time for this extra-curricular activity.

Mission control in Houston was in on the communication loop, as they would be during the actual blast-off.

In Washington, American astronauts and Soviet cosmonauts were gathered for the signing of the "Peace in Space Treaty" that would prohibit the placement of nuclear weapons in space. It was a joyous occasion, though it was clear to everyone that the elephant in the room was the race to the moon.

Despite the glitches I actually thought I might make it out of there by dinnertime. Sally was back in Houston, so it wasn't a question of a romantic evening, but it was Friday after all, and none of us would have minded being out in a timely fashion for once.

Then suddenly, at 6:31 PM, we heard the words that I still hear in my dreams:

"Fire!!!"

"We've got a fire in the cockpit!!!!!"

*"We've got a **bad fire**………* **GET US OUT! WE'RE BURNING UP!!!!!!!"**

Gus and Ed had jumped out of their seats and groped back for the hatch.

There was a brief, piercing scream followed by a hollow, crackling silence.

Inside the control room, we froze.

Outside, the pad crew sprang into action and rushed to the capsule with fire extinguishers raised high, only to be stopped short by the toxic smoke and the white-hot hatch. Inside, the flames lapped the pure oxygen and devoured everything in sight. Again and again, the pad crew rushed towards the inferno, only to be forced back.

In Houston, Sally suddenly let out a muffled wail: The three cardiograms had just gone flat.

Gus, Ed, and Roger were dead.

On the launch pad, everyone was still frantically yelling, "Get them out!!!" "Get them out!!!" When the pad crew finally opened the hatch, they found only a pile of black and silver death. Gus and Ed were slumped over the back of their couches under the hatch, while Roger's head hung limply on his chest. Their spacesuits hideously soldered to the seats, the martyred astronauts remained in place until 1 A.M. when they were finally extricated from their charred, molten capsule and taken to a makeshift morgue. No one had anticipated such a need.

The capsule eventually cracked in two like an overcooked egg and belched smoke for hours.

**

On Tuesday January 31st, a state funeral was held for the three astronauts. Their caskets were slowly paraded through the streets of Washington. Gus was buried at Arlington, the graveyard of dreams, and Roger was buried there later in the day. Ed was buried at West Point, his Alma Mater.

At the cemetery I couldn't shake the memory of Gus greeting me on my first day at NASA – how green and eager and intimidated I was, how quickly he had put me at ease. His warmth; his vitality. Now, he lay at my feet inside a wooden box. I thought, *he'll never know if we make it to the moon.* All seven Mercury astronauts were present, as was John Young. And of course, Lyndon Johnson. At any other time it would have been a special thrill to stand next to the President of the United States of America. My thoughts, however, were with Betty. She stood straight and still, with that dignity military wives seem to acquire with their wedding rings.

As we stared at the turned earth on this frosty January day, four aircraft in tight formation came streaking towards us, low to the ground, shaking everything but the headstones. When they got close, jet #2 peeled off, up and away, leaving a gaping hole in the formation – the traditional missing man formation. That glaring gap summed up the churning emptiness inside all of us.

A few weeks later, a ceremony was held at the Cape, and a bronze plaque was dedicated: "In memory of those who made the ultimate sacrifice so others could reach for the stars. God Speed to the crew of Apollo 1."

Melancholy settled over the Cape. Most of us had never dealt with death. The astronauts were better equipped for it, having served in the armed forces, losing wartime colleagues and friends. For the controllers, engineers, and myself, however, this was a first. See and Bassett had died in a plane crash. Somehow that was different. This was so… bizarre, coming during a routine run-through. The capsule had been sitting on an empty Saturn rocket, for heaven's sake! Our nightmares had been populated with rockets blowing up at liftoff, capsules drifting off into space, vehicles burning up in re-entry – not a fire on the pad. Not that in the end it really mattered, but somehow it seemed that the astronauts deserved a more heroic death.

Behind it all lurked the thought that this could perhaps have been prevented. An accident in space could reasonably be considered an act of God. An accident on the ground during a low-risk rehearsal – that was something else. Did we all share in the blame? No snowflake in an avalanche ever feels responsible. We all believed that we'd dutifully fulfilled each and every one of our little obligations. Yet we'd all seen Gus hang a lemon on the capsule. Had we done enough to look at the bigger picture? That lemon now loomed as large as a grapefruit and tasted twice as bitter.

We were conditioned to show up for work bright and early, seven days a week. No more. Everything was put on hold while the Apollo fire was investigated. "GO Fever" had been a way of life, but it was now gone, replaced instead with somber reflection.

There had always been critics of the space program. Understandably so. The billions that were being spent could have been spent on education and health. We were spending billions of dollars on the Vietnam War. Could we really afford this space folly?

From my perspective this was shortsighted thinking. With each liftoff the imagination of every boy in America took flight. The space program inspired thousands of teenagers to consider the sciences as a career. If nothing else, it might motivate them to finish their homework! What price could you attach to that? Getting to the moon was symbolic of mankind's unlimited potential and would open the door to space exploration. Once that door was open, who could tell what the benefits might be?

Wernher von Braun, always the space enthusiast, had put it eloquently when addressing Congress: "When Charles Lindbergh made his famous first flight to Paris, I do not think that anyone believed that his sole purpose was simply to get to Paris. His purpose was to demonstrate the feasibility of transoceanic air travel. He had the farsightedness to realize that the best way to demonstrate his point to the world was to select a target familiar to everyone. In the Apollo program, the moon is our Paris." Of course in Lindbergh's case, there had also been the little issue of prize money.

The spectacular successes of the space program so far had kept the NASA critics at bay. The public had been riveted by every new exploit and knew every astronaut on a first name basis. The fact that we were racing the Soviets had added further spice to the adventure.

Presently, the death of three astronauts, two of them iconic figures, gave the boo-birds the opening they'd been waiting for, and they pounced. An investigation determined that a spark probably emanated from the confusion of wires near Gus's left foot. The astronauts' deaths were deemed avoidable, and NASA appeared increasingly sloppy as the investigation progressed. Funding cuts loomed, as if that would make things safer. Hearing upon hearing was held, the future of Apollo hanging more precariously in the balance each time around. It took the President of the United States to end the wrangling. Using his considerable political savvy and the full weight of his office, Lyndon Johnson talked down the naysayers, urging NASA to learn from its mistakes and move on. He was right, of course. As every test pilot knows, when you develop a new aircraft, you're going to lose some hardware and some pilots. Grissom knew that. White knew that, and so did Chaffee. They would have wanted us to go on. Hell, they would have been furious if we hadn't.

I poured this all out in a letter to Mal.

**

The Review Board would determine that the astronauts had passed out fifteen to thirty seconds into the fire. Although they had suffered some burns that must have been excruciating, they had actually died of asphyxiation from the toxic smoke. It was determined that the fire had indeed started around a wire near Gus's left foot. The wording of the report could be interpreted to mean that the fire was Gus's fault, and with the memory of Gus's *Liberty Bell* sinking, the press focused on Gus-the-screw up. Many of us took huge offense to this: Deke called every reporter and Congressman he knew to set the record straight. He owed it to Betty and the kids.

The hatch came under criticism. It took fourteen turns and various procedures to open it from the inside; in such a crisis, even a big, athletic man like Ed White had no chance. Already before the accident, it had been slated for replacement. The Apollo 2 hatch would be lighter and could be opened in twenty seconds. That might not have saved Grissom, White, or Chaffee, for the new hatch was still designed to open inwards. With their clumsy suits, they probably couldn't have made it out. The simple, awful fact was that a fire on the ground had never entered into any planning. The fear had always been that an outward-opening hatch might accidentally blow open in space – a fear ironically fueled by Gus's own mishap with *Liberty Bell*. Now that a hatch had fatally blocked three astronauts, NASA would have to take its chances again with an outward-opening model.

Overall, 1,341 changes were made to the Apollo capsule. It took 150,000 men and women a year and a half to implement these changes.

From the earliest days of the Mercury program, we had debated what the oxygen content in the capsule should be. Some advocated a normal air mixture, while others pushed for pure oxygen. There were good arguments in both directions. Normal air is a mixture of oxygen and nitrogen, and at sea level, the pressure is around 15 lbs/in^2. A pure oxygen system would allow you to function at just 5 lbs/in^2. If the capsule were filled with normal 15 lbs/in^2 air, each time the astronauts donned their 3 lbs/in^2 spacesuits they'd have to slowly work *down* to it. This elaborate procedure would be necessary to gradually rid their bodies of nitrogen and eliminate the threat of the bends. Normal air systems were also heavier than their pure oxygen equivalents.

In consideration of all of these factors, the proponents of pure oxygen had won out. The scales now obviously tilted the other way. NASA could simply not afford another fire.

As strange as it seems in retrospect, we'd never realized how flammable Velcro is, and we'd never given any thought to all the paper in the capsule. The flight plan alone was over a foot thick! We learned the hard way that aluminum is violently combustible in pressurized oxygen.

**

The astronauts had not been the only victims of the fire. As with many tragedies, the human toll continued to rise far past the date of the event itself. Ed White's wife Pat would commit suicide a few years later, and a few engineers, riddled with guilt, went off the deep end. This was an area where NASA failed. The doctors could monitor the tiniest physical sign and symptom of an astronaut, but they knew little about providing emotional support.

****

In the midst of our gloom, our mourning, the government investigation, the second-guessing, and all the backbiting, "Penny Lane" arrived like an angel on a cloud. The song was ever-present; it emanated from every radio, every store, and every car. Each time I heard it, a little ray of sunshine entered my soul. This was clearly McCartney's song. I could not identify any of the other Beatles. It was a piano tune, a nostalgic Victorian dream portraying a section of Liverpool. The scenes depicted in the song captured a mood and an era, much as a Norman Rockwell painting might. There was the banker, the barber, the fireman and his fire engine, and the nurse selling poppies from a tray. The instrumentation was mostly classical, and instead of a guitar solo we were treated to a high-pitched wind instrument, the snappy piccolo trumpet. Very strange! Another new sound.

The B-side complemented "Penny Lane" as an ode to childhood. It was also a dream, but an anguished Lennon dream. The title was taken from an orphanage, and the song mixed themes of abandonment, despair, no – hope! and certainly confusion. The arrangement was as tormented as the theme. Lennon's voice was detached, distant, and even hesitant, as he reflected on escapism and the meaning of life. The words served to convey both a mood and a message. It was the song John had written in Spain. Nothing was "real."

After the clear-cut, exalted high of "Penny Lane," "Strawberry Fields Forever" took you down to a nebulous, existentialist part of Lennon's brain. While Lennon played a simple guitar and took care of the singing, the others addressed a progressively more complex arrangement of guitars, muffled drums, and various instruments. Mal would explain to me later that they'd gone through multiple, multiple iterations of the song. No song to date had so drastically changed in the studio. McCartney had added a slow, childlike introduction on a new instrument called a mellotron – a funny-sounding piano, and with the other Beatles had progressively layered in all the studio sounds they could tastefully muster. When they were done, John liked the first half of one version and the second half of another version. In typical fashion he left it to George Martin to join the two.

There was but one problem: the two halves were recorded at a slightly different pitch. What to do? By precisely slowing down the second version and speeding up the first, Martin was able to change its pitch and create a seamless splice.

Ian Fleming's "Q " had nothing on George Martin.

As the song faded out, you thought the song was over. Instead, a barrage of sound appeared briefly, with perhaps a clarinet, an oboe, and some mumbo jumbo lyrics before disappearing for good. The gibberish would be the center of a major controversy two years later.

According to Mal, "Penny Lane" and "Strawberry Fields Forever" had both been targeted for the Beatles' next album, a record tentatively centered on the theme of childhood and Liverpool. It had been a long time since any kind of Beatle release, however, and the band was pressured into releasing the songs as a Double A single.

****

With everything at NASA shut down, Sally and I decided to finally take up Mal on his offer. He had invited us before, but we were so busy, and London was so far. The long distance now looked like a plus. I would turn thirty on February 14th, and going to London was suddenly the perfect birthday present.

Houston was a reasonably large city, but upon arriving in London, we were shocked. Shocked by everything: People in the street appeared to be from another planet. Mal had directed us to Carnaby Street, the capital of fashion, the epitome of swinging London; and swing it did. Gone apparently were the days of staid, discreet, "elegant" clothes. The skirts were short, the hair was long, the ties were wide. Sally had brought her trendiest clothes, but her 'miniskirts' were still inches too long in comparison. Some of the skirts and dresses were made of brightly colored vinyl – taxicab yellow, hot pink, lime green. The op art look was "in" – kindergarten collages come alive; I could just see Sally wearing one of these back in Houston. Not a chance.

With every door that opened, music floated out into the street. All was "mellow," "groovy," "far out." I felt a bit the square peg in the round hole, although my job was truly the farthest out... Sally insisted

I wear my white T-shirt or my button-down shirt, but not both. And fortunately, the plastic pocket penholder had stayed in Houston.

The big moment was to be our meeting with Mal at the EMI studios. We hailed a taxi and inched our way to the studio on Abbey Road. I'm not sure what I was expecting, but it didn't appear to be a studio from the outside. You could easily drive right by and miss it. It was boxy, smallish, and set back from the road by a few parking spots.

Mal greeted us at the door and gave us a hug. I introduced him to Sally. He still wore the black-framed glasses, but the hair was longer, his pants were fire engine red, and a paisley shirt hung loosely over his large frame. He led us inside with a finger to his lips. We walked upstairs to a cramped space. The consoles reminded me a bit of my own control room. We were introduced to George Martin, who shook our hand briefly and then thoughtfully turned his gaze back down to his prize pupils. A large glass pane overlooked an expansive studio, filled with musical instruments and tea cups.

And there they were.

They didn't fit the image we'd had of them, and it took me a few moments to take in the scene.

They all wore moustaches. Apparently, Paul had been in a moped accident and had split his lip. The moustache was there to cover it up. It hadn't taken long for the others to follow suit.

McCartney wore grey pants lined with thin stripes and a shirt that clashed wildly with his pants. John had on a frilly vest that you'd get arrested for in Houston. He studied his guitar through thin, round glasses. Harrison sported a jean jacket and black pants smattered with red and white oval patterns. Resting on his nose were heart-shaped tinted glasses. He removed them shortly after I got there. I couldn't quite make out Ringo. There was something else... Yes, that's what it was, their hair was short! Longer than mine perhaps, but shorter than everyone else's in town. Between their hair, their moustaches, and John's glasses, I wouldn't have recognized them on the street.

Though reels of tape were spinning, they didn't seem to be recording any specific song. Lennon was strumming an acoustic guitar and humming a slow melody. Paul sat at an organ that had been altered to sound like a "celeste," George Martin explained. In the shadows,

Harrison was tuning his guitar, and Starr watched from behind his drums.

"I need it more dreamy," said Lennon, looking in our direction.

McCartney was tinkering with a melody, in a tempo similar to John's tune.

"Dreamier, dreamier," continued Lennon.

George Martin slowly slid the levers up and down the console until John appeared satisfied.

Meanwhile, McCartney had hit upon a melody that was different from Lennon's, while complementing it quite nicely.

Lennon's lyrics made no sense, but conjured up amusing images: plasticine porters, looking glass ties, kaleidoscope eyes. McCartney shouted out, "newspaper taxis," and then "cellophane flowers," to which Lennon gave him the thumbs up. Harrison now got into the act, throwing out his own fanciful gibberish. Ringo hit his cymbal and laughed.

The chorus seemed to be "Lucy in the sky with diamonds," or something to that effect. It didn't make any less sense than the rest of the lyrics. After a few iterations, Paul had a suggestion.

"The chorus should be stronger. We can all come in on this here."

With that, he pounded out the chords and belted out, "LUCY IN THE SKY-Y WITH DI-I-IAMONDS" – and stopped to look around. They all nodded.

Paul counted in.

"4, 3, 2, 1, Lucy in the Sky-y with Di-i-iamonds," they all sang together, while Ringo got busy on the drums. It was the first time I'd heard them sing in unison, and it was riveting. The chorus presented a stunning contrast to the dreamy melody of a few moments ago. Without fully realizing it, I had inched forward to the edge of my chair. These were the Beatles I'd been waiting for.

The four of them went through the melody and chorus over and over and over again. I'm sure there were subtle differences each time, but I couldn't tell. Mal whispered over to us, asking if we were bored. I really wasn't. I was quite used to this kind of repetition, it being similar to our launch simulations.

Eventually, John, George, and Ringo got up to leave. Paul picked up his bass guitar and, listening to the playback, began to try out different riffs. He seemed to be going through endless permutations of notes and tempos. "He'll be here for hours," noted Mal. Just then he put down his guitar and headed up to the control room with Lennon in tow.

As he walked, Lennon would bob his head in a slightly spacey way. He didn't look 100% steady on his feet, reminding me of astronauts returning to their recovery ship. Mal introduced us. I actually shook Lennon's hand. The meeting was brief.

"Richtman, Dutch Richtman."

"He spells it R-i-c-h-t-m-a-n, but pronounces it RICH-men," Mal felt obliged to clarify.

"RITCH-men, RICH man, Rich MAN. Sounds Jewish. It's OK, Eppy is Jewish. You're not queer are you?" "Uh, no." I introduced him to Sally, perhaps subconsciously looking to prove my sexuality. I desperately wanted to say something memorable, but of course could think of nothing.

Lennon grabbed a pack of cigarettes from the console and out he went. McCartney hung out a little longer. "You're an astronaut?"

"Not really…" I fumbled through an explanation of my job.

"A couple of years ago – *Mal was it that long ago?* – I posed for Richard Avedon in a NASA astronaut suit. I fancied for a few moments what it might be like to fly into the heavens. They didn't have a helmet for me to try on."

McCartney in an astronaut space suit! If I'd been a little quicker, I might have commented on the perfect fusion of our society's icons; or in the same spirit, perhaps hummed, "*Into* the Sky-y With Di-i-iamonds." Instead, I lamely nodded and McCartney returned to the studio.

Mal pulled me aside. "John's like that. He wrong-foots everyone. You want to go for a drink?"

I was torn. Part of me would have been quite happy to stay in the studio watching McCartney work on more bass lines. Which one would he finally pick? But it didn't seem appropriate to hang around, not to mention that it would bore Sally. We drove off to one of Mal's watering holes.

"So what did you think?" Mal called out to me in the back seat.

"Wow! is all I can say."

Mal grinned. He looked like some kind of fairytale giant in his bright clothes. Sally, who was 5'5", seemed petite beside him.

"Yeah, I always feel like I'm part of history. Neil and I are the only ones down there with them. Some of these songs at first sound wimpy, or like they're going nowhere. Lennon was boring me a bit with his Lucy before you arrived. And then, like a magician yanking out a rabbit, they pull it together. D'you note McCartney's melody on that celeste? I bet he'll come up with a great bass line too. With George, it's kind of "still waters run deep." Doesn't say much, but his insight's always great. Lets Paul and John slog it out and slips in a key word here and there."

We reached the pub, parked, and went in. Our first London pub! It looked just like the movies. Sally smiled at me happily, and I felt proud I could offer her this. Mal brought our drinks back to the table.

"While you're in London, you should check out the guitar scene. It's hot. A band called Cream is setting the place on fire; they're a trio consisting of drum legend Ginger Baker, bass guitar virtuoso Jack Bruce, and guitar god Eric Clapton. He really is revered like a deity around here. You'll see "Clapton is God" scrawled on buildings, here and there. But do you know who's *really* hot? He's American, maybe you know him? Jimi Hendrix?"

"No." It didn't even ring a bell.

"Arrived without a penny in September. Chas Chandler, bass player for the Animals, brought him over. Within a week, every big name guitarist was showing up to watch him play. John and Paul have seen him a number of times, and Eppy even booked him for his Saville theater. Brian Jones of the Stones had the best line when talking about Hendrix' shows: "It's all wet down front from all the guitarists crying." I noticed that Mal still twirled his glass when he spoke.

"Even Clapton?"

"Are you kidding? He permed his hair into an Afro." Sally giggled at the idea. White guys with Afros hadn't shown up in our world yet. Then she took a sip of her drink and made a face. She'd insisted on trying a "shandy," a traditional British pub drink combining beer and lemonade; warm of course. I slid over my pint of Guinness so she could share. We talked about London and music for a while longer, then I changed the subject.

"So Mal, I've heard things at work that made me think of you." With that, I proceeded to tell him about Gordo and Deke's UFO encounters. Mal was silent a few moments.

"Dutch, there's a lot of stuff out there you don't know yet. There's a reason for the position you're in."

Me? I wasn't making the decisions or heading out to the moon. I just did my job. Another silence, while I tried to figure out what he meant.

"And here's a little bit I'll throw your way: John'll write a song for you."

"Lennon?"

He nodded.

"Why?"

Mal just arched his eyebrows. A thin smile pulled up along the left side of his face. His black plastic glasses suddenly looked even larger.

"You'll see."

Mal explained that he couldn't invite us to dinner because he was temporarily living at Paul's house in St. John's Wood. "Just doing whatever he needs, you know." He seemed embarrassed about it so we didn't press, though we did wonder where his wife and kids were. We'd been looking forward to meeting them.

As we walked out, a woman was coming in. She and Mal exchanged surprised looks, and Mal introduced us – it was Ringo's wife, Maureen. Mal spun around and went back in with her. I guess he wasn't in that much of a hurry.

Sally and I did the tourist things for a couple of days – The Tower of London, Buckingham Palace – and had great fun sitting in pubs listening to people talk. I wanted to go to Liverpool and Stonehenge (Sally wanted to hop the channel to Paris), but we didn't have time. Before heading back to Houston, however, Sally had me accompany her to a hospital in Wrightington where something called a "hip replacement" was being developed. Doctors were removing arthritic hips and replacing them with high-tech metal and plastic. I was struck by the surgeons' astronaut-type outfits (worn to minimize the risk of infection).

"I hope they perfect this in time for my dad," said Sally. Her father often complained of hip pain.

"We'll be lucky if it's in time for us," I replied, thinking of NASA and how long everything was taking.

We returned home with music in our heads: "Mellow Yellow," "Georgy Girl," "Happy Together," "Love is Here and Now You're Gone," "The Beat Goes On," "Knock on Wood," "Sweet Soul Music," "New York Mining Disaster 1941" (the Bee Gees' first hit).

Shortly thereafter, I noticed a small bit in the local paper: "Warner Reprise announces the signing of guitarist Jimi Hendrix." I bought his album, *Are You Experienced?* Mal had told me about Hendrix, but no amount of warning could have adequately prepared me for his sound.

"Purple Haze" and the album *Are You Experienced?* burst onto the scene in a way that reminded me of "I Want To Hold Your Hand" three years back. It was the first of many tremors that would shake the music world in the months to come.

From the metronome-like beginning to the wailing guitar, this was a sound like none other. I could only compare it to the power of our rockets. Hendrix' style arrived fully formed: One day he was a sideman for Curtis Knight and the Squires, and the next day he was taming hurricanes of sound. *Are You Experienced?* would not reflect his most sophisticated effort, but it would define him. The tree of music had just sprouted a whole new branch – hard rock. Hendrix's guitar playing defied classification. You felt yourself pushed out, spun back, and constantly gyrating at the end of a mad musical yo-yo. The guitar wasn't merely amplified to the sky; it was twisted and distorted in every possible manner, yet melodious and thrilling.

Other classic songs from Hendrix's offering included "Hey Joe," "Fire," "Foxy Lady," and "The Wind Cries Mary." Left off the American album (again @#$!) was "Red House," a pure blues song with blistering guitar licks.

The question of who was the better guitarist – Hendrix or Clapton – would quickly dominate backyard conversations, and both received considerable ink in serious music publications such as the fledgling *Rolling Stone* magazine. Eric Clapton and Cream had the pedigree. Clapton had been with the Yardbirds and then with John Mayall's Bluesbreakers. Bass player and singer Jack Bruce was classically trained and was already well known in music circles. The same could be said of drummer Ginger Baker, he of the two bass drums. When the three had joined forces, there had been a noticeable stir in the music world.

No such stir was created when bass player Noel Redding and drummer Mitch Mitchell were teamed up with Hendrix upon his arrival in England. Nevertheless, inventing guitar solos and guitar fills that no one had even dreamt of, Hendrix was quickly recognized as being in a league of his own. In my book, even though Eric Clapton was a blues guitarist extraordinaire, I gave the nod to Hendrix (as did Clapton himself). It didn't hurt that, by and large, he wrote his own material and was more than passable as a lyricist.

Both guitarists were masters of the wah-wah pedal, a pedal that would allow the guitarist to modulate distortion as he was playing. Being a first-rate guitarist now meant being agile with your feet too.

At this early stage Cream won the battle of the album cover art. The cover of *Are You Experienced?* was merely a photograph of Hendrix's band as seen through a fish-eye lens, matted with an ugly chartreuse color. The Cream offering, *Disraeli Gears*, was wildly original – a collage of graduated pink, yellow, and orange patterns *(the late Prime Minister would have been aghast)*. The cover was truly "psychedelic," a word lately added to the English language, suggesting something psychotropically induced or enhanced. Cream, admittedly, had a head start in the art department, this being their second album. The Hendrix team would catch up.

The major songs off *Disraeli Gears* were "Sunshine Of Your Love," "Tales of Brave Ulysses," and "Strange Brew."

Another supremely talented former Yardbird guitarist waited patiently in the wings, intently studying the style and success of Hendrix and Clapton. His day would arrive two years hence with bandmates Robert Plant, John Paul Jones (really), and John Bonham. His name was Jimmy Page, and the band, of course, would be Led Zeppelin.

****

In late April I received an urgent message from Kranz. The Russians were sending up Komarov. This was the same Vladimir Komarov who had commanded the first three-man mission back in 1964. He was going up in the brand new, un-tried Soyuz ("Union") capsule that was halfway between an Apollo and a Gemini capsule. It was suitable for three astronauts. It had been fitted with a docking collar, but there was no tunnel within the collar. Cosmonauts would have to perform a space walk to get from one spacecraft to the other. Nevertheless, it was good enough to take to the moon, or at least around it. Soyuz would make use of the latest in energy technology, solar panels, rather than batteries or fuel cells. Rumor had it that if this mission went well, the Soviets could sent a Soyuz around the moon as early as November – the perfect exclamation mark on the 50th anniversary of the Bolshevik Revolution.

Kranz said the specifics of this mission were still sketchy. From what he understood, three astronauts would take off the next day in Soyuz 2. The two capsules would rendezvous and dock, after which two cosmonauts from Soyuz 2 would perform a space walk, join Komarov in Soyuz 1, and return to earth with him. A pretty ambitious plan considering their long absence from space and, as we would later find out, serious failures in the three unmanned Soyuz flights. It would be the first real Soviet rendezvous, the first Soviet docking, the first true Soviet space walk (like Ed White, Leonov had merely floated), and the first *double* space walk. Apparently, even without Khrushchev, the Soviet government continued to pressure their space planners; a Soviet triumph coupled with America's recent tragedy would be a tremendous political victory.

Considering the difficulties we'd had with our own spacewalks, I wondered how they would pull it off. I did not have to wonder very long.

When Komarov reached orbit, he launched into a by-now-typical Soviet diatribe: "On the eve of the glorious historic event, the fiftieth anniversary of the Great October Socialist Revolution, I convey warm greetings to the peoples of our homeland who are blazing mankind's road to communism."

He was crowing a little prematurely, for Komarov's problems started shortly thereafter. One of the two solar panels failed to deploy. There were also guidance problems, and the weather at the Baikonur launch site was poor. Soyuz 2 was cancelled. Komarov's mission now simply turned into a shakedown cruise of the Soyuz capsule.

The mission's problems weren't over.

His main radio failed, so he went to his backup.

The Soyuz capsule was designed to be piloted from central headquarters, with the pilot as a backup (consistent, one might say, with the centralized communist system). When the ground-controlled navigation system went kaput, Komarov was forced to go manual. He found control of the spacecraft to be difficult.

Komarov flew out over the communication dead zone. For hours he was incommunicado. When Soviet ground control finally regained contact with Soyuz 1, they found themselves dealing with a distraught cosmonaut in a tumbling spacecraft. It was clear that Komarov had to come down from space, and it was equally clear that with a wobbly capsule he might not survive re-entry.

The Soviets hastily arranged for Komarov and his wife Valentina to have a private, perhaps final, conversation.

Komarov fired the retro-rockets and initiated re-entry. With the automatic control system out of order, Komarov continuously fired and adjusted his thrusters to maintain the alignment of his bucking beast.[16]

He somehow survived re-entry, but if Komarov thought his biggest problems were behind him, he was wrong. They were above him. As the capsule continued to tumble, his parachutes became tangled and never deployed.

He was buried in the Kremlin with full honors.

The Soviets were right back with us at square one. Both the Americans and the Soviets seemed to be playing a celestial game of Candyland®. Just when you thought you were reaching the top of the board, you'd land on Plumpy, and down at the bottom you'd be again!

Years later we discovered that Komarov hadn't been the first cosmonaut fatality. In an incident eerily similar to ours back on March 23rd, 1961, Valentin Bondarenko had thrown an alcohol pad near a heater in his pressurized, oxygen-saturated isolation chamber, and had incinerated himself before anyone could get to him.

This death, however, had as big an impact on the Soviets as the death of the Apollo 1 astronauts had had on us. Never again would they send up a cosmonaut in an unproven spacecraft. Again, we all had to ask ourselves whether this race to the moon was worth it. The

---

16 Just as Cooper had done on his Mercury flight.

Soviets, of course, didn't have constituents to worry about. You could be sure they were still in it.

****

London, 15ᵗʰ May, 1967

Dear Dutch,

You won't be surprised when I tell you that the song you heard the boys practicing is now officially called "Lucy in the Sky with Diamonds." [Many people would come to believe that the title of this trippy song stands for LSD, but Mal told me it sprang from a classroom picture drawn by John's son Julian.]

Much, much has happened since you were here.

Paul's come up with the idea of having the Beatles play as another band altogether, under a different name. This would free them from having to play songs that fit the Beatles mold. In keeping with the crazy-named bands of the day, he's dreamt up "Sgt. Pepper's Lonely Hearts Club Band"! Then, he thought the whole album should be a show. It would open up with a short intro tune; the song would end with an emcee introducing the next act, "Billy Shears," and without interruption would segue into "With a Little Help from my Friends." Paul wrote this specifically for Ringo to sing. He and John spent hours at John's home working on the lyrics. John came up with a great line: "What do you see when you turn out the light? I can't tell you but I know it's mine"! Another line was, "What would you do if I sang out of tune, would you throw tomatoes at me?" but Ringo refused to sing that. He had visions of fans throwing tomatoes at him if the band ever went back on tour. So the line was changed to "Would you stand up and walk out on me?"

Anyway, that's it for the "show." The title song is reprised at the end of the album, but the remaining tunes on the album don't have a particular theme or thread.

Paul's been into this album more than any of the others, probably because Jane's been on an extended acting run in the States[17]. She's very serious about her career — thinks it more important than spending all her time with Paul. John's been helpful of course, but he's been busy exploring

---

17 Girlfriend Jane Asher.

illicit substances with George. George has himself just come back from India; he's gone even more completely bonkers — if that's possible — over everything Indian. It looks like being back in the studio is becoming more of a job than a passion.

Ringo's learned to play chess with Neil.

Wait until you see the actual cover. The last one was a little adventurous, what with Klaus's black and white sketches — but that was nothing. This one's in spectacular color. It's cost a fortune, and EMI's not at all happy about it. The Beatles' art dealer friend, Robert Fraser, hired artist Peter Blake and photographer Michael Cooper to produce Paul's vision. Paul wanted a floral arrangement, and after multiple brainstorming sessions, it's come down to this: the Beatles resplendent in brightly-colored satin Victorian military uniforms (Paul and George subtly wearing their MBE medals), looking down at an ornate floral arrangement spelling out "Beatles" and surrounded by cardboard cutouts of sixty-two people — friends, heroes, you name it. Bob Dylan, Stu Sutcliffe, Edgar Allan Poe, Marilyn Monroe... And guess who had to track down these people (or their estates) and get their written approvals??? You guessed it. I never realized that, as a roadie, this would be part of my job description. EMI did nix some people outright: Gandhi, Jesus, and Hitler (thrown in by John, of course, just to shock). Mae West first said she didn't want to be associated with any Lonely Hearts Club Band type of thing, so we had to explain.

And for kicks, the boys threw in their dummies from Mme Tussaud's wax museum — these were the "old" Beatles; the mop tops, the matching outfits, and the like. The wax dummies appear to stare down on the floral arrangement as if witnessing their own funeral. Just a little subtlety in case the listener couldn't already tell from the music: The old Beatles are dead.

Another amusing touch is a raggedy-Ann doll with the words "Welcome the Rolling Stones" stitched across the front. And there are the marijuana plants, but we won't get into that. Sgt. Pepper was first going to be called Doctor Pepper, but it turns out that you have a soda by that name. A small nightmare, all this just for an album cover. (Lil's complaining I'm not home enough; it's harder for her now with Gary and Julie in tow. But somebody's got to make a living.)

The lyrics will be printed right on the back of the album; this will be a first. Much work has been expended on these lyrics, and the boys are eager to highlight this aspect of their craftsmanship (and no more listening to a song over and over again to try to catch that word!).

By the way, the album opens up like a book. I think this is also a first. Paul wanted artwork by a group called The Fool for the inside cover, but he got voted down. Instead you'll see a portrait of the four in their Victorian military outfits. Each album will contain little party favors — paper cutouts of Sgt. Pepper himself and other goodies.

A splendid time is guaranteed for all!

The album is top, top secret, so I can't send you an advance copy. I hear that for once the album will be identical on both sides of the Atlantic.

Last month I went with Paul to Denver and then to L.A. and San Francisco. (Sorry I couldn't stop over.) The Denver bit was to surprise Jane on her birthday. Sodding big mountains there. Paul wanted to see them up close, so we went on a bit of a hike, froze our arses off, and then flew to California on a jet kindly lent to us by Frank Sinatra! Remember three years ago when he thought the Beatles were "an abomination?" The jet had cool black leather seats and a fully stocked bar, which we greatly appreciated.

In San Francisco, we checked out the music scene. Paul met with John Phillips of the Mamas and the Papas. (No, the Beatles would not oblige him by playing in his upcoming Monterey Music Festival, but Paul encouraged him to include Jimi Hendrix.)

We also hung out with the Jefferson Airplane and other bands with crazy names I can't remember. And, in the wacky name category, there's a writer Ken Kesey, who goes around the country in a psychedelic bus with a bunch of nutters calling themselves the Merry Pranksters. Paul's already got an idea for his next project. He'll base it on the Pranksters and will call it the Magical Mystery Tour. Never a dull moment here.

Groovingly Yours,

Mal

It was June 2nd, and there I was in line with everyone else. It was a little embarrassing, to say the least. People seemed to be half my age. I'd let my hair grow since the trip to London. It went over my ears, covered my collar, and swept forward over my forehead. My T-shirt was tie-dyed, and bell-bottom jeans covered the heels of my boots. The boots weren't pink like Eric Clapton's, but I wasn't a complete geek.

Ooohs and aahs emanated from all corners of the store as people ripped the cellophane off their new record. This only heightened the excitement for those of us still on line.

The record did not disappoint. Mal had alluded to the efforts that had gone into the cover art, but the visual feast offered up by the album nevertheless took me aback. The little yellow rim at the top, the blue sky, the many, many figures and little objects – it looked like one of those "I Spy" pictures that would come around many years later. And there, in the middle of the cover, were the new Beatles, dressed in their Victorian military outfits; Paul in blue, John in yellowish green, George in red, Ringo in bright pink. And they all still had short hair! Just when I'd let mine grow, theirs was short! And they all still wore mustaches.

The lyrics were printed on the back. I started to read them, wondering what the melodies would be. Would the song be fast? slow? A Paul song or a John song?

The album indeed opened up like a book. The four Beatles smiled and welcomed you into the show. I picked up off the ground the sheet of colorful cardboard cutouts, not too sure what to do with them.

Triumphantly, I arrived home; Sally had been patiently waiting. I popped open a beer, turned off the noisy AC, reverently placed the black vinyl disc onto the altar of the turntable, and sat back for the show.

There came the distant sounds of an orchestra warming up … and then WHAM the guitar lick kicked in!

"It was twenty years ago today, Sgt. Pepper taught the band to play." Not much of a song really, but sung with verve by McCartney. It was short and it ended with "so let me introduce to you, the one and only Billy Shears, Shears, Sheeeeeeears." Without a break it blended right into the next song. A Ringo song. And not a throwaway. It was actually catchy. "I get by with a little help from my friends… I'm gonna try with a little help… I get high with…"

I get HIGH?

Had I really heard that?

That was daring!

Once more, without a break, the song segued into the next.

And I recognized it! It was the song I'd heard them rehearse back in February!

I liked it. The body of the recording was dreamy, nonsensical, and filled with flights of fancy. And, naturally, having been there during its creation, Sally and I could relate to it.

"Being for the Benefit of Mr. Kite" was a circus song, completely in keeping with the Victorian uniforms on the cover. There were dancing horses, flying acrobats, hoops and garters, and a hog's head of real fire. My favorite part was the twenty-second fadeout which included a new little melody and some fierce calliope. To Sally's annoyance, I had to play back those last twenty seconds a few times over before allowing the needle to proceed onto the last song, which opened with the mellow sounds of... a harp. It was a wonderfully crafted tale of a young woman who leaves her parents' home without so much as a word. She leaves "a note that she hoped would say more." The song encapsulated the disconnect between the generations. Her parents had given her "everything money could buy," but something was still lacking. This was Sally's song. "Something inside denied to her for so many years" struck a deep chord within her, as did the *finale,* "She's leaving home, bye, bye..."

I was startled by the little tear in the corner of Sally's eye. I thought she had a good relationship with her parents, but later that night, she told me things about her teenage years I'd never heard before. Surprising what a song can bring out.

I got up to turn the AC back on for a few moments and got myself another beer.

The first side of the record had been positively colorful, both visually and musically. The old Beatles were indeed dead and buried. Yet it had only been three years since "I Want To Hold Your Hand."

The opening song on the second side was Harrison's. All the instruments were Indian. The title was "Within You Without You," as in "the world goes on within you and without you." It was a spiritual song with a message, as most of Harrison's songs would be from here on in. By design the song had a slow, droning sound, and you either liked it or you didn't. I thought it was one verse too long.

The next song quickly perked up the mood. It had McCartney written all over it. It was a throwback to what my parents might have listened to. It could never have been released as a Beatle song proper – it was just too far removed from the world of rock'n'roll – but as a song performed by Sgt. Pepper's Lonely Hearts Club Band, it would be a good fit. In typical McCartney fashion we were introduced to characters he'd created: Vera, Chuck, and Dave. Disdained by every rock 'n' roll purist, "When I'm Sixty Four" was nevertheless destined to become a classic[18].

In the following song we would meet "Lovely Rita," the meter maid, another product of McCartney's imagination. It was produced in a light-hearted vein similar to the previous track, except that it fades out over a crescendo of grunts, groans, and sighs, some lecherous panting, and, finally, a short post-climactic piano chord.

"Good Morning, Good Morning" ends over the sounds of various animals: a cat's meow, a dog's bark, a horse's whinny, a pig's grunt, a lion's roar, an elephant's trumpet, and, lastly a chicken's cluck that just happens to be in the same pitch as the guitar note which opens the final song of the show. That would be "Sgt. Pepper's Lonely Hearts Club Band (reprise)," a faster version of the opening song. You think it's the last song of the album, but no, as it fades out, one hears the quiet strumming of a guitar. A new song, a little goodie bag to take home after the show.

It sounds at first like a pure Lennon song. It's in the same style as "Strawberry Fields" or "Lucy in the Sky," but more chilling; but it's also a McCartney song. Both writers in their own style are approaching musically the concept of A Day in the Life of Joe Somebody. It reminded me of their diverging childhood reminiscences, "Penny Lane" and "Strawberry Fields." Lennon contributes an otherworldly song about the dying rich, the Albert Hall, holes in Blackburn, and other non-sequiturs. The piece is sung with a voice that would send shivers up the spine of any mammal. Lennon ends the first portion of the song with an unused bit of McCartney's lyric, "I'd love to turn you on." It's an apparent reference to drugs – and an automatic BBC radio

---

18 In the 1960s, sixty four was an age at which you were expected to be old and doddering.

ban. The songwriters would explain that they simply wanted to turn people on to reality.

McCartney's approach to a Day in the Life is bouncy, pedestrian, no-nonsense, and down-to-earth. "Woke up, got out of bed, dragged a comb across my head." The verse ends with "I took a smoke and I went into a dream" (grounds for another radio ban), and the song abruptly reverts back to Lennon's eerily detached vocal.

Between the Lennon and the McCartney sections, McCartney initially left 24 musical bars empty, to be filled in somehow at a later date. Mal sounded an alarm clock to signal the end of the 24 bars. It was to be removed during final production, but at the last moment was left in; it fit so well with the start of the McCartney lyric ("woke up...")!

To fill the 24 empty bars, McCartney conjured up an extravagant, avant-garde solution that would cost another bloody fortune. Only the Beatles might have gotten away with this: an entire orchestra hired and brought into the EMI studio. In the druggy, childish, festive atmosphere of the day, some of the musicians were asked to don a clown's red nose, a request that was met with less than unmitigated enthusiasm. Then they were asked to play their instruments from the lowest to the highest note in the space of the 24 bars, at any tempo they wished. The result was a tornado of sound that swells and swells, until it climaxes with the tiny sound of that alarm clock. The maelstrom of sound is repeated at the end of the song, immediately after which the song ends on a long E chord played simultaneously on the lower end of four pianos. The excitement, the climax, the exhaustion... Mal was one of the four piano "players" and he described the technical difficulties:

"Paul wanted to end the song and album in dramatic fashion, a loud piano chord that would last as long as possible. We brought in as many pianos as possible, which turned out to be four. Paul, John, George (Martin), and I were instructed to strike the lower E chord at precisely the same time. Do you have any idea how difficult it is for four people to strike their pianos at precisely the same moment??? You'd think it would be a snap. We had to repeat the bloody exercise nine times until it sounded just right! The crashing sound of the pianos was then allowed to quietly drift away for close to a minute, until it disappeared entirely."

A quiet, peaceful end to a psychedelic adventure.

After a few moments of silence, Sally nodded slowly. It had been worth the wait. The peacock had fanned its feathers. Sally sidled up next to me to go over the album cover. Was that really Bob Dylan? We could only identify some of the faces in the crowd. Sally got up, turned the record over, and placed the needle on the first track again. There came the distant sounds of an orchestra warming up...

The musical extravaganza was even more satisfying the second time around, as I started to pick up on the varied instruments and sounds. It looked and sounded as though the Beatles had jumped out of a black and white world into big pools of Day-Glo.

I wondered how much grander the album might have been with "Penny Lane" and "Strawberry Fields," instead of their substitutes, "When I'm 64" and "Lovely Rita." I seemed to be the only one harboring those thoughts, for the album could hardly have received a more glorious welcome.

The arrival of *Sgt. Pepper* was one of the major cultural events of the year. Critic Kenneth Tynan called it "a decisive moment in the history of western civilization." You could not escape it. It was the featured story in every newspaper, every magazine, every cocktail party, and every dinner conversation (except at NASA). It was hailed as a masterpiece within days of hitting the record stores. It scored an A+ in every category: quality, variety, originality, cover art... The Beatles had channeled the musical and social trends of the day and showered us with a psychedelic splash. A quasi-religious awe soon surrounded the album, and the record landed the Beatles on the cover of *Time* magazine. The Beatles, and by extension the entire world of rock'n'roll, had arrived. They were now to be taken seriously.

For the Beatles, this was their moon landing.

Despite *Sgt. Pepper*'s immense success, Lennon would later say that it was not his favorite album. Hard drugs had progressively taken their hold on him, and it had been harder and harder to get him out of bed and into the studio. His four major contributions to the album (not counting his input into "With a Little Help from my Friends") were, in a way, lazy. All were inspired by what he could see from his bed: his son's grade school drawing ("Lucy in the Sky"), a poster for a 19th century circus from which he lifted all the lyrics ("Mr. Kite"), a Kellogg's cornflakes television commercial ("Good Morning, Good Morning"), and clips from the day's newspapers ("A Day in the Life"). *Sgt. Pepper* also marked the beginning of McCartney's tenure as unofficial musical producer/manager alongside the official producer, George Martin. Though Lennon was a major artistic contributor as were Harrison, and to an extent Starr, *Pepper* had clearly been McCartney's baby. Finally, with Brian Epstein increasingly unavailable and unpredictable as a result of his substance abuses, McCartney had gradually filled the void. As useful and even necessary as this might be if the Beatles were to remain a unit, in the back of his drug-addled mind, none of this was particularly to Lennon's liking.

To celebrate the release and instantaneous success of *Sgt. Pepper,* Brian Epstein hosted one of his famous all-out parties. He had been roller-coastering for months from the peak of elation to the trough of despondency, eased only by drugs and alcohol. There was no pill for what ailed him. On this night he was as proud as could be, and all was well. Even so, for Epstein dark clouds always sullied the brightest of times, and today was no exception. The success of *Sgt. Pepper* had proved the Beatles right and Brian wrong: they could sell an album without the benefit of touring. And without touring, would there be a need for Brian in the Beatles' life? His contract with the boys would come to an end in October. Would they renew it? The subject had not been brought up yet, but Brian worried. Paul didn't show up for the party. Should he take this as an omen?

There were other parties celebrating *Sgt. Pepper,* and seated at one of the press parties was a young, blonde American photographer, who'd made a bit of a name for herself photographing rock stars. Her name was Linda Eastman. She left with all the other photographers, but noted that McCartney had not been completely unfriendly. It was their second meeting. They had connected back in May at the *Bag O'Nails,* where Paul commonly mingled with Eric Clapton, Steve Winwood, the Animals, the Who, and other members of British rock royalty.

****

If Kennedy's Presidency and the development of the Mercury program represented the first phase of the '60s, and the Beatles, the Gemini program, and the Civil Rights movement embodied the middle phase, then the Spring of 1967 saw the beginning of the third and final phase.

It was the era of Peace, Love, Violence, Sex, War, Drugs, Demonstrations, and overall Grooviness. 1967 – the Summer of Love. American parks turned into a riot of color and marijuana smoke. No one stayed off the grass.

All the summer needed was an anthem.

The Beatles had been selected to represent the U.K. in a worldwide television show, the first ever satellite broadcast. 400 million people were expected to watch[19]. Lennon had been ruminating over a song about love and about the one-ness of the Universe, a continuation of the cosmic awareness provided him by LSD. The lyrics had a gibberish aspect to them, but their author did not mean for them to be nonsense. This was a spiritual song about the limitless, celestial coming together that would declare itself if we only opened our eyes to cosmic love. Without necessarily grasping the depth of the lyric, the television producers were thrilled with the overall message. On June 25th, the Beatles gathered in a festive studio. They sang the song in front of a carefully selected audience which included Eric Clapton and Mick Jagger, decked out in a smashing silk coat. The studio was festooned with balloons and spiritual symbols from around the world. Parts of the instrumentation had been pre-recorded (a full fifty seven takes, mind you), but the singing was live as were the bass, lead guitar, and drums. Lennon was nervous and forgot to spit out his chewing gum prior to the show; he was more relaxed at the end and launched into "She Loves You, yeah, yeah, yeah" during the fadeout.

The song, "All You Need Is Love," was a hit.

I was quite frankly astonished to receive a copy of the song in the mail. Mal had not sent me a single in a long time. There was no need to play the disc as I had heard the song repeatedly on the radio. It was Sally who noticed a few days later that the *flip* side of the record had been signed. "To Dutch, John." There was a rudimentary sketch of a face underneath the signature. How about that? Autographed to me! Why the B-side, though? Who cared about "Baby You're a Rich Man"? Sally and I dutifully sat down to listen. The song starts with an instrument that I had never heard before (typical, I thought). It has a

---

19   It would not be broadcast in the U.S.

chugging rhythm and is constructed like "Lucy in the Sky." A hazy, lazy verse sung by Lennon, followed by a more rousing chorus. The lyrics could have been rejects from the A-side ("What did you see when you were there? Nothing that doesn't show"). I got the message. You can be a rich man too, if you open your eyes to the love in the universe, etc... But what did that have to do with m...

I got it. Ha-ha.

Dutch Richtman. RICH-men, Rich-men, Rich Men, Rich Man, "Baby You're a Rich Man." A little gift from Mal's extra-terrestrial friends perhaps? They *knew* in February that Lennon would be writing this? And what, called Mal to tell him? It was more likely John had already started writing the song back in February. Mal would have to do better than that. Anyway, I now had Lennon's autograph. Perhaps if I played along with Mal, I could get a few more.

The summer of '67 saw the flowering of the hippie movement, the capital of which was the Haight-Ashbury section of San Francisco. Hippies followed Dr. Timothy Leary's admonition to "turn on [to drugs], tune in [to reality, man], drop out [of society]." The trend gradually spread to the entire country. Theirs was a childlike vision of the world in the spirit of Jean-Jacques Rousseau and William Wordsworth. People were innately good, not only innocent at birth, but possessing the potential to remain that way – although, alas, society corrupts us all.

This philosophy was hardly the mainstay of Beatle music, but it did fit in with the band's general view of life. Harrison had said to Maureen Cleave (as part of that infamous Beatles and Jesus series a year earlier), "Babies when they are born are pure. Gradually they get more and more impure with all the rubbish being pumped into them by society." And of course, in "She Said, She Said" Lennon had sung, "When I was a boy, everything was right." The hippies' existence consisted of railing against the vices of their parents' generation as well as wishing for peace and love, code words for psychotropic drugs and sex, as far as I was concerned. At the extreme they lived in communes, where they were "liberated" from society's rules, i.e. free to have sex with whomever they wanted at any given time. The endless war in Vietnam provided convenient fuel for the hippie ire and fire against the

establishment. From my vantage point I didn't see hippies as contribut-
ing much to our society, but they certainly added color and inspired
wonderful music.

In short order every musician would wear wildly colored clothing
(specifically *not* color-coordinated) and devilishly long hair. The theme
of peace and love would provide an endless source of songs.

**

A new phenomenon was occurring in the American music world:
album sales were increasing, both in absolute numbers and in relation
to singles. This coincided with the rise in popularity of FM radio stations, where disc jockeys began to expose the public to artists' non-Top
40 works. By 1967, album sales surpassed those of the little spinning 45
RPM discs that had dominated the music industry.

****

Somewhat overshadowed by *Sgt. Pepper* in June of 1967 (what
wasn't?) was the newest Bond movie, *You Only Live Twice*. Bond had
plunged to the ocean floor with *Thunderball* and was now flying off
into space. This was a radical departure from Ian Fleming's plot in the
book of the same name. The reviews were mixed, the receipts weren't
as strong as for the previous movies, and it had to compete against
another Bond movie!

Harry Saltzman and Albert Broccoli owned the rights to all the
James Bond books – except the first one, *Casino Royale*. Rival producers decided to make their own James Bond movie. Not wanting to go
head to head with the high-tech Saltzman and Broccoli productions,
they went with a light-hearted spoof. Despite an all-star cast that included comedian Peter Sellers, it was a disaster. Director after director
begged off, and the result was awful. What amused me most was the
opening scene: "Les Beatles" is seen scrawled on a wall.

Although it was fashionable at the time to see *You Only Live Twice*
as an inferior Bond film, I saw no problem with it. On the contrary, I
gave the thumbs up to the opening scene, where a car full of thugs is
plucked out of the sky by a helicopter and dropped into the ocean; I noticed no drop-off in Connery's performance, despite his own personal

misgivings. Best of all, obviously, was the combination of James Bond with the space race. Nobody at NASA was going to quibble with the technical details. SPECTRE had mastered the space rendezvous as well as we had! In fact the SPECTRE spacecraft that gobbles up American and Soviet capsules looked quite like our own alligator-like ATDA! The movie would perhaps stoke the public's (and Congress's) continued interest in our space program.

****

I found myself conflicted about drugs in general. It wasn't a moral issue. Was getting high a great deal worse than getting sloshed? It was really an issue of who did what. Proper society got drunk, hippies got high. Dylan and the Beatles were different. They gave us "Mr. Tambourine Man" and "Lucy in the Sky." I gave them a pass. But honestly, did our society really need more noxious substances? The conservative side of me said 'no.'

Nevertheless, some of our non-NASA friends were starting to try pot. Sally and I had been offered some. Sally was, if anything, more anti-drug than I was, and we felt uncomfortable being around others who smoked. They laughed at things that weren't funny; then they were awkwardly silent; then they were famished.

The four Beatles were far ahead of our friends, demonstrating the range of outcomes that can follow a sampling of drugs. McCartney found marijuana to be his substance of choice and had no need to go beyond his few little forays into the world of LSD. He indulged in just enough cannabis to improve his mood and creativity, but not enough to interfere with his workaholic nature. Starr developed a dependency on a more classic drug, alcohol. Lennon became the poster child for every parent's nightmare: marijuana led to LSD, which led to heroin, which led to addiction, withdrawal from the world, paranoia, and destruction of his social fabric.

Harrison eventually decided that chemicals would not provide the path to self-awareness; the Maharishi would. His opinion was cemented once and for all when he visited the Haight-Ashbury section of San Francisco. He'd expected to find enlightened youth deep in heavy discussions. He found, instead, aimless dropouts swarming around him in a drug-induced stupor as if he'd been the Messiah. That marked the end of his LSD experience. When his wife, Pattie, pointed out an upcoming lecture on transcendental meditation by the Maharishi Mahesh Yogi, this struck a powerful chord. George was in. And if George was in, the others would be also. The lecture was a success, and they all agreed to go for an extended session in Bangor, Wales later in the summer.

On the night of August 27th, Brian Epstein phoned his recently widowed mother, who was still in deep mourning. He phoned her often, chats that comforted them both. Following the conversation he reached into his drawer for a handful of pills, climbed between the sheets, and waited for the tablets to take effect. This was his usual routine, but this night was different. His heart pounded more urgently than usual, sweat spilled from his brow onto his pillow, images swirled, and his eyes glared wildly – then slowly faded. Soon, only the whites of his eyes showed between half closed eyelids, and his mouth slowly settled into an ungainly rictus.

Bangor, 28th August

Dear Dutch,

Tragedy has struck.

Brian Epstein died yesterday.

I've never seen John's face so white. We were up in Bangor getting an introductory lecture from the Maharishi when we got the call. His housekeeper found him dead in his bed. There's lots of speculation about suicide, but none of us believe this. Eppy was very attentive to his mother; he wouldn't want to put her through this sort of grief, not while she's still recovering from his father's death. He's binged on all sorts of substances and required repeated drying out sessions at various clinics, but he wasn't suicidal. We think he took one too many pills.

I don't know what to think. It's really hard to take in. The poor bastard. He had such a complex about not being good enough, when of course he was bloody marvelous. Paul wishes he had told him that more often, but of course that's just how you think when somebody dies.

Mal

Sally and I were sad about Brian, but mostly for Mal and the Beatles. We hadn't met Epstein in London. There did seem to be a lot of death going around.

Mal wrote again over the ensuing weeks.

Dear Dutch,

We're still adjusting to Brian's death, especially the impact on the business side of things. For a while we ran around like chickens without a head. Brian was the only one who knew where the contracts were, what the contracts said, what deals were in the works, etc... You could go crazy thinking of all the things Brian took with him to the grave.

However, Brian wasn't as essential as he'd been in the past, at least not in the same role. Paul's been the first to snap out of the shock, and I've noticed him taking the lead in the group's discussions

Would you ever think of "Apple" as the name of a company? The Beatles' accountants have advised them to diversify — the only alternative to giving all their money to the taxman. They're forming a company. Robert Fraser, the art dealer, gave Paul a Magritte painting depicting a green Granny Smith apple in place of a man's face, and Paul suggested to the others that they name the company Apple! How boring would it be to name it Beatles Inc. or something like that? If you're going to be original, you need an original name. The others all agreed, so Apple it is! There's also the little pun on Apple Corps...

The boys have some cool ideas. This is not going to be some stuffy, money-grubbing company. They'll audition musical acts without putting them through a torture chamber, and they'll open a store selling hip clothes at reasonable prices.

The Beatles are also set to film and record *Magical Mystery Tour*. There's no real script. We're getting on a brightly-painted bus that says "Magical Mystery Tour" and driving through the countryside. We've hired actors to fill out the bus. Paul's written a title song. I'm not crazy about it, though I like the piano fade out. (I hope you're burning these letters.) A better song is one he wrote at the top of a mountain in the South of France, "Fool the Mountain," "Fool on the Hill," actually. I got to travel with him.

But the BEST song in the movie is going to be another nutty song of John's called "I Am the Walrus." Where to start? It's a bit like "Strawberry

Fields." There's not much to it if you just play it on the guitar. The melody consists of two repeating notes — like a police or ambulance siren. The lyrics could have been taken out of "Alice in Wonderland." John was clearly on acid when he wrote this. But what a production! This is where THE BEATLES (and George Martin) come into play. What sounds, what rhythm changes!

The Magical Mystery Tour bus takes off tomorrow — and I have no idea where we are going... If you never hear from me again, look on the moon!

Mal

At the top of the "what were they thinking?" list that summer was the pairing of Jimi Hendrix with the Monkees, both on tour in the first year of their fame – the world's greatest guitarist alongside four actors pretending to be a band. The young teenagers who flocked to see the Monkees screamed, "We want Davy!"[20] during the gyrations of this wild man from Borneo. Needless to say, Hendrix soon begged off the tour.

In October *Rolling Stone*'s inaugural issue appeared on the news-stands. A black and white picture of John Lennon taken from the set of *How I Won the War* graced the cover.

****

Astronaut Alan Bean was starting to wonder what was happening. He seemed to be doing well in training, but he hadn't been assigned any mission; the numbers were starting to work against him. His story was looking more and more like Aldrin's. Both were capable men who'd been getting lost in the shuffle. Aldrin had been rescued from the numbers' game by the death of See and Bassett, and on October 27th, the Japanese fable granted Bean a similar gift: C.C. Williams, the lunar module pilot on Conrad's crew, crashed his brand new T-38 when the controls apparently jammed. On the verge of quitting the astronaut corps for lack of a mission, Bean was in.

---

20 Davy Jones – the Monkees' lead singer

When Deke announced the crew assignments for the upcoming Apollo missions, he had Wally Schirra commanding the first crew, followed by Commanders Jim McDivitt, Frank Borman, Tom Stafford, Neil Armstrong, and Pete Conrad.

Al Bean would be the lunar pilot with Conrad on the sixth Apollo mission. He and Conrad were a good bet to be the first to walk on the moon! Such a reversal of fortune was remarkable – to be surpassed only by Aldrin's.

****

The Beatles released the movie *Magical Mystery Tour* the day after Christmas. It was a bust. The release consisted of a black and white showing on British TV. Critics of every stripe roundly and loudly panned it – the first egg laid by the otherwise very golden Beatle goose. On the other hand, the accompanying album, released in time for Christmas, was a major hit. Personally, I thought the album represented a considerable dip in value. Much of it could have been titled "1967's Greatest Hits," and most of the first side was inferior by Beatles' standards. Yes, there was the standout "Fool on the Hill," but everything else was somewhat sub-par: "Your Mother Should Know" ("When I'm Sixty-Four" redux), "Blue Jay Way" (Harrison's morose meditation), and "Flying" (the instrumental that never gets off the ground). The title song was weak, except for the piano fade-out as pointed out by Mal.

The Beatles' year ended with McCartney's yin-yang, stalker-lite "Hello Goodbye" reaching the #1 spot ("I don't know why you say good-bye, I say hello").

Except for their very un-magical movie, it had been a banner season for the band. 1967 had seen the release of "Penny Lane," "Strawberry Fields Forever," *Sgt Pepper's Lonely Hearts Club Band*, "All You Need Is Love," "Hello Goodbye," "I Am the Walrus," "Fool On The Hill," and the *Magical Mystery Tour* album. A lifetime's work for even the most successful act. Mozart could not have had a better year.

Ironically, the Beatles didn't have the best-selling album of 1967. Nor the second, nor the third. The Monkees took the top two spots with *The Monkees* and *More of the Monkees*. Then, in successive order, came the soundtrack to *Dr. Zhivago*, *The Temptations' Greatest Hits*, the soundtrack to *A Man and a Woman*, *S.R.O.* by trumpet-playing Herb

Alpert, *Whipped Cream* (Herb Alpert again), and *Going Places* (Herb Alpert *again* again). Finally, rounding out the Top Ten was *Sgt. Pepper's Lonely Hearts Club Band.*

The Beatles could take some comfort in knowing that they had the top *rock* album of the year. *(And in time would out-sell all the others ahead of it on the list.)*

On a similar note the Beatles sold more singles than any other act that year, but none of the records individually cracked the top ten in total sales. Their best seller, "All You Need Is Love," came in at #30.

1967 hadn't spawned only Love. In a more confrontational spirit, bands like the Jefferson Airplane, the Doors, the Buffalo Springfield, and the Grateful Dead had been giving the finger to the Man. The next year would see the youth of the Western World take their message to the streets – and it would not be a pretty sight.

For other illustrations, see www.intotheskywithdiamonds.com

12. You are GO for TLI

Dear Dutch,

Greetings from Rishikesh, India!

I'm sitting in the shadows of the Himalayas, looking out at the stunning Shivalik mountain range. The holy Ganges River splits the town in two, and the water is actually quite clean!

We've signed up for a spiritual massage of sorts at the feet of the Maharishi. It's a sizable crowd: There's Donovan, Mia Farrow, her sister Prudence, Patti's sister Jennie [Harrison], Mike Love from the Beach Boys, not to mention a lucky photographer, and a bevy of students just coming through.

Paul and John amble about in loose, white pajama-like garb. They strum their guitars most of the day, and I'm hearing bits of many new tunes. John's nose has gotten pink from the sun. It's a real holiday for me too: No equipment to carry around!

Just before leaving for India, we endured mega-sessions at the studio. Everything had to be wrapped up by 15 February, the date of our departure. The boys needed to contribute four new songs to a Beatles' movie that they're contractually tied to. It'll be a cartoon. They're not excited about it, but it gets them out of having to act in a movie again. They were lucky to have three unused songs from last year, two noisy songs by George, "It's Only a Northern Song" and "It's All Too Much," and a simple little McCartney song, "All Together Now." The fourth song is a terrific Beatles cooperative effort, "Hey Bulldog." John came in with a melody and an absurd Walrus-like lyric; Paul added a piano lick and whipped up a furious bass line, and they were off to the races. They were howling away, having the best of times. A film crew was on hand to film a promo for the upcoming single, but instead they got ten hours of the Beatles hamming it up on "Hey Bulldog."

John also contributed a wonderful song, "Across the Universe," which is hazy and poetic. The lyrics alone stop you in your tracks.

"Words are flowing out like endless rain..."

265

'Wait 'til you hear this one.'

I thought for sure it would be the A or B-side of a single, but John wasn't completely satisfied with the production.

The key song of these sessions was the Beatles' latest radio release, "Lady Madonna." Everyone was enamored with it the moment Paul sat down to play it. It's an ode to motherhood, if you wish, but the lyrics are secondary. It's plain fun. Paul played a rollicking boogie-woogie piano, and all of them had a jolly good time singing cartoon-like *pa-pa-pa-pa*'s and what not. It'll be out soon, if it isn't already. With a single on the radio, it won't be so obvious that the Beatles are far away.

We all left for India on a very high note!

I'll make sure to send you some beads!

 (d'you like my new signature?)

P.S. Did I tell you, I've been made an 'executive' at Apple? And Neil's now the managing director. I never thought I'd be in business.

****

While the kings of rock'n'roll sought spiritual peace in India, violent student demonstrations wracked and roiled much of the world.

In New York City, a fellow named Mark Rudd led a group of rudderless students in their takeover of Columbia University's Administrative offices. This group of no-goodniks seemed happy to join any cause that would excuse them from studying. At least that's what it looked like from Houston. Racism, capitalism, and the war in Vietnam were their alleged causes.

In Paris, led by red-haired Daniel Cohn-Bendit, students also took to the streets to fight L'Homme. Like Mark Rudd, Cohn-Bendit offered no constructive contribution and he was never heard from again. These demonstrations did, however, help bring down both Lyndon Johnson and Charles de Gaulle.

April 4th, 1968, was a day I'd been looking forward to for some time. In the absence of any manned mission, the testing of rockets was the most exciting thing around. Though he'd lost out to the Air Force in the Gemini program, von Braun had been assigned the design and construction of the monstrous Saturn rockets. On November 9th, 1967, the first Saturn V had been launched with great success (retroactively, if not confusingly, named Apollo IV), the second had been launched with equal success in January, and now it was time for Apollo VI, the third launch of a Saturn V.

The Saturn was an impressive beast, weighing more than a Navy destroyer. It was hard to imagine getting such a hulk off the ground, let alone accelerating it to 17,500 miles per hour. As the countdown began, we retreated to the safety of the Launch Control Center, a comfortable three miles away. At the time of the first Saturn launch, no one had completely anticipated the visceral power of this new rocket. When the five F1 engines had ignited in a tidal wave of red flames and grayish smoke, a powerful rumble had quickly shaken the whole building, ceiling tiles had fallen on reporters' desks, and the corrugated metal sheets covering the press viewing stands had been wrenched loose. These structures had now been beefed up, but the rumble still vibrated every molecule in our bodies – all before the slightest sound reached our ears: From three miles away, we would have to wait fifteen seconds for the sound of the blast to reach us!

Two and a half minutes after liftoff, spent of its fuel the first stage was jettisoned, and the second stage, S-II, took over.

That was the end of our successful launch.

The rocket began to experience severe vertical vibrations ("pogo"). Two engines shut down. With only 60% thrust at its disposal, the guidance system took the rocket on a stormy ride into a lopsided orbit. The rocket shut down as planned. Two and a half hours later, Mission Control went to restart it.

In vain.

We were able to separate the Command Module from the rocket and simulate a re-entry and recovery, but overall it was quite a downer.

Momentous news spared us front-page embarrassment in next day's papers: Martin Luther King Jr. had been assassinated.

President Lyndon Johnson, himself a longtime voice for racial equality and harmony, pleaded for calm. His admonitions fell on deaf ears, and America was treated to riots from "California to the New York Island, and from the redwood forests to the Gulf Stream waters." Antiwar protesters had been hammering Johnson for months.

(The cruel couplet "Hey, hey, LBJ/How many kids did you kill today?" was being chanted in demonstrations all across the country.) Now with Blacks ignoring him and his hated rival Bobby Kennedy on the rise, Johnson sensed the walls closing in on him from all sides. He announced that he would not seek re-election in November and called it a career. This was the President elected in a landslide less than four years earlier! It was remarkable and it angered me. I was beginning to agree with the students about the war (though it made me sick, the way these privileged kids treated returning soldiers, mostly working class kids who couldn't afford college deferments), but Johnson had stood by NASA, and he'd pushed through a lot of compassionate (if expensive) social programs. I just didn't think the guy deserved such vicious attacks. Anyway, he was the President. That meant something where I came from.

The assassination had already pushed space exploration out of the public mind, or at least into a corner – there simply seemed to be more pressing problems – and Johnson's resignation would be another nail in the coffin of space travel. Each budget of the last few years had been carving out ever-greater chunks from NASA's allocation. Without Johnson, one of NASA's biggest supporters, where were we headed? Assuming we could reach Kennedy's goals, then what? Every post-Apollo project had been slashed, and it was not even certain that all the Apollo missions would fly.

With the exception of January 1967, this would be the gloomiest time for me at NASA, the time most filled with self-doubt *(Sally did her best to lighten things up. When I told her that due to budget cuts we would have to tighten our belts, Sally promised to go right out and buy one).* If we didn't succeed in landing a man on the moon by the end of the decade, would Congress scrap the project altogether? What were Sally and I going to do after that? Industry for me, I supposed; hospital work for her. Quite a comedown from The Race to the Moon.

These dark musings were brought to an end by the news that Apollo VI's problems had been identified and were easily correctable – so correctable that NASA made a striking announcement: the next Saturn flight, Apollo VII, would be manned.

****

London, 12ᵗʰ June, 1968

Dear Dutch,

I'm just back from New York in my new capacity as Apple Executive! I don't really have a title, but do a little of everything – meetings and publicity and whatnot. It's really not so different from what I've always done: make sure the details are attended to, keep everyone happy, and try to do my own thing as well, which in this case means finding talent. I'm very excited about that part.

But really, I feel proud that the boys trust me to do this. There've been times I've felt a little bit overlooked, y'know. Just good old Mal, always available to fetch tea and new socks, and deal with the lassies.

I don't know if you saw John and Paul on Johnny Carson when we were in New York. Too bad Johnny was on vacation. Some guy, Joe Garagiola, took his place. (I know he's a famous baseball player.) John says it's the most embarrassing interview he's ever given.

But bloody hell, besides my rise in the world of Apple, there've been some ugly things going on. Where should I start?

As I was telling you, the Beatle entourage went to learn at the feet of the Maharishi in beautiful Rishikesh. For a while we all enjoyed a relaxing time. Donovan took a liking to Jennie and wrote a song called "Jennifer Juniper." John learned a picking technique from Donovan that he practiced over and over again. It's wonderful, if exhausting, to watch his enthusiasm for any idea that catches his fancy. But then, John was bummed to discover the Maharishi's very, shall we say, earthly fondness for female companionship; he's sure to write about that![21] Ringo left early. He couldn't stomach the food.

More seriously, I thought this would have been a good time for John to re-connect with Cynthia.

No GO! No GO! as you would say.

After a few days in Rishikesh, John asked to have his own bedroom. It became very awkward. On the one hand I was telling Cyn to keep her chin up, while on the other I would run down with John every morning to see if there was a letter from his new love interest.

---

21 And indeed Maharishi would undergo a gender change and become "Sexy Sadie."

On the flight back from India, John's a little tipsy and he regales Cynthia with every affair he's had since their marriage. He practically rolls out the scroll. Essentially every woman who's been to their house, including her girlfriends, is on the list; cruel.

No sooner does the plane land in London that John urges Cynthia to go off and take a little holiday in Greece, while he busies himself in the studio.

Big mistake!!! I don't know what she was thinking. Maybe she just wanted to be away from him too. Lil said she hoped Cyn found herself some hand-some Greek fellow, but that's not Cyn.

When she comes back on the morning of the 20th, who is sitting in the sunroom having breakfast with John?

The stalker!

Joko, Yoko, whatever her name is! And she's wearing Cyn's bathrobe! Neither John nor the woman seems the least bit perturbed by Cyn's arrival. The end.

Cyn feels like she's the intruder. She stammers something about the three of them going out for a bite. Without looking up, John simply says, "I don't think so."

Can you imagine?

Cyn's replayed the scene in her head a million times, thinking of all the things she could have done, should have done, and would like to have done. (Don't we all!) She's angry with John and Lil's angry with me. I'm innocent! (Well, not really. I've helped the boys hide their affairs. But that's my job, innit?)

Then, the very next day, John tells Cyn that everything is really fine, that he still loves her, that he's busy recording with the guys, and that, since he has to go to New York with Paul to announce the start of the new Apple venture, a little time off in Italy would be good for her.

She goes. Tells Lil she just wants to be away from that horrible woman. Lil told her to get lots of shoes on John's account.

She's barely in Italy, when John serves her with divorce papers. Adultery is the pretext.

Adultery? Cyn?

How would John even guess who was with her in Italy? All I know is that our good friend Magic Alex, the self-styled electronic wizard with a misplaced opinion of himself, is presently driving a shiny white Mercedes, courtesy of John. It's really revolting.

And let me tell you, this Yoko has not been very nice. It's "The Count of Monte Cristo" revisited. She's now making life miserable for everyone who mistreated her during her quest to land a Beatle; that would be everyone, as far as she's concerned.

And John is more than playing along. It's the drugs. Yoko's opened his eyes to a very dark world. She's slid into him like a long key in a deep lock. They're inseparable, even when they go to the loo.

Do you know Robert Fraser? He had sworn he'd never let this woman within a mile of his gallery. So where does John want the woman's next exhibit? Fraser can't say "no" to John.

Yoko sends Tony Bramwell out to fetch her this, to get her that. He had to run around town the other day, looking for special cameras so John and Yoko could film people's arses. John even filmed his own erection, for God's sake. He's got it in his head that every aspect of his life is art — art that should be shared with everyone.

He has a project. He's calling it *Two Virgins*, in honor of their fresh start. (The other guys had a few choice comments about that.) The record consists of her wailing; I tried listening with a straight face. Get this: He wants a full frontal nude picture of himself and the woman on the cover (black and white 'coz it's more *artistique*), with a nude picture shot from the back on the flip side. He wants to show the world that he and Yoko are just plain folk. (Does the world really care?)

And plain they are. I can't see anyone getting off on this sorry sight. No one at Apple is pleased. The Beatles' accountant has resigned. He doesn't want to be associated with us anymore. Paul is furious. He doesn't give a hoot what John does, except that John's behavior reflects on all the Beatles.

John's printed verses from Genesis on the sleeve, you know — Adam and Eve, "And they were both naked, the man and his wife, and were not ashamed." Well, maybe *they* aren't ashamed... And to boot, it's on the *Apple* label (an as yet unbitten apple...)!

Ringo's funny: "I don't really see what's wrong with this pict... oh my yes, he's got his willie hanging out, hadn't really noticed."

There are surprises on the McCartney side too.

He's fallen head over heels over that American photographer, Linda Eastman. I've met her a few times and she's a pretty classy gal.

The problem was Jane. He was officially engaged to her since Christmas. And it's really too bad because she's a classy lass too. But she's got her career, and she's always on some tour because of this or that play. Paul needs a more traditional woman, someone who can be to him what his mum was to his father.

Jane found him in bed with some chick (not Linda), and it was over. I think Paul intended for Jane to catch him so that she would break the engagement, not him. John may have confessed to Cynthia about his affairs for the same reason. Lil says they're both cowards.

Anyway, both Paul and John have new love interests, though they couldn't be more different. One radiates warmth, the other sucks the life force out of a room.

John is committed (he should be committed!) to sending all kinds of messages to the world. Peace, hunger, you name it. Speaking of hunger, Ms. Ono orders the most expensive caviar every day, and from what Tony says, they don't even eat it all. So much for saving the world from hunger. I think the heroin cuts into their appetite.

Did I forget to mention that?

The lovely lady has turned John onto heroin. So now he's even more paranoid. It's the whole world against the two of them.

It tears me up to see him destroying himself.

Cynthia's looking better and better!

I'm looking at four separate Beatles here. There used to be a like-mindedness among the four of them that was striking. You could ask any one of them a question about politics, religion, music, and he would answer, "Well, we believe..." This "we believe" is over. It's been a gradual process, and I guess it's part of getting older, but the last few weeks and months have been like an earthquake splitting them apart.

The boys (I should stop referring to them as "the boys") have a good batch of songs to record. John insists that he and Ono are but one person, and so demands that she be present in the studio. That violates the unwritten rule about wives and girlfriends at work, but John will hear none of it.

The first time was quite a sight.

272

When he walked in with Yoko on his arm, we all stiffened, and all conversation ceased. It was frosty smiles all around. In quick succession the boys' faces registered indignation, annoyance, and resignation. "Well let's get on with it, we've got company," Paul finally said, studiously avoiding eye contact with the newcomer. John laughed, but the laugh had a hard edge.

They ran through a couple of tunes, but without much spark and without the usual banter. Her mere presence doused the flame of creative wackiness that normally warms the studio. You should have seen her at his shoulder like a bird of prey, the two of them continuously engaged in spirited whispering. She doesn't make the slightest effort to be friendly. Occasionally a glint of mischief shines in the depth of her eyes, but that's it. Her face is as impassive as the back of a guitar. (Or is it just a mask that she keeps in a jar by the door?)

Ever the diplomat, George Martin addresses her with controlled politeness, ("My dear, I do believe you are interfering with that microphone").

She had a "suggestion" the other day before quickly relapsing into a surly silence. A suggestion! George H. was seriously ticked. All these years he's played second fiddle to John and Paul, and now little Miss Screecher is going to step in ahead of him with a suggestion? I don't think so! It's clear that with all his telepathic strength George wishes her away.

For Paul, however, the survival of the Beatles is the number one priority. This is why, after a few tense moments, he graciously "discussed" her suggestion. Another time, during the recording of "Sexy Sadie," she wondered aloud whether the Beatles could do "better" on a certain take. I thought George would leap over the amp and deck her. John sensed that she had crossed the line. He quickly interjected, "Well maybe I can." George's eyes narrowed and hardened ever so little.

Although nowhere as disruptive as Yoko's presence, there are other little annoyances. The *producer* in Paul's soul is gradually moving to the fore. While the drumming arrangements were once solely Ringo's province and the lead guitar George's, Paul's come to clearly visualize just how he wants each instrument to sound, especially on his own songs. He'll tell Ringo to play the drums this way; he'll diplomatically suggest to George that the solo go that way... Mind you, he's always done a bit of that, much to everyone's benefit, and no one ever thought twice about it, but now everything's taken as an offense. They used to yell and curse at each other, and then laugh it off. Nowadays, the slightest perceived slight is cause for silent snickering.

Even the levelheaded Ringo is so exasperated that he temporarily quit. In his absence Paul recorded the drum track for "Back in the USSR."

Such is the current state of affairs.

Yours,

Mal

Mal as a business executive? Sally and I couldn't imagine it. It was exciting to think that maybe the Beatles would do for the music business what they'd done for music.

The stuff about John and Yoko was both surprising and not. "I don't know how anyone could keep a marriage together in that kind of life," said Sally. Yoko didn't sound like the sort of woman I'd choose if I could have my pick of girls, but Sally said she thought that was the point. "She doesn't treat him like a prince. She doesn't swoon. She stands up for herself. I would guess it's refreshing."

"She sounds crazy."

"John's a bit crazy, too. "

"But his is the good kind."

She smiled and pinched my cheek, as she does when she thinks I'm being naïve. "That may be true, but if you live inside that kind of creative mind, it's probably a relief to be around someone else who does too, even if they're not so talented or charming."

"I think if I were John Lennon, I'd insist on charming."

In June, John F. Kennedy's brother, Bobby Kennedy, was assassinated after winning the Democratic California primary for President. It seemed like America was plunging off a cliff. When would these assassinations stop? The media started pressing for gun control – long an LBJ issue, though not a Kennedy one. The NRA was at that time a sleepy organization, disdainful of politics. All that would change.

Sally cried for the family – especially those eleven fatherless children. I joked that with eleven kids, Bobby probably didn't even remember all their names. I didn't mean it – it was just one of my typical lame responses to emotions I didn't completely share. I was very upset about the assassination, but I didn't feel it as personally as Sally did. She'd been moved by his speeches, while I was more skeptical.

"JUST SHUT UP!" she shouted. I was stunned. This was the first time she had yelled at me in six years! Her anger was usually quiet and contained.

"Okay," I said. "I'm sorry."

"What's happening to our country?" she sobbed. "And what's wrong with eleven children?"

I tiptoed out. "Nothing."

She backed down. She was conflicted about kids in general. If she hadn't been, she would have left me long ago. Sally had dreams. She wanted to travel. She thought about being a nurse with the Red Cross. Some nights, she'd talk about raising horses or learning to sail – sailing around the world. I really had no idea if any of this would ever happen, but she was afraid of being tied down.

I didn't watch the funeral with her because I really *was* disturbed. What *was* happening to our country? I liked the changes of the '60s – civil rights, the music, the sexual freedom. I hated to think that societal disintegration was an inevitable result. I wondered what the decade would have brought if we'd never gotten involved in Vietnam.

**

I'd filled Mal in on the problems with the Saturn V, and I heard from him at the end of July.

London, 30ᵗʰ July, 1968

Dear Dutch,

Although they were away most of the spring and have been buried in the studio since their return, the Beatles are all over the news. United Artists has released the *Yellow Submarine* movie.

Truth be told, they've had nothing to do with this dazzling cartoon. It's not even their voices. The producer is Al Brodax, creator of the Beatles television cartoon series. There's really no connection between the two pro-ductions. This cartoon is PSYCHEDELIC! The rapid change of colors is phenomenal and the artistic work is beyond belief. The script calls for the Beatles to rescue the people of Pepperland, who've had music taken away from them by the Blue Meanies. A sub-plot involves rescuing Ringo, who has pushed a button in the Yellow Submarine and has been ejected into the sea. (This rescue-Ringo theme has worked well in the previous movies.)

Ringo tells me that little kids come up to him in the street and say, "WHY DID YOU PUSH THAT BUTTON?"

We've all enjoyed the movie. The Beatles appear in person at the very end of the movie, and they've contributed four musical tracks. "All Together Now" would make a great nursery school song, if not for the line "Black, white, green, red, Can I take my friend to bed?"

"Only A Northern Song" is an inside joke: Northern Songs is the publisher of the Beatle catalog to which none of the Beatles have any rights ("It doesn't really matter what chords I play, what words I say ... as it's only a Northern Song"). "It's All Too Much" appears at the end of the movie, and personally, by the time the song comes around, it really is all too much.

Alas, my favorite song, "Hey Bulldog," has been cut out because Al Brodax doesn't care for it[22]. He should have cut out "It's All Too Much." Don't tell George I said so! A number of previously released Beatles songs pepper the movie (pardon the expression) with great effect.

The movie was very relaxing for everyone, except for a fidgety John: He formally unveiled the new woman in his life.

The coming out party has not been a major success. A couple of weeks ago, he and Yoko put on an art exhibit consisting of boxes. The two of them showed up completely dressed in white. For the finale they released white balloons carrying a tag that read, "You are here." John asked people who found the balloons to write to him, care of the gallery. Most of them told him to go back to his wife. They criticized him for his hair, Yoko, his money, becoming an artist, you name it. The critics were just as cruel. If you thought the reviews of the *Magical Mystery Tour* movie were bad...

They had another "exhibit" a few weeks ago, consisting of two acorns — One printed with "'John,' by Yoko Ono" and the other saying "'Yoko,' by John Lennon." They buried them on the east and west sides of Coventry Cathedral in the name of peace. John got savaged for that, and I guess I wouldn't call it art, but what's wrong with peace?

---

22 It was reinstated years later for the re-issue of the movie.

John's dug in. "I was never cuddly," he tells the papers. "You just want me to stay in my own bag." I think the problem is Yoko. She never smiles. The woman's as serious as a heart attack. After the acorn exhibit, the reporters had her sliced and diced into sushi in time for the morning papers.

John has gone from being the darling of the press to the object of derision. He doesn't understand why. He's really madly in love with this woman and doesn't get it that by pushing her on people, he's just making things worse. It's putting quite a bit of stress on all of us.

Thank God, *Yellow Submarine* appears to be a major hit.

Mal

****

In August the Soviets watched Czechoslovakia with a jaundiced eye, as the Czech government gradually allowed limited freedom of speech and appeared to be inching towards the West. On August 21st, Brezhnev sent tanks into the streets of Prague, and Czechoslovakia was solidly back in the Communist camp.

****

NASA planners had the next three flights thoroughly planned out – or so they thought: Schirra, along with two astronauts to-be-determined, would perform the shakedown cruise of the Saturn V rocket and the Apollo capsule. They would circle the earth for over a week, checking out every possible system. This would be the Apollo 7 mission.

Apollo 8, with McDivitt, Schweickart, and Scott, would repeat the Apollo 7 mission, with the major addition of the Lunar Module (LM). McDivitt would be the Commander, Scott, the Command Module pilot, and Schweickart, the Lunar Module pilot. The LM was to be stored in the nose of the Apollo rocket. The Apollo capsule would disengage itself from the Saturn rocket, turn 180°, and dock nose-first with the LM. The astronauts would check out the functions of the lunar module and practice maneuvering in space, the two spacecraft connected like a pair of Siamese twins joined at the cranium.

Borman would be the Commander of Apollo 9, the riskiest mission to date. He and rookie astronaut Bill Anders would enter the LM, separate themselves from the Apollo capsule, and fly the Lunar Module in space. They would then meet up with the capsule and dock with it.

In August 1968, the astronauts for missions 7, 8, and 9 were actively training for these missions.

A few problems crept into this carefully mapped out schedule: The lunar module was not going to be ready by December 1968, the planned launch time for Apollo 8. Reading Soviet tea leaves as well as it could, NASA saw the Soviets preparing to send men around the moon.

Without a lunar module, Apollo 8 would not be much of a mission. It was foolish for Apollo 8 to simply be a repeat of Apollo 7– unless Apollo 7 encountered serious glitches. Now that the space race was heating up again, it was important to move forward.

****

On the bigger front, the war in Vietnam was progressing poorly. We'd seen Operation Rolling Thunder, Operation Starlite, Operation Crimp, Operation Birmingham, Operation Attleboro, Operation Cedar Falls, Operation Pegasus, and had won them all. We'd inflicted far greater losses than we'd incurred. We remained unsuccessful, however, in discouraging the North Vietnamese Vietcong from invading South Vietnam. Their major Tet Holiday offensive earlier in the year had been a failure, but they remained unfazed. The American public was growing restless. Revered television anchor Walter Cronkite pronounced the war a stalemate. On March 16th, renegade American soldiers slaughtered civilians in the village of My Lai, and when word of this filtered back home, the balance of public opinion was altered forever.

The American image was taking a beating. Good news – any news – would have been welcome.

****

At NASA, a little micro-rocket took off inside George Low's head: What if we sent Apollo 8 to the moon? Not to land on it – but to *orbit* the moon?

It would be a major scientific and public relations coup. America could stand proud again. The race to the moon would be back on the public radar, and we'd be ahead!

There were a great deal of ifs… but with greater and greater vigor, Low went back and forth on this like a tongue to an aching molar:

- Von Braun would need to have a souped-up Saturn V (Vb) rocket ready to go. (Pushing the Apollo capsule into earth orbit was one thing, swinging it out into space was quite another.)
- The Service Propulsion System (SPS) rocket at the back of the Service Module, designed to get the astronauts out of lunar orbit and back to earth, would have to be tested and deemed ready.
- Then there was my area: could we have continuous voice communication with the crew, a quarter million miles out in space?
- Finally, the Slide Rules poring over charts and computers had to finish solving the celestial equations needed for the timing and duration of every single rocket burn.

These were many ifs indeed.

George Low set out to poll the head of each unit. There was no question what answer he was looking for.

Von Braun reminded him that the Saturn Vb would be fired without a test flight; the rocket would get its space baptism with the lives of three men on the line; the Slide Rules wouldn't have the opportunity to test their equations on an unmanned Apollo, etc…etc… Yet, one by one, each Director came back with the desired answer: Yes, if NASA were willing to take these risks, we could send three astronauts to the moon by the end of the year.

It wasn't clear what exactly the astronauts would do when they reached the moon. Swing around the moon and return to earth – or slow down, allow themselves to be caught up in lunar orbit, spin around the moon a few times, fire up the SPS rocket, shoot out of lunar orbit, and fly back to earth? Asking the SPS rocket to first decelerate and then accelerate the spacecraft obviously added another major set of risks to a mission that was already full of them.

Somewhat to my surprise, NASA decided to go for broke. Apollo 8 would circumnavigate the moon a number of times before returning to earth.

It was a mixed blessing for McDivitt. He and his crew had been training for a Lunar Module mission. Borman et al. were also training with the Lunar Module, but were not quite as far along.

Deke decided to flip-flop the crews: Borman would fly the Lunar Module-deprived Apollo 8, while McDivitt would continue to be the first astronaut to test the Lunar Module, now slated for Apollo 9.

Needless to say, there was a great deal of behind-the-back whispering concerning this little switcheroo. Did McDivitt have a say in this? Would McDivitt not have preferred to go to the moon? Was McDivitt really that far ahead of Borman in the Lunar Module training? Did Deke and Borman's friendship going far back to their days as Air Force test pilots play a role? It certainly made for lively gossip among a group of men not usually prone to this form of entertainment.

**

If Deke didn't already have his hands full with the swapping of the Apollo 8 and 9 crews, he suddenly found himself faced with an unexpected medical situation:

Mike Collins suffered from persistent neck pain and was told he needed spine surgery. He would be back with the program if all went well, but not in time for Apollo 8. Deke could have pushed back the entire Borman-Collins-Anders crew to a subsequent flight, but instead he plucked Jim Lovell from the Armstrong-Lovell-Aldrin backup crew. Borman and Lovell of course knew each other *intimately* from their two-week Gemini mission, and this eased the decision-making. For Lovell this meant that he would <u>not</u> be flying the Apollo 11 mission with Armstrong and Aldrin, a relatively minor issue at this particular time.

For Anders the change in mission from Apollo 9 to Apollo 8 was even-Steven: he had trained for months on the Lunar Module, suddenly for nothing, but now he had a chance to be the first man to circle the moon.

Fred Haise was placed on the backup crew with Armstrong and Aldrin.

Not for long.

All the talk about going to the moon was idle chatter, of course, since Apollo 7 had yet to get off the ground and wasn't scheduled to do so until October. The Apollo 8 moon mission would consequently be kept secret. Von Braun would work on the Saturn, the Slide Rules would work their equations, and we would all wait to see what Apollo 7 had to offer.

****

Violent protests in Chicago marred the Democratic Convention that would nominate Vice-President Humphrey. The protesters appeared again to be ne're do well, long-haired hippies clamoring against our society and the war in Vietnam. A word was said, and the Chicago police all too happily jumped in. The clubbing, the dragging, and the screaming were all duly filmed for television. The country was horrified.

Against this backdrop the Republicans could have nominated any moderate, and he would have beaten the hapless Humphrey hands down. They did not. They chose Richard Milhous Nixon. It was a strange choice – not just a loser, but the guy who lost to *Kennedy*. Nixon still looked as uncomfortable in his skin as any man could. He was the politician least likely to bridge the generation gap and brought new meaning to the term "square."

Americans would be choosing between the amiable Humphrey and the dour Nixon. Humphrey suddenly assumed responsibility for the Vietnam War, and through no fault of his own, he now symbolized the disarray and lawlessness of the Democratic Left. Nixon embodied "law and order," '50s style.

At NASA the choice was not automatic. The scenario was reminiscent of the '64 campaign. The Democrats had supported the Apollo program from the start, while Republicans had supported the program only to the extent that it was absolutely necessary. Nixon, on the other hand, projected an aura of stability. He'd been a naval officer, while Humphrey's hernia had kept him out of the army. Most of all, the Democrats were seen as responsible for everything left-wing and destructive: riots, violence, hippies, the Black Panthers, the occupation of universities, etc... while Nixon, regardless of his charisma-challenged personality, seemed to be the guy to restore some kind of sanity to this country.

It was a close call. I really did not care for Richard Nixon.

****

London, 20ᵗʰ August, 1968

Dear Dutch,

John has practically abandoned Julian now that Yoko has entered his life. He is doing unto his son what his own father once did onto him. Ironically, it is Paul who occasionally visits and consoles the boy.

This sad scene has had a small plus side: Paul feels sorry for the little tot, and upon returning from a visit with him, he sat at the piano and played us a song: "Hey Jules, don't make it bad, take a sad song and make it better," hum hum "...the movement you need is on your shoulders" — to which he quickly added, "Don't worry I'll change that, sounds like a parrot," waving his hand as if warding off imaginary critics.

"No you won't, it's a great line," replied John. Yes, everything you need is right there within your reach.

The song takes off in various directions, and at one point, John thought the song was written for him. He liked the overall message, especially the bit about "you have found her, now go out and get her" — Paul's presumed blessing for John to go out and get Yoko. Paul was happy to have John on board, regardless of the reason.

Paul changed the name of the song's protagonist to Jude.

Capitol has been pressing the Beatles for a single (there hasn't been one since "Lady Madonna" last winter), and the Beatles are equally eager to kick-start Apple (remember Apple?). This looks like it could be it.

For the B-side we have a raucous, fuzz box-heavy rocker called "Revolution." John is telling all the so-called revolutionaries to cool it ("But when you talk about destruction, don't you know that you can count me out"). Having said that, he's been hanging out with a lot of these revolutionaries, and they scare him. On the slow version of the song (it'll come out on the next album), he caves in somewhat, murmuring "in" right after "count me out." But he really <u>means</u> "out." "You can't achieve peace through violence," he always says.

We've been seeing some good 'Apples'. A fellow named James Taylor comes to mind. We've also opened up a clothing store on Baker Street for which the boys commissioned a stunningly bright, red and blue mural. (If it were up to me, I would have chosen your countryman Peter Max to do this.) Nothing so exciting has happened on that street since Sherlock Holmes.

It's been a total fiasco. The community objected to the mural, and we had to paint it over with a boring solid color. I agreed with John on this one: this stultifyingly dull bourgeoisie is exactly what we're supposed to be fighting.

The boutique itself has lost money hand over fist. Many people came in only to steal, which I guess they thought was alright because the Beatles are rich, and everybody should share everything or some rot, and the employees weren't so honest either. The idea of rounding people up for the bobbies isn't our style, you know, so one day, we simply decided to give everything away. People queued all night. The feeding frenzy was impressive. We were not witnessing humanity at its best.

Why don't you come back for a visit?

One of the Capitol execs is flying here out of Houston and returning a few days later. I can arrange for you and Sally to join him. He owes me a favor. (I got him some autographs.)

Mal

It was an offer we couldn't refuse. Things were quiet in Houston, and I cleared it with Kranz. In early September, Sally and I flew out to London. Mal fetched us at the airport and advised us to head right for the EMI studio. Apparently this was a session for the ages, and you never knew when the next one would come 'round. It was already the middle of the evening, but the action was just warming up.

We arrived to what was arguably the loudest noise I had ever heard. (Even during rocket launches, we sat a few miles away.) The lighting was dim, and I could just barely make out the figures. The red lights of the amplifiers dotted the darkness. Booming bass notes bounced off the walls, cymbals crashed, guitars screeched in protest, and voices howled "Helter Skelter" (a British amusement ride). I looked over at Sally and then at Mal. "The last take of this song was 27 minutes long. Isn't it great?" I knew Sally didn't think so. I was rather enjoying this semi-jam session. The guys were clearly having fun, and from the seamless stops and starts, appeared to know where they were going. Nevertheless, looking over at Sally I thought it best to call it a night. Mal took us to the hotel. The band was in a groove, and his absence would go un-noticed.

The next day we met him for lunch. He hadn't changed in the last year and a half, but his clothes now looked like they'd been bought in New Delhi. His neck was ringed with a row of yellow beads.

Mal talked a lot about his job at Apple and the scouting of bands. He filled us in on the general mood; it wasn't good. Lennon had no patience for anything but his songs, and he wasn't into spending hours perfecting the arrangements. Studied harmonies were out of the question. Yoko had to be with him at all times. Still, every now and then, he seemed to take pleasure in the sessions. You never quite knew which John would show up. Harrison was no happier than Lennon, but less vocal. Ringo gamely bided his time.

Mal suggested we come back to the studio in a few days. Mid-morning would be best. No guarantees as to who would show up or what kind of song they'd be rehearsing. They might even be listening to playbacks the whole day.

We arrived promptly at 10 A.M. to a near-empty studio. George Martin and engineer Geoff Emerick stood in the control room; at the far end sat Maureen (Starr). Mal re-introduced us. Sally sat next to Maureen. After a few pleasantries (were Americans ever going back in space? etc...), the door opened briskly on a good-humored Paul McCartney. His hair was longer, his moustache was gone, and he hadn't shaved in a few days. Sally summoned up all her courage and inquired about the beads around his neck. "Ask Mal!" he answered playfully.

After discussing some technicalities with George Martin, McCartney went down into the studio and picked up an acoustic guitar. He played a progression that had a classical ring to it. He played it repeatedly and then seemed to tire of it. He moved to the piano and began tinkering. He toyed with a single riff, over and over again. Over this riff McCartney started to mumble "happy, happy birthday to you," "it's your, it's your birthday today." It sounded like he had a birthday party that night.

Little by little, the other Beatles (and Yoko) arrived. I hadn't realized how petite she was. Only a sliver of her face showed between two rivers of long dark hair. Harrison and Lennon grabbed their guitars. Harrison was nattily dressed, as was Ringo. Both sported shirts with ruffles. Lennon wore a grubby, non-descript T-shirt.

Ringo acknowledged Maureen with a lazy wave of the hand. I don't know what the Beatles were originally scheduled to record that morning, but Lennon, Harrison, and Ringo seemed interested in joining the budding composition. "This could turn out to be like the "Hey Bulldog" session," Mal whispered.

The lyrics didn't seem to go anywhere ("You say it's your birthday … we're gonna have a good time…"), and the melody was somewhat simplistic. Suddenly, while the three guitarists vamped around on their respective instrument, a new melody arose – "yes we're going to a party party" – and then there appeared a *third* melody in a new key – "Birthday, I would like you to dance, Birthday, take a cha- cha- cha- chance." As if reading each other's minds, the song abruptly reverted to the original riff. They did this over and over again, progressively connecting the various parts. By mid-afternoon, they were done. Mal explained that they'd be back in the evening to record the song they'd *really* meant to work on that day.

The Beatles made their way up to the recording booth before leaving. Lennon was hardly recognizable, his face pale, his hair long and greasy. He was agitated and silly. Yoko stood behind him bashfully, once trying to interject something, but her voice was so soft we couldn't catch the words. John put his hands together, as if in prayer, and he fluttered his eyes. His head weaved to and fro. "I remember you! Rich Man! Baby You're a Rich Man!" With that, as if catching a shifting breeze, he spun around and walked off.

I was again left with the painful longing to have said something – anything – that would have been memorable.

As we were leaving London, Mal asked off-handedly if he might pay me a visit at Mission Control. Tit for tat I suppose. How could I say 'no' after all he'd done for me? I promised I'd look into it. Truth was, he'd never get security clearance. I couldn't shake his request though, and it nagged me throughout the flight home. Sally had wondered about Mal's extreme generosity in arranging our visits to the Beatles' recording sessions. I had chalked it up to his friendly nature. Perhaps he did this for everyone. But could it be that Mal had an ulterior motive? Was he warming up to me to reach his extra-terrestrial friends? I hated to think that way.

****

Four days later, the unmanned Zond 5 splashed down in the Indian Ocean after having swung around the moon. The Soviets were back in the race.

The Apollo 7 flight was always going to be a biggie. Of course all manned flights had been "biggies," since each represented an American "first" in one area or another.

But when it came to sheer size, this would be biggest of the biggies.

No man had ever sat on top of such a machine: it stood thirty-six stories tall. The supporting tower for the Saturn rocket soared higher than New York's United Nations building. The Saturn would not have fit on a football field; it was twice as tall as its successor, the Space Shuttle. Various sections of the rocket had been transported to the Cape by *barges* – for no train or truck could carry them. The first stage alone had the power of 500 jet fighter engines or 86 Hoover dams. It would lift the 6.4 million lbs rocket to an altitude of thirty-eight miles in two and a half minutes. When taking off it would create the loudest man-made sound after the atomic bomb, et cetera.

More importantly, Apollo 7 was our first venture into space since the Apollo 1 tragedy. Apollo 2 through 6 had been unmanned. We literally and figuratively could not afford another failure.

And who could forget that Apollo 6's rockets had, to a large extent, failed? The engineers were rather certain that they had found the problem and fixed it. *Rather* certain. Prudence would have dictated another unmanned launch, but that was not going to happen. As Wally Schirra put it, when you worked on the Apollo program, you were always in a locomotive with a bunch of other locomotives barreling down behind you.

After the multiple crew switches, Deke had finally settled on veteran astronaut Wally Schirra and two space rookies, Donn Eisele and

Walt Cunningham. Walt was the "Lunar Module Pilot," though of course there would be no lunar module on this flight. (Not to mention that even in the Lunar Module, the Lunar Module "Pilot" would not be doing any piloting: The mission Commander would be doing the piloting. The "Pilot" would be a cross between a navigator and a systems engineer, reading the dials and advising the Commander during the LM's flight.)

Donn's last name was pronounced EYEz-lee, but everyone got tripped up. When Jim Webb, head of NASA, introduced the astronauts to President Johnson, he called Donn "I-SELL." From then on it was the Wally, Walt and Whatshisname show. It had a certain ring to it. Donn wasn't too thrilled. After all, what was so hard about Eisele?

As the only astronaut left from the Mercury missions, Wally was now the big cheese among the astronaut corps. He could be a fun guy – we all remembered his Santa Claus hijinks on Gemini VI – but he was also opinionated. Wally wasn't impressed by rank or by the initials that followed somebody's name. Once he'd made up his mind, it was hard to get him to budge.

One opinion he held very strongly was that engineering and safety came first. Showmanship and public relations were a distant second, and science not directly related to the flight was lumped together in his mind with public relations. He had already chafed at the experiments suggested by NASA scientists during the Mercury program, and his opinions on such matters had not changed. That was too bad, considering the Apollo 7 flight plan. It was loaded with public relations events and experiments.

Being in space for more than a week posed a peculiar problem for Schirra: like many of the astronauts, he was a smoker. That had not been a problem during his Mercury flight, and he'd been fine with the short Gemini flight, but eleven days! He knew, however, that he had no choice, so he managed to quit. No sooner had he done so than coffee was also banned from the flight. Coffee, after all, was without nutritional value. It took up room. It wasn't necessary.

No coffee! Wally hit the roof. This had to be another idea from some pointy-headed scientist. He wasn't a robot; he was a man (a man without cigarettes) spending eleven days in confined quarters. What was wrong with a little java to make him happy? Wally lobbied at every possible level. Finally, he convened a breakfast meeting and arranged for the coffee to be missing. Everyone groused; the meeting quickly came to an end. Wally won that one, but he had even tougher battles ahead.

Ideal launch conditions called for light winds heading East out to sea. If a mission had to be aborted within seconds of takeoff, the winds would carry the capsule gently out over the ocean. Westerly winds, on the contrary, would pull the parachutes over hard ground, and the landing could be fatal.

Awakening in the pre-dawn night of October 11th, Wally could see that this was going to be a windy day. Wrong-way windy, blowing in from the ocean. NASA thought it was worth the risk. It was a grumpy Wally who climbed into the capsule.

The countdown progressed smoothly. Eisele commented on the burps and gurgles of the fuel lines and valves. Talk about being in the belly of the beast!

5...4...3...2...1... A column of flame appeared, instantly followed by a vast turmoil of smoke. The flame roared greedily while the booster built up thrust. The hold-downs peeled off in unison, the spidery fingers of the orange gantry pulled away, and slowly, very slowly, the booster began its rise. Within moments, freed from the weight of the spent fuel, the Saturn broke through the sound barrier. Schirra ticked off each abort point as the Saturn continued to carve its thunderous arc.

And the wind? NASA's gamble had paid off. No abort, no landing in the middle of Florida. Still, Schirra felt justified in his pre-launch complaints.

This was the first rocket truly made for manned flight, and whether the Saturn was intentionally designed that way or not, Schirra appreciated the mild acceleration, especially when compared to the 10 Gs he'd pulled in his Mercury capsule (uh, spacecraft – Schirra still hated the word capsule) or the 5 to 6 Gs of the Gemini-Titan rocket.

Once in orbit, the astronauts separated themselves from the S4B, the only stage of the rocket that was still around, and turned the Command Module (capsule...) 180° back towards the S4B to simulate the capture of a Lunar Module. One of the panels on the S4B failed to open completely. Had the mission called for the real retrieval of a Lunar Module, it would have been a failure right there and then.

Fortunately, the mission called for no such thing, and Wally, Walt and Whatshisname gamely moved on.

The Command Module was downright roomy compared to its Mercury and Gemini predecessors. It was 12 feet high and 13 feet wide at its base. It was made of steel, titanium, and an aluminum alloy. The control panel included 24 instruments, 566 switches, 40 event indicators, and 71 lights. Most importantly, the rat's nest of wires that had been the downfall of Apollo 1 was no longer present – or at least safely tucked behind a panel.

Taking his first rest, Wally took a few moments to collect his thoughts. He was now the only astronaut to have flown in the Mercury, Gemini, and Apollo phases of the race to the moon. Perhaps he'd been a little testy with NASA personnel, but darned if they didn't always add on irrelevant fluff to these test-pilot missions! He would retire after this mission. Walking on the moon was no longer on his wish list. The opinions of others didn't matter to him; he would stick to what he thought was right. Even so, he wondered if he could behave for eleven days. And he did – until the very next day… when he awoke to the sound of Eisele having an argument with Mission Control (possibly the first argument in space). "When Wally hears about this he's going to be pretty damned annoyed!" And indeed, Wally was.

NASA had planned on having Wally, Walt and Whatshisname host the very first television transmission from space, and the flight plan called for this broadcast to take place the next day. NASA now wanted to move it up twenty-four hours.

Wally did a slow burn. Every minute of the flight plan had been honed for hours on end, and he could see no good reason to change it. A dangerous part of the mission lay ahead. The crew needed no unnecessary distractions, and that was all there was to it. A parade of NASA officials tried to get Wally to change his mind, but it was No Go. Instead, he and the crew prepared to approach the S4B again. The astronauts earned a few grey hairs as they came to within a hundred feet of the gyrating machine. They then relaxed … with a cup of coffee.

The following day the whole world saw the side of Wally that NASA had been waiting for: Wally the showman. The world tuned in as Wally, Walt, and Donn gave a guided tour of the Command Module. Wally invited the audience to participate. "Keep those cards and letters coming, folks!" The show was a big hit and it was high-fives all around in Mission Control. The crew would win an Emmy award.

The good cheer did not last long. The crew came down with head colds. All three of them.

They would bring new meaning to the word "cranky." And who could blame them? Was there anyone on earth who could say, "Oh come on, it can't be so bad..."?

Cranky and bored.

NASA's concern (paranoia?) about a fire on board had precluded the astronauts from bringing any reading material. This might have been a good time to read Jules Verne's *From the Earth to the Moon* or HG Wells' *The First Men on the Moon*. Though everyone at Mission Control felt sorry for the astronauts, the crew did not endear themselves by wondering aloud what "genius" had devised this or that experiment. I was surprised to hear Schirra sling mud at Kraft and Slayton.

And yet the worst was yet to come.

American astronauts had always donned their spacesuits and helmets upon re-entry in case of sudden, fatal de-pressurization[23]. These helmets fit quite snugly; you could easily scrape your nose putting them on. Schirra thought it was critical for the astronauts to use the pinch-your-nose-and-blow technique to help equilibrate their inner ear, what with their colds and clogged sinuses. Deprived of this ability, they risked rupturing an eardrum during re-entry.

NASA insisted on the spacesuits. Schirra dug in.

Not being a doctor I had no horse in this race, but I had to figure that the NASA doctors knew what they were talking about. Death from de-pressurization was more serious than a ruptured eardrum. Schirra, however, continued to see NASA physicians as sick doctors bothering well astronauts. He compromised Schirra-style: they would don the spacesuits and put on the helmets at the slightest hint of depressurization (assuming depressurization were willing to hint at its arrival).

The splashdown took place without a hitch. No ruptured eardrums, no depressurization.

The Apollo 7 now held the record for longest spaceflight; more time, in fact, than all the Soviet missions combined. Because the factory had designated our Command-Service Module "CSM 101,"

---

23 As would happen to three Soviet cosmonauts just a few years hence.

NASA announced with great fanfare that Apollo 7 had been 101% successful. Privately, Kraft made it clear to the crew that they would never go in space again. Not while he was flight director.

And never did they go.

****

With the long Apollo 7 mission behind us and the excitement building over the upcoming Apollo 8 flight, I'd hardly had time to think about music; but towards the end of November, there it was, a large envelope postmarked from Great Britain and Mal's unmistakable handwriting.

Inside was a white album. Stark, glossy minimalist white.

It was a double album. You opened it like a book, and each side contained a record. Embossed off-center in a slightly up-sloped direction were the words "The BEATLES." There was no obvious title. The number A12 0 2 was printed at the bottom right, as if it were a special edition for a select few million people. (Each album was indeed printed with a different number.) As I opened the album, I was greeted by a 5x7 glossy color picture of Lennon, a pimple on his forehead and shoulder-length hair parted down the middle. Simple round glasses completed the picture. Behind it was a picture of McCartney, unshaven and un-smiling. There were also pictures of Harrison and Starr, both neatly coiffed and dressed in the style of the day. If you didn't know any better, you'd have thought Harrison and Starr were the headliners, with Lennon and McCartney as the grubby sidekicks.

There was a poster. On one side were the lyrics to all the songs and on the other a collage of pictures, including one of a naked John sitting cross-legged on the floor (no privates showing).

If they were looking to convey a fresh image by way of their graphics, they were successful, though I'm not sure I cared for this latest direction.

Paper-clipped to the record was a short note from Mal: "Check out Revolution #9. There's something in it for you." This, it turned out, was track 5 of side 4 – the next to last song on the album. I would later discover that the number 9 held a special significance for Lennon. He had been born on the 9th of October, his mother had lived at house #9, Brian Epstein first heard the Beatles on the 9th of November, they had gotten their first record contract on the 9th of May, and he had met Yoko on the 9th of some month. Of course, any number between 1 and 31 could have been equally connected to dates and places in his life, but John had a thing for the number 9. He had written "The One after 909" as a teenager, and here was another "number 9" song. It would not be his last. The number 9 would then make one final appearance in his life, in a most unwanted way.

The song was not encouraging. You could not even call it a song. It was more of a sound collage, with the words "Number 9" intoned throughout the song. Interspersed was gobbledygook, "you are born, you are naked" and so forth.

This new style was truly un-enjoyable, and I couldn't even see what was in it for me – though I discovered a few weeks later that I'd been a little hasty in my judgment.

As for the rest of the album, there was a lot to take in.

Thirty songs.

Starting with the "art" work of the cover, it looked to be the anti-Pepper album. I suppose that once you've climbed a mountain, you want to climb a very different one the next time. There were no exotic instruments, no groundbreaking arrangements, no groundbreaking songs at all. No songs that moved you in epic fashion.

In fairness to the band, they had released "Hey Jude" and "Revolution" just a few months earlier – two songs that clearly moved you, albeit in completely different ways. "Hey Jude" had been uplifting. "Take a sad song and make it better" offered a universal warmth that everyone could relate to. The fadeout consisted of the repetitive, rising na na-na na-na-na-na, which was longer than the song itself! At close to seven minutes, it pushed the limits of Top-40 radio. George Martin could have faded out the outro during the song's production phase. He had not, and for good cause. The song intensifies and swells, as McCartney scat sings over an ever-widening range of growls and octaves. It was hard not to get swept along, and millions did, making "Hey Jude" the Beatles' best selling single up to that point. It stayed atop the charts for two months straight. Thirty-six years hence, *Rolling Stone* would list it as the best Beatle song ever.

"Revolution" was, as Mal had said, a toe-tapping rocker, laden with fuzz-distorted guitars. "You say you want a revolution…" and with that, Lennon had gone on to lay out his political views, as would soon be his wont. To the radicals, the song was a sell-out. Sniffed the *New Left Review,* the song is "a lamentable petty bourgeois cry of fear."

Mal told us about a big flap with a radical paper in London called *Black Dwarf.* Its writers had been offended when "Revolution" was first released. Lennon wrote a furious response to the editors, full of scorn for those who only wanted to tear things down; he ended it with "You smash it – and I'll build around it."

Sally liked that.

The album, soon to be nicknamed *The White Album,* represented a hodge-podge of styles, each song a reflection of the author's whimsy. Some songs involved mostly one Beatle – McCartney's "Blackbird" and Lennon's "Julia," for example, both of which featured handy guitar work. Also one-man shows were McCartney's "I Will," an easy-going love song to no one in particular, and "Mother Nature's Son," his ode to the down-home country boy.

Two songs could have been released as singles, the opening, foot-tapping "Back in the USSR" and "Ob-La-Di, Ob-La Da."

Two songs consisted of three melodies cleverly woven together, McCartney's "Martha my Dear" and Lennon's "Happiness is a Warm Gun," each to great effect.

There were two naughty songs, "Why Don't We Do It In The Road" (McCartney) and "Happiness is a Warm Gun" (Lennon feeling his finger on *herrrr* trigger), an entire animal farm (a raccoon, a pig, a blackbird, a monkey, a walrus, an eagle, a worm, a sheepdog, a tiger, and an elephant), and three raucous songs (McCartney's "Helter Skelter" and "Birthday," as well as Lennon's "Everybody's Got Something to Hide Except Me and My Monkey").

Joining Michelle, Eleanor, Lucy, Vera, and Rita, a rash of new women were added to the Beatle pantheon: Molly, Prudence, Sadie, Julia, and Martha [*though Martha was actually McCartney's dog).*

Ringo made his writing debut with the harmless "Don't Pass Me By."

The Harrison song that appeared on Side 1, "While My Guitar Gently Weeps," was an instant classic. As with many a Harrison or Lennon song, its first incarnation was a light, melancholy melody. The lyrics are both simplistic and soulful. The song opens with the patented

McCartney sound: a slow set of devastatingly effective notes reminiscent in their simplicity of "Ticket to Ride," "Strawberry Fields," and "Lucy in the Sky." Though layered with a rich piano sound, the song's signature instrument is the guitar, a guitar that fits the title of the song like few others. It was the most beautiful guitar solo I'd ever heard from George Harrison.

Except that, as I would ultimately discover, it was not Harrison playing the guitar; it was his friend Eric Clapton. I thought it was slightly insulting for the Beatles to bring in another lead guitarist, but it was Harrison himself who'd invited the guitar legend – the ultimate incarnation of "leaving your ego at the door"!

You could quibble over this or that song, but, over all, the album rather satisfied my appetite for fresh Beatles music. Apparently it did everyone else's, as it would go on to be the best-selling album of the 1960s. "It's the bloody *White Album!*" McCartney would later say to would-be critics.

****

Nixon won the election by less than a percent of the popular vote, but a comfortable Electoral College majority. Humphrey carried his home state of Minnesota, the Northeast, Montana, Washington, and Texas. Independent George Wallace took four southern states, and Nixon took the rest. I was more depressed than I thought I'd be. I didn't see Nixon connecting with my generation any time soon.

I was distracted from these thoughts by the Soviets' launching of Zond 6, an un-manned spaceship that circled the moon and returned safely to earth. They were ready to send a manned mission. Based on the relative position of the planets, the Soviet window of opportunity for a lunar flight was the first week of December, the best day being the 6th. The cosmonauts were in a clear position to steal our thunder. The cover of *Time* magazine's December 6th edition showed an American astronaut and a Soviet cosmonaut running full stride towards the moon.

Needless to say, December 6th was a stressful day. Every ring of the telephone had us jumping with the expectation of bad news.

Yet the 6th came and went without a Russian space flight.

Nor would there be one on the 7th or the 8th.

What was going on in Russia???

We didn't learn the truth for another 20 years: The Zond 6 flight had not gone as smoothly as advertised. The Zond capsule had lost pressure during re-entry and had landed excessively hard. Either incident would have killed the cosmonauts. To their credit, the Soviets were not going to take a chance with a manned flight until they had these problems solved.

****

With no Soviets in sight, the Apollo 8 astronauts readied themselves in their capsule. Only one astronaut was really needed for this mission, but there were three astronauts aboard; all three had been given official-sounding titles: Borman was the Commander; he sat on the left and controlled the dreaded abort handle; had this mission gone to the lunar surface, Borman would have piloted the lunar module and led the expedition onto the moon. Lovell was the "Command Module Pilot"; he would have been in charge of flying the Apollo capsule and docking with the Lunar Module, had one existed. Anders was the "Lunar Module Pilot," an exaggeration under the best of circumstances and again a complete misnomer, since there was no lunar module.

Lovell's wife, Marilyn, was at the Cape with their children, while Susan Borman and Valerie Anders stayed behind in Houston. Only Marilyn was resolutely optimistic. Valerie was apprehensive at best. Susan was practically in black.

A pale paper moon hung low over the Cape. The Saturn stood and steamed, a tower of bestial froth. The capsule sat atop the rocket, a fist at the end of a muscular arm, poised to deliver an uppercut to the communist world.

At 6:51 AM, on December 21st, the five F1 engines at the base of the rocket fired simultaneously. For nine seconds they gradually built up thrust. The clamps released, and the growling Goliath emerged from a cauldron of orange and grey clouds. Slowly it rose, the shockwaves again violently shaking the television booth four miles away. News anchor Walter Cronkite feared out loud that the building would collapse. With unrelenting pounding, the F1 engines accelerated the missile to 6,000 miles per hour. At the precise moment, all five engines shut down, the first stage of the rocket was jettisoned over the Atlantic, and the astronauts were flung forward with tremendous force. Just as suddenly, they were slammed backwards, as the second stage kicked in. Relieved of the first stage's hefty weight, the rocket now gathered speed even more rapidly. For six minutes, the engines of the second stage hammered away, accelerating the astronauts to 15,000 miles per hour. The engines crisply shut down as planned, the connecting bolts blew, and the second stage was sent tumbling off into the ocean. The third stage lit up, sending the screeching spacecraft to a speed of 17,400 miles per hour.

All of a sudden, barely six and a half minutes after liftoff, all was quiet. Apollo 8 was in orbit. The astronauts fine-tuned their trajectory and checked out all their systems. Now came the wait.

Mission control was doing its own checking. If all systems were GO, the astronauts would be given the green light to proceed. If any glitch were found, it would be thumbs down and a disappointing ride back to earth.

Flight Director Cliff Charlesworth, all of thirty seven years old, called the roll, polling each console down the line for the GO / NO GO signal.

It was GO all around.

2 hours, 50 minutes, and 31 seconds into the mission, the astronauts heard the words they'd been waiting for: "You are GO for TLI." This stood for trans-lunar injection. CapCom Mike Collins was prosaically giving them the go-ahead to leave earth orbit and head for the moon.

This laconic techno speak belied the major evolutionary step forward in Man's exploration of his Universe. Until now, astronauts had always stayed relatively close to the earth, at least in astronomical terms. This time, the astronauts would no longer be going around in circles. They were going somewhere; they had a destination! For the first time ever, Man would now be leaving the confines of his planet – atmosphere and all – and heading for another World. He was no longer a sailor fishing within sight of the shorelines, but an explorer heading out into the vast, unknown ocean.

To wrench themselves from earth's orbit, the astronauts would again fire the third stage of the Saturn rocket, boosting their speed another 7,000 miles per hour.

It would be the first of four do-or-die moments in the Apollo 8 mission, and it would be either sweet victory or a day of infamy for the brilliant astrophysicists who had long planned this defining moment.

The astronauts needed to ignite the Stage 3 booster at precisely the right instant to rendezvous with the moon three days later. The Apollo capsule would be whipping around the earth at 24,000 miles per hour. The earth, as it spins on its axis, moves through the sky at 66,000 miles per hour along a curved orbit. The moon travels right to left at 21,600 miles per hour along its own curved orbit.

The moon is 239,000 miles from earth.

In football terms, it would be the ultimate quarterback bomb.

The Apollo 8 trajectory was actually even more complicated than that, for crossing paths directly with the moon would have done them no good. They would have crashed headfirst, and they would have been dead on arrival. Instead, they had to arrive sixty miles *in front* of the moon to be captured by its gravity and become an orbiting satellite. If they arrived a few moments too soon, the moon would still be too far away to exert sufficient pull. Apollo 8 and its human cargo would fly off into the universe never to be heard from again. If they arrived a few moments too late, they would be too close to the moon, and the moon's gravity would pull the spacecraft down to a fiery death. (Well, a short little fire, since there is no oxygen on the moon.)

None of this was on the astronauts' minds as they prepared to ignite Stage 3 of the Saturn rocket. Their job was simply to fire the rocket at the precise moment.

"4...3...2...1 GO! 28,000 ... 30,000 ... 34,000 ... 35,000..." Lovell read off the ship's speed in feet per second. Five minutes and seventeen seconds into the burn, the craft reached the exit velocity of 35,452 feet per second, the engine shut down – and they were off into outer space.

"You're on your way – you're *really* on your way!" exclaimed Chris Kraft. I turned around to look at him. I don't think I'd ever seen him get so excited. But yes, Man was off into space. And *quickly*.

Zipping along at a 24,171 miles per hour clip, the astronauts were traveling faster than any human in history. 35,452 feet per second. I tried to imagine what that represented. A plane flies at around 35,000 feet. Therefore, at that speed, an airplane taking off would reach its cruising altitude in... one second. And since 24,000 miles is the circumference of the earth, at 24,000 miles per hour it would take but an hour to circle the earth!

Shortly after leaving earth orbit, the crew jettisoned Stage 3 and maneuvered the spacecraft 180° to get a fix on the discarded rocket. In doing so, the astronauts were in for a shock: There, in their window, was Planet Earth.

The ENTIRE planet.

No one had ever seen it before, and they just stared.

"This is what God sees," thought Borman.

The crew wasn't paying attention to us down in Houston, until Borman pinched himself out of his reverie. "We see the earth now, almost like a disc."

None of us quite appreciated what Borman, Lovell, and Anders were seeing.

Mike Collins said, "Gee, that's nice, take a picture," or something to that effect.

A few thousand miles into the heavens, the astronauts continued to stare. The bright blue ball was receding into blackness. They were all alone, just the three of them, traveling through space – an endless black box of unblinking diamonds.

The pilot says to the passengers: "I have good news and bad news. The good news is that we're making good time. The bad news? We're completely lost."

The astronauts were making good time. It would be three days, however, before anyone knew if they were on target or completely lost.

Though the Apollo capsule was relatively roomy compared to its Gemini predecessor, it was still somewhat cramped. Shortly into the flight, Lovell accidentally activated his life vest. Borman and Anders got quite a chuckle from Lovell's sudden inflation, but of course it was no laughing matter. Lovell could hardly move, and if he deflated his vest in the spacecraft the deadly CO_2 would overwhelm the filters. It was time to improvise. Lovell lowered himself until the valve of the vest could be introduced into… the urine dump. (An astronaut was supposed to relieve himself by introducing his private parts into a hose. The urine would then be expelled into space.)

The urine dump trick worked, and Lovell resumed his human shape.

It was soon discovered that the urine dump had an undesirable side-effect, regardless of how it was used: each expulsion acted like a small jet propulsion, which then required a compensatory rocket correction. It was pretty straightforward, as soon as we figured out why all these little adjustments were necessary[24].

To keep the direct sunlight from overheating one side of the capsule, Borman started the spacecraft on a slow, steady spin – the barbecue mode. For the next few hours, the astronauts coasted. They could sit back and reflect on the moment.

****

The similarities between Jules Verne's *From the Earth to the Moon* and our Apollo 8 flight were striking. In Verne's adventure, Americans are the first to send men to the moon. They fire up three men. (One of them is French, *bien sur*.) The voyage takes 97 hours and 20 minutes (close enough). Verne chose a southern launching site to bring the space rocket as close to the Equator as possible. Verne explained that this maximized the centrifugal force of the earth and helped fling the spacecraft into space. Specifically, he chose Florida. He recognized that the capsule didn't have to be powered all the way to the moon because, past a certain point, the gravity of the moon would take effect. Finally, his space explorers used retro-rockets to slow themselves during their approach to the moon.

**

Anders slipped into a fretful sleep. Without a pillow, he was constantly awoken by a sensation of falling. Borman had it worse: A day

---

24 The correction orders had to come from Houston. The computers on board Apollo 8 were more rudimentary than today's calculators.

or so into the mission, he got sick. He began to vomit, and soon even treated his buddies to diarrhea. Lovell and Anders found themselves groping about trying to capture bits and pieces of poop.

They needed to discreetly alert us to this sensitive situation. As part of our openness, everything the astronauts said could be heard by the entire world. We had anticipated the need for a private communication and had devised a system whereby the astronauts could talk into a tape recorder. The tape would be transmitted at high speed to Mission Control, and we could then listen to it in a separate room, away from prying ears. Of course, we could only listen to tapes whose existence we knew of! The astronauts had to tell us that they were transmitting a tape, though they'd rather not be too obvious about it, lest the press start asking questions.

This led to a series of oblique suggestions on the part of the astronauts. "Ahem, how's the voice quality on those tapes?"

Silence.

Realizing that we hadn't listened to the tapes and had no idea what they were getting at, the astronauts followed up with banter along the lines of, "Gee, we're really wondering how those tapes are sounding."

Finally, we got it.

Despite its comic aspect, the doctors were concerned that Borman might be suffering from the radiation he'd been exposed to when the capsule had crossed the Van Allen radiation belts. Fortunately, Borman recovered uneventfully.

52 hours after TLI, at 2:29 PM Central Standard Time, Man, for the first time, made the transition from earth's gravity to the gravity of another planet. The tug of earth's unrelenting gravity had gradually slowed the capsule, but now, as they entered the moon's gravitation field, the capsule accelerated again.

The astronauts had a television camera and were scheduled to transmit six broadcasts *("And now Live from the Moon...")*. They did this with more grace than their predecessors, even though Borman, like Schirra, had fought to keep such entertainment out of the flight plan. As the spacecraft hurtled on further and further into space, there was time for a little levity. Anders showcased how a toothbrush would just float in mid-air wherever you put it. "And he brushes regularly," Borman chimed in.

Flying backwards towards their target, the astronauts could not see the moon. Instead they watched the earth shrink away. As space pilots, theirs was not to dwell on beauty or philosophy. That kind of thinking had already gotten Carpenter into trouble. Their job was to stay focused on the flight plan. Nevertheless, Lovell couldn't resist mentioning how struck he was by the magnificence of the earth; he marveled that he saw no sign of his home planet being inhabited. NASA didn't ask him to expand upon these themes, and Lovell left it at that.

Sixty and some hours into the mission, a shiver went up Anders' spine: over a portion of the sky, large swathes of stars were gradually disappearing. A black veil was gradually moving across their window.

THE MOON!

All three pulses shot up simultaneously, as the astronauts recognized the magnitude of the moment. They were the first humans to see the moon up close, and would soon be the first humans to see the far side of the moon from *any* distance!

Before long, the moment approached that would tell them if NASA's calculations had been correct. Valerie Anders wasn't completely optimistic. Kraft had given her just a fifty-fifty chance that her husband would come back alive. Bill had made a tape for her to be played if he failed to return, and in her mind she'd already made funeral plans.

In order to slip into moon orbit, the spacecraft needed to slow down at precisely the right moment, down to a very specific speed. To this end the astronauts would fire the hefty SPS rocket at the back of the Service Module. Everything had been pre-calculated – but this was the first real, live test of the SPS. There was no backup.

5...4...3...2...1 the rocket fired automatically. The three astronauts instantly went from weightlessness to crushing pressure against the back of their seats. They could feel the vibrations of the rocket, but could not hear it. No atmosphere, no sound.

After four minutes, the rocket shut down as quickly as it had turned on.

The waiting game began.

Too much of a slowdown, and they would speed towards the moon's unfriendly surface. The first humans would arrive as lasagna. Had the rocket burn stopped prematurely, on the other hand, the three astronauts would disappear into deep space. Their oxygen would slowly run out, and they would drift towards eternal peace into the feathery down of a noble cause valiantly fought.

For what seemed an eternity, the astronauts could only *sense* the moon's presence by the blackness that gradually took over the entire skyline.

Since the moon was but a sliver of a crescent when viewed from the earth[25], this meant that the moon lay roughly between the earth and the sun. The near side of the moon was mostly dark; the far side would be mostly bright!

And suddenly, sure enough, brilliant sunshine filled the capsule. There they were: Ms. Moon and Mr. Moonlight in living color!

Not completely in color, though; perhaps beige. "Looks like plaster of Paris or some sort of grayish beach sand," intoned Lovell.

There were enormous craters, many more than on the near side, and long, long shadows.

As they flew further behind the moon, the astronauts' voices began to break up and then disappeared altogether. The radio crackled on a while longer, then nothing. The mass of the moon blocked all communications.

The astronauts were on their own.

Yet another waiting game began. It was somewhat reminiscent of re-entry into earth's atmosphere, with its communication blackout and resultant nail biting. "We'll see you on the other side" were Lovell's last words before the onset of radio silence.

The other side?

****

London, 19th December, 1968

Dear Dutch

I was in America again for your Thanksgiving holiday; sorry I couldn't invite you! George and I went up to Dylan's place in Woodstock, NY, a small town in the country. Marvelous food; everyone sat around after dinner with guitars, while the children frolicked. Fantastic!

Things aren't so great back here. Despite the immense success of the *White Album*, the recording sessions were stressful. Yoko hasn't just

---

25   Though less so than when they blasted off three days earlier.

replaced John's former wife. She has replaced his mother, his mistress, the mother of his children, his musical collaborators, his producer, his favorite political activist, and all his friends and prior relations! We mean nothing to him anymore.

John has also played with another band. Albeit a one-off adventure, it was somewhat unsettling to see him play with another group. The band called itself the Dirty Mac, and consisted of Eric Clapton, Keith Richards, Mitch Mitchell (Jimi Hendrix's drummer), and Yoko Ono as the "singer." On one number, she just wails. Clapton does his best not to look at her. It's not a keeper.

The following will give you an idea of where John's head is at: Apple had negotiated for John to provide a Christmas message to a magazine. The magazine planned on releasing it as a little plastic disc stapled to the magazine. What was John and Yoko's Christmas message? The gradually fading heartbeat of a dying fetus — Yoko's. I mean, talk about a way NOT to get sympathy for a miscarriage! Although, really, I am sorry for them.

Apple settled out of court.

To their dismay, the Beatles recently discovered themselves to be contractually tied to yet one more movie. Acting out a script is a non-starter, and they've done the cartoon bit. The band has therefore decided to simply create a movie of themselves recording their new songs. They'll be killing two birds with one stone.

The movie producers have reserved the Twickenham studio. Sound familiar? That's where they filmed *A Hard Day's Night*.

It's fair to say that neither John nor George is taking a particular interest in the Beatles. Paul has tried to rally the troops. Playing to a live audience, getting back to their roots, this would energize the band, no? Paul's actually managed to stir up a bit of a discussion. Where to perform this live concert? John thought a lunatic asylum would be appropriate. Yoko came up with the idea of playing in front of twenty thousand empty seats. John applauded wildly and nearly fell off his chair. The others just stared.

Happy New Year!

Mal

****

At 4:30 AM, we would hear the astronauts again. If their voices appeared before or after 4:30 AM, the crew was doomed. Doomed to crash or doomed to disappear in space.

We did not even need to hear their voices. The crackling of the radio would announce their arrival.

It was a moment of high drama, and Susan Borman was trying on her funeral dress. I sauntered down the three flights of stairs and out onto the duck pond in the central plaza. I lit a cigarette and ran back in. If the astronauts were lost in space, what would happen to the space program? This was only the second manned flight since the Apollo I fire. Would the public tolerate the loss of three more astronauts? Borman and Lovell were well known to the public from their Gemini VII flight. Funds would be cu…

The radio was crackling! There they were!!!

"He.lo H…ton"

And right on time!

Yes! They were in lunar orbit! There were high fives all around; the tension was broken. The astronauts were now in cruise control.

It was Anders' job to take pictures of the lunar surface. His photographs would be combined with those of the unmanned Surveyor in planning for the eventual lunar landings. Anders had been given this assignment as a consolation prize, a present to make him feel useful, but Anders took the job seriously and began clicking away. The capsule disappeared behind the moon for a second time without any of the excitement of the previous pass.

As the capsule re-emerged from behind the moon, there were a few moments of silence in our headsets. "Hello, hello, hello, Apollo 8 do you read me?" There was a worrisome silence, but in fact there was no danger. Anders, Borman, and Lovell had noted a spellbinding sight:

The earth was beginning to appear over the lunar horizon.

Seen from the moon, the earth would be the exact opposite of a paper moon. It was just about full. A full earth, one might say.

The sparkling blue earth was the only object of color in the entire sky. An awestruck Anders was tempted to take a picture, but this was not in the flight plan. It had never dawned on us earthlings that the *earth* might make for an interesting picture. We already knew the earth, who needed a picture? After a short discussion and Borman's

prodding, Anders got the go ahead. *("You are GO for a picture of earth,"*
I mused.)

Anders proceeded to take the picture *heard 'round the world* – arguably the picture of the 20th Century:

An earthrise over the moon.

The picture soon graced a United States stamp. It would be the featured picture on the world's first Earth Day the following May, and it fairly shocked the world into protecting Mother Earth.

Yet, for all its fame, the picture we saw was not exactly the picture that Anders took. Anders took the picture the way he saw it, with the moon on the right, a vertical horizon, and the earth appearing just to the left of the moon. For public consumption, the picture was turned clockwise ninety degrees to look more the way an earthling would think of an earthrise!

When he snapped the picture, Anders was oblivious to any importance anyone might ever attach to it, and he dutifully went back to taking pictures of the colorless moon. It featured every shade of grey, and nothing else. More importantly there were no signs of life. Had the Selenites all gone into hiding? There were no footprints, hoof prints, or any other prints for that matter. For those who had speculated that all life would be on the *far* side of the moon, it was a major strikeout. Both sides of the moon appeared equally desolate.

There were many un-named craters, and the astronauts named three of them Grissom, White, and Chaffee. Chris Kraft also had a crater named after him. I thought the astronauts could have thrown Kranz a bone, but I suspect that the list was drawn up ahead of time.

It was December 23rd. I thought I'd throw in a little levity by reminding the astronauts that they only had two more days of shopping left until Christmas. Kraft screwed up his eyes without humor.

**

The astronauts now entered their ninth and final revolution around the moon. Communication with earth would…

"Revolution number 9," exclaimed Kranz. "10 minutes to go."

Revolution #9? Where had I heard this??? Why of course… I swiveled towards Kranz, but he was focused on his console. He hadn't attached any particular meaning to "Revolution #9." It was just the ninth revolution, no more no less.

As the astronauts disappeared behind the moon and out of touch for the next to last time, I took off my headset and pondered Kranz' proclamation. It now became clear to me why Mal was so keen on that cut from the White Album. There would indeed be a Revolution #9 on this mission to the moon.

But so what?

It was now Christmas Eve.

Borman had told me that he would have a message for us back on earth, and I had agreed to remain quiet after his message. I had no idea what he had in mind, nor did anyone else at NASA. There had been a discussion of what, if anything, Borman and the astronauts should say on the occasion of Christmas. NASA had left that up to the astronauts. This kind of latitude would never have been permissible in the Soviet system. The time had come.

Borman announced that all three of the astronauts would give their final impressions of earth's only natural satellite. A hush descended over Mission Control, and all eyes turned towards the large television screen.

Revolution #9.

Borman began speaking. At that very moment, Anders accidentally turned off the video portion of their transmission. No one dared interrupt Borman.

"My impression is that it's a vast, lonely, forbidding-type existence or expanse of nothing (…) it looks rather like clouds of pumice stone, and it would certainly not appear to be a very inviting place to live or work. Jim, what have you thought most about?"

"Well, Frank, my thoughts were very similar. The vast loneliness up here at the moon is awe-inspiring, and it makes you realize what you have back there on earth. The earth from here is a grand oasis in the big vastness of space."

Lovell had a deep voice that lent gravity to his words. I couldn't help but feel shivers. The astronauts' words and pictures would forever alter Man's perception of his planet. It was now Anders' turn, and his thoughts were less lofty, more clinical, more down to earth, so to speak.

"The lunar sunrises and sunsets (...) bring out the stark nature of the terrain." He paused, and I thought it a good time to point out the lack of a television signal. Anders quickly corrected that. He continued:

"The moon is quite light, and the contrast between the sky and the moon is a vivid, dark line."

After a few more descriptive exchanges, the astronauts fell silent again. As the Apollo capsule neared the lunar night, the shadows along the lunar surface grew long,.

Borman had spent an inordinate amount of time prior to the flight pondering what his words should be at this very moment. He had canvassed friends and colleagues in search of the perfect words. This had caused him more grief than any portion of his training. He was a pilot, not a poet, and he struggled for inspiration. After considering multiple options, he was confident that he had found the perfect answer. The time to deliver had arrived.

"We are now approaching lunar sunset, and for all the people back on earth the crew of Apollo 8 has a message that we would like to send you," Borman began.

Once again, the hum in Mission Control dissipated. We all focused on the television screen. Around the United States and in much of the world, all activity ceased while we waited to hear the Christmas message. Certainly the crew would deserve to congratulate themselves, NASA, and our American way of life for their technological achievement. Borman, however, had other ideas.

"In the beginning, God created the heaven and the earth. And the earth was without form, and void."

A murmur went through Mission Control. The astronauts were reading the Bible!

"... and darkness was upon the face of the deep."

The three astronauts took turns reading a few lines from Genesis. You couldn't help being moved, regardless of your religious beliefs.

Borman was the last to read, and when he finished there was silence. Fortunately, he had discussed this with me ahead of time. Thus, I was able to refrain from blurting out, "Right on, man" or "Dude, that's cool!" There was just empty silence, and we were left to ponder the spiritual impact of the moment.

Revolution #9. I thought back to the recurring lyrics of the composition. "You are born, you are naked." Lennon had meant it for Yoko and their new relationship. I could see, however, where Mal was coming from. On the ninth revolution, the astronauts in outer space had read from Genesis – our culture's theological interpretation of Man's origin, the origin of the Earth, the origin of the Universe. God – the ultimate extra-terrestrial.

Mal had been prescient about "Baby You're a Rich Man" the year before, and now somehow he had known that something spiritual (extra-terrestrial, in his mind) would happen on the ninth revolution. These thoughts were taking me to uncomfortable places, and I preferred not to dwell on them.

Critical point # 3 in the mission was coming up: TEI, or Trans Earth Injection. The astronauts would fire up the SPS engine one last time, and head out of lunar orbit. The issue facing them was now exactly the same as the one they had faced on the way in: The SPS had to ignite at precisely the right moment. Too soon, too late, too short a burn, or too long a burn, and they would be dust. One last time they silently sped behind the moon, and for the second and last time, the crackling of the radio would announce triumph or despair. Out of sight and out of radio range, the astronauts fired the SPS for two minutes and eighteen seconds. Controllers whose shift had long ended milled around with us, and waited. The quiet of the room was broken regularly by CapCom Ken Mattingly's steady invocation. "Apollo 8, Houston," … "Apollo 8, Houston" … Suddenly, Lovell's voice rang out. "Houston, Apollo 8. There is a Santa Claus!" He was right on cue.

The long journey to terra firma would now begin.

It was not without drama: In working the computer, Lovell accidentally knocked out the I.M.U designed to provide the re-entry's navigational data. If the capsule weren't properly oriented, the heat shield would be ineffective. Lovell had to re-enter navigational data into the computer by aligning the capsule with a star – any star. Given a field of view of only 1.8 degrees, there were some tense moments while Lovell searched and searched for any recognizable bright star. Finally, he was able to line up Sirius and Rigel. I'm sure I'd learned about these stars during one class or another. I was just glad that my life didn't depend on identifying them.

From here on in, the journey was more lighthearted than on the way out. The main goal of the mission had been accomplished.

The fourth and final critical point was still to come. They had to make it back alive.

The key to a non-fatal re-entry was the angle of the capsule's approach. At 25,000 miles per hour, striking the earth's atmosphere would be akin to a flat stone hitting water. If the capsule came in at too shallow an angle, it would bounce off the atmosphere as surely as the stone skipping off the pond, and it would be *hasta la vista* Apollo 8. Too steep an angle, the capsule would burn up like the many meteorites that never reach the earth.

As usual, we would not know for sure until the end of the re-entry blackout whether they'd found the critical angle. From down in Houston, their approach looked good, and sure enough, following the usual broken-pencil period, the three parachutes deployed and the charred capsule made an uneventful splashdown.

The reception the astronauts received, however, was anything but uneventful. The first men to fly away from earth! The first men to see the moon up close! The first men to see the far side of the moon! The first men to safely re-enter earth's atmosphere from outer space!

The astronauts landed on the cover of *Newsweek* and were named *Time*'s Men of the Year *(whom did they displace at this late date? Mark Rudd?)*.

It had been a moment of dramatic, inspiring scientific triumph, ending a politically and socially dismal year.

**

With the unqualified success of Apollo 8, it would soon be time to formally announce the crew of Apollo 11.

For illustrations, see www.intotheskywithdiamonds.com

13. Magnificent Desolation

The success of Apollo 8 had heightened expectations of a moon landing by the end of the decade, and Deke had promised to name the upcoming crews in short order. Apollo 9 and 10 were already spoken for. The astronauts of Apollo 11, however, remained to be determined. The backup crews had always rotated to the prime crew position three missions down the line, which meant that if he maintained this tradition, the Apollo 8 backups, Armstrong, Aldrin, and Haise, would be the prime crew of Apollo 11.

This mission, however, would obviously be special. The crew of Apollo 11 would get the first crack at a moon landing. Were these astronauts really the best of the lot? Did it matter one way or the other that Armstrong was a civilian? Who would best represent NASA and America?

Then again, Apollo 11 hardly had a lock on the first moon landing. Any significant glitch on Apollo 9 or 10 would push the first landing to Apollo 12 or even 13.

Fielding phone call after phone call from well-wishers giving a little "friendly" advice, Deke fiddled with the pieces on his chessboard. He moved Haise to Apollo 13 and replaced him with the now-healthy Michael Collins. Other than that, in the end, he left everything in place.

On Monday January 6th, 1969, Deke made it official: the prime crew for Apollo 11 would consist of Neil Armstrong, Eugene "Buzz" Aldrin, and Michael Collins.

***

A few days later, the upstart American Football League's New York Jets defeated the established National Football League's Baltimore Colts in Superbowl III. The event featured a pre-game guarantee by New York quarterback Joe Namath that the Jets would win – a bold prediction that led to serious cringing in the coaches' corner. The Jets were newcomers and major underdogs. The victory led to the merger of the two leagues.

***

London, 9th February, 1969

Dear Dutch,

Apple's cutting down on staff members. I'm still here, but my title on the company books is now "office boy." Some promotion. For a while I nearly felt important in a slightly creative way, but it seems all I do once again is fetch and carry. I find it difficult to live on what I take home each week, and I dream of being like the Beatles and their friends who buy fantastic homes... I always tell myself — look, try to give and you will receive. The enemy is ego. I know that, but it still hurts. At other moments, I remember how much I love them, and then nothing is too much trouble.

Mal asked half-seriously whether there might be a place for him at Mission Control. I wondered all over again whether I was reading too much into his requests. I had to break it to him that anyone without major security clearance would be considered a Soviet spy until proven otherwise.

It's not easy for the boys either. Considering their mood, I wonder why the four even bothered to come in on the day after New Year. Of course, there was that small matter of the cinematic obligation. It was clear, however, that they were just fulfilling an obligation. The studio used to be a creative workshop, but now it's just a place of work. They were here to arrange, rehearse, and be filmed.

Rehearse for what? They still had not decided.

Rehearsing for a concert perhaps, or possibly a television special, or maybe it would not be a rehearsal at all, but simply a demonstration of how a Beatle record is made. Nobody knew. This would have to be a solution in evolution.

Since the hysteria of Beatlemania has long died down, Paul again brought up the issue of playing to a live audience. George was a bit of a downer: he declared he wasn't going on any tour and he wasn't leaving the country. John was often stoned or bored; or he giggled; it was hard to get a straight answer from him or keep him on topic for very long. He used humour and funny faces to deflect his lack of focus. In any case, he was clearly in no position or mood to go on any tour.

A compromise was reached: They would play live, but just once, at a place to be determined. The album would be recorded live, without any overdubs. The raw Beatles! The real anti-Pepper album! Yeah! John was all for that.

Early in the month, Paul walked in with a rollicking song called "Get Back." The chorus, "get back to where you once belonged," summed up the spirit of the day, and the whole movie/concert project was dubbed "The Get Back" sessions.

On the heels of "Get Back," John and Paul combined melodies to create the melodiously raw "I've Got a Feeling," quickly parodied by John as "I've Got a Hard On." Cast against type, Paul delivered the throat-scorching parts and John provided the balm. It was John, however, who simply *had* to throw in the line "everybody had a wet dream." Another future ban from the BBC. My job was to go around transcribing and distributing the lyrics three times over, so Paul, John, and George could stay on track. There were many problems with the whole production. Where to start? Wrong setting, wrong time of day, wrong temperature, wrong attitudes...

The stage was cold (in every way). We could practically see our breath. How do you play an instrument in such temperatures? What kind of acoustics and what kind of atmosphere do you get on a movie stage? By contract, we could only be there from 9 to 5. They were joking, no? The boys don't usually come *into* the studio until after 5 PM. 9 AM, why John's just going to bed! And, of course, there were lights. Bright lights, colored lights! At one point, the spotlights all turned red, giving one of their arguments the appearance of a quarrel from hell. The black shadows threw every frown into a devilish grimace, every guitar into an evil pitchfork. Fortunately, there were many light-hearted moments, and most often, when things got a little dicey, they would whole-heartedly launch into an oldie.

Paul was eager, John was spacey, George was peeved, Ringo was exasperated. Paul would throw out ideas in the hope that one would stick; the others just punched the clock. Certain of how he wants his songs arranged, Paul's become less tolerant of others' contributions. At one point Paul commented obliquely on one of George's guitar parts. That was one comment too many for George. "Fine, I'll play it anyway you want me to," George shot back with more than a little sarcasm, "or I won't play at all if that's what you'd like." I hope they don't put that bit in the movie. [They did.]

John arrived with just one semi-complete song, a fair one at that, "Don't Let Me Down," a plea to Yoko. The song would be his main contribution to these sessions. He was enamored with it and played it constantly. It has the same structure as "Lucy in the Sky" and "Baby You're a Rich Man" — the dreamy melody and then the loud chorus. Except that instead of "newspaper taxis," "plasticine porters," and "kaleidoscope eyes," you have "she do me," "she does me good," "she really done me." (Was his son just learning declensions?) Of course, John knows exactly what he's doing. I heard him tell Paul, "When you're drowning, you don't say, 'I would be incredibly pleased if someone would have the foresight to notice me drowning, and come and help me,' you just scream."

Much to my delight, John at some point launched into "Across the Universe," the song I so liked last year. To my chagrin, however, the boys quickly moved on.

George arrived triumphantly with a couple of keepers. His relationship with his wife Pattie is strained (his affairs are no secret), and as with his bandmates, he finds solace in composing. He's really been keen on "All Things Must Pass," the fruit of his meditations, and for a while, the three other Beatles pitched in on the arrangement. Before long, however, their attention shifted to another song. George was furious. Always so little time for his songs. He shouldn't have been so prickly. Many songs got short shrift. John was doodling with a solid song titled "Child of Nature," and *that's* gone nowhere too[26]. Nevertheless, George quit the set. He didn't say anything. He simply up and left for a few days. John was nonplussed. "Fine," he said, "we'll get Eric [Clapton]."

George returned after being coaxed by Paul, Ringo, and even John. He agreed to play and share his toys, on condition that the band record elsewhere. No one had a problem with that, on the contrary. It was decided that they would play in the basement of Apple's offices on Savile Row. With that, all the equipment was brought over. Guess who did most of the lifting? The mood improved at once. There was light-hearted banter, and it nearly seemed like old times.

While walking down the street, George found yet another way to keep the peace: he literally ran into keyboardist Billy Preston (Preston used to be

---

26 Later released on the *Imagine* album (with different lyrics) as "Jealous Guy."

in Little Richards' band), and bodily dragged him into the studio. Respected as he was, he had the same effect on the boys that Eric Clapton had had the year before. They all behaved, and Billy had a nice little solo on "Get Back."

Paul rallied the troops with some quality songs. After "Get Back" and "I've Got a Feeling," came "The Long and Winding Road." Then he wrote "Two of Us" specifically for him and John to harmonize on, something they hadn't done in eons. Perhaps being physically close would capture some of that old magic. (It didn't.)

And then the clincher: Angsting over the future of the Beatles one night, Paul had a vision of his mother Mary telling him that everything would be alright. A bearded, subdued McCartney walked into the bustling studio, sat at the piano, and oblivious to all around him, played out the chords to his new song. "When I find myself in times of trouble, mother Mary comes to me, whispr'ing words of wisdom, let it be." Quiet gradually descended over the room. Sessions usually started with some wisecracking, jamming, and banging of drums, but this morning was clearly different. The song itself was different; it was both somber and uplifting; you felt like bowing your head. Written in a prior century, it would have been a religious hymn.

When Paul finished, the room was silent for a while. John and George nodded. How do you argue after a song like that?

"I'm a little embarrassed," Mal went on to say. "There's a little twist to this song that maybe I'm not supposed to talk about. It was in India that Paul first had the idea for this song, and I was the one in his dream saying "let it be." The words were originally "When I find myself in times of trouble Brother Malcolm comes to me." Then, one night, Paul had a dream about his mother. He asked me if I minded his changing the lyric to 'mother Mary.' It just sounded better. Can you imagine, Paul asking ME if it's OK?

There was a deadline for these sessions: Ringo had a commitment at the end of January for a part in the movie, *The Magic Christian*. The four of them finally decided to play live somewhere, but each suggestion withered on the vine. I can't remember whose brainstorm it was, but someone suggested a concert on the roof! On the roof! Right there on the roof of 3 Savile Row! The city below would be our audience. It would create a bit of mess in the streets. John loved that! George didn't half mind either. If

John was excited, well then Paul would go along too. Perhaps if John had fun he'd want to play live again.

I, of course, would be in charge of trudging all the gear up the stairs.

When the time came, the boys trotted up to the roof — and it was cold! Cold and grey. Ringo's red mac and George's lime-green pants added a splash of color. John threw on an ill-fitting fur jacket. They launched into "Don't Let Me Down." John forgot the words and adlibbed some gobble-dygook. At the end, he gave Paul a big grin — *ah, yes just like the good 'ole days!* "Get Back" and "The One After 909" were delivered smoothly. There were no singing parts for George. He didn't much care. Again, they went through "Don't Let Me Down."

Then came the chaos. As traffic came to a standstill below and every pedestrian looked up at the sky to see where the music was coming from, the Man struck back. Bobbies and pipe-smoking inspectors knocked on the door and climbed over from the neighboring townhouses. We were a "public nuisance." John was giddy with excitement, but after a third go at "Get Back," I had to pack everything up. (You'll see me in the movie to the right of Ringo during much of the performance.) The gals sitting off to the side clapped wildly at the end of the show. Ringo's wife, Maureen, was the most exuberant of the bunch, and Paul publicly thanked her ("Thanks, Mo'!"). John quipped, "I hope we passed the audition!"

The original plan had been to record the Beatles live and raw, but the resulting tapes were deemed inadequate for public distribution. We only released "Get Back" (with "Don't Let Me Down" on the B-side). It has been a very long time since the last single release (measured in "Beatle months"), and the public has just gobbled it up.

I would have thought they'd release "Let It Be," but they let me down. Cheerio,

MAL

Sally and I couldn't understand why Apple or *somebody* didn't pay him more — surely they could afford it. Not that we thought they should buy Mal a house, but certainly they could pay him a decent salary. Sally reminded me that we didn't know what he was paid, really, or if he was spending it on drugs. Even so, the story about "Brother

Malcolm/Mother Mary" made me think he was more than a gofer – a dogsbody, as he would say.

Mal revealed so much because I was both far away and an American working for NASA – I got that. In the early years he was just tickled and proud to be giving me the inside scoop, and now he could also vent. Still, I was never sure why the letters continued, year after year. Sally said my letters about NASA and the race to the moon were a fair trade, that Mal needed a connection to space and the great beyond; but I felt like I got more than I gave. I wondered if he felt the same.

****

While working on the deficiencies of their Zond capsule, the Soviets were busy putting together a monster rocket, the N-1, that would rival if not better the Saturn 5. The inaugural launch took place on February 21ˢᵗ. The big bruiser took off without a hitch, and all was well for an entire minute. Then fire erupted between two of the stages. The broken-hearted range officers had to destroy the rocket, and it exploded in a bonfire of embarrassment. Wreckage was strewn for thirty miles, taking along much of the Soviet spirit.

**

The Lunar Module was finally ready and was quite a sight. It was 22 feet 11" high and 31 feet wide at the landing pods. It looked like a kindergarten contraption – a stack of geometric forms sitting on four skinny legs, each glued to a dish. Designed to fly in the vacuum of space, there was no need for it to be in the least bit aerodynamic, and certainly no one would ever accuse it of that! Once again, the ungainly appearance of a spacecraft would give no hint of its remarkable sophistication. The upper portion was designed to house the astronauts. There were no seats, since they were unnecessary in a low gravity environment. In the belly of this upper portion lay the rocket that would launch them off the lunar surface and back to the mother ship. The lower, box-like part contained the rocket that would slow the craft as it approached the lunar surface. It would also serve as the launching platform upon departure from the moon. Because every ounce of weight translated into pounds of fuel, even the screw heads had been shaved.

The lunar craft had initially been referred to as the bug, but that was too undignified. It had been re-baptized "Lunar Excursion Module" (LEM), but "Excursion" lent an air of frivolity. "Lunar Excursion Module" was therefore shortened to Lunar Module. The "LM" would still be pronounced "lem."

It was presently ready for real-life testing, and for James McDivitt, Dave Scott, and Rusty Schweickart, three years of training would now come to fruition.

This mission would lead to another first: the first flight of a craft that had no possibility of returning safely to earth. To survive, McDivitt and Schweickart had to successfully dock the LM to the command module. Failure to do so would lead to endless orbiting of the orphaned craft and the eventual death of its crew.

There was no Plan B.

On a less dramatic note, I would once more have to communicate with two spacecraft simultaneously. Since it wasn't always possible to identify the astronauts by the mere sound of their voices, it was decided to formally name the two vehicles. The astronauts chose *"Gumdrop"* for the command module and *"Spider"* for the LM. There was no arguing with the merits of the metaphors, but NASA was none too pleased. How undignified!

February 28th was the target date for the mission, but the crew came down with colds!

Colds!

What was happening to our astronauts???

Finally, on March 3rd, the low, massive, rumbling sound emanating from North Eastern Florida announced the take off of Apollo 9.

The crew's first task was to dock with the Lunar Module, folded like origami at the top of the Saturn. As previously practiced by Apollo 7, the Command/Service module would separate from the upper stage of the Saturn (the S-IVB), turn 180º, fly back to the Lunar Module, and dock with it. The docking mechanism between the Command Module and the Lunar Module was hellacious, requiring perfect alignment and the locking of sophisticated latches.

On Day 2, the astronauts successfully plucked *Spider* out of the S-IVB. McDivitt and Schweickart crawled out of the nose of their capsule and into the LM.

Problems arose on Day 3. Schweickart was scheduled to perform a space walk, but was gradually overcome with nausea and vomiting. A fart in a spacesuit might be funny, vomiting, on the other hand, could be fatal. On day 4, Schweickart felt well enough to float away and test the definitive Apollo space suit.

Day 5 was the big event: after an endless series of checks and re-checks, *Spider* pulled a hundred miles or so away from *Gumdrop*. Jim and Rusty fired the descent stage and were able to modify *Spider*'s orbit. They fired the *ascent* stage, kicking out the descent stage into oblivion and simulating a liftoff from the moon surface. Finally, in an elaborate mating dance, *Spider* docked securely with *Gumdrop*. (I thought *"John"* and *"Yoko."*)

Success! The Lunar Module had passed its first test.

It remained to be seen how it would function in lunar orbit after a 325,000 mile journey.

That would be for Apollo 10.

****

London, 5ᵗʰ May, 1969

Dear Dutch,

I wish I could give better news, but I can't. Very little is going on in the studio; I just run stupid errands. A couple of weeks ago, I had to tell George, "I'm broke." I've been feeling down because I'm in the red. The bills are coming in, and Lil and the kids are suffering because I haven't asked for a raise. George was gracious and helped me out a bit.

The boys amble in, here and there, to tinker with this or that song. George came in on his twenty-sixth birthday to work on two new tunes, "Old Brown Shoe" and "Something." He polished up "All Things Must Pass."

Thought was given to releasing a *Get Back* album featuring the new songs, the jam sessions, and the studio chatter. They even took a rather original picture for the cover: the four of them went back to the building where they'd had their picture taken for their first album, they climbed up the same stairwell, and struck the same pose. Since the *Get Back* sessions, Paul has shaved his beard, but John has let his grow. Seven years have passed since the original picture. An eternity... It would have made a great cover, except that there's no album! Normally, the Beatles record a song,

listen to the playback, and tweak the song indefinitely until everyone is satisfied. Here we have hours upon hours of multiple takes —some only partial
— of multiple songs in random order. None of the Beatles volunteered to
sift through the hours of tape. The project has been shelved (even "Let It
Be"!). I feel bad for Glyn Johns, who has spent the better part of a month
putting an album together. I think they'll simply wait for the for the movie
release to reconsider the issue — whenever that'll be.

Linda is pregnant, so she and Paul got married in March. Pete [Brown],
Neil, and I were the only ones present from the Beatles' entourage. I was a
'witness'! The three other Beatles had something else to do — or perhaps
Paul didn't invite them, or only half invited them — I didn't want to ask. Many
female fans came to boo the loss of the last available Beatle.

Ironically, on the very same day, George's home was raided for drugs!
Bit sticky. Paid a fine. I didn't venture too many questions.

John and Yoko also got married. John used the occasion to change
his name from "John Winston Lennon" to "John Winston Ono Lennon." He
likes the nine o's in their combined names! (By the way, was I right or was
I wrong with respect to "Revolution #9"?) To avoid the press, they jetted
on moment's notice down to Gibraltar, where they tied the knot. They were
formally photographed in their rumpled white outfits, and they flew out just
as quickly as they'd flown in.

John is the subject of ridicule everywhere he goes, but he doesn't care.
The more he's seen as a wack job, the more it sharpens his resolve. After
avoiding reporters on the day of their wedding, John and Yoko actively
courted the media during their honeymoon. The latest light bulb to go off in
John's head had the two of them promoting a "bed-in for peace." For days,
he and Yoko stayed in their Amsterdam Hilton room, inviting reporters to
watch and listen to them pontificate in their white pajamas. There were
peace signs everywhere, and all John talked about was Vietnam. In the end,
he simply made the *proponents* of the war look sane.

John's next stunt was to conduct interviews from within a cloth
bag. John and Yoko formed "Bag productions," and we were treated to
"baggisms"...

Always finding his own life to be the greatest source of musical inspiration, John has written a song about his marriage and his honeymoon. "The
Ballad of John and Yoko," he's called the song, with a straight face no less.

He clearly does not see (or revels in) the irony of the word "ballad" being attached to His Silliness. There is nothing deep, lyrical, or poetic about the verses, just a straightforward narrative beginning with the paperwork, the travel to Gibraltar, the honeymoon in Amsterdam, etc... And just to show how far he's come from his "Jesus" apologies three years ago, he specifically wrote "Christ, you know it ain't easy ... you know they're gonna crucify me." So there.

Having written the song in a hurry, he wanted to record it in a hurry, and get it out to the public in a hurry. (For, surely, the public thirsted for a song about the difficulties he had ditching his lovely first wife in exchange for her humorless replacement.)

There was no question of getting the Beatles together in a hurry.

There was, however, one person he could reach out to, who could arrange the song, play all the instruments, and get the record done overnight.

John called Paul.

Thinking this might smooth over some of their differences Paul eagerly came over. It was actually fun. Both Paul and John were in fine spirits. In the middle of one take, John yelled out to me, "un string avec caput, Mal!" and I got him a guitar string. Then, a few moments later, with Paul on drums, John urged, "Go a bit faster, Ringo!" to which Paul replied "OK, George." With a little multi-tracking, Paul played bass, drums, and piano, and took the harmonies; John sang the lead and played the guitar. This time, it was Paul who was having trouble here and there, in particular where the song suddenly stops and John yells, "Think!" Paul had to repeat the drum part a few times. He eventually slammed it home, and they went on to have a jolly time.

The song actually reached #1 — *while* "Get Back" was still on the charts, no less. I guess the public really IS interested in John and Yoko's story.

On the Apple front, things are going from bad to worse. The finances are a mess, and therefore, so are the boys'. (Not like mine aren't a worse mess. I've got about 70 pounds to my name, but I won't whine about that anymore. Promise.) They all realize that someone's got to be brought in to clean things up.

Paul's father-in-law, Lee Eastman, is a well-known New York lawyer in the art world. (Original family name: Epstein. Can you believe it?) Mr.

Eastman has delegated his son John to help out the Beatles. John's closer to them in age, he's amiable enough, and being related to a Beatle, he can be completely trusted. The perfect choice. Or so Paul thinks.

As far as John's concerned, this John Eastman represents all he detests: he's got the preppy look; he's a phony (the family changed their Jewish name Epstein to Eastman to be more WASPy); he's young, but he's square; he's an agent of THE MAN, the very MAN that he and Yoko have been fighting against. In fact, Lee Eastman has represented the very artistic establishment that so ridiculed Yoko when she lived in New York. "Mr. Epstein" John calls him to his face.

Paul has been completely taken aback. And because it's family, it's become personal!

Out of the frying pan and into the fire, John has aligned himself with a truly unsavory character. The man's name is Allen Klein. He's also a New Yorker, but he couldn't be more different from John Eastman. He's a foul-mouthed, loutish, rotund boor. He's an accountant, and I must say, he starts with a reasonable premise: the music industry often cheats its musicians. By threatening costly audits and behaving in ways quite unbecoming a gentle-man, he negotiates more favorable terms for his clients (notably the Stones, the Animals, Donovan) — and alienates everyone in the process. He takes a sad song, makes it better, and then burns down the studio.

John sees him as his alter ego — direct, unconventional, street smart, anti-establishment, uncompromising, endowed with a roguish charm, and completely oblivious to what anyone might think of him. To Klein's credit, he's done his homework, and he knows what buttons to push; knows all of John's lyrics; has assured Yoko that he can get her films distributed with a one million dollar advance; has told George that the Beatles are a four-man band, not a one-man band with three sidemen; all should be equal! This is music to George's ears, of course. So guess what? George and Ringo have quietly sided with John. It's "the in-laws against the outlaws," John likes to say.

Alas, John is also completely insensitive to the harm Klein is causing the Beatles: Dick James is the Beatles' publisher. He owns a major stake in each and every Lennon-McCartney composition. His life story's been the polar opposite of Pete Best's when it comes to luck: Whereas Pete was dumped just as the Beatles became popular, Dick James signed up the Beatles after hearing just one early song over the telephone ("Please Please Me"). Without anything more than that phone call, he has become immensely rich. Well, all this negative publicity around John has led him to beg off and sell his shares — and he did so without giving the Beatles first dibs on their own songs! This is all because of his desire to avoid Allen Klein at all costs.

Paul doesn't grasp why John, George, and Ringo might consider the Eastmans to be partial to him. John, George, and Ringo, on the other hand, don't see that Allen Klein wins battles, but loses wars.

EMI doesn't want to get involved in the squabble and has put the Beatles' earnings in escrow. Now, no one is getting any money. The guys are furious. Paul blames John for having brought in a gangster; John blames Paul for trying to ram his in-laws down everyone's throat.

I don't see a happy ending...

Mal

It upset me to hear that the Beatles were drifting even further apart. There were many bands I loved, but it would be an understatement to say the Beatles were special. I was also surprised. Heck, I thought if I'd been lucky enough to produce what the Beatles did —and I'm not even talking money or fame – I'd hold onto it. After a few drinks, though, I felt that surely the Beatles would stay together; so many millions of people wanted them to. That had to create some kind of psychic centripetal force, no?

I also thought the Apollo program would have inspired songs about the race to the moon, but it did not. In his happy-go-lucky "Eve of Destruction," Barry McGuire had written, "You may leave here for four days in space, but when you return it's the same old place." We had been treated to "The Martian Hop" and to the Byrds' "Mr. Spaceman." Creedence Clearwater Revival had written "It Came Out of the Sky," and Laika, the dog that had died in *Sputnik 2*, came back as the Finnish instrumental group Laika and the Cosmonauts; but that was essentially the extent of the connection between the world of rock'n'roll and the world of space. The keystone – and only significant member – of the Space Rock genre would be David Bowie's "Space Oddity," featuring Major Tom marooned out in space and staring longingly at planet earth.

Commander Bond returned to earth in his sixth and last picture of the decade, *On Her Majesty's Secret Service*. Saltzman and Broccoli flipped-flopped this production with *You Only Live Twice*, just as they'd done with *Doctor No* and *From Russia With Love*. In Ian Fleming's work, Bond marries "Tracy" at the end, only to have her gunned down by bad guy Blofeld. Bond then gets his revenge in *You Only Live Twice*. On the silver screen, there is no connection between the two movies.

The movie, nevertheless, hews close to Fleming's plot. Secluded on the top of a steep, snowy Swiss mountain, Blofeld hypnotizes women, who will soon unwittingly fan out into the world and wreak devastating havoc. (As would soon happen in California.) Bond must infiltrate the devil's lair.

The film was Connery-free. A highly publicized, worldwide search had been carried out for Connery's replacement. Consideration had been given to Timothy Dalton and to Roger Moore, the lead actor in the British television show *The Saint*. The nod had finally gone to Australian model/actor George Lazenby. You never know when the biggest decision of your life is going to come around, and for Lazenby it was now. Despite reasonable reviews, Lazenby decided to avoid being typecast the way his predecessor had. He turned down the opportunity to do a second film – and quickly schussed into oblivion.

For the first time, the title of the theme song was different from that of the movie. "We Have All the Time In the World," sang Armstrong (Louis, that is). These are Bond's last words to his dying wife, Tracy. Louis Armstrong himself had but little time left in this world, passing away shortly after the recording.

****

While we were mostly focused on the upcoming Apollo 10 flight, training was in high gear for the eventual *landing* of a Lunar Module. Apollo 9 had demonstrated that the Lunar Module was space-worthy and could dock with the Command Module. Astronauts now needed practice landing it. For this, NASA developed the Lunar Landing Research Vehicle (LLRV), a bed frame of sorts with four legs, a main engine, and a multitude of small jets. It was not too dissimilar from a helicopter, and before you knew it, all potential Lunar Module pilots were going to helicopter school.

Though Lunar Module pilots would be standing at all times in the LM, the LLRV pilot sat down for the sole purpose of having an ejector seat. And a good thing too, for on May 6th, pilot Neil Armstrong hit the ejector button just seconds before the LLRV crashed and burned.

A little helium tank problem.

**

It was time to give the Lunar Module its *lunar* baptism. Tom Stafford, Gene Cernan, and John Young would be in charge of Apollo 10. They would fly to the moon à la Apollo 8, except that Stafford and Cernan would lower the Lunar Module near, but not *onto* the lunar surface. There was talk of landing on the moon since they would be so close! But it was idle chatter. This particular lunar module had always been targeted for orbital flight testing and was too heavy to take off from the moon. NASA might have chosen to wait for the next LM off the assembly line, but elected not to.

On May 18th, *Charlie Brown* and *Snoopy* took off (only a very slight improvement in the names). The astronauts received the GO for Trans Lunar Injection, three days later they were orbiting the moon, and on Day 4, Stafford and Cernan waved Young good-bye. Their goal was to scout the Sea of Tranquility, the proposed landing site of Apollo 11, which sat on the moon's equator, just right of center. The sun would be rising over the Mare Tranquillitatis, throwing long dark shadows that would heighten the landscape.

The descent of the Lunar Module went smoothly. At forty-seven thousand feet, Stafford ignited the rocket of the descent module, the lower, boxy portion of the LM. Had this been a moon landing, the descent rocket would have decelerated them down to the lunar surface, but here it merely lowered their orbit and allowed the astronauts to loop around the moon for a closer inspection of the projected landing site. Stafford then fired the ascent rocket, hurling the descent module towards the moon and shooting the LM back towards the Command Module.

Did Stafford ever consider for a moment a little deviation from the flight plan to actually land on the moon? It had to be tempting. It would have been suicide, but he would have been the first to walk on the moon. I probably spent more time contemplating this than he did.

Communications were not as smooth as I would have liked. We could communicate with *Charlie Brown* and with *Snoopy*, but the two had trouble talking to each other. Their antennae always seemed to be pointing the wrong way. We would have to fix this prior to the moon landing.

As the LM sped back towards the Command module, a scream of "Son of a bitch, something's wrong with the gyro!!!" interrupted my ruminations.

Was that *Snoopy* or *Charlie Brown*???

Snoopy. Cernan to be specific.

The LM was flipping around like a fish out of water.

It was Gemini 8 all over again: An out-of-control spacecraft. If Stafford and Cernan failed to identify and control the problem, they would be unable to dock with the Command Module, and... the rest was obvious.

A stillness swiftly descended upon Mission Control.

Nothing seemed wrong from down here. Just as suddenly, the astronauts discovered a switch in the wrong position. They were back on track. *Snoopy* and *Charlie Brown* docked, Stafford and Cernan crammed themselves back into the Command Module, the three of them said goodbye to *Snoopy*, which was jettisoned off into space, and they all returned to earth uneventfully.

It was a most successful mission. A remarkable aspect of the flight was the number of nasty calls NASA received regarding Cernan's use of an expletive – and NASA's subsequent lecturing to the astronauts on the use of "cuss" words in space. What a bunch of wet noodles! I'd have liked to see *them* with their ass in a sling, whipping around the moon.

A few days later, NASA's Sam Phillips publicly announced that on July 16th, Apollo 11 would leave for the moon.

And, by the way, the crew would attempt a moon landing.

**

As the Lunar Module sped towards the moon, it became clear that even with the descent rocket braking at maximum power, it was going too fast. "ABORT!" ordered Mission Control.

Too late. The three-second delay in our communications had done them in. The astronauts were splattered across the Sea of Tranquility.

Moments later, another Lunar Module hurtled towards the moon. Out of the blue, the computer conked out. (The astronauts' computer held a grand total of 64 Kb of memory.) We would have to abort. All at once, an alarm went off. We considered the importance of this new alarm, but in doing so, we allowed the moment for the Abort to pass.

Splat.

Fortunately, all this was taking place over at SimSup's – our simulation training area.

We always seemed to be getting ourselves into the "dead man's box," the part of the velocity/altitude/time plot from which no safe landing or abort is possible. In pilot's lingo, we were behind the power curve. And time was running short. Apollo 11 was being readied on the launch pad.

**

A number of side issues gradually came to the fore.

What should the crew do when they got to the moon? (Have a picnic? Secede from the Union? Sacrifice a goat?)

One strategy called for a single member of the crew to take a few steps on the moon, pick up a handful of small rocks, and take off. Period. The plan would be as simple as possible. Weren't there enough risks to begin with? This plan did not please the scientific community. Why go through all the trouble to land on the moon without gathering as much information as possible? Scientists had been planning for this landing as far back as 1965. They had developed an instrument package, called ALSEP, to be left on the lunar surface. Two people were required to deploy it.

Science won. Both astronauts would walk on the moon.

But who should go out first? This decision would impact all the history books to come.

One contingent felt strongly that the Lunar Module Pilot, Eugene "Buzz" Aldrin, should get out first. This contingent consisted of Buzz and his father.

Yes, his father.

Gene Senior had been an aviation pioneer and had lobbied for his son from the get-go. He had lobbied for a flight on Gemini and now this. Some thought Buzz was being a bit of a NASA-hole, others thought "no, an assholenaut," but in fairness, nothing ventured nothing gained.

The best argument for the Lunar Module Pilot-first approach was that on the Gemini missions it had been the Pilot, not the Commander, who had walked out of the capsule. But two arguments carried the day in favor of the Commander-first group: the more senior member of the crew should get the goodies. If Gus had been alive, he would have been the first man on the moon. Secondly, and most importantly, the exit hatch of the LM was in front of the Commander. It would have been silly for the Pilot to shimmy by the Commander ('scuse me, 'scuse me) just to get out first. End of discussion.

And what about lunar germs? We'd seen no evidence for such a thing, but who could say there weren't any? And what if the astronauts came back infected by these germs? Mightn't they spread among a population never before exposed to such creatures, and perhaps kill off humankind and take over the earth? Someone with too much time on their hands had to be thinking of this, but we couldn't be too cautious, could we? Many hours were spent thinking of how to get our "contaminated" astronauts from their capsule onto the ship and how to best quarantine them.

It was decided that upon splashdown, the capsule's hatch would be doused with disinfectant, that the astronauts would don biological isolation garments, and that they'd be hustled into the Mobile Quarantine Facility, a fancy term for a big container. Our heroes would be quarantined just like suspect cattle. Somewhat nicer quarters, but not much.

Finally, there was the critical issue of what to name the Command and Lunar Module. This would not have been an issue, but for the fact that NASA had had a small canary with *Snoopy, Gumdrop, Charlie Brown* and the like. A little dignity! We were potentially talking First Man on the Moon. This time around, NASA insisted on having a say.

Julian Scheer, head of NASA public relations, put forth *Columbia* for the Command module. It had an American sound to it, and it gave a subtle nod to Jules Verne whose *Columbiad* had circled the moon a hundred years earlier[27].

---

27 In a back-to-the-future kind of way, Verne returned the favor by naming one of his space voyagers "Ardan," surely a combination of Armstrong and Aldrin.

Jim Lovell suggested *Eagle* for the Lunar Module. No explanations required.

Columbia and *Eagle* it was.

**

Uncharacteristically, the Soviets revealed their next venture: They would take another pass at launching the most powerful rocket ever. The media discussed *ad infinitum* why the Soviets would suddenly change their approach to public relations. They'd always informed us *after* the fact.

On July 3rd, the Soviets trotted out another herculean N-1 rocket, with essentially the same results. Ten seconds into the launch, it exploded with the force of a nuclear weapon, obliterating the entire launch complex and the last of the Soviet morale.

**

Involved with the minutiae of putting together a space flight, none of us other than the SimSup team had given much thought to failure. But as the launch date approached, you couldn't help it. This flight would be so different from the others. Prior missions had had multiple goals. If one failed, you simply focused on the successes. This mission had just one goal: walking on the moon. If the Apollo astronauts failed, the entire mission would be a fiasco. There would be no sugar coating.

Publicly, NASA emphasized mission safety. Better fruitless than fatal. If Armstrong did not feel it safe to land on the moon, he had strict orders to abort and return to earth; there would be no shame. Armstrong had already proven himself on Gemini 8. Like many of his fellow astronauts, he had liquid nitrogen running through his veins. We knew he wouldn't panic. If Armstrong decided to abort the mission, then surely that would be the right decision. We'd just try again.

Yet, money aside (and this mission *would* cost a pirate's ransom), the entire world would be watching. Every single prior mission had been designed specifically for this event – the moon landing. There were no "alternate goals." Faced with mixed signals, it would be next to impossible for an astronaut offered the chance to be the first man on the moon to abort the flight. Everybody knew this, but it went unspoken. NASA talked "safety," "trust," and "It will be Armstrong's decision."

One night, I discussed with Sally something else no one at NASA could publicly discuss. There was, after all, an intermediate type of failure: death.

In this scenario Armstrong and Aldrin would walk on the moon, but wouldn't make it back alive. They would go down in history as the first men to walk on the moon, the first men to walk on a planet other than earth, and yet if they died, the mission couldn't really be a success, could it?

Did it matter *when* they expired? The lunar module had to successfully take off. If the rocket failed, Armstrong and Aldrin would die on the lunar surface. There was a bit of romance to that. Songs and books would be written about the two astronauts resting in peace on the lunar surface.

The lunar module could take off successfully, but fail to rendezvous with the Command Module up above. Collins would return home alone, leaving Armstrong and Aldrin to circle the moon for all eternity.

Again, I could see a certain romance to this.

The list went on. The SPS rocket that would boost the Apollo capsule out of lunar orbit could fail, leaving *all three* astronauts stranded in perpetual orbit around the moon. The SPS had already proven itself on Apollo 8 and 10, but you never knew.

How much of a success would the mission be if the astronauts perished at the last moment? The lunar portion of the mission would obviously have been a success. Armstrong and Aldrin would go down in history as the first men on the moon, but there would be a major asterisk next to their names.

This was all idle pillow talk. The reality was, there remained a bevy of details to check, re-check, and re-check again. The entire Cape was in overdrive.

In the eye of the storm was the Apollo 11 crew. It had been decided that to minimize their stress (and the risk of catching a cold!), we'd keep admirers and politicians away. Even President Nixon was turned down when he asked to have dinner with the crew on the eve of the launch (some dinner companion...). Instead, dinner on July 15th was a quiet affair including just the crew, their backups, Deke, and a couple of support guys.

Reveille was at 4 AM.

There was one last examination with Dr. Berry, Dee O'Hara, Sally, and the rest of the medical team. A few miles away and awash in columns of white light, the Apollo 11 rocket quietly awaited its big moment.

And then it was time. The van, the elevator, the white room, the capsule, the wave good-bye, the sealing of the hatch.

NASA had donned its Sunday best for the occasion. Flags snapped smartly in the warm wind. A quarter million people lined the roads and the beaches. It was THE hot ticket in town. Lyndon Johnson was there; so were Charles Lindbergh and camera crews from the world over.

On Wednesday morning the 16th of July, at 9:32 AM, they were off. Half way engulfed in a turmoil of flame and cloud, the Saturn gradually tore itself from the pad and majestically began its ascent. The crowd craned its collective neck, as the 20th century obelisk gradually made its way up to the heavens.

They orbited the earth and fired off into deep space to the spot where the moon was expected to be three and a half days hence.

Before there was time to breathe, news arrived that the Soviets had just fired Luna 15.

???

Was there any chance of the two spacecraft colliding?

No, the Soviets assured us that the trajectories were different. Luna was simply going to pick up some rocks off the moon and return – just before our astronauts. The goal was presumably to prove that you didn't need humans to pick up a few lunar stones. A machine would do.

We ignored Luna 15. The astronauts pressurized the Lunar Module, and Armstrong and Aldrin went in for their first inspection. For one and a half hours, the duo took the world on a televised tour of the spacecraft. But they had some competition. Ted Kennedy, the only surviving Kennedy brother, had driven off a bridge at Chappaquiddick. He'd survived, but his female passenger – not his wife, mind you – had drowned. There'd been a delay in notifying the police. A bona fide scandal. Could he ever run again for office?

At 8 A.M., on Sunday July 20th, I promptly sat at my console. The familiar smell of stale food, burned coffee, and sour cigarette smoke was vaguely comforting.

Time again for the White team.

Although all teams worked in unison, there was always a bit of jockeying among Flight Directors to see who would draw the plum assignments. Our assignments had been given to us earlier in the year. It would be on our shift that Armstrong and Aldrin would attempt a moon landing.

On this mission the White Team included Bob Carlton, an Alabamian nicknamed the Silver Fox for his prematurely silver hair, Don Puddy, a tall fellow from Oklahoma, and twenty-five year old Steve Bales, who stood out with his large, round black-rimmed glasses. Carlton's handle was CONTROL, and his job was to monitor the LM's propulsion system. Puddy worked with me in communications (TELMU), and Bales' specialty was computers and guidance (GUIDO).

The Apollo crew had already been up a while, going through their checklists. Their trajectory looked good. They were neither going to crash onto the lunar surface nor disappear into endless space. They were going to be pulled into lunar orbit just like Apollo 8 and Apollo 10.

Behind the moon, Armstrong and Aldrin crawled out of *Columbia,* the Command Module, and into *Eagle,* the Lunar Module. The disconnection first required venting the air out of the short tunnel that bridged the two spacecraft. A small amount of air remained in the tunnel following the venting, and the separation was accompanied by a little pop.

Right on schedule, *Columbia* and *Eagle* came back 'round to the near side of the moon.

"How does *Eagle* look?" we asked.

"*Eagle* has wings," answered Armstrong.

Collins fired his thrusters for eight seconds, moving *Columbia* and *Eagle* further apart.

Collins examined *Eagle* from all possible angles, while Armstrong and Aldrin checked and re-checked every switch, dial, and circuit breaker. This little tango went on for forty minutes or so, and soon they were behind the moon again and out of touch.

It was 2 PM Houston time.

On the far side of the moon, Eagle began its descent. The astronauts had their backs to the moon, while the LM's radar scanned the surface.

As *Eagle* swung around to the near side, my heart skipped in a big way: We'd lost communication. Kranz was apoplectic. He shut the doors to the control room. Either you were in or you were out.

We could speak to *Columbia,* and *Columbia* could speak to *Eagle,* but *we* couldn't speak to *Eagle.*

This was my turf, along with Don Puddy's.

We swung into action, asking Armstrong and Aldrin to tip the LM this way and that way, favoring this and that antenna. We picked up their signal again using the aft antenna, but it was touch and go. No sooner did we connect, that the ham-in-a-skillet sound would come on again. We'd have to do better on future missions.

They were now ten miles above the moon, the low point of Apollo 10's descent; somewhat familiar turf up to now, if a single flight could count as familiar turf.

They were given the GO for PDI – Powered Descent Initiation to the moon, a whole new ballgame.

Finally we'd be finding out what the lunar surface was made of. Although un-manned probes, such as the Surveyor, seemed to have landed without difficulty, no one knew *for sure* what the surface would be like in the Sea of Tranquility. Cornell astronomer Thomas Gold predicted up until launch time that the lunar surface would consist of a thick, fluffy, powdery substance that would swallow up the Lunar Module and its two inhabitants. He had recommended that the astronauts drop weights onto the surface before landing to make sure they didn't sink.

Armstrong and Aldrin had no time for such thoughts. Armstrong rotated the lunar module to the upright position and could now see where they were going. Aldrin's eyes were fixed on the console.

The descent rocket fired at full throttle, braking *Eagle* as it hurtled towards the surface.

Aldrin read off the numbers to Armstrong.

Then came the first bit of bad news.

"12-0-2 alarm," said Armstrong without much agitation in his voice.

12-0-2 alarm?

What the heck was that? Who could remember? Time to abort? We'd learned from the simulations that there was no time to dawdle.

A sudden chill set in.

But wait! 12 0 2, 12 0 2, A12 0 2, yes, this sounded familiar! The number stamped...

Steve Bales suddenly remembered too, as if my epiphany had instantly sharpened his memory. 12-0-2 was a minor overload signal.

He went for it.

"We're GO on that, Flight!"

Whoosh, like air leaking from a tire, we all started jabbering again. Not for long.

"12-0-1 alarm" radioed Armstrong.

????????

More of the same.

"We're GO on that, Flight," said Bales, a little more laconically this time around.

Though the alarms in and of themselves did not signal anything dangerous, a rapid string of alarms could shut the computer down and abort the mission. These alarms, therefore, still gave us cause for concern.

Three thousand feet above the moon, Armstrong and Aldrin had a much more serious issue to deal with. The Sea of Tranquility was hardly tranquil. Armstrong was staring down at a giant maze of tumbled boulders. If they landed there, the LM would be resting at a cockeyed angle, and could never take off. The little "pop" that had taken place during the separation of *Columbia* and *Eagle* had nudged the Lunar Module just far enough downfield to compromise the landing.

Armstrong would have to improvise.

Unfortunately, there were no fuel provisions for that. They had precious little of it left, and the gauge was now practically useless – like a car with the needle on Empty. Still we had to make some estimates.

"Sixty seconds," drawled Carlton. Sixty seconds of fuel left.

Aldrin reeled off the data: "Lights on. Down 2.5. Forward. Forward. Good. 40 feet. Down 2.5. Picking up some dust."

Picking up some dust! They were getting close. And still no place to land.

In all the simulations, the LM had by now landed or aborted. We were way in the red zone.

Armstrong's voice was calm, but sensors showed his heart ominously thumping away.

CapCom Charlie Duke echoed Aldrin with some reassuring banter, "We hear you, we copy you."

Deke nervously punched him in the arm and told him to shut up. We only wanted to hear the astronauts' voices and Carlton's fuel estimates.

The papers in Gene's hands were soaked with perspiration.

"Thirty seconds."

Get out of there Neil, get out! Punch out! PLEASE!

"Forward ... Drifting right. CONTACT LIGHT."

"OK, engine stop. ACA out of detent. Modes control both auto. Descent engine command override off, engine arm off. Four thirteen is in."

"Houston, Tranquility Base here ……… the *Eagle* has landed."

Landed?

Landed??? With all those boulders around?

Not crashed, but landed?

There were whoops and tears and hugs all around.

Man had landed on the Moon.

Finally.

Five deaths.

Ten years.

Dozens of astronauts.

Hundreds of engineers.

Thousands of workers.

Centuries of dreaming.

A zillion hours of overtime work.

Up in Eagle, all was silent.

Armstrong and Aldrin allowed their pulses to calm down as they collected their thoughts.

Now what?

Would the Lunar Module gradually sink into the ground?

Would alien forms come out of underground caves?

There were contingency plans for the Lunar Module to take off again within a minute. All looked good, however, and when calm returned to the Control room, we gave them the green light.

"OK for T1." We were giving them at least one minute. When all continued to look good, both from down here and from up there, we gave them an okay for T2, a second minute.

Until now, the lingo had been GO / NO GO. But what would "GO" mean once the Lunar Module had landed? Go back up? Go on out and walk on the moon? I had successfully lobbied to have the lingo changed to Stay / No Stay.

The next milestone would be the twelve-minute mark when *Columbia* would be orbiting up above them. After that, barring an emergency, it would be a couple of hours until *Columbia* would swing around again.

No, all the data looked normal.

"Good show," exclaimed Collins as he flew over.

It was now time for a rest. Our shift was over, and we passed the baton to Windler's Black Team.

Armstrong and Aldrin were too excited to rest and asked if they could start their lunar exploration early. The baton was thus just as quickly passed to Charlesworth's Green Team that'd been assigned to the moonwalk. After six hours of system checks, Eagle had been depressurized, and the astronauts were ready to go.

It was July 21st, 1969.

The hatch opened, and Armstrong's eyes took in the scenery. The shadows were long; the clarity was stunning. In the distance lay the boulders that could have been their graveyard. Now he turned back, momentarily facing Aldrin, and took a deep breath. The grainy black and white television transmission showed Neil slowly backing down the ladder.

He first stepped onto one of the landing pods and then back up onto the ladder, just to make sure he and Aldrin could get back in.

"I'm going to step off the LM now."

With that, he let go of his last link to earth and took a step onto the lunar surface.

"That's one small step for man, one giant leap for mankind."

At least that's what we heard. In his mind he said, "That's one small step for *a* man," but in all the excitement that's what came out. We all knew what he meant.

Armstrong allowed himself an imperceptible smile. He was a team player and would always remain an aw-shucks type of guy. But Lady Luck was finally smiling on him. There were no official astronaut rankings, but he'd been the *last* in his group to fly in space. His Gemini mission had largely been a bust; he was hardly a good luck charm. And what'd happened after that flight? Dave Scott, his co-pilot, had been kicked upstairs into the Apollo training, while he, Armstrong, had had to toil on yet another Gemini backup. And now ... the first to walk on the moon. The first human to take a step on a planet that wasn't called earth. He would be remembered forever.

It wasn't Armstrong's style to dwell on this type of issue. He quickly turned to the task of checking his footing. He launched himself forward with a few stiff steps forwards, backwards, left, right.

"The surface is fine and powdery. I can pick it up loosely with my toe."

Every part of the moonwalk had been carefully choreographed, with very little left to improvisation. As per the script, Armstrong immediately whipped out a pooper-scooper type of device and collected some soil. Should he suddenly have to abort the mission, at least he'd have a sample to show for his efforts.

As Aldrin peered down from the LM, a flood of conflicting thoughts and emotions ran through him also. To think that he Edwin E. "Buzz" Aldrin had been *this* close to being the first on the moon. But heck, he was part of the first *mission* to the moon! Yes, but he was the more educated, the more thoughtful, the more accomplished of the two astronauts. He had *deserved* to be the first. Of course, sure, he had to be grateful for being there in the first place. Had See and Bassett not bought the farm, he'd still be pushing pencils behind a desk.

The little tug of war between Aldrin the Devil and Aldrin the Angel was interrupted by a crackling voice in his headset: Armstrong was giving him the go-ahead.

Re-assured by Neil's few steps, Aldrin alighted more quickly. "Magnificent desolation!" he exclaimed.

Armstrong took pictures of Aldrin bouncing down the ladder and out onto the moon. Aldrin looked down and took a picture of his lunar footprint.

Armstrong and Aldrin placed a plaque on the moon. It read:

HERE MEN FROM THE PLANET EARTH
FIRST SET FOOT UPON THE MOON
JULY 1969, A.D.
WE CAME IN PEACE FOR ALL MANKIND

They planted a stiff version of the American flag – unfurled forever in the windless atmosphere, and saluted – an emotional moment for any American.

They had come for all Mankind, but it was, after all, an American moment. It had been a ten-year, two-country Olympic event, and America had just won the Gold.

The astronauts deployed the contentious ALSEP science package, spoke to President Nixon, and collected rocks. The phone call from Nixon was the ultimate long-distance call, but struck me as a little trite. "I want to congratulate you…" And what exactly had been Nixon's role in the race to the moon? While holding the telephone receiver with one hand, he was slashing the NASA budget with the other, thank you very much.

Up above, Collins bided his time. Despite his front row seat, he was the only human incapable of watching the lunar broadcast.

A little over two hours later, it was over. The astronauts laid a medallion on the lunar surface bearing the likeness of the Apollo 1 patch – *Grissom, White, and Chaffee,* and made their way back to the Lunar Module.

Despite our exhaustion, Sally and I didn't sleep that night. My whole body was tingling with pride and awe. We tottered through our neighborhood in the early morning hours and looked up at the crescent in the sky. "Hey, guys," Sally called out. "Send us a postcard."

"We should do something."

We went home and called Mal. It would have cost a fortune if anyone had answered.

Now came the anticlimactic portion of the trip, the second half of John F. Kennedy's pledge "... and returning him safely to earth." This was like climbing down from Mount Everest. Not as exciting, but just as dangerous.

As they readied the LM for takeoff, alarm bells went off again, indicating a potential problem with the radar. This would be an even bigger problem on the way back than on the way down; the computer and radar were a heck of a lot more important in their search for little *Columbia* above than it had been in their quest for the moon below! In order to meet up with Collins, Armstrong and Aldrin needed to fly off the lunar surface within a narrow period. Time was therefore of the essence. Urgent calls were placed to the MIT team that had done the programming. Eventually, it was determined that one of the switches for the rendezvous radar had been set to "AUTO" instead of "MANUAL" (after all those checks!).

During the checkout, Neil also discovered that his lunar backpack had knocked off a circuit breaker. After some high-level discussions, we came up with a low-tech solution:

"Jam in a pen," we told him. It worked.

At 1 PM, on July 21st, they were set to leave.

"9..8..7..6..5.." *by the way, Luna 15 ended up crashing into smithereens on some lunar rocks ...* "4..3..2..1," and off they went. The take-off was nearly instantaneous, like firing an arrow into the sky. "That was beautiful!" exclaimed Aldrin.

Eagle was able to chase down *Columbia*, rendezvous, and dock. Collins was glad to have some company again.

The big engine at the back of the Service Module – now considered 'ole reliable – fired right on cue, and the three musketeers headed back towards earth. Re-entry was the last nerve-wracking part of the mission, but the three red and white parachutes opened as planned.

President Nixon announced, "this has been the greatest week in history since Creation." Perhaps there was a touch of hyperbole, but it sure felt like the greatest week. Certainly no single event had involved so many people over such a stretch of time.

The astronauts had a little indignity foisted upon them at the end of their mission: BIGS. As per the pre-flight decontamination plans, as soon as the capsule's hatch was opened, the three astronauts were quickly wrapped in Biological Insulation Garments. And so it was that the first lunar voyagers were ceremoniously dropped from a helicopter onto an aircraft carrier and into a large metallic box punctuated by a narrow glass window, just wide enough for three heads. The astronauts peered out, while the rest of the world peaked in.

From magnificent desolation to magnificent isolation...

While the astronauts lay zoo'ed up in their quarters, scientists quickly busied themselves with the cache of moon rocks and the rolls of film. When the pictures were laid out, we were in for a mild shock: The only astronaut on film was Aldrin. Aldrin alighting from the Lunar Module; Aldrin walking on the moon; Aldrin saluting the flag.

Aldrin hadn't taken any significant photographs of Armstrong! He'd taken pictures of the moon, of the lunar module, of his footprint... Was Armstrong's picture not in the flight plan? All the First-Man-on-the-Moon pictures were photographs of the second man! The only photographic evidence of Armstrong's presence on the moon was his reflection in Aldrin's visor and some grainy black and white film. That was it.

**

There was a small personal downside to this spectacular success. The focus of our lives, the entire reason for our being, was now gone.

We'd fulfilled Kennedy's vision and had won the space race. The engineering aspect of the Apollo program was over. We'd proven that we could mold Man and Machine into a unit that was capable of landing on the moon and returning to earth. There were still a few items to work out; transportation on the lunar surface, for example. Could we build a functional moon buggy? This was little stuff, however, compared to landing on the moon and returning. The remaining issues were mostly scientific and simply weren't going to be as sexy.

And speaking of science, scientists around the world were ecstatic. Rarely had the expression "to hit paydirt" been so apt. Analysis of the Apollo 11 rocks answered the age-old question of where the moon had come from.

It came from us.

It was formed at the same time as the earth, and appeared to be made of the same elements.

While it was party time for the scientists, for the rest of us it was time for a little reflection. We looked around at the remains of our personal lives, and for many, the battlefield was ghastly. The married guys with children (long-neglected children), whew… For those not yet divorced it was time to re-discover their families.

What exactly had we done? Had it been worth it? So much time, so much money. These were questions we'd asked many years ago when we first embarked on this gargantuan project, but now that it was over it seemed appropriate to revisit the subject. The goal had been to show the world what a free society could accomplish. Had we done this? Did anybody care? Had we won anyone over? Would anyone remember? Yuri Gagarin and Alan Shepard were long forgotten. How long before the world would forget Neil Armstrong and Buzz Aldrin?

Gus had given his life. So had Ed and Roger. And so had Komarov.

I like to think it was worthwhile. The rockets, the race, the pictures of the moon, the vision of the earth! Had these not all brought an un-paralleled sense of excitement and possibility? Had the fragility of our earth not been revealed to us – an iridescent blue gem in the emptiness of our universe?

But mostly, in those days, I thought it was just the beginning. Sally and I might not get to the moon, but others would. Man would go to Mars, maybe the outer planets. It wasn't too much to think that outer space colonies would come of age in the 21st century. And if UFOs were real, and contact were made, what would we discover?

****

The crown jewel of musical hippiedom lay just ahead. On August 15th, 1969, a half million young souls descended near Woodstock, NY, onto Max Yasgur's farm. For three days they reveled in the epitome of sex, drugs, and rock'n'roll, topped by Jimi Hendrix' brilliantly unnerving rendition of "The Star Spangled Banner." The happening has deservedly grown to mythic proportions, but America at the time was more transfixed by a grizzly set of events: the Manson murders.

Charles Manson, a career criminal, fancied himself a hippie, a composer, and an interpreter of the Bible – and Beatle lyrics. He was charismatic, delusional, devious, and he talked a group of middle-class men and women into murder. He never killed anyone himself. The goal was to foment revolution. Violent revolution. On the night of August 8th, Manson ordered his Los Angeles "family" to 10050 Cielo Drive. Their orders were to kill. And kill they did. The pregnant actress Sharon Tate and four others were chased around the property and repeatedly stabbed until they died. The scenario was repeated the next night in another home. The killers used the victims' blood to scrawl "Helter Skelter" on the walls. Manson said he had received this apocalyptic vision of death and revolution from the Bible, and the lyrics from the Beatle song of the same name.

Was this what we could expect from hippies? We knew it all along, didn't we?

****

London, 29th August, 1969

Dear Dutch,

Congratulations on the moon landing! I know they couldn't have done it without you. Still, I bet it was more fun at Woodstock. Wish we could have been there — except that we're hardly a band anymore. I hear Joe Cocker played "With a Little Help From My Friends," so in some way we were there!

I went to Hyde Park for a musical tribute the Stones gave to their founder and lead guitarist, Brian Jones. They released thousands of half dead butterflies into the sky. Brian was only twenty-seven; he'd been found at the bottom of a pool.

Following his Amsterdam bed-in, John flew to Toronto. (He couldn't get into the States due to a marijuana arrest.) He repeated the bed-in thing, this time adding a new song, "Give Peace a Chance," to his peace promotion;

it's been released through Apple as a record by the Plastic Ono Band and credited to Lennon-McCartney — a gift from John to Paul in gratitude for his help on "Ballad." (Can it get more complicated?) As soon as the bed-in ended, John and Yoko were... deported! Not that they did anything wrong. They were in Canada on appeal and they lost their appeal. I'd say they made pretty good use of their time.

The Beatles had another meeting with Klein. He puffed contentedly on his cigar and tapped its ash off onto the floor. Through a mouthful of toast, he laid out his plans for extracting concessions from EMI. Would the Beatles sign an agreement allowing him to represent them? Yes, of course they would, hissed Lennon, coming across the table like a whiplash. What was there to discuss? He was hardly in a conciliatory mood, and his cold eyes were getting chillier by the minute.

"NO!" said Paul, practically spitting out the word. He couldn't even look at Klein. There was an argument. Ever the conciliator, Ringo tried to fend off the disagreements and weariness that hinted of the breakup.

Paul thought Ringo would eventually side with him. But, no. Et tu Brute?

Ringo quietly sided with John and George again. Soooooooo, majority wins. Despite his refusal to sign the contract, Paul is now represented by Klein, whether he likes it or not. To the outside world it looks like the four are still a band. Obviously, they are not — at least not in the traditional sense of the word.

Paul, ever the optimistic Beatleaholic, has been successful on at least one front: he has caressed and cajoled John, George, and Ringo into coming together to the studio, and has twisted George Martin's arm into producing one more Beatle album. He's even agreed to have a large bed moved into the studio for Yoko, as John won't come without her; she's pregnant and in delicate health (from a minor car accident)!

It actually feels good to be back at the EMI studio with George Martin at the helm.

One of the new songs features an ethereal three-part harmony. It is transcendentally beautiful. The song is double-tracked twice, so it sounds like nine voices. It's so peaceful and choir-like that you'd think Paul wrote it, but it's John's song. He says he heard Yoko playing Beethoven's "Moonlight Sonata," played the chords backwards, and composed a melody around them. There's something nostalgic about watching the three of them work

on these harmonies over and over again. It reminds me of the old days...
"This Boy" ..."Yes It Is" ... "Think for Yourself."

Another one of John's songs has been totally revamped right here
in the studio. It started as a little chippy-choppy song, with the opening
Chuck Berry line "here come 'ole flat top." Paul's slowed it down. He's added
a moody, heavy bass riff, and a piano line, and Ringo's added some creative
drumming. George plays an echo-drenched guitar. For the first time in a
long while, this has been a true collaboration by all four Beatles. They've all
"come together" over John's song. The boys are thinking of it as an opening
track for the album.

Paul has come in early to sing with the gruffest morning voice possible
a song he's been working on since the spring. He gulps, he coos, he growls,
he screams, everyday a different sound. He's by himself, so he can sing to
his heart's content.

Ringo has a composition, as he did on the *White Album*, but this one's
better. He composed it while on a visit to an octopus hatchery in Sardinia.

Have you ever heard of the Moog Synthesizer? It creates otherworldly
sounds when you just click this key or push that button. The boys have just
been introduced to it, and Paul's played the instrumental solo on "Maxwell's
Silver Hammer" by cleverly running his finger on the machine's ribbons.
Paul's convinced that "Maxwell" should be the Beatles' next single, but John
and George won't hear of it. Too frilly. John is veering towards minimalist
music, and George is all things spiritual these days. Neither has the stomach for another vaudevillian song, no matter how macabre and avant-garde
the lyrics might be. Nevertheless, Paul has had them rehearse the song
over and over. It might not have been best to hammer away at this song on
John's first day in the studio. He and George are just counting the days.

George, nevertheless, should be grateful. He has a breezy song ["Here
Comes the Sun"] that reminds me of Paul's "Mother Nature's Son," and
Paul has spent a great deal of time on it. It's just George, Paul, and Ringo.
John's been a no-show.

These are all random songs, and you either like them or you don't.
The *piece de résistance* of this album is the fifteen-minute finale. Paul
and George M. have devoted considerable thought and time to the ending
of what could possibly be the last Beatle album. Scouring the cupboard to
cook up one last flaming pie, they've dug up bits of unused songs and have

created a little symphony, complete with an overture and recurring musical phrases. The piece builds to a climax, a final arc of harmony fills the air, there's a little epitaph, and it's over.

Paul listened to it for the hundredth time, tinkered with this or that switch on the console, signed off on it, shook George Martin's hand, and walked out without saying a word. The door shut behind him with shivering finality.

Thought was given to calling the album *Everest* (after the cigarette brand) and flying off to Tibet for a photo shoot. The imagery would have been appropriate, for the Beatles have reached the pinnacle of their world.

No one had the slightest inclination to fly to Tibet — or anywhere else. The hell with it all, said Paul, why not step outside into the street and take some pictures? The album can be named after the street. This, they finally agreed upon. Paul drew up a little sketch for the planned shoot, and a few days later, with the hot August sun swelling the mercury into the '90s, out they went. As the boys crossed Abbey Road a few times, photographer Iain Macmillan stood high on a ladder and reeled off a roll of photographs. This had to be done quickly while a compliant bobby held up the traffic. Back and forth they went, John leading the way, his voluminous beard aging him far beyond his twenty-eight years. Paul took off his sandals.

Studying the transparencies, Paul thought one stood out, and there you have it, *Abbey Road*, perhaps the Beatles' Last Will and Testament[28].

Paul has diplomatically allowed John and George's best songs to precede his.

London, 20th September, 1969

Dear Dutch

I never finished my last letter to you, and I'm including it with this one. It's been a very down time.

A concert promoter contacted John. Would he attend a rock concert in Toronto? Impulsive as he is, John said he would go *if* he could perform. His plan was to promote the music he and Yoko had been composing. The promoter was thrilled and agreed. There was just one problem: John had

---

28 Although they had no way of knowing it, August 20th, 1969, would indeed mark the last time the four Beatles would be in the studio together.

no band! He called Eric Clapton, who was literally getting off the plane from his final gig with Blind Faith. Would Clapton get back on a plane and join him in Toronto? Yes! They rounded up our friend Klaus Voorman to play bass, Alan White to handle the drums, and off they flew. They had never played together and had no set list. They rehearsed in the First Class section of the plane. Sitting with them was the owner of Schick razors, an amusing irony considering John's beard. Upon arriving, John was informed that his Plastic Ono Band would perform at midnight, between Chuck Berry and Little Richard. Chuck Berry and Little Richard! John was terrified enough to be playing live for the first time in years — but un-rehearsed and sandwiched between his childhood heroes? He and Clapton shared some drugs backstage, and John threw up. The Plastic Ono Band played classic '50s songs, the crowd was pumped, and no one cared how unpolished the band was. At the end of the set, John had a little surprise for the audience. He placed his guitar against the amplifier, allowing the feedback to wail unabated. Out of a bag that had been sitting off to the side of the stage came Yoko Ono. She launched into a seventeen minute version of "Don't Worry Kyoko, Mummy's Only Looking For Her Hand in the Snow," a series of ear-splitting shrieks that suddenly made the feed-back sound soothing. John was elated. As far as he was concerned, the performance was a tremendous success. He would never have admitted it to his face, but Paul had been right: playing live is what it was all about. Of course, playing with Paul or any other Beatle was out of the question. John needed to move on.

Upon his return to England, John demanded a meeting with Paul. The *Abbey Road* sessions hadn't gone too badly, and Paul had some ideas. The next Beatles project...

"It's over," John said.

Paul was incredulous, but he was used to John's impetuous nature. Surely he could humor him as he'd done for the last year and a half.

John was adamant. This was it. "Don't you understand?" John shouted. "It's OVER! I want a divorce, just like the divorce I got from Cynthia! Can't you get it through your bloody head?" And with that, he stormed out with Yoko in tow.

Do you know of a band that could use my services?

And in the end…

"We should invite him to visit us," Sally said.

"Good idea – but he probably can't afford it. He only ever traveled with the Beatles."

"I can't stand that they've broken up. I feel like someone's died." We didn't listen to every Beatle record that night, but we tried.

On September 26th, Capitol released *Abbey Road*. Like "Get Back" earlier in the year, it was an instant hit, rapidly outpacing the sales of *Sgt. Pepper*. You'd have never known the Beatles no longer existed. John had yet to make public his "divorce."

The reviews were uniformly positive, especially with regards to the final seventeen-minute medley. The piece turned in by John Mendelsohn of *Rolling Stone* was typical:

> Side two does more for me than the whole of *Sgt. Pepper*, and I'll trade you *The Beatles (White Album)* and *Magical Mystery Tour* and a Keith Moon drumstick for side one.

Contrary to most other critics, he even liked "Maxwell's Silver Hammer," a song about a homicidal medical student.

> Paul McCartney and Ray Davies [of the Kinks] are the only two writers in rock'n'roll who could have written "Maxwell's Silver Hammer," a jaunty vaudevillian/music-hallish celebration wherein Paul, in a rare naughty mood, celebrates the joys of being able to bash in the heads of anyone threatening to bring you down. Paul puts it across perfectly with the coyest imaginable choir-boy innocence.

The contrast between the merry melody and the macabre lyrics was indeed entertaining.

Tipped off by Mal's letters, I could easily see the underlying meaning to the lyrics that would have escaped most reviewers. Mendelsohn, for example, would write "Then, just for a moment, we're into Paul's "You Never Give Me Your Money," which seems more a daydream than an actual address to the girl he's thinking about."

Girl?

Money, funny papers, negotiations, breaking down? No, this was not a girl he was talking to.

Nor was he addressing a girl when he sang about picking up his bags, wiping a tear and stepping on the gas.

A number of songs took on a radically new meaning, when the context of the recording sessions was factored in. "Octopus's Garden," for example, was Ringo's harmless, child-like tune. There's nifty guitar by George Harrison throughout, and the song is clearly fun and cheerful, as the *Yellow Submarine* meister returns to the ocean depths. This time, however, he's not rescuing anybody, nor is he having fun with his fellow Beatles. Instead, his fellow Beatles are the problem. He'd like to get away from it all, escape the turmoil around him. He'd like to be at the bottom of the ocean below the storm in his little hideaway. Sad Ringo.

"Carry That Weight" featured an equal double entendre with a reprise of the melody from "You Never Give Me Your Money" and a return to the "breakdown" motif ("you're gonna carry that weight").

Abbey Road opens with the slow, swamp rock, bass and tom-tom driven Lennon song, "Come Together," that Mal had described. Considering his decision to break up the band, it was a curious title. It did represent the Beatles at their best, however, with a driving McCartney bass, and a subtle, clever drum contribution from Ringo. The "Come Together ... over me" chorus was full of double meaning, which, flowing from John's pen, could hardly have been coincidental. It's a wonder it wasn't banned from the radio[29].

"Something" was the song that Harrison had been working on through the spring. It was worth the effort, a sweet song with just enough raw emotion ("I don't know, I DON'T KNOW," courtesy of

---

29 It was, in fact, temporarily banned by the BBC.

John Lennon) to keep it from being syrupy. Frank Sinatra would call it his favorite Lennon-McCartney song!

The throat-ripping production Mal had referred to was "Oh! Darling," an Elvis Presley send up. The song is all about the ferocious vocals, and upon its release, instantly joined "Long Tall Sally," "Twist and Shout," "Helter Skelter," and "I'm Down" in the Beatle catalog of riveting vocal performances.

Mal had not prepared me for the last song on the first side, "I Want You (She's So Heavy)." It starts with a slow, hypnotic guitar riff, awash in echo and white noise. The white noise gets louder and louder, the song gradually draws you in to its whooshing whirlwind of sound ... and stops.

Just stops.

And does so in the middle of the riff when you'd least expect a song to stop. It's the end of the first side, so you're just left with silence.

"Because" was the song with the three-part harmonies – another song featuring the Beatles at their best. It literally transposes you to another dimension.

Holding the album in my hands and studying the cover as I listened to the music, I found the picture of the four Beatles to be visually arresting. I suppose I wasn't the only one. The picture would be widely imitated for many years hence – remarkable, considering the little time that had been expended to its planning and execution. Even the near blank *White Album* had taken longer! But what was so special? It simply depicts four men crossing a street.

For one, they are all dressed in a solid color. John is in his white suit. (Was it always the same one? How many did he have? How often was it cleaned?) Behind him comes Ringo, dressed in black. Behind him is Paul, in a casual grey suit. Bringing up the rear is George, all in blue denim.

The sky is very, very blue.

There's a casual and satisfying geometry. In the middle of the picture, the tree-lined street disappears straight back into the distance, while the Beatles walk in a straight line, left to right; a gentle, inverted T.

But there's more. In a classical painting, the line of perspective draws you in. What here was so visually arresting?

It was Sally who pointed it out to me: all eight legs are straight.

Outside of a parade, the odds of four people being in the exact same phase of gait are quite low. And indeed, when one looks at the outtakes of the photo shoot that day, in only one frame do we find this concordance. No wonder McCartney quickly picked out the best shot.

As Mal had said, there you had it, *Abbey Road*. The Beatles had sublimated the pain of their fractured relationships just long enough to produce one last sparkling jewel.

"Paul is dead, man, miss him, miss him"

A funny thing happened shortly after the release of *Abbey Road*. Someone called radio station WKNR in Michigan to say that they had found hidden clues into the Beatles' recordings. These strongly suggested that Paul McCartney had actually died in 1966 and had been surreptitiously replaced. The rumor took wings when WABC in New York picked up the story. (W-A-Beatle-C, as it liked to call itself in the early days of Beatlemania.) An army of aficionados suddenly devoured every Beatle record all over again, poring over every groove, forwards, backwards, and sideways. The CIA would have been proud.

As the list of clues grew, the rumor circled the globe faster than a new Beatle song.

Many of the clues were obscure, and you had to be a believer. In the groove between "I'm So Tired" and "Blackbird" is a little bit of mumbled sound. Why would the Beatles leave nonsensical sounds at the end of their songs? Perhaps there was a secret message. An enterprising listener noted that if you played the gobbledygook *backwards* (something you can do on a vinyl record), it certainly sounded like "Paul is dead, man, miss him, miss him." And if you did the same with the end of "Strawberry Fields," you could be talked into hearing "I buried Paul" (or "I'm very bored" or "Cranberry Sauce"), right?

In Revolution #9 a voice repeatedly intones, "Number nine, number nine." The word McCartney has nine letters. More significantly, when played backwards, "Number nine, number nine" sounds like "turn me on, dead man; turn me on, dead man." When the entire track is played backwards, it sounds like an awful collision. (Fact was, some thought this applied to all Yoko Ono recordings.)

On The *White Album's* "Don't Pass Me By," Ringo sings, "you were in a car crash and you lost your head."

How much more obvious can one get?

Then there were the visual clues (so many, where to start?): In the *Magical Mystery Tour* movie the four Beatles are wearing white suits adorned with a carnation on their lapel. The carnations are all red – except Paul's, which is black. Oooooooo, black.

The *Sgt Pepper* sleeve, so rich in imagery, was chock-full of clues: Paul is wearing an arm band that reads "O.P.D." Officially pronounced dead, of course! There is an open-palmed hand directly over his head, an Eastern symbol of death! The wax models of the Beatles appear to be looking down onto their grave; there's a bloody glove on the doll off to the right; on the back of the album, George is pointing to the words "five o'clock" – the time at which Paul died, naturally; if you place a flat-edged mirror through the center of Sgt Pepper's drum, the word "die" appears, and a diamond symbol points up to Paul.

On the cover of *Abbey Road,* a VW Beetle is parked on the sidewalk. The license plate reads "28IF." 28 if what? Paul would be 28 IF he were still alive, obviously! Paul is holding a cigarette. In his RIGHT hand! Everyone knows he was left-handed! And why is he leading with his right leg, when all the others are leading with the left? He is out of step with the others, is he not???

Scientists got into the act. Dr. Henry Truby at the University of Miami analyzed Paul's voice before and after 1966, the year of his alleged demise. Applying sound spectography to Beatle songs, he determined that the voice that sang "Yesterday" was suspiciously different from the one that sang "Hey Jude"!

How could so many clues not be right?

It didn't help that McCartney had taken this particular moment to go into seclusion up on his Scottish farm.

Of course, many of the clues were in the eye of the beholder, and some had rather pedestrian explanations. McCartney picked a black carnation because he couldn't find a red one. OPD was more specifically the Ontario Police Department. "I buried Paul" was simply "I'm very bored" (or "Cranberry Sauce?"). And McCartney was twenty-seven, not twenty-eight when *Abbey Road* was recorded. It was obvious to any sane person that this "Paul is dead" adventure was just an amusing distraction, but all in all, it served as a reminder of how easy it is to retroactively find clues that confirm a pet belief.

Given the major importance of the subject, *Life* magazine felt compelled to send a team of reporters to McCartney's farm. He was none too pleased to see them. The Beatles were dead, and he had no use for a ridiculous rumor about his own death. This was not the usual jovial Paul who greeted them. He threw them off his farm, then he promptly reconsidered; he let them take a few pictures and gave a short testy interview. "Paul Is Still With Us" was *Life*'s cover story on November 7th. An informal black and white family portrait of the McCartney family graced the cover.

In the article, McCartney was quoted as saying

> The Beatle thing is over. It has been exploded, partly by what we have done, and partly by other people … The people who are making up these rumors should look to themselves a little more. There is not enough time in life. They should worry about themselves instead of worrying whether I am dead or not.

"The Beatle thing is over"?

Neither the press nor the public caught on to this little factoid. Surely this was just a temporary little spat. Had the Beatles not just released their first album in a year – and a great one at that?

McCartney could thank Lennon for wrenching the spotlight back. Lennon announced with fanfare that he was returning his MBE award in protest of British foreign policy (and in remonstration against his latest song, "Cold Turkey," slipping down the charts). The medal had been proudly displayed at his Aunt Mimi's house, and she was appalled to find out after the fact why Lennon had come to "borrow it." Most of Britain joined Aunt Mimi in her revulsion.

****

To accommodate a little dash of piloting spice, Apollo 12 was pushed back from October to November. Why not? What was the rush?

The unmanned Surveyor 3 had for thirty-one months been sitting in the Ocean of Storms – and Apollo 12's new task would be to land within walking distance of the Surveyor[30].

The crew consisted of Pete Conrad, Al Bean, and Dick Gordon. All Navy guys. They baptized the Command Module *Yankee Clipper* and the Lunar Module *Intrepid*.

It was the last crew I would work with and possibly my favorite. Al was an artist – he took night classes in oil painting, and Pete was still a hoot. Whereas Wally Schirra had been a prankster (putting apple juice in the urine sample had been one of his favorites), Pete was simply quick-witted. His jousts with Sally had been priceless.

Sally: Should you guys not learn Russian? What if you're captured? Would you not want to know what your enemies are saying?

Pete: Yeah, like *"you die at dawn"*…

Another time, Sally was trying on an astronaut's space suit for fun.

Pete: Aren't we the sexy one.

Sally: Yes, I have one in every color, and it makes for great evening wear.

You don't tire of a launch. As a warning to those of us who might have been lured into complacency, liftoff on November 12th flirted with disaster. Flags strained in the wind, while thunder and lightning played about.

The behemoth made it off the launch pad, but thirty-six seconds into the flight, we lost all contact with the crew. Inside the capsule all the alarms had gone off at once, and the instrument panel was ablaze with warning lights. This was beyond anything the astronauts had experienced during simulations.

When I finally re-established contact, the news was not good.

"We just lost the platform," declared Conrad. The platform was a critical part of the Command Module guidance system.

---

30 *Sea of Tranquility? Ocean of Storms? Ironic names for a celestial body without obvious water. How about Tsunami of Worries?*

Pete had more bad news: The fuel cells were down and the Command Module was running on its battery.

"I'm not sure we haven't been hit by lightning."

They had, and the circuits had overloaded. To continue the mission or not? J. Aaron would be the Steve Bales of Apollo 12.

"SCE switch to Aux," he instructed the crew. The platform and fuel cells were back up. Nevertheless, data still needed to be re-inputted into the platform, and Dick Gordon had relatively little time.

Could the parachute system have been damaged? If so, the poor guys were doomed, regardless; might as well let them go to the moon.

It was a GO.

Intrepid's ride down to the moon lacked the drama of its predecessor. Conrad and Bean landed the Lunar Module within sight of *Surveyor*, though once again, they came close to running out of fuel.

Getting out of Intrepid and onto the moon was a little tougher for Conrad than it had been for Armstrong. He was short, and *Intrepid*'s legs had not compressed quite as much as *Eagle*'s.

"Whoopie! Man, that might have been a small one for Neil, but it's a long one for me!" he exclaimed.

Not quite as poetic as Armstrong either.

Conrad found himself leaning far forward to compensate for the weight of his backpack. He ambled about, adjusting his balance, and a half hour later called for Bean.

In Houston we were set to watch the television transmission of the second moon landing, when the picture on the screen suddenly turned to snow. The sun had momentarily caught the aperture of Bean's camera and burned out the circuitry. So much for the sound and light show. We would have to settle for sound. Fortunately, Conrad was providing the running commentary, all the while humming and laughing in his trademark giggle. He was obviously enjoying himself.

Bean marveled that a piece of foil could be flung as far as a football punt. He reached into his pocket for his silver astronaut pin, and, facing the Surveyor, flung it as far as the eye could see. *(Lennon could have given him his MBE, I thought.)* Of course, upon his return to earth, Bean would be receiving the *gold* astronaut pin of the space veteran.

The astronauts collected more rocks and set up scientific instruments. This included a seismometer to quantify moonquakes, a magnetometer to search for magnetic fields, another gizmometer to assess high-energy subatomic particles emanating from the sun, and a central transmitting station to relay all these data back to earth.

Al Bean, ever the artist, made a mental note of all the paintings he would create when he returned home. All too soon it was time to go.

The return was uneventful. A few people watched it on television.

***

On December 7th, a small piece in the Houston papers caught my eye. A black spectator, Meredith Hunter, had been stabbed to death during a Rolling Stones concert at the vastly overcrowded Altamont Speedway in California. Stabbed by a Hell's Angel hired to provide security, no less. The symbolism of a black man being murdered, while icons of the peace-and-love decade sang "Sympathy for the Devil" was sobering.

The '60s movement had floated on a utopian cushion of music, love, drugs, and childlike innocence. This murder, along with the Manson massacre of the past summer, would dramatically darken the collective reverie. Had the ideals of the '60s just been smoke and mirrors?

Or was it just that the moon was in Scorpio?

To many, it seemed that the young generation's faith in itself had been dealt a blow as fatal as Meredith Hunter's. To others, the central message of *LOVE* would endure forever.

For illustrations, see www.intotheskywithdiamonds.com

14. Stay Groovy

As we awoke on January 1st, 1970, there was nothing to suggest any imminent changes to the new decade. Same President, same music, and we were still fighting the Communists. Yet, many of the ideals and icons of the '60s wouldn't make it through the first year. Only the long hair would last. Jimi Hendrix performed glorious sets at New York's Fillmore East on New Year's Eve, and it was downhill from there.

Janis Joplin and Jimi Hendrix would both die from drug overdoses in the fall of 1970, and Jim Morrison would follow a year later. Eric Clapton and John Lennon barely escaped their own heroin addictions. The Beatles would officially break up on April 10th, 1970, and three days later, without the lucky charm of the 1960s, Apollo would come this close to biting the dust.

On March 29th, 1973, the United States signed a treaty with North Vietnam and pulled out its troops. Two years later, Saigon fell. Whether the U.S. never gave the military enough support to win, whether the war was hopeless under any circumstance, and whether we had ever needed to be there in the first place would be a matter of historical debate for decades to come.

***

Remarkably enough, all Apollo missions to date had met with success. That streak came to an end with the flight of Apollo 13. Captained by James Lovell, who by now was logging more hours in space than any other space voyager and was heading to the moon for the second time, the Apollo 13 mission literally blew up in space. An oxygen tank in the service module exploded just as the astronauts were leaving earth's atmosphere. The cause was eventually traced back to a handling error a few years back. Bleeding electricity and oxygen while piling up carbon dioxide, the capsule made it back to earth on a wing, a prayer, and magical scientific improvisation in Mission Control. Gene Kranz played a key role in pulling the troops together, and he would later be portrayed by Ed Harris in the movie *Apollo 13*. Lovell might not have walked on the moon, but he had one last time lived up to his nickname "Lucky."

Apollo 13 had taken off at 13:13 military time and exploded on April 13, a vindication for all the triskaidekaphobics of the world, if ever there was one.

For Alan Shepard, the Japanese fable touched his life one last time. He was cured of his inner ear problem. Having flown in space for only a few minutes back in 1962, he was raring to take another shot at it; he was in the right place at the right time and was named Commander of Apollo 14. Of the seven original Mercury astronauts, he would be the only one to walk on the moon.

The following September, Congress cancelled Apollo flights 18 and 19. There would be just three flights to the moon after Shepard's, and that would be the end of Apollo. Besides handling the heartbreak of the pilots slated to fly the cancelled missions, NASA had to deal with the fury of the scientific community: the first scientist-astronaut, geologist Jack Schmitt, had been penciled in for Apollo 18.

What to do?

Should the Lunar Module pilot of Apollo 17 be pulled off in favor of Jack Schmitt? The three members of the Apollo 17 team had trained together many years in preparation for their mission. The astronaut pulled from Apollo 17 would forever more lose his chance to walk on the moon.

Should the entire Apollo 17 team be scrapped in favor of the Apollo 18 crew? Astronauts Dick Gordon, Vance Brand, and Jack Schmitt did not have a problem with that!

Or should NASA let things be and leave the scientific community to argue with Congress?

Once again, the lines were clearly drawn. The astronauts were outraged at the thought of a last minute switch, and the scientists thought it essential. Hadn't the scientific community been promised at least one slot on Apollo? And wasn't it science that underlay the intellectual and economic achievements of the 20th century – and the hope for more? The astronauts would face personal disappointment, but the scientists were working for the world community and our future. I felt closer to the astronauts, but I thought the scientists made a better case.

The scientists won.

X-15 pilot Joe Engle was out, geologist Jack Schmitt was in. When he jumped onto the lunar surface, he would be the first, last, and only scientist to walk on the moon. He and Gene Cernan traveled along the lunar surface in their moon buggy, and they analyzed rocks, soil, and the lunar atmosphere for close to 24 hours. On December 16th, 1972, Cernan took one last look at the moon behind him and shut the Lunar Module's door.

He would be the last human on the moon for generations to come. It was an emotional moment at NASA, yet a moment that went largely unnoticed by the American public. It had lost interest.

In some ways, the Apollo program had been a victim of its own success: Anders' famous picture of our fragile blue earth stood in stark contrast to the ugly pictures of our wanton neglect. On June 22nd, 1969, barely a month before the first moon landing, the Cuyahoga River near Cleveland had literally caught fire (again). Local citizens lamely joked that you didn't drown in the river as much as decay in it. Pictures of the unnatural event were broadcast throughout the land. Were we at war with our own planet? Technology and industry were the villains in this conflict, and the public was no longer in the mood for expensive, repetitive technological achievements presenting no immediate benefits.

The production of Saturn V rockets was discontinued, and much of the tooling and machinery was lost or destroyed.

Lyndon Johnson died without fanfare in January 1973, his death eclipsed by the very public trial of the Watergate conspirators; the Manned Spacecraft Center was quietly named after him.

Deke finally made it into space. The cardiologists cleared him and he flew the 1975 Apollo-Soyuz mission. The Americans docked with the Soviets, shook hands, signed documents, returned to earth, and formally ended the American-Soviet competition.

****

Released from each other's critical eyes, each Beatle could now fully pander to his own proclivities. McCartney could be sentimental, Lennon could explore his tortured soul, and Harrison could preach. Like the characters in the Wizard of Oz, each Beatle found himself lacking a little something: Harrison lacked a commercial interest; Lennon lacked a feel for studio production; McCartney lacked Lennon material to sink his teeth into; Ringo lacked a band. They *all* lacked a filter, appearing to release whatever tune, song, or message came to mind. The results would be uneven.

In early 1970, Lennon asked Phil Spector to produce his new single, "Instant Karma." Appreciating Spector's work, Lennon gave him the *Get Back* recordings, with instructions to make something decent of the endless tapes. The material had lain fallow for the past year, none of the Beatles having expressed an interest in revisiting the road kill.

When he heard the raw recordings, Spector was subject to the same urge that had once seized McCartney upon hearing the demos of "Strawberry Fields," "While My Guitar Gently Weeps," and so many other nascent Lennon and Harrison songs: the need to produce! Spector added some strings here, some female back up singers there, and in the end, produced a very credible album. He rescued from oblivion Lennon's poetic masterpiece "Across the Universe," tacking it on to the album, even though it had been recorded an entire year before the *Get Back* sessions.

When the album came out in May 1970 as *Let It Be*, the songs "Let It Be," "Across the Universe," "Get Back," "The Long and Winding Road," and "Two of Us," made it well worth the price of purchase – with an honorable mention to most of the other songs. Given a wide choice of takes for each song, Spector chose one version of "Let It Be" for the single and another for the album. (The former has a much better Harrison guitar solo). Either way, it was a major hit. Despite Spector's input, the album still had a live, unpolished feel – as intended – and you either liked it or you didn't. Said Lennon, "He was given the shittiest load of badly recorded shit with a lousy feeling to it ever, and he made something out of it. He did a great job." He took a sad song and made it better. George liked it, so did Ringo, and so did I.

McCartney hated it.

In fact, he loathed it. He particularly despised the idea that his songs were arranged without his approval – he, the perfectionist, who had always fretted over the tiniest detail of every Beatle song.

Ringo had momentarily left the band during the recording of the *White Album*; George had long hinted that he'd had enough; Lennon had said outright that he wanted a divorce, and it was Paul each time who had coaxed everyone into hanging in there. But now, Paul himself had had it. Every Apple move seemed to be a source of irritation, and

Let It Be was the last straw. The love that once bound him to his band-mates had grown cold.

In April 1970, McCartney released his first solo album, the eponymous *McCartney*. Not being in any mood to field questions from the press, he instructed Derek Taylor at Apple to draw up a list of questions likely to be thrown his way. McCartney would provide the answers. This little Q & A exercise was printed up and distributed with the record.

"Are you planning a new single or album with the Beatles?"… "Do you foresee a time when Lennon-McCartney becomes an active song-writing partnership again?"

Paul: "No"

To those in the know, this was no major bombshell. It came as a major shock, however, to a worldwide audience that was still reveling in *Abbey Road* and *Let It Be*. The public blamed the breakup on the messenger – McCartney, of all people.

Lennon should have been pleased by McCartney's pronouncement, considering his unrelenting lobbying for the band's dissolution. He wasn't happy at all. It was *his* turn to be incensed. Not about the Beatles' break up; with that he was quite content. No, HE had formed the band, and it was HE who should have made the announcement. Not to mention that it was HE who had first proclaimed his firm intention to leave the band, and it was HE who had been talked into keeping his intentions quiet.

Paul could have given a flying fig.

Thus began the mudslinging between Lennon and McCartney. The poisoned darts, in fact, came mostly from an irritated Lennon, who was unable to goad McCartney into public retaliation. Then again, McCartney had no partner egging him on. McCartney had retreated with his wife and children to an isolated farm high up in Scotland and was content to regroup and write songs. Where Lennon's attacks were direct and cutting ("Crippled Inside," "How Do You Sleep at Night?"), McCartney's responses were subtler – as with the picture of one beetle screwing another on the back sleeve of his *Ram* album. It would be years before the bitterness of this musical divorce would subside.

Lennon and McCartney both placed their marriages ahead of their careers and reputation, a noble sentiment that served their families well. To that end, they both pushed their wives front and center, the reluctant Linda and the atonal Yoko. Blinded by love, John and Paul were oblivious to the catcalls.

To those able to look past Linda and Yoko and willing to tiptoe around the sub-par material, it was apparent that both McCartney and Lennon remained capable of superior songwriting. Much of the public, however, was unwilling to make that effort, with many a defiant Beatle aficionado making a concerted effort not to purchase any McCartney or Lennon music. Giving peace a chance was one thing, giving John and Paul a chance was quite another.

The major beneficiary of the Lennon-McCartney feud was Harrison. Merely leaving his wife at home made him look brilliant.

Major praise was heaped upon Harrison's triple-album release, *All Things Must Pass*, although to my ear not every song was wonderful. It should have been a double, or even a single album. But George had stocked up so many compositions in his musical attic! On a peculiar note, Harrison drove his producer Phil Spector batty with his desire for multiple takes of each song – the same perfectionism that George had come to resent in his last years with McCartney and the Beatles.

Ever amiable, Ringo remained on good terms with all his former bandmates. He had it tougher with Maureen, and they divorced. Ringo subsequently married James Bond actress Barbara Bach in a relationship that has endured. From Beatles to Bach. Ringo successfully battled his own drug of choice, alcohol, and recorded enough quality songs to remain on the musical radar. His major claim to fame in his post-Beatle life, however, was far removed from the world of music. He endeared himself to an entire generation of kindergarteners as one of the main voices in the wildly successful children's series, *Thomas the Tank Engine*.

Lennon would spend the rest of his life distancing himself from his career as a Beatle, repudiating even the very quality that had made his songs such a success: craftsmanship. In his Beatle days each of his songs had been tweaked, stroked, harmonized, massaged, and enhanced until the best possible production had been achieved. Now, Lennon had no patience for this. He had once said that *Please Please Me*, the Beatles' first album, pleased him most because it had been recorded in a single day. He could now finally get back to that style of (non) production.

The result was a string of brilliant songs, some of them hits, some not, sounding mostly like nasal demos than a finished product.

Still addled by heroin and prodded by Yoko in whose orbit he was now firmly fixed, John went on the attack against all manners of demons. He moved on to politics, pushing a feminist/leftist agenda in ways that were often more irritating than convincing. I thought it ironic that he'd been a revolutionary force in the days when he just meant to write music, and was now mostly an annoyance when he preached revolution. Not that he ever *really* preached revolution. From his Central Park apartment in New York, he enjoyed bumping fists and high-fiving the radical elements of society while giving vocal support to the working man he'd never been.

Yoko Ono was widely blamed for the break up of the Beatles, but this was a bum rap. In 1970, as they approached thirty years of age, the Beatles' interests were pulling them apart. They'd been together practically every waking hour since they were teenagers, and it was time for each to have his space. Yoko Ono's role in the breakup was simply to hasten it, to poison the well, and to ensure that the four Beatles would never play music together again[31].

Lennon was as committed to finding spiritual satisfaction as Harrison was ("God is a concept by which we measure our pain," he had sung, and indeed he was in much pain), but his path could not have been more different. Where Harrison had found THE path to God and Krishna and had remained unwaveringly dedicated, Lennon hopscotched from one medium to the next, under the close guidance of his wife. He never did find the answer.

The number 9 continued to play a major role in John Lennon's life. He penned a song, "#9 Dream," and a son, Sean, was born to him and Yoko on October 9th – his own birthday.

Late one night in December 1980, Lennon was returning from a recording session in downtown Manhattan. Upon reaching his home,

---

31　The closest they ever came to a reunion of sorts was in May 1979 when Eric Clapton celebrated his wedding to Pattie Boyd ("Layla") by inviting all his musician friends to come jam. George came (no hard feelings seeing his ex-wife marry one of his best friends). So did Paul. And so did Ringo. John called a while later to say that he would have loved to come, but never got the invitation. What could have happened to that invite?

he was met by Mark David Chapman, who shot him dead. It was the 8th of December in New York, the 9th of December in Liverpool. He had just released "Starting Over" after a five-year absence from the music scene.

Following his death, *Rolling Stone* printed a cover picture of John Lennon. The picture was one of many taken by photographer Annie Leibovitz just prior to his murder. From that multitude, Yoko Ono chose the cover photo. It was not a picture of John the Beatle, John the performer, John the philosopher, John the happy father, or even John the happy husband. Instead, the photograph depicts a stark naked Lennon in a fetal position, his arms tightly wrapped around a fully clothed Ono. His eyes are closed while she looks impassively away. This image of their unusual relationship was her gift to the world to remember John by.

As oft will happen, death was a good career move for John and Yoko. The word "weird" was expunged from Lennon's "weird genius" appellation, and Yoko became the Grande Dame of Rock, even smiling and occasionally poking fun at herself.

For McCartney, who'd fought the hardest to keep the Beatles together, there followed a period of uncertainty. *"When an astronaut has landed on the moon, where does he go from there?"* McCartney asked. Do you form a new band that will compete with the one you just left? No, you talk your wife, the photographer, into joining your band to send a clear message that you're not even trying.

McCartney's genius lay in many areas – songwriting and performing, to name but a few. As he'd demonstrated many times over as a Beatle, he was also a master at taking to a higher level songs that lay outside his compositional realm. He was a *producer*. Unfortunately, he no longer had the Lennon and Harrison songs to work with, a lose-lose proposition all around.

Macca, as he was known among intimates, would re-invent himself, though perhaps not as much as Ringo. Inspired by David Bowie, or perhaps just following the fashion of the times, McCartney shaved his beard and morphed into an androgynous Star Trek-meets-Ken and Barbie figure. He formed a band called Wings featuring himself, Denny Laine, his wife Linda, and a rotating cast of guitarists and drummers.

Mining a seemingly endless vein of mellifluous melodies and musical doodles, he enchanted an entire new generation of teenage girls too young to hold him up to an impossible bar. It was mostly Beatles-lite music, and they loved it. As a short-term career move it was brilliant. Many recordings flew to the top of the charts ("Uncle Albert/Admiral Halsey," "Another Day," *Band on the Run*, the frilly "Silly Love Songs," and the saccharine "My Love," to name but a few). He would also write "Mull of Kintyre," the highest selling, non-charity single ever in Britain, pen the popular James Bond theme "Live and Let Die," and continue to fill arenas around the world.

Alas, having transiently taken a header into the syrup, there would be some damage. In the late 1970s, *Rolling Stone* wrote, "This ex-Beatle has been lending his truly prodigious talents as a singer, songwriter, musician, and producer to some of the laziest records in the history of rock and roll." His commercial success had indeed been a Faustian bargain: The new McCartney image made it difficult for his fan base to stay on board, and his new public image would persist long after he'd shed his Wings. His most popular songs slowly cast him as a purveyor of the trite and contributed to a temporary, yet steep, slide into critical irrelevance. It would be years before the unforgiving critics and public would give him another look, and it was not until 1999 that he was inducted into the Rock 'n' Roll Hall of Fame as a solo performer. (His daughter, Stella, could be seen at the induction ceremony sporting a T-shirt that read "About F...ing Time.")

And yet...

And yet... within each of his albums lay compositions that consistently revealed a thoughtful and clever songsmith, songs that would have comfortably fit on any Beatle album – a treasure trove of outstanding material for anybody with the inclination to scratch below the surface.

***

Mal's letters dwindled after the Beatles' breakup. He remained an employee of Apple until 1974, but his relationship with the Beatles was up and down; he was depressed and a bit lost. He penned me a brief note when he and Lil broke up and a more enthusiastic one when he moved to L.A. in search of excitement. Yet again, no job came close to providing the status he'd become accustomed to in his years with the Beatles. Mal's final letter to me was about something Lennon told him on the phone from New York – that he'd seen a UFO out his bedroom window.

Mal took to drink and drugs. One night, in January 1976, he apparently went over the top. His girlfriend called the cops. Mal was threatening. They shot him, and he died.

There was a funeral in L.A. None of the Beatles attended.

Mal was cremated, and his ashes were sent to England – and lost in the postal system. Lennon joked that they should look in the dead letters' file.

That gave me a twinge.

I thought about Mal's death and his missing ashes for a long time. Could this all have been part of a bigger plan? Had Mal somehow been reunited with his extra-terrestrial connections? What if I'd gotten him into Mission Control?

"Alarm A12- 0-2." I would never forget that.

***

In 1970, the EMI studio in London, home to nearly every Beatle song ever recorded, was re-baptized "The *Abbey Road* Studio" in honor of its most famous denizens. It would *retroactively* be referred to in this fashion forever more.

And what if the Beatles had not broken up? What if they'd taken a break from recording, gone their separate ways, and returned one or two years later with fresh material? The album, this time called *Everest*, might have looked something like this:

Side 1: "Maybe I'm Amazed," "Imagine," "My Sweet Lord," "Every Night," "Jealous Guy," "Junk."

Side 2: "All Things Must Pass," "Give Me Some Truth," "You're Sixteen," "Uncle Albert/Admiral Halsey," "Another Day," "Instant Karma."

Some would say it was their finest album.

**

In 1979, Allen Klein was convicted of tax evasion and served two months in prison.

****

As for yours truly, I'd dedicated ten years of my life to NASA, and it had been worth every minute. It was now time to move on. Mal, Deke, and Gordo had had their effect on me: I took more of an interest in UFOs, though I never did quite figure out what to make of them. I had long stopped making fun of people who thought they saw them streaking through the sky. I had not held it against presidential candidate Barry Goldwater for claiming that he'd chased a UFO while flying his F-86, nor was I critical of President Jimmy Carter for saying he had filed a UFO report while Governor of Georgia, and nor did it diminish Ronald Reagan in my eyes when he swore he'd seen a UFO while flying on official business as Governor of California. Ed Mitchell, Apollo 14 astronaut and sixth man to walk on the moon, stated publicly that UFOs exist, and Gordo himself eventually came out of the UFO closet.

My last interaction with NASA took place in the early 1990s, when Purdue sent me a reunion/fund-raising letter. The figureheads for this campaign were none other than Neil Armstrong and Gene Cernan – the first and last men to have walked on the moon. At the reunion, we reminisced and talked about how happy Gus would have been to be included. We made a point of finding Betty.

After her split with Ringo, Maureen married Isaac Tigrett, who was in the process of creating a music club in London. The concept, quite original at the time, was to mix food and rock 'n' roll. Tigrett and his partner, Morton, even had a motto for their restaurant: "Love All – Serve All." Eric Clapton was rumored to be donating a red and black Fender guitar that would hang on the wall. Opening day was set for June 14, 1971, and they were hiring. Mal mentioned this in passing – he'd always been fond of Mo. Sally and I looked at each other. Could this be for us? Not as a career move of course, but maybe as a reprieve from reality? Sally had always said she didn't want to be tied down! It would mean moving to London and starting in an entirely new direction, but yes, as McCartney had said, when you've landed on the moon, where do you go from there? The music-eatery was to be called

The Hard Rock Café. Sally and I signed on to be assistant managers – a role we were both used to. We got married in '74; we invited Maureen, but she couldn't make it.

It took me a while to adjust to every day life. I hadn't been at work very long, when one of the girls we hired came to me in tears. (In tears!) "We have a *major* glitch in the coffee machine."

I stared blankly. *(A "major glitch"! A "major glitch!!" A major glitch is when a light turns on in John Glenn's capsule, a major glitch is when Gordon Cooper's fuel cells conk out, a major glitch is when Gemini 8 spins out of control, a major glitch is when the alarm bells go off during the first lunar landing, a major glitch is when Apollo 13's oxygen tank blows up in space. Never mind.)*

"Well of course, lassie, we'll get it fixed."

And then, of course, the occasional irate customer would walk in and start in on me with the type of line we'd all be hearing many times over during the next few years:

"What's the mater mate, the Americans can put a man on the moon, and you can't make a cappuccino?"

Yeah, right. Stay groovy.

THE END

Footnote

The main character, Dutch, bears no intentional resemblance to the real Manfred "Dutch" von Ehrenfried, hired by NASA in 1961.

Mal Evans was the Beatles' roadie and bodyguard. All events and statements pertaining to Mal are true (or plausible) with the following exceptions:
- He did not travel to Hamburg with the Beatles in their formative years and did not start working at the Cavern until 1962.
- His thoughts pertaining to UFOs and all things extra-terrestrial are conjectural and not based on his statements or writings.

The Houston Astros were called the Colt .45s until 1964. The Astrodome was built in 1965.

Dutch and Sally are fictional characters.
Thoughts attributed to Gene Kranz are speculative but in keeping with his autobiography.

All historical events are real.

A few intentional "errors" were created to facilitate the flow of the narrative:

The signing of the Parlophone contract was somewhat convoluted: On May 9th, 1962, the Beatles (in Hamburg) received a telegram from Brian saying a contract had been secured with Parlophone with the first recording session set for June 6th. In fact, it was as much a recording test/audition as it was a session. The contract was offered following the session, signed later that month, and backdated to the 4th to cover the June 6th session.

Lennon's Rolls Royce listed as being yellow in 1966 was in fact black. The psychedelic yellow paint job was applied in the spring of 1967.

It was actually Wendy Hanson, Epstein's assistant, who was in charge of obtaining permissions from the people featured on the Sgt. Pepper cover. She'd left Brian in late '66, but Brian begged her back specifically to handle what he thought was an impossible task.

Two Virgins was recorded on May 19th, but the cover photo was taken in October, and the record was released in November.

Ringo walked out on the White Album recording session on Aug 22nd 1968

Bibliography

Bakich, Michael: The Cambridge Planetary Handbook.
    Cambridge University Press. Cambridge, 2000.
    Basic planetary physics.

Barrow Tony: *John, Paul, George, Ringo and Me.*
    Thunder's Mouth Press. 2005
    The Beatles from the point of view of their publicist.

Bean, Alan: *Apollo.* Greenwich Workshop, Shelton CT, 1998.
    Spectacular paintings of the Apollo missions to the moon by the
    fourth moon walker.

The Beatles : *The Beatles Anthology*, Chronicle Books, 2000.
    This is the *National Geographic* of the Beatles books. You mostly
    look at the pictures, but the text is worth the read. Little snippets
    of interviews chronologically laid out by subject matter. An easy
    read.

The Beatles: *Let It Be…Naked – Fly on the Wall.* Apple Records, 2003.
    Sound bites of the Beatles recording *Let It Be.*

Beattie, Donald A: *Taking Science to the Moon – Lunar Experiments and
    the Apollo Program.* The Johns Hopkins University Press. Baltimore
    and New York. 2001.
    Re ipse loquitur. The moon voyages as seen from a scientist's point
    of view.

Benson, Harry: *The Beatles Now and Then.* Universe, New York, 1998.
    Intimate photographs of the Beatles on tour (including Paris and
    New York, February 1964)

Boomhower RE: *Gus Grissom. The Lost Astronaut.*
    Indiana Historical Society Press, Indianapolis, 2004.
    Gus Grissom's life told in straightforward fashion.

Bramwell, Tony: *Magical Mystery Tours – My Life with the Beatles.*
    Thomas Dunne Books, St. Martin's Press, 2005.
    Bramwell grew up with the Beatles and produced their first "music
    videos."

Brown Peter, Gaines Steven: *The Love You Make.* New American Library (McGraw-Hill originally), New York NY, 1983.
Terrific behind-the-scenes book by Peter Brown, Brian Epstein's associate.

Bugliosi, Vincent with Gentry, Curt: *Helter Skelter: The True Story of the Manson Murders.* 1974
Billed as the #1 true-crime bestseller of all time. Certainly one of the most revolting.

Chaikin, Andrew: *A Man on the Moon.* Penguin Books, New York, 1994.
Gripping narrative of the Apollo missions.

Clapton, Eric: *Clapton – The Autobiography.* Broadway, New York, 2007
Riveting and remarkably well-written. Colorful vignettes of his times with the Beatles (and a painfully honest account of his battle with addiction).

Collins, Michael: *Flying to the Moon. An Astronaut's Story.*
A Sunburst Book. Farrar, Straus, Giroux. 2nd ed, 1994.
Geared towards children, the book nevertheless has all the essentials of this Apollo 11 astronaut's flight to the moon.

Codigan, Patrick: The Revolutionary Artist – Lennon's Radical Years.

DeCurtis, Anthony: *In Other Words.* Hal Leonard, Milwaukee WI, 2005.
Insightful interviews with the world's biggest rock stars.

Edmonds, Mark: Here, there, and everywhere.
Mal Evans' unpublished diaries.
The Sunday Times, March 20 2005.

Farmer, Gene and Hamblin, Dora Jane: *First on the Moon – A Voyage with Neil Armstrong, Michael Collins, Edwin E. Aldrin, Jr.* Little, Brown, 1970.
The story of the first astronauts to the moon – with a little help from their friends.

Fleming, Ian: *Live and Let Die.* Penguin Books, 1954
    "   : *From Russia With Love.* Penguin Books, 1957
    "   : *Doctor No.* Penguin Books, 1958
    "   : *Goldfinger.* Penguin Books, 1959
    "   : *Thunderball.* Penguin Books, 1961
    "   : *On Her Majesty's Secret Service.* Penguin Books, 1963
    "   : *You Only Live Twice.* Penguin Books, 1964

Freeman, Robert. *The Beatles – A Private View.*
Mallard Press, New York. 1990.
Pictures from the photographer of five early Beatles album covers.

Giuliano, Geoffrey: *The Lost Beatles Interviews.*
Penguin Books, New York, 1994.
A wonderful collection of Beatle interviews (with an afterward by Timothy Leary)

Godwin, Robert: *Apollo 8, The NASA Mission Reports*, Apogee Books, 2nd Ed, Burlington, Ontario, Canada, 2000. Technical summary of the mission.

Gould, Jonathan: *Can't Buy Me Love.* Harmony Books, New York. 2007 Well crafted account of the Beatles' story, with a strong smattering of social commentary and song analysis.

Grissom, Betty & Still, Henry: *Starfall.*
Thomas Y Crowell, New York. 1974.
Gus Grissom's life, through wife Betty's eyes.

Grushkin, Paul & Selvin, Joel: *Treasures of the Hard Rock'n'roll Café.*
Rare Air Media, Chicago IL, 2001. Beautiful pictures of rock'n'roll' memorabilia from the Hard Rock Cafés around the world.

Hall, Rex, Shayler David J: *The Rocket Men. Vostok & Voskhod, The First Soviet Manned Spaceflights.* Springer Praxis, Chichester UK 2001. The space race from the Soviets' point of view.

Hall, Stephen, Clark Robert: *Spirits in the Sand – The ancient Nasca lines of Peru shed their secrets*, National Geographic, pp. 56-79, March 2010. The geoglyphs of Peru.

Harrison, George: *I Me Mine.* Simon and Schuster, New York, 1980. Mostly a collection of Harrison's lyrics, preceded by a few pages of a (possibly fictitious) interview with Derek Taylor.

Harry, Bill: *The Ultimate Beatles Encyclopedia*, Hyperion, 1992. Excellent reference for the Beatles world from a Beatles Liverpool buddy.

Hendrix, Jimi: *The Lyrics.* Hal Leonard, Milwaukee, 2003 Though Hendrix is known for his virtuoso guitar, the lyrics to Hendrix' compositions are worth reading.

Heppenheimer, TA: How America Chose Not to Beat Sputnik Into Space. *Invention & Technology* magazine, Winter 2004, pp 44-48.

Hertsgaard, Mark: *A Day in the Life. The music and artistry of the Beatles*. Delta book (Dell), New York, 1995.

Clever musical analysis from one who has listened to the archival tapes. Hertsgaard's musical tastes within the Beatles' canon fortuitously agree with this authors'.

Kane, Larry: *Ticket To Ride. Inside the Beatles' 1964 Tour That Changed the World*. Running Press, Philadelphia, 2003.

Day by day account of one of the zaniest tours ever.

Kozinn, Allan: *The Beatles*. Phaidon Press, London, 1995.

Rock critic pens a (relatively) concise biography (200 pages). Superior prose.

Kranz, Gene: *Failure Is Not An Option*, Berkley Books, New York, 2000.

Superb, backstage technical insights from one of the key Apollo "Flight" directors.

Kurlansky, Mark. *1968. The year that rocked the world*. Ballantine books. 2004

All the dirt on the Columbia University protests.

Leary, Timothy, Metzner, Ralph, and Alpert, Richard: The Psychedelic Experience: A Manual Based on the Tibetan Book of the Dead.

Lennon, Cynthia: *John*.

Crown Publishers (Random House), New York, 2005.

Convincing account of her relationship with John Lennon, though she does not completely appreciate why she might have become uninteresting to John despite all her good qualities.

Lewisohn, Mark: *The Beatles Recording Sessions –The official Abbey Road Studio Session Notes*. Harmony Books, New York. 1988.

The Bible of studio notes.

Lewisohn, Mark: *The Complete Beatles Chronicles*.

Harmony Books, New York, 1992.

The Beatles week by week. A variation on the above.

Mailer, Norman: *A Fire on the Moon. Life* magazine, pp25-41, August 29th 1969.

Mallon, Thomas. *Aurora 7*. Harcourt, 1991.

Scott Carpenter's flight narrated as a historical novel. A fun time capsule of 1962.

McDermott, John with Eddie Kramer: *Hendrix – Setting the Record Straight*. Warner Books. New York, 1992.
Thorough and readable. Pictures by Linda McCartney.

Miles, Barry: *Paul McCartney – Many Years From Now*.
Henry Holt, New York 1997.
Written by a long time friend of his, this McCartney biography is practically an autobiography. A must.

Neal, Valerie; Lewis, Cathleen; and Winter, Frank: *Spaceflight*.
Smithsonian Guides, MacMillan, New York 1995.
A lavishly illustrated paperback summarizing Man's 20th Century adventures in Space.

Neary, John. "The Magical McCartney Mystery".
Life magazine, November 7th, 1969.

Neufeld, Michael: *Von Braun. Dreamer of Space. Engineer of War*.
Alfred A. Knopf, 2007.
Everything you'll ever want to know – and more- about this brilliant, controversial rocket builder and visionary.

Noebel, David A: *Communism, Hypnotism and the Beatles: An analysis of the Communist use of music, the Communist master music plan*.
Christian Crusade Publications. 1965
Funny or scary, depending on how you look at it.

Patterson, R. Gary: *The Walrus Was Paul. The Great Beatle Death Clues*.
Fireside/Simon and Schuster, New York 1996.
An exhaustive account of the "Paul is dead" drama in the Fall of 1969.

Reynolds, David West: *Apollo The Epic Journey to the Moon*.
Tehabi Books/Harcourt, San Diego, 2002.
Uncommon pictures and illustrations (including a detailed map of Cape Kennedy).

Rosen, Michael J: *My Bug*. Artisan, New York, 1999
Pictures, cartoons, short stories, all pertaining to the VW Beetle.

Rolling Stone magazine #980, August 11th 2005 p.54

Roylance, Brian: Blinds and Shutters – Michael Cooper.
Genesis/Hedley, London 1990.
Deluxe compilation of /tribute to the Sgt Pepper photographer

Rubin, Steven Jay: The Complete James Bond. Contemporary Books, Chicago, 1990, 1995.
Wonderful vignettes about every actor, director, set design, gadget, location, etc...Dictionary style.

Saltzman, Paul: *The Beatles in Rishikesh.* Viking Studio/Penguin Putnam, 2000 /*The Beatles in India –Limited Edition* (2005).
Unique, colorful photographic essay of the Beatles in Rishikesh.

Schirra, Wally, Billings RN: *Schirra's space.*
Naval Institute Press, Annapolis Maryland. 1988.
Concise autobiography. Schirra doesn't mince words when it comes to scientists and doctors.

Sculatti, Gene: *100 Best Selling Albums of the 60s.*
Barnes and Noble books, New York, 2004.
Shepard, Alan & Slayton, Deke: *Moon Shot.*
Turner Publishing, Atlanta. 1994

Smith, Joe: *Off the Record.* Warner Books, New York. 1988
Short, poignant interviews.

Spignesi Stephen and Lewis Michael: *Here, There and Everywhere – The 100 Best Beatles Songs.* Black Dog and Leventhal, New York, 2004.
It is always fun to check out other people's idea of the "best" Beatles songs (complete with explanations).

Staten, Vince: *Do Bald Men Get Half-Price Haircuts?*
Simon and Schuster, New York 2001. Pages 56 and 93.
The Beatles kill the barbershop and hair tonic business.

Sulpy, Doug and Scheighardt: *Get Back – The Unauthorized Chronicle of the Beatles' Let It Be Disaster.* St. Martin's Griffin, New York, 1994
Day by day, sometimes minute by minute chronicle of the *Get Back/Let It Be* sessions in January 1969.

Swenson Jr. L, Grimwood JM, Alexander CC: *This New Ocean. A History of Project Mercury.* The NASA Historical Series. NASA, Washington DC, 1966.
Encyclopedic, technical history of the Mercury program.

Testa, Bridget Mikntz: *Mission Control. Invention & Technology* magazine, Spring 2003.

Thompson, Dave: *Cream.* Virgin Books, London 2005.
All you need to know about Eric Clapton, Jack Bruce, and Ginger Baker in their Cream days.

Thompson, Gordon: *Please Please Me. Sixties British Pop, Inside Out.* Oxford University Press, New York, 2008.
The *other* British 60s acts.

Trynka, Paul: *The Beatles – Ten Years That Shook the World.* Dorling Kindersley (DK)/Mojo, London, 2004.
Lavishly illustrated in DK style.

Turner, Steve: *The Gospel According to the Beatles.* Westminster John Know, Louisville KY, 2006.
An analysis of the spiritual movements that underlie the Beatles' lyrics.

Unger, Irwin and Unger, Debi: The Times were a changin'. The sixties reader. Three Rivers Press, Crown Publishing Group, Random House, 1998.

Verne, Jules: *De La Terre A La Lune – Trajet direct en 97 heures 20 minutes [From the Earth to the Moon].* Librairie Hachette.

Verne, Jules: *Autour de la Lune [Around the Moon].* Librairie Hachette.

Von Braun, Wernher and Ordway III, Frederick I.: *History of Rocketry and Space Travel.* J.G. Ferguson, Chicago. 1966
Detailed book by the masters.

Ward, Ed; Stokes, Geoffrey, and Tucker, Ken: *Rock of Ages. The Rolling Stone History of Rock'n'roll.* Rolling Stone Press (Summit Books, Simon and Schuster), New York 1986.
Seamless, scholarly analysis of the great ages of rock.

Wells, H.G.: *The First Men in the Moon.*

Wenner, Jann: 20 Years of Rolling Stone – What a Long, Strange Trip It's Been. Friendly Press. New York, 1987
Selected interviews (including John Lennon), articles, illustrations, and photo shoots (Annie Leibovitz' December 3rd and December 8th 1980 John Lennon photographs)

Whitaker, Bob: *The Unseen Beatles.* Collins, San Francisco, 1991.
Classic pictures from one of the official Beatle photographers.

Wolf, Tom: *The Right Stuff.* Bantam Books. New York, 1979.
The story of the Mercury program told in the ultimate literary style. A must.

Zimmerman, Robert: *Genesis – The Story of Apollo 8.*
Dell, New York, 1998
Excellent narrative of Apollo 8's epochal flight to the moon.

Web pages:

Burley, Leo: www.independent.co.uk/arts-entertainment/music/features/jagger-vs-lennon-londons-riots-of-1968-provided-the-backdrop-to-a-rocknroll-battle-royale-792450.html
Lennon and Jagger's view of revolution in 1968

Cadigan, Patrick: http://books.google.com/books?id=EpaGf45wjNcC&source=gbs_navlinks_s
Quotes Lennon as saying that McCartney's inspiration for "Let It Be" came from a dream about Mal Evans ("…Brother Malcolm comes to me")

Elsas, Dennis: www.denniselsas.com http://wfuv.streamguys.us/archive/8790.asx
Colorful one-hour radio broadcast exploring the Beatles' New York arrival in February 1964.

Evans, Mal: Diaries, as discussed by Mark Edmonds http://www.timesonline.co.uk/tol/life_and_style/article424674.ece

Froman, Sandy: The History of Gun Control, part 2. http://www.wnd.com/news/article.asp?ARTICLE_ID=56156

Geller, Uri: http://www.urigeller.com//megg.htm
Lennon tells Geller of his UFO/alien experience. It is different from Pang's (see below).

Pang, May: http//abcnews.go.com/video/playerindex?id=4384271
Television interview with May Pang, Yoko Ono's assistant and Lennon's lover during the "lost week-end," an eighteen month period during which Lennon lived in L.A. with Pang. Pang states that she and Lennon saw a UFO, which Lennon quickly drew on a manila envelope.

http:// aa.usno.navy.mil/data.docs/Moonphase.php. Phases of the moon for the past centuries [Apollo 8]

www.time.com/time/magazine/article/0,9171,870817-1,00html.
Feb 21 1964 *Time* quote.

http://www.timesonline.co.uk/tol/life_and_style/article424674.
ece?token=null&offset=36&page=4 Mal Evans in the USA with
The Band

www.rollingstone.com/artists/thebeatles/albums/album/206268/
review/594
Rolling Stone review of *Abbey Road*.

www.youtube.com/watch?v=PeGT34R2il4.
Paul McCartney interview with Howard Stern (Sirius radio, Jan 14
2009). McCartney explains how he came up with the idea for the
name and cover of *Abbey Road*.

Miscellaneous

Brodax, Al: personal communication during a presentation at
the Harvard Club in New York. Mr. Brodax did not care for "Hey
Bulldog" and he chose to remove it from the American version of the
Yellow Submarine movie. Of the four Beatles, Mr. Brodax felt closest
to George Harrison.

References and footnotes can be found at
www.IntoTheSkyWithDiamonds.com

Index

Grissom, Gus 14, 15, 23, 41, 42, 43, 53, 60, 61, 62, 71, 94, 97, 108, 154, 155, 156, 157, 197, 227, 228, 233, 305, 338, 371, 373

H

Haise, Fred 203, 280, 311
Ham, the chimp 44, 45, 60, 64
Help! 159, 161, 167, 180, 187
Hendrix, Jimi xv, 148, 240, 242, 243, 248, 261, 303, 342, 357, 373, 375
Hey Jude 292, 351
Hippies xv, 256

I

I Want To Hold Your Hand 121, 242, 250

J

Johnson 77, 81, 94, 113, 125, 147, 148, 173, 179, 185, 203, 231, 233, 266, 267, 268, 287, 331, 359

K

Kennedy, John xv, 33, 34, 38, 43, 44, 54, 55, 56, 57, 62, 72, 75, 76, 94, 98, 107, 108, 113, 117, 122, 123, 124, 127, 129, 148, 204, 254, 268, 274, 281, 331, 339, 340, 375
Khrushchev, Nikita 9, 10, 38, 63, 98, 147, 244
Kirchherr, Astrid 37, 212
Klein, Allen 322, 323, 343, 367
Komarov 243, 244, 245, 341

L

Lennon, Cynthia 19, 59, 80, 116, 166, 222, 269, 270, 272, 346, 374
Leonov, A 155, 161, 164, 165, 244
let it be 315
Lovell, Jim 95, 177, 181, 182, 183, 184, 185, 198, 225, 280, 295, 297, 298, 299, 300, 301, 302, 304, 306, 308, 329, 357
Low, George 21, 76, 278, 279
Lucy in the sky with diamonds 238

M

Magical Mystery Tour 248, 260, 261, 262, 276, 347, 351
Maharishi 258, 259, 265, 269
McCartney NASA astronaut 239
McDivitt, Jim 95, 163, 177, 227, 228, 262, 277, 280, 318
Meet the Beatles 128, 153

N

Nikolayev 93, 94
Nixon xv, 33, 34, 38, 281, 282, 294, 330, 338, 340

P

Paul is dead 350
Penny Lane 235, 236, 251, 253, 262
Popovich 93
Presley, Elvis 17, 126, 129, 134, 349
Purdue 14, 22, 23, 60, 94, 95, 117, 177, 207, 367

R

Redstone rocket 10, 24, 38, 39, 40, 45, 47, 48, 50, 51, 60, 71, 72, 156, 157, 158
Revolution 292
Revolver 211, 212
Rolling Stones xv, 92, 115, 125, 129, 149, 168, 169, 199, 222, 224, 247, 355
Rubber Soul 186, 188, 199

S

Saturn rocket 204, 229, 231, 267, 268, 275, 277, 279, 281, 286, 288, 295, 297, 317, 318, 331, 359
Schirra, Wally 14, 32, 78, 94, 96, 97, 108, 110, 112, 157, 158, 177, 178, 179, 182, 183, 184, 185, 227, 228, 262, 277, 286, 287, 288, 290, 300, 353, 376
Scott 118
Scott, D 177, 200

Made in the USA
Middletown, DE
17 June 2020